CURSE OF THE NECRARCH

NECRARCH VAMPIRE Radu the Forsaken lurks in his castle, engrossed in dark experiments and his quest for power. When he discovers that a long lost artefact is buried in a nearby Empire town, the lure of its possession is too great for him to resist. It is rumoured that the relic dates back to the time of Nagash and has the magical ability to elevate him to the level of this legendary sorcerer. The Empire will be his to control. Gathering an army he attacks the town, slaughters the inhabitants and seizes the artefact.

Now Reinhardt Metzger must assemble a force of men, hunt down the vampire and destroy it before it can unleash a plague of pure evil onto the Empire. With the odds set against him and time running out the fate of the Empire is in his hands.

More Warhammer adventure from the Black Library

VAMPIRE WARS – THE VON CARSTEIN TRILOGY
(Contains the novels: *Inheritance, Dominion* and *Retribution*)
by Steven Savile

Also available

ANCIENT BLOOD
by Robert Earl

THE VAMPIRE GENEVIEVE
by Jack Yeovil

A WARHAMMER NOVEL

CURSE OF THE NECRARCH

STEVEN SAVILE

To Marie,
For loving me and saying so
For loving me for my faults, not despite them
You make me want to be the hero of my own life.

A BLACK LIBRARY PUBLICATION

First published in Great Britain in 2008 by
BL Publishing,
Games Workshop Ltd.,
Willow Road, Nottingham,
NG7 2WS, UK

10 9 8 7 6 5 4 3 2 1

Cover illustration by Ralph Horsley
Map by Nuala Kinrade.

ISBN 13: 978 1 84416 553 7
ISBN 10: 1 84416 553 1

Distributed in the US by Simon & Schuster
1230 Avenue of the Americas, New York, NY 10020.

See the Black Library on the Internet at
www.blacklibrary.com

Find out more about Games Workshop
and the world of Warhammer at
www.games-workshop.com

Printed and bound in the US.

THIS IS A DARK age, a bloody age, an age of daemons and of sorcery. It is an age of battle and death, and of the world's ending. Amidst all of the fire, flame and fury it is a time, too, of mighty heroes, of bold deeds and great courage.

AT THE HEART of the Old World sprawls the Empire, the largest and most powerful of the human realms. Known for its engineers, sorcerers, traders and soldiers, it is a land of great mountains, mighty rivers, dark forests and vast cities. And from his throne in Altdorf reigns the Emperor Karl-Franz, sacred descendant of the founder of these lands, Sigmar, and wielder of his magical warhammer.

BUT THESE ARE far from civilised times. Across the length and breadth of the Old World, from the knightly palaces of Bretonnia to ice-bound Kislev in the far north, come rumblings of war. In the towering Worlds Edge Mountains, the orc tribes are gathering for another assault. Bandits and renegades harry the wild southern lands of the Border Princes. There are rumours of rat-things, the skaven, emerging from the sewers and swamps across the land. And from the northern wildernesses there is the ever-present threat of Chaos, of daemons and beastmen corrupted by the foul powers of the Dark Gods. As the time of battle draws ever nearer, the Empire needs heroes like never before.

ran beside the castle wall, skirting the edge of the lake and then ran the length of the skeletal trees before emerging on the plain. From any sort of frontal approach the illusion of the island fortification was perfect.

There were no guards shivering against the bite of the cold as they walked the walls.

There were precious few left to defend it from the dead and every one of them knew that nothing as fragile as flesh could save the living.

The buildings beyond the frozen lake lay in tatters, walls torn down, the clay tiles of the roofs shattered and trodden into the dirt along with the bones of their lives: brothers, sisters, mothers, wives, sons and daughters left to rot in the muck of defeat. It had been a vibrant town no more than a month ago. Like so many remote settlements the town was a haven that had sprung up around the castle to serve the needs of its defenders. For years it had been nothing more than a few wooden buildings. Then little more than a year ago those had been replaced with stone houses, giving the doomed settlement an air of permanence.

Felix Metzger stood on the battlements, a solitary point of calm amid the chaos of the thick falling snow. It settled in his grey hair and across the shoulders of his cloak and his bronze plate armour. Bitterness frosted within him. Down in the small courtyard the remnants of his knights stood over campfires, burning anything the enemy might find useful come dusk and their victory. Five hundred of them had defended the castle; thirty remained. He was immune to the cold, this mortal cold at least.

Another cold had settled inside him ever since he had begun thinking of himself as a dead man walking. It was not in his nature to admit defeat, but this creature with its vile, twisted bramble of a soul had undone him and everything he loved. He was broken inside. All he could think of was one final act of defiance, one last tilt. His home would fall, that was a foregone conclusion. The question now was the price he claimed for it. He had lived with the notion that an army was like a snake, sever its head and another would grow to take its place, but the denizens of death were different, mindless in their devotion to their liege, this accursed Korbhen who clung to the shadows, afraid of honest daylight.

Cut off his head and perhaps they would all fall?

Metzger was a simple man who lived for the people under his protection. He did not crave the glory of combat, the thrill of steel ringing on steel, the frenzy of bloodlust nor the calm that came in its wake. That did not mean he feared death, either, only that he did not seek out the endless winter night like some men he knew. This new death of the Winter War was different. When the dead did not stay dead, how could the world as you knew it be trusted? When friends rose up at your back, suddenly enemies desperate to feed on the marrow of your bones, how could you look the living in the eye let alone raise a hand to strike down the dead?

His charge was simple: hold the castle and keep the pass open.

Even after all this time fighting them, Metzger understood little of his enemy, and that bothered him. A good soldier knew his foe intimately, and used that knowledge to his advantage, but after years of chasing vampiric shadows he knew as little now as he had on the first day he had taken up his sword. His head swarmed with a flurry of questions every bit as chaotic as the snowstorm that buffeted and bullied him. How did their vile resurrection work? How could they be bound once more to life and yet remain dead? Did Morr relinquish his hold on their souls or cherish them, leaving the flesh to rot? Were they robbed of an afterlife, cursed forever to live a half-death? Could they think and act of their own volition?

There was one question that haunted him more than any other: was there anything left of them, the real them, when they came back? Could they remember? Could they be saved?

Like so many other good men he wrestled with guilt and grief, unable to come to terms with the conflicting emotions that warred within him when he was forced to take up arms against the faces of men he had once called friends. Yet that was the nature of the conflict. Death wore familiar faces.

He watched a black bird of ill-omen battle through the sky thick with snow and alight on the ruined section of what had been the Temple of Sigmar in a flurry of black wings. A pale, cadaverous figure greeted the bird, taking it in its withered hands and holding it up to its face as though listening to the raven's caws. With the snows intensifying, the crook-backed figure shuffled away from view. It was easy to imagine those malignant shapes clawing out across the frozen lake to pierce the hearts of every last man huddled in the dubious safety of the redoubt. His fears were like that now, as insubstantial as shades, worming their way into his mind, undermining his resolve. It was easy to fear the unknown, natural even.

He was not a coward though, no matter how strong fear's grip on him. He was Felix Metzger, Knight of the Twisted Thorns. His strength was the flame-scalloped blade in his hand.

Metzger reached down instinctively for the reassuring comfort of his sword, letting his fingers linger on its hilt.

'Give me strength,' he whispered, his words carried away from his chapped lips by the wind. Its only answer was a mocking lament, low and mournful, the voices of all the dead returning to plague him.

He drew little comfort from the knowledge that it would all be over soon, for better or for worse.

Dusk closed in, its darkness more stifling for the swirling snows.

Metzger's men huddled around their lanterns, watching them burn down with dread. Lanterns, bonfires and torches, anything that offered light had become more important than swords now that the hard-faced moons had emerged. Men tended the fires religiously, making sure they did not burn down during the night, for if they did there would be no light. The one thing they knew, without doubt, was that the dark was their enemy's territory.

Metzger shivered; it had nothing to do with the cold. He had never truly understood dread, even though he had lived through all of it, birth and death.

He had crouched beside his own son as he drew that final shuddering breath. His life, the lives of all he cared for, had been reduced to blood and ash. Now, on this gods forsaken castle, within this lake of ice, staring at the ruined walls of the temples, oast houses, granaries and mills, imagining the damned they sheltered, now he understood it. Dread was so much more than fear.

Metzger turned his back on the fallen town and walked back down the narrow stone stairwell carved into the wall to join his brother knights. He was desperately hungry but they had precious little in the way of food left. Like everything else the harsh winter and the drawn-out siege had worn their stockpiles down to nothing. The conversations hushed, the men looking expectantly towards him.

There were ten faces around the fire, and ten more around the one across from it. Ten more were gathering faggots to feed the flames. They were running painfully low on firewood and had taken to burning anything that would light. The beast was toying with them. Metzger had no rousing words to lift their spirits. His brother knights knew as well as he did what they would face during the darkest part of the night; they had lived most of their lives either hunted by or hunting the beasts. That was the curse of the time they had been born into and that was how he thought of the dead, as beasts, monsters. Metzger hunkered down and rubbed his hands briskly before the low burning camp-fire.

'I want these roaring, lads, I want the fires licking the sky and turning night to day before the hour is out. Anything we've got, burn it. It ends here so let's go out in a blaze of glory. The bronze armour is going to shine like the sun when I walk out across that draw-bridge.'

Sarbin, the youngest of the knights, looked up at him. There was no hope in his pale blue eyes. 'You're going to sacrifice yourself, then?'

'No, lad. I'm going into the belly of the beast and I am going to cut its heart out,' Felix Metzger said with all the confidence he could muster. With the elegiac wind cutting across his words they sounded like hollow bluster.

'Then let us stand beside you.'

'No, lad. This is about honour. Men of my line have been charged with protecting this fortress for two hundred years. This is a line that can never be broken. Whether I live or die, these walls are Metzger every bit as much as my flesh is, and my father's was. I will face the beast alone.'

Leiber rose, a look of utter disgust on his hawkish face. 'No. With all due respect, that's not the way it is going to be, sir. We've stood with you this far. We will stand with you at the end. We are not children to be sheltered from pain. We are men of the sword. We pledged our lives to protect this place and its people. If we die trying we die with honour.'

The others grunted and nodded their agreement.

'This isn't the end, my friend,' Metzger said. He meant it. Live or die, this wasn't the end. The vampire's kind infested the Empire, like rats carrying their stinking pox of unlife into every town and village. 'This isn't the last battle. There will always be another beast that rises to wear the mask of evil. Human or inhuman monsters, this world of ours is made for them. When we stop fighting the monsters, that is when we succumb to true evil, my friend. Remember, the sun also shines on the wicked.'

'Yes, but it burns these ones to a cinder,' Koloman said, grinning at his gallows humour. The man's weasel-like nose twitched, throwing long shadows across his acne-pitted skin.

'That it does. Now I will have no more arguments, you'll have those fires blazing and that is an order.'

'They'll burn, but we will not let you take the long walk alone, sir.'

And he knew they wouldn't. They were good men.

Metzger left the circle, confident they would disobey him. They were brothers to the bone, not merely warriors. More, they were the Twisted Thorns. They would stand together and die together.

He sat alone, gathering his thoughts for a while. The world around him seemed so much more vital now that he had entered his last few hours, the colours more vibrant, the cold of the snow more chilling, the wind in his face brisker.

Metzger occupied himself so as not to brood, for what would be would be. He checked the fastenings of his greaves, methodically oiled the individual joints of his gauntlets and adjusted the lie of his mail shirt beneath the heavy bronze breastplate. It needed no thought; he had done each a thousand times over a thousand nights of conflict during his life. There was comfort in the preparations; they offered the illusion that he was in control of his destiny, that this last night was his and not the beast's. Last of all, he drew his blade, a mighty flame-scalloped sword, and lay it across his knees. The blade had tasted the blood of hundreds of men over the course of their time together and not once had the edge failed him. Metzger raised the crosspiece of the bronze hilt to his chapped lips and kissed the cold metal. 'One last time, old friend,' he whispered.

Behind him the first of the bonfires spat and cackled as the men threw more kindling on it. He saw them hacking up the refectory table and the oak benches, feeding them to the flames along with tapestries and other flammable treasures. The shadows of the flames danced all around him.

Metzger pushed to his feet.

He was an old man feeling every one of his years as he walked slowly through the falling snow towards the huge winch that would open the castle's wooden drawbridge. The ice that had filmed across the ground cracked, the sound rolling around the hills. It was an omen, Metzger decided. The thaw was coming. The snows could not last forever. Two more ravens flew in over his shoulders, resting on either side of the portico. As one, they craned their necks to gaze down at him with their jaundiced eyes. He did not care. The sound of the ice cracking could mean only one thing: the great winter was drawing to a close. The long night of the vampire counts faced the inevitable dawn that humanity had been longing for, and with the sun would come true death for the children of the night. With each successive step Metzger drew himself a little straighter, a little taller, sloughing the weight of the years and the burdens of so many failures from his shoulders.

The light from the fires blazed all around him, orange and red tongues licking at the sky. They lit up the spires of the citadel and the chapel and the length of the high curtain wall, throwing eerie shadows across the parapet walks along the barbican and the drum towers.

Metzger grasped the winch and turned it one cog at a time until the gates stood open, and strode out onto the wooden drawbridge.

He did not need to turn to know that the last remnants of the Twisted Thorns were gathering behind them.

The gatehouse dwarfed him, the keystone of its arch more than half his size again. The bronze plate caught every movement of the flames, transforming him into the sun as he drew the great blade and demanded, 'Face me!' at the top of his lungs.

The Knights of the Twisted Thorns emerged from the castle behind him and formed a line, blades drawn.

The wind shifted, skirting the wall walk, bringing back with it the stench of the desecrated town beyond the frozen lake. The stink battered him back a step, but he recovered his balance quickly. He heard the scurry and scuttle of movement across the lake and the rasp and slither of insidious voices. He waited, the snow gathering in the chinks of his armour, squirming down his neck to dribble slowly and uncomfortably down the curve of his back. Visibility was poor but he knew they were coming.

'Face me, coward, one leader to another,' he bellowed, sending the challenge at the barred gate. 'Do away with the darkness and the shadow. Or are you afraid?'

Behind him one of the knights began to beat slowly on his shield with the flat of his sword. Another took up the beat a moment later. Then another until all of them were beating out a slow taunting rhythm. Metzger raised his sword, taking it in both hands. The flames danced along the length of the blade, bringing the cold metal to life.

Shadows thickened along the expanse of the ice lake. He could feel their eyes on him. The scrutiny made his flesh crawl.

With the snow swirling around him, Felix Metzger walked slowly out onto the ice, the cacophony of swords on shields ringing in his ears.

'Face me,' he yelled again.

He saw long, delicate and utterly bloodless fingers reaching out of the snow towards him, black nails thick with crusted dirt. The long fingers became a hand, each fine bone picked out in sharp relief against the slack white skin.

Metzger's breath caught in his throat as the snows parted around the pallid, bald pate of the beast. The vampire revealed itself. It was not the beast he had imagined in his nightmares.

'You would face me, little man?' the creature wheezed, its voice a grating death rattle. It was less, and yet more than he had expected: less monstrous, more human. Bloodless lips parted on crooked and chipped tombstone teeth. The incisors appeared to have been filed to sharp points. 'Here I am. Bring your sword and cut me down if you would.'

It shuffled forward two paces, crook-backed and wizened.

'Cut me down, hero of the Empire, if that is what is in your heart.'

The vampire threw its bony arms wide. The creature's clothes hung on it like rags. Snow devils swarmed around its legs. Clumps of white hair matted at the base of its skull. Only its black eyes set deep in the hollows of its head betrayed any sort of strength or cunning. They were soaked in moon madness.

Metzger stepped forward, licking his lips uncertainly. This was Korbhen? This decrepit thing? The swords of his men still rang out, matching the pounding of his heart. He stared at the beast he had hunted for so long, at a loss to explain its frailty. 'Evil wears countless faces,' he told himself, peering snow-blind into the darkness beyond Korbhen's cadaverous figure. He was looking for the trick. This wretched thing could not be the vampire that had plagued his protectorate. It could not possibly have the blood of so many staining its ruined hands. There had to be another, some monster with the strength to tear asunder the rules that bound his world together, capable of reaving the veil between life and death, capable of all the evil he had been forced to live through.

The vampire moved slowly, as though age had calcified its brittle bones and even this little movement was tortuous. Metzger stepped forward to meet it, feeling faintly ludicrous brandishing his great sword at such a pitiful creature.

'Death would be a mercy,' Felix Metzger said.

'What would you know of death? Have you lived in its shadow for so long that you claim to know it?' Korbhen reached out a filthy fingernail and tapped it against the burnished bronze breastplate, matching the rhythm of the swords hammering shields behind Metzger. Each light touch placed a deeper and deeper chill in his heart. The vampire leaned in close, its bloodless lips grazing Metzger's ear as it whispered, 'You think you can stop me with your big sword?' The vampire's malevolence saturated its voice. Metzger felt the chill thrill of the beast's sharpened teeth graze the skin beneath his ear. He lurched back to the sound of the creature's mocking laughter. The sudden shocking intimacy of the gesture chilled his blood more thoroughly than the snow or the wind ever could. Sickness clawed at his craw. He had thought he was prepared. He had been a fool.

The sound of drums intensified, taken up within the anonymity of the snow out over the lake and back towards the ruined town. They grew louder and louder in his ears with every heartbeat as the creatures sheltering within the snow hammered on the ice with fist and claw, drowning out the efforts of Metzger's men.

'You think a little fire and noise frightens me, Metzger? Yes, I know your name. I know all about you, Felix Metzger. The dead whisper to me, telling their tales, but then they fear me. The dead fear me. Can you comprehend the power instilled in these old bones?'

He saw them, indistinct shadow-shapes, leering faces, hungry eyes glittering in the swirling snowflakes, twisted and deformed. Not one or two, but hundreds of them writhing in the shadows out on the ice. Some of their faces bore the marks of their deformity, the skin slipped, eyeless sockets hollow, the cartilage of noses rotten away. With others it was less obvious, limbs shrunken, claws instead of hands, spines twisted, feet clubbed. The creatures lurking in the ward were truly monstrous.

'What are these monsters?' he breathed, his question barely a whisper.

'You have your soldiers, I have mine,' Korbhen said, licking his pale lips.

The creatures came out of the snow, moving with shocking speed, their vile visages twisted and brutal as they hurled themselves at the line of knights. The Twisted Thorns surged out onto the ice to meet them.

The vampire's gaze held Metzger apparently incapable of movement as some wretched mesmerism gripped his muscles. By sheer force of will the old knight broke free, bringing his flame-scalloped blade up. He lunged at the vampire's heart.

The creature moved with a speed and force that belied its apparent frailty. The bones of its face contorted, the line of its jaw distending as the beast's thin, bloodless lips curled back. Even as Metzger buried his blade deep in the vampire's gut, thrusting up beneath the ribs spittle frothed from its mouth, silvered by the moon, as the vampire bared its fangs. In that moment, the hollow nothing between heartbeats, Felix Metzger saw the beast for what it was, but by then it was too late. The vampire threw itself further onto the knight's sword, teeth tearing out

Metzger's throat with shocking savagery even as the warrior's blade missed its heart by the merest fraction.

Metzger lost his grip on the blade.

It did not fall to the ice.

The sound of drumming on the ice drowned out the bronze knight's screams while the necrarch fed with barely controlled frenzy.

CHAPTER ONE

Beneath the Bone Garden
Kastell Metz, Deep in the Heart of the Howling Hills,
Middenland
The Autumn of All Our Fears, 2532

'Peace! I want peace! Is that so much to ask?' Radu raged against the dying night. He clawed at his skull, raking the mottled flesh of his scalp with thick crusts of nail and then turned and slammed his clenched fists against the wall. Had there been blood in his veins it would have run from the deep graze he tore into his skin.

Radu's footsteps haunted the vast subterranean chamber as he paced back and forth, back and forth, beneath the spectre of failure.

He wore a tattered black cloak over a close-fitting, brown, tailored topcoat and a blood-red cravat that covered his throat. The cravat was held in place by a five-pointed black iron pin, its head worn down by years of thoughtless caressing while the vampire worried through a conundrum. The cloak was spattered with smears of blood and alchemical treatments that had seared holes in the coarse fabric. The topcoat was of a cut that had ceased to be common centuries before, worn ragged at the cuffs to expose flesh that had rotted through to the bone.

A pustulent reek pervaded the creature's lair with no breeze from the world above to stir it. Thin ribbons of turgid water dripped through the grave dirt and fell fifty feet to the floor, drip, drip, drip, leaving stagnant puddles to gather across the hard stone.

As Radu walked behind the single source of light, an oil burner, he cast an emaciated silhouette against the distant wall. As he stalked around the rim of the two great pits in the centre of the chamber his shadow stretched out, thin fingers growing impossibly long, ears taking on a bat-like sharpness to their shape even as all the strength seemed to be hollowed out of his form.

Every inch of the walls was covered in mad intricate scrawls in countless languages, pictograms, and numerals. There were drawings, far more complex than any cave drawing, rendering concepts as art in a struggle to capture the essence of their meaning. Snatches of enchantment and incantation were inked in beside precisely rendered alchemical formulae. It was all packed so closely together that the walls had ceased to make any sense to anyone but their creator. So many secrets, so many discoveries, had been blotted out by Radu's hand as more ideas began to take root in his diseased mind.

'Why do you vex me so? What is so difficult to understand? This noise! This noise! How am I supposed to concentrate with this infernal racket? There is always so much noise.'

The chamber was shrouded in complete and utter silence.

The ceiling, fifty feet above his head was a vast writhing mass of leathery bodies, bats nesting in the chill confines of the cavernous enclosure. Moonlight leaked in through the vents the bats used for their passage to the world above.

'Go! Now!'

His two thralls, Casimir and Amsel, ever faithful, shared a look and emptied the bones they carried into the great pits. Then they shuffled out, leaving him alone with his despair. Radu was not to be reasoned with.

More bones were gathered in piles spread out across the granite floor, hundreds of thousands of them of all shapes and sizes. Decay had set in, leeching the marrow from the largest. Porous craters speckled the balls of the joints where calcification had already begun to occur. They had been in the dirt too long with nothing to preserve them from the ravages of the elements. Radu picked up one the size of his forearm and hurled it at the mocking shadows. It shattered on the painted wall.

'Must you always weep, woman? Day and night, so much wretched sobbing. You wear my patience thin. Were you not already dead I would give you a reason to sob your heart out.' He turned away from the wall to face the spectre of a girl, a maid, standing in the centre of the largest pile of bones. She was naked and clutched at her chest, which still bore the savage

wound that had killed her. The place where her heart
should have been lay empty, her ethereal torso
stripped back to bear the empty cavity. Tears streaked
her cheeks, and her blue eyes were haunted by a
melancholy so deep and profound that even without
the wound to bear witness he knew she belonged to
the dead of this place, bound still by grief or hate. She
crossed her arms over her breasts when she saw him
leering.

Hopping from foot to foot in a mad caper, Radu
snatched up another bone and hurled it through her
shade, cackling madly as he did so. She threw up her
arms amid his rising laughter, losing substance and
solidity before his eyes. He hurled a third bone,
through her tears. 'Now, go woman, lest you would
have me reeve your soul, shred it and banish it to that
darkness from which there is no haunting? Go, you
are disturbing my work!'

She was already gone and only the ragged whisper
of her weeping remained.

Grinning fiercely, Radu scattered the bones at his
feet, dropped to his knees and began to paw through
them, discarding some and stacking others reverently.
He scrambled forward, pulling a piece of charcoal
from his pocket and began scraping it across the hard
stone, trying to record an idea that flowered fully
formed in his mind. The charcoal stick snapped under
the insistent pressure of his urgent writing. Cursing,
Radu hurled a piece of the broken stick away in disgust and bent down again to continue, only to have
lost the thought. He stood and scuffed his feet over
the half-finished drawing, knowing that whatever it

had been, the notion was lost to him now. It would return, in time, or it wouldn't. So many ideas didn't.

He sat amid the bones. The stench of the swamp still clung to them. The creature had been dead for so, so long, but the bones remembered. He let his crooked fingers linger, stroking the length of a single vertebrae almost half his size. 'My beautiful one... you will rise again in majesty. You will soar.' As his fingers touched the bone an image of the creature swelled in his mind, the mighty beast owning both land and sky. 'Soon, my beauty, soon.'

The greatest of all the bones, the skull of some enormous beast with its massive ridged brows and over-sized canine jaw, stood like an altar at the far side of the chamber. Even stripped of scale and flesh it had a daunting presence. Beside the skull row upon row of dusty tomes were stacked haphazardly, some open on cracked spines, others bound in human skin so brittle that he dared never open them lest their secrets be lost for eternity. Such knowledge had been amassed beneath the graveyard: words unspoken since antiquity, ancient wisdom, glimpses into the darkest arts, thoughts and philosophies from races long since lost to the world. Radu whispered the words of a simple incantation, causing one of the countless bones to rise up, separated from the rest, only to fall as his concentration slipped.

Screams filled the room, echoing off the walls as a coterie of spectres shambled through his workshop, none of them whole. Each bore the deformities of life, though in the shadows the illusion of wholeness survived. As they passed through the light the glamour-flesh failed and the wounds that undid them, noose burns, knife-wounds, gaping holes, hideous burns and the bloated rot of decay was exposed. They dragged ruined limbs, remembering the agonies of life.

'Begone!' Radu screeched, cursing the damned even as they fled his wrath. The shades disappeared into the charcoal-smeared walls.

Someone coughed behind him; an absurdly polite gesture. Radu wheeled around to see that Casimir had crept back into the subterranean chamber. His face bore none of the ruin that marred Amsel's, but death was new to Casimir. His long white hair, cinched in a ragged knot of string at the nape of the neck, had lost the lustre of life but had yet to flake away with the desiccated skin of his scalp. Like Radu, he wore an immaculately tailored suit that had seen better days. Moths and maggots had eaten clean through the wool weave in several places. The leather of his left shoe had rotted through, baring pallid white flesh and thick ridges of bone.

'What?' Casimir shuffled uncomfortably. Radu enjoyed his uncertainty. 'Speak up, man. What do you want?'

'I had a thought about the work, master,' Casimir said not meeting his eye.

'You had a thought about the work? How splendid. A thought. Did you catch it and write it down or did it flit like a bat out of your little brain?'

'It is about the bones, master,' the thrall said, and there was something almost sly about the way he said it that rankled with Radu. The necrarch sneered, 'The bones?'

'Yes, master.'

'Well are you going to share this thought of yours or am I going to have to pry your tongue out and have it whisper in my ear all by itself?'

Casimir tugged self-consciously at his ear and shuffled from foot to foot. Radu smiled, appreciating the deference. With his rotten cheeks the expression was far from friendly. Casimir craned his head towards the skull, speaking sotto voce, 'If bones are like stone, is it possible they absorb the memories of things that happen around them?'

'Possible,' Radu mused, intrigued by the notion that a skull might retain the memories of the departed.

'If we can cause those memories to stir, perhaps the beast can remember itself.'

Radu's smile turned cruel. 'You think it falls apart because the beast cannot remember what it was? Preposterous.'

'No, master,' Casimir said his tone shifting again, wheedling, 'not precisely. May I demonstrate? It is far more effective to see than to hear.'

Amused, Radu gestured towards the pile of bones. 'Go ahead.'

Casimir drew back the ragged sleeves of his topcoat, like a prestidigitator undertaking the simplest legerdemain. He took a small alembic from the depths of his pocket. It contained some sort of cloudy white distillate. Casimir uncorked the tube and began to chant slowly, the rhythm of his words building momentum as he agitated the liquid. He crumbled something in his fingers and added it to the alembic, causing the liquid to shift from white to chartreuse. Next, as his incantation intensified, he withdrew a fragment of glass, which he crushed and flaked into the mixture. The chant took on speed. His words were precise, each syllable clipped so that they did not run into one another. He knelt, still gently agitating the alembic, and drew a small bone-handled knife from the same pocket he had taken the glass tube from. His eyes had rolled into his skull, the pupils disappearing. Still his hands moved with uncommon surety, as he deftly peeled away slithers of bone from one of the larger vertebrae. The bone went into the alembic, the final ingredient.

Radu watched with barely masked fascination, quite perplexed by Casimir's trance. The distillate had turned perfectly clear before Casimir ceased shaking it. Then, with surprising aggression, the thrall shattered the alembic in the centre of the bones and raised his face to the distant ceiling. The bats above mirrored the agitation below, their leathery wings astir as one by one they woke from their graveyard sleep.

'Rise!' Casimir shouted, all meekness vanishing from his voice. At the sound of his cry hundreds of bats burst into shrieking flight, their shrill screeches deafening in the confines of the subterranean chamber. Curious acoustics made the noise move around them in the same tight spiral as their wild flight. 'Rise!' Casimir commanded again, driving the bats towards the vents and out into the first shadows of twilight.

Radu was not watching the bats. He stared, rapt by his thrall's theatrics as Casimir beseeched the bones to miraculously come to life. He wanted to laugh, but he felt a frisson in the stale air that had not been there a moment before. Something was happening. Casimir punctuated each new word with a sharp flick of the wrist, urging the bones to rise. No, not the bones, Radu realised, captivated by the genius of his underling. It was no mere reanimation. It truly did appear as though Casimir's invocation conjured the memories out of the bones, his exhortations willing a vaporous ghost of what once had been into the air so that, for a moment at least, the great beast's skeleton dominated the huge chamber.

Radu gazed upon it with nothing short of awe, though he masked it well. It disturbed him that his thrall had rendered the physiognomy of the wyrm so beautifully. He moved forward, reaching out to touch the ghost-light as the memory of each bone came together to complete the whole. Just as it was no mere reanimation, it was no mere illusion either. Radu's calloused fingers thrilled to the touch, the energy flowing from the ghost-light through him as blood once had. 'She is beautiful,' he breathed, captivated by the thickening of the memory. The longer Casimir maintained the invocation the stronger the memory of the bones became. The first red muscles coagulated around the sheen of bone and then the fatty white of sinew and more, huge pulsing sacs of lung and pounding heart within the cage of bone, and still more as Casimir's words gave it body.

The more the great wyrm remembered itself, the more Radu forgot himself.

The ghost of fire roiled in the guts of the beast.

Sinew and tendon slowly plated over with ethereal scales.

The ghost-memory was so real that Radu turned to look back over his shoulder at the huge skull still on the stone floor at the other side of the room. The wyrm dwarfed him, standing almost ten times his height, barely caged within the huge chamber, the remembered wings spanned tip to tip two hundred feet, and were furled up at the beast's sides as it lowered its massive head to stare at the jumble of broken bones before it.

'Beautiful,' Radu said again, and the ghost opened its jaws to breathe fire. He stood unmoving in the heart of it as twin gouts of flame seared the air around him, but there was no heat. The flames roared, turning everything to blood. Radu stared as the unforgettable fire coiled around him, cradling his corrupt flesh in what should have been a cleansing flame that stripped him down layer by layer, from flesh to bone to soul. Then the fire in the beast's heart burned out, as though it understood that its shade was no match for its true form, that death denied it might and majesty, and the last lingering lick of flame played with his outstretched hands.

The great door slammed behind him, the sound resonating through the stones of the floor and walls. The unexpected noise disturbed Casimir's concentration, causing the memory of the bones to unravel as quickly as it had come together. The thrall shrieked his pain as the flame vanished from around his fingers, leaving the flesh untouched. The breaking of the spell brought Casimir to his knees, hands pressed against his temples as the backlash of magic tore into him. Radu had no pity for the thrall's failure. He turned to see Amsel shuffling into the room, the crook-backed thrall dragging his lame foot. He clutched a large sack of bones.

His eyes glimmered with the last moment of the memory's reflection. He dumped the bones into the nearest pit. 'The master is strong in death magic.'

Radu looked from Amsel to Casimir; he was right, he was strong in the ways of the death wind, but Casimir had just done something that he had never even imagined.

He recalled the sly tone that Casimir had used before raising the memory of the bones. Hearing it again in his mind it sent an icy shiver down the length of Radu's spine.

He watched his thrall with distrust as he gathered the remains of the alembic from within the pile of bones.

'The distillate, of course. Yes, I had ventured such an invocation months ago, but judged it little more than pretty lights. You disappoint me, Casimir, I had hoped you had something of interest to show me.'

'Sorry, master,' the thrall said, but this time Casimir defiantly met his eye.

CHAPTER TWO

Deeper than Bones
Kastell Metz, Deep in the Heart of the Howling Hills,
Middenland
The Autumn of All Our Fears, 2532

AMSEL SOUGHT REFUGE in the darkness.

He moved slowly, dragging his ruined fingers across the stones.

'Casimir, Casimir, Casimir: master's favourite, master's lickspittle, master's chosen. Casimir the ugly, Casimir the liar, dirty stinking Casimir with treachery in his heart. Why can't the master see like we can? How does the traitor blind the master to his ambitions? How can the master not see?' And at the root of his grief, 'Why does the master ignore us? Why? How have we wronged the master? How have we disappointed him that he chooses to ignore us in favour of that damned Casimir? What of us? What of Amsel, oldest, most loyal, what of me?'

The dark was his friend. It did not judge. It did not mock. It did not flaunt its superiority.

There was so much secret darkness hidden within the castle: chambers long sealed away, lost to cobwebs, spiders and ghosts; passageways that reached out like wizened fingers beneath the lake into the belly of the hills; the warren of cells that had housed the screams of countless fallen foes banished into that same darkness that Amsel craved; the crypts with their sarcophagi and effigies, stacked with rotten grave goods; and then there were the true secrets, the places only he had found, deep in the foundations of the castle where the stones rooted into the hills; the walls that were not walls, that slid and moved beneath his touch, their mechanisms rusty but still serviceable. These were the dark places he returned to again and again. Some were shown to him, others found. He had not yielded up all the secrets of the castle to Radu, some he kept for himself.

He dragged his lame foot behind him, his gait a lopsided shuffle-drag, shuffle-drag. As he moved down the claustrophobic passageways he breathed a single word again and again, snuffing out the alchemical globes that stubbornly held some trace of light in their glass hearts. The globes were Radu's creation, meant to be used up above, to light the hovels of the coterie of the damned that they had gathered to them. He had stolen a few, using their long light to help root out more nooks and crannies where he could be alone to think and scheme.

His footsteps echoed their peculiar echo. He heard the mockery of eternity in them, the deformities of his flesh that would stay with him forever and beyond. His flesh was a cloak that even in death he could not cast off, a weakness he could never be free of. He loathed it, just as he loathed all flesh.

In the darkest places of his mind he imagined stripping the world of its flesh, turning the perfect footsteps of the living into a haunting reminder of their mortality, and draining out the sustenance that was blood from their veins and scorching the meat with hideous fire until nothing of the flesh remained. He kept those thoughts behind his wretched face, secret, hidden for now.

The master would not overlook him for long. Oh no, Radu the Forsaken would see him as he finally shed the shadows. Until then he would find peace down below, deeper than bones, where the others never came. Radu had made the vault beneath the cemetery his haven, and rarely left, living in the filth of his experiments. Casimir clung to the high places, tending the ravens and laying his plans to oust them all. Only Amsel truly understood the nature of the castle, but then he had lived there longest.

The passage ended in a stone wall that was not there. Amsel closed his eyes as he stepped into and then through the false wall. Beyond it lay a thick door that still bore the vestiges of the familial crest of the first inhabitants of Kastell Metz all those centuries before.

It was a sigil he associated with the first master of the castle, Korbhen, though it was not the great necrarch lord's mark but one he had stolen from the castle's inhabitants.

The mysteries of Korbhen's horde had lain hidden behind that door for so long: pages written in the blood of his sire, on pages cured from his flesh and bound in his skin as he moved towards ascension, unburdened by the bonds of flesh. Those pages contained all the wisdom of the creature that was Korbhen's father in death, and such secrets they were. Precious few remained.

He would make the new master value him. He would bring him a treasure such as his greed could only imagine. The thought thrilled him. The master was wise. He had foreseen all eventualities, even this, the arrival of a rival. His fingers went to his throat, feeling out the vein where once his pulse had been so strong. He wore the wound still that had welcomed him into this second world of ghosts and shades where blood meant so little.

Unlike so much of his life before, he remembered still the heady tang of the blood kiss as if their lips had just parted. His entry into a second life had been so much sweeter than his entry into the first, his mother squatting in an alley, amid a mulch of rotting cabbages, cauliflowers and seed potatoes that had been thrown out from the market the night before. She told him later that she had almost abandoned him to the animals and let them eat their fill, but something had stayed her hand.

It was not love, for she had never loved a thing in her life, not even the men she rutted with; not compassion, for the life she cursed him too was worse than death at the jaws of the dogs. Perhaps it was hate, because she surely hated him every day of his stinking life. In comparison his second birth, into death, had been tender despite the pain. He would do anything for the master who shared his blood, and to think that he had first turned up at the gates of Kastell Metz looking to kill him.

Amsel opened the door.

The familiar smell greeted him before he set foot inside. The pages retained the perfume of their maker even after all this time. He stood in the doorway, breathing it in. There were two low shelves in the centre of the room, and glass cabinets against one wall. Where there had been so many treasures now there was only broken glass and empty shelves. The wonders were gone, save for the single sheet that lay beneath the glass of the last one. Korbhen had pillaged most of the arcane treasures before abandoning the castle in search of von Carstein's book, lost all these years since the fall of Drakenhof at the end of the Winter War.

He looked down at the single sheet of sun-cured skin in the last cabinet. The bloody ink had paled to the point of illegibility.

Amsel cleared the splinters of broken glass away with great care and lifted the skin of the great vampire out. He handled it reverently, but still it was brittle beneath his clumsy fingers. A fragment from the edge crumbled away, taking half a word with it. Amsel could not read the text; it had taken him three centuries to learn his letters and how to inscribe his own name. These words were older than any language he had mastered in the years since. All he knew was that this one page contained secrets so great that they would damage Casimir in the new master's eyes, restoring his reliance upon Amsel. The master had promised him.

'The master is wise,' Amsel crooned, cradling the page to his chest as he left the hidden chamber. He walked slowly. He did not breathe light back into the alchemical globes. There was no need; he knew every twist and turn intimately and he preferred the darkness.

'WHAT IS THIS, fool?'

'I found it, master,' Amsel said, still not showing the blood-inked side of the cured page to Radu.

'You disturb my studies to show me something you found? What are you, some kind of child needing my approval? A kitten bringing me a gift? You should be more like Casimir. He applies his intellect to the problems we face, he does not squirrel himself away in the dark, making his home down with the rats. Show me this treasure, then and let me judge its worth,' Radu said with disgust. Radu had been in a vile temper for days. The beast refused to rise; no matter what invocation he applied, the bones remained bones.

The threshold of death was not so great or daunting that it could not be crossed. Something stymied the necrarch's work, some piece of wisdom he lacked. Ignorance made a monster of him. He paced the perimeter of the workshop, scratching out formulae and pictograms as his anger and frustration rose. An entire stretch of wall was now solid black, whatever had been beneath it lost forever, and as he scrubbed out the writing he raged. Amsel moved quietly, creeping through the detritus strewn across the workshop floor soundlessly; soundlessly because he heard the vile name Casimir trip off the new master's tongue.

The way Radu said it, the syllables dripping with acid as they left his mouth, brought pleasure to Amsel's withered heart. He lurked, hoping for more, a hint as to the reason behind the loathing, but Radu fell silent, scrubbing and scrubbing at the charcoal erasing all traces of the words beneath. When he hadn't uttered a sound for the longest time, Amsel dared approach with his prize.

Still the master vented his scorn upon him.

'Paper? You bring me paper? Does it have words on it, this miraculous paper, or is it blank?'

'It is not paper, master,' he said, holding it up before his face and inhaling to emphasise his point. 'You can still smell the fragrance of the man beneath the skin.'

'Cured flesh? Well it isn't the best writing material, the ink fails to take to it, over time it fades. I suppose that is why it is blank, anything interesting must have soaked into the flesh. Here, let me have it.'

Amsel lowered the page from his face and gave it to Radu. The necrarch turned the page over in his hands. His eyes betrayed nothing as he saw the faint scratchings of the dead language that remained. He mirrored Amsel, lifting it to his nose to inhale the essence of the man who had sacrificed his flesh for the word. Still his dead eyes showed no hint of pleasure as he breathed deeply of the brittle skin.

'There is nothing remotely interesting about this find of yours. You bother me with trifles. The markings are gibberish, the man himself of no consequence. I am disappointed, Amsel. I thought more of you than this. Go, and do not bother me again unless you have something of worth to say.'

Amsel held out his hand to take the page back.

'Oh no, I shall keep this, I think,' Radu said. 'I am sure I can get some use out of it. I can bleach the remnants of ink from it and use it again to record one of my own formulae, perhaps.'

'The master is wise,' Amsel said, leaving Radu alone with the page and its hidden secrets, satisfied that he had planted the seed of curiosity no matter how vehement the necrarch's denials.

ALONE, RADU EXAMINED the page.

He did not recognise the script, which in itself piqued his curiosity. He had mastery of thirty-seven tongues, more than even his own sire. He had dedicated decades of his existence to the accumulation of languages, of graphology and syntax, the similarities so many tongues had at their roots, showing a common heritage, and so much more. Yet here was a page unearthed in his own home in a script he had never seen, bearing no similarity to any of the tongues he was familiar with.

Which, he surmised, meant it was no script at all, but if not a script, then what?

The blood used to ink it had faded to the point that some symbols were obscured, and around the edges of the page decay had claimed more than a few others.

There were several repetitions within the markings, the same brush strokes rendered again and again, where other symbols appeared but once. Curiously, a few of the symbols were misplaced on the page, slightly above the line of the rest, or slightly below.

The penmanship was so intricate that it was difficult to imagine that the displacement was due to carelessness, which meant it was almost certainly deliberate.

'A cipher,' Radu mused, guessing the nature of the page, but what secrets did it unlock? And more pertinently, how could he ever hope to possess those secrets even after deciphering the page?

Secrets within secrets? His mind raced with the possibilities.

Some of the symbols were relatively simple, intersecting lines, spheres and hemispheres, others were more intricate. The repetitions would be the key. In any language certain double letters revealed the intent of the cipher's creator, but without somewhere to begin it would prove if not impossible, then incredibly difficult to work any meaning out of the greater text.

His fingers lingered on the cured skin, recognising the stench of death upon it. Though it possessed no magic of its own, this was no mere page that Amsel had rendered unto him. He needed to know more about the page, and where the thrall had found it. Had Amsel recognised the taint of the blood kiss that still clung to the skin? Radu crouched over the page, inhaling its intoxicating perfume once more. He imagined the layers of fragrance hidden just below the most pungent: the streets the vampire walked, the flesh he tasted, his desires and discoveries all seeped into that single page so long ago. He would have done almost anything for the chance to inhale them, drawing the essences of all those forgotten memories into him that he might learn from them.

Laying the page aside, he went in search of Amsel.

Considering the underground labyrinth and the above ground sprawl, the castle was huge, with countless hiding places for the lame thrall. That Amsel knew it far better than anyone else, having lived all of his life within the walls, exploring its dark and deep places, made him almost impossible to find if he did not want to be found.

Though they all had chambers within the towers, Amsel was a nester by nature and had several nooks and crannies that he had feathered for comfort out of the life of the castle, all below ground. It would take him the best part of the night to track down the errant thrall if he had to traipse to even half of them. The alternative was to have the others look for him.

Loath to leave his workshop with so much undone, Radu chose the lesser of two evils. He pushed open the great double doors of the workshop, for a moment wearing their shadows like ethereal wings, and stalked out. He would have Amsel brought to him in the high tower, close to the soothing radiance of Morrslieb and Mannslieb, and as far away as possible from the places where Amsel felt so comfortable.

The workshop was annexed to the old cells, hollowed out from the rock beneath the graveyard, and linked to the main keep by a narrow twisting passageway. Damp seeped through the smooth stones, lending them a gloss that caught the glow of the alchemical globes. The ceiling was low, barely clearing the height of Radu's bald head, and the floor sloped upwards as it neared the cells, causing him to hunch slightly as he walked. The texture of the stones changed, as well, from natural stone cut away to inlaid blocks used to hold back the weight of the dirt. The new material brought with it new odours, most redolent the musk of the grave dirt it held back and the brackish water that stagnated in it.

He found two lost souls in the cells, Rakeh and Rane. The twins looked at him with the disturbing cataract-filled white stare they shared. It was the only thing they did share: Rakeh was thin to the point of emaciation, hollow eyes and sallow skin, his long greasy hair pure white, while Rane was rotund and ruddy, with spikes of ebon-black hair greased into points.

'Find Amsel, and when you do, bring him to the Galas Tower. I shall be with the ravens, enjoying the moons.'

'As you wish…' Rane said, dusting off his meaty hands on his coarse apron.

'…master,' Rakeh finished.

THE WIND CARRIED the dreams of mortals, spilled by twitching sleep-fevered lips and whipped away.

Radu braced himself against one of the machicolations, the twin moons casting his twisted shadow down to the abutments below. A few of Casimir's ravens slept with their heads beneath their oily black wings, creating the illusion of a row of headless guardians ringing the tower. They were not his chosen watchers; the carrion eaters lacked the finer qualities of his beloved bats who could find their way unerringly without sight, using echolocation to sound out the landscape they needed to navigate. Yet many of his kind craved the company of the death eaters, seeing them as some sort of kindred creature. They did make a better meal, he thought, looking at one of the fat-bellied birds.

The hills were laid out before him like waves crashing up against the shore of his home. The lake, alive with small ripples agitated by the breeze, had taken on a sickly green pallor from the moon's glow.

The waters had risen, effectively isolating the castle. A peculiarity of the mechanisms he had devised caused the tidal ebb and flow of this land-locked lake high in the Howling Hills. It had been no huge feat of engineering but rather a subtle enchantment of the subterranean waters, causing them to swell with the rising of the moon, and the water level of the lake to rise just as a real tide would.

Behind the curtain wall, the castle's ward teemed with its own peculiar life. From his vantage they looked like ants marching in chaotic lines, intersecting but somehow never colliding. He spent so much of his life below ground, wrapped up in his experiments that he sometimes forgot about the coterie Amsel had gathered here, offering them refuge in the anonymity of the mountains. They were damned, one and all, deformed children cast out by bitter parents, bagged and thrown in the rivers to drown, culled by shanks and left to die in the dirt, wretched creatures tainted by sickness and deformity to become freaks in their parents' eyes. The castle was their sanctuary, Amsel the one they followed. Radu suspected it was his thrall's club foot that made him sympathise with the freaks, styling them as his own coterie of the damned.

The trapdoor opened behind him.

Without turning, Radu said, 'You found him?'

'Huddled…' Rakeh answered, his reedy voice betraying his eagerness to please.

'…in the crypts,' Rane finished.

'Excellent.' Radu turned to face the three of them as they emerged. 'Now leave us.'

'Yes…'

'…master.'

The wooden trap closed behind them, fitting snugly into the chiselled stone. Like so much of the castle the fit was precise, the craftsmanship undeniable. Alone with the birds, he said to Amsel, 'These tortured souls you collect, the deformed urchins unwanted by the rest of the world…' and left the sentence hanging.

'Yes, master?' Amsel said, shuffling towards the stone crenellations.

'Why do you tend to them? Are you thinking, perhaps, of turning them against me?'

'No, master.'

'Are you sure, Amsel? Do you harbour ambitions? Do you look at me and think perhaps you might usurp me?'

'No, master.'

'Then, why do you seek out the sick and the lame and bring them to my door?'

'Not the sick and the lame, master,' Amsel said, staring down at his feet as though the worn-smooth stone beneath them was the most interesting thing in the world.

'No? When I look at them that is what I see, the freaks of the Empire given refuge. What are they then, if not your private army?'

'Tainted,' Amsel said, as though that one word explained it all.

'Tainted?' Radu repeated the word, his inflection more quizzical, as though the word explained nothing.

'Their deformities mean they are less than human.'

Radu turned back to the edge of the battlements and peered down at the shuffling legions of wretched souls that had erected hovels within the ward of the castle, at the filthy tarpaulins that covered them, forming a tent-city where the stables and latrines had once been.

'Good. Never forget, your freaks exist under my sufferance, not yours, Amsel. Like everything in this place, they are mine.' The moon bathed his white face with its deathly pallor as he craned his neck, leaning in threateningly. 'Tell me, do you plan on making a study of the degeneration? It could prove interesting... useful even. Study, dissect, find the secret and replicate it. Perhaps you should look into harnessing some of the more interesting taints as they manifest.'

'Yes, master.'

'Good, good. Now, this thing you brought me...' Radu said, leaving the rest of the sentence hanging.

'Yes, master?' Amsel said, shuffling towards the stone crenellations.

'Although it is quite worthless, it intrigues me. I would know more of its origins. Where did you happen upon it? Somewhere within the castle?'

'Yes, master.'

'That was an invitation to tell me more about your discovery, Amsel.'

'Yes, master.'

Radu swallowed down his frustration. 'I will try again. Where did you find it? Describe everything to me, leave out no details, I would paint as full a picture in my mind as may be painted from words alone.'

'Yes, master. It was in one of the old places my sire used to haunt, master. There are many such troves, now plundered, within the roots of the main keep.'

'Indeed,' Radu mused, 'and you just stumbled upon it today?'

'Yes, master, or no, master,' Amsel said, enigmatically. He twitched visibly, casting fretful glances left and right as though distrustful of the open sky. Radu enjoyed his discomfort.

'Well, which is it? It cannot be both,' Radu said, impatiently.

'The inference was that I knew it was there all along, master. To that, the answer was no, master. The words themselves suggested I happened to find it by accident, to that the answer was yes, master.'

'Are you playing games with me?'

'No master, I am being precise, as you taught me. I sought to please.' There was something about the way the thrall said it that suggested a different truth hidden within his subservient words.

'So this was the first time you had been in this hidden chamber?'

'No master, not the first, but the first time I had fallen through the wall.'

'You are making no sense, Amsel.'

'I would show you, master. The old walls, many of them are not what they seem.'

'Show me,' Radu said, his curiosity getting the better of him.

Gratefully, Amsel opened the trap and led him down into the old tunnels, down and down, deeper than the bone yard, deeper than the crypts, deeper than the very first stones of the keep, and still down.

HE FOLLOWED THE cripple to a dead end, only to see Amsel shuffle through what appeared to be solid stone and disappear behind the illusion.

'Follow, follow,' Amsel's urgent voice said, apparently from nowhere.

'Curious,' Radu muttered, reaching out tentatively. He felt the familiar tingle of magic as his fingers penetrated the wall. It was not strong, but it was effective. Even this close, the stones appeared solid. He brushed the illusion aside like a spider's web and stepped through to the other side. The passageway continued another dozen feet, ending in an open door. 'And you say you simply stumbled through the wall by mistake?'

'Yes, master,' Amsel said, turning his face away from him. Radu did not believe him for a moment. He approached the door, noting the sigil carved into the heavy wood. It was a crest he was intimately familiar with.

He pushed the door fully open and walked inside the room. With a single whispered command he brought a faint bluish light to life in his palm. Its radiance, though meagre, was enough to see that there was nothing left but broken glass and empty shelves. He walked through the debris slowly, his long fingers lingering over every inch of bare wood and shattered glass as though his touch could be enough to draw back some of the knowledge the room had once held. The light emphasised every crag and crease of his bald head, ageing him centuries with its callow caress.

'And there are more such rooms?' he asked.

'Yes, master, many more, hidden away by the old families of the castle.'

'And you know them all?'

'Oh, no, no master, not all. A few, I have found a few.'

'And they were all pillaged like this one, or did they perhaps have something of value left?'

'Nothing, master. All looted like this.'

'Korbhen,' Radu muttered. It was the only logical solution. 'Well there is nothing here. It is all a waste of time, like the page itself.'

'Yes, master.'

CHAPTER THREE

Shadow Tongues
Kastell Metz, Deep in the Heart of the Howling Hills,
Middenland
The Autumn of All Our Fears, 2532

RADU RETREATED TO his rooms to be alone with the
page.

He pored over the symbols, certain that the clues to
cracking the cipher lay in the raised letters and the
dropped ones. The flaw in the scribe's work seemed
far too deliberate to have been anything else. Laying a
fresh vellum beside the page Radu recorded each of
the raised letters first, curious to see if they made any
more sense removed from the clutter of the text. He
repeated the process with the subscript letters, scratching carefully on the blank page, each symbol rendered
in smooth script, and utterly meaningless. The second
set of symbols, released from the rest, made no more
sense.

A different language perhaps?

A substitution code?

Could it actually be as simple as that? He counted the symbols he had just copied, but there were twenty-nine different ones, too many for the alphabet.

Just one word, a single one, would give him a place to begin.

He looked for matching pairs of symbols, reasoning that they must represent double letters, but even with that it was a long stretch to even interpreting a four letter word from the apparently random twists and squiggles of bloody ink.

Frustrated, he sent the pot of ink sailing across the room to explode in a Rorschach stain all over the soft white stones of the wall. He stared at the stain for a full minute, looking for some kind of fortuitous pattern hidden within it, but there was no such divination waiting to save him from the torments of ignorance.

He turned back to the page yet again, convinced there had to be something in it he had overlooked, something so painfully obvious that he had dismissed it in search of a deeper meaning.

There was nothing.

The symbols were not alchemical. They were no language he had ever encountered. Were they perhaps numerical? No, a base of twenty-nine was a nonsensical counting system, so not that.

'But what?' Radu railed at the document, his gnarled fingers inches from tearing the page up in frustration. 'WHAT?'

Why go to such extreme lengths unless you are trying to hide something truly valuable?

Nights of obsessive study did nothing to illuminate the text. Radu cracked his knuckles, drumming his thick dirt-crusted nails on the wooden surface of the writing table. Radu cracked the bones in his neck, rolling his crook-backed shoulders. He dreamt of the page, the symbols blurring and moving, lifting off the page and rearranging themselves to taunt him. He heard the whispered voices of the night gaunts promising the truth if he burned the page, and laced in and out of the hallucinations, a face conjured for the skin and blood to own, a face to demand answers from.

He awoke on the sixth morning in a tangled mess of sweat, the inside of his coffin lid bearing the frantic scratch marks where during his slumber he had tried to claw his way out of the box.

It wasn't until he walked back into the workshop to see Casimir hunched over the scattering of bones that it occurred to him there was more than one way to skin this particular cat.

'I have a task for you, a test.'

'Master?' Casimir asked, looking up.

'I have prepared a challenge, to evaluate your learning, Casimir. You show signs of aptitude, but signs are not always correct, omens turn sour, hope fades. I would see how well you apply process to a conundrum. If you fail me, your time here is done. Is that understood?'

'Yes, master,' Casimir said, standing and brushing the bone-dust from his hands. 'You are wise, master. I shall not fail.'

'I trust not,' Radu said, smiling callously. 'You will accompany me to my tower. I will watch your methods with interest.'

'Of course, master.'

* * *

RADU STOOD BY the empty fireplace, watching as Casimir pored over the sun-cured skin. His cheek ticked every time something struck him as interesting, Radu noted, wondering if perhaps the same tell would give away more truths in different circumstances. He chose, very deliberately, to remember it.

As he expected, Casimir approached the problem much the same as he had, noticing the irregularity of the script.

'It is a key of sorts,' Casimir said eventually.

'Indeed it is. Good. Is that all you have gleaned from it thus far?'

Casimir touched the skin for the first time, lifting his index finger to his lips and licking the residue off.

'No, master. It was not made this day, or any day recently. The blood is old.'

'Very good. Tell me more.'

'I believe the page is cured skin.'

'It is.'

'Old blood and cured skin, testaments and revelations were often made on such, were they not?'

Radu nodded, the thought had crossed his mind, but surely if the page were part of some religious revelation it would have been at least vaguely intelligible. What was the point of the gods using mortals as conduits if they did not record their wisdom in a way that was readily open to all?

'The symbols appear to mean nothing, but I suspect they must or you would not have set the challenge.'

'Indeed,' Radu said.

Casimir raised his index finger to his nose, inhaling its fragrance as though it held the intoxicating tang of martyrs' blood still on it. 'Could it be that the blood itself is the key?' He looked at Radu for encouragement. With none forthcoming, he touched the script, tracing his fingertip over the curl of symbols. 'Yes,' he said, breathing the gift of death in to his lungs. 'Most curious. Not a religious revelation then, given the nature of the blood.'

'Your reasoning?'

'There are few instances of blood rites recording written words, and bar a few of the darkest practices, none are particularly religious in nature. The presence of blood, a poor substitute for ink at the best of times leads me to believe that there is more here than a few words of worship.'

'Indeed,' Radu said, his smile genuine this time. 'So if not the wisdom of some deity, what?'

Casimir placed his hand flat on the page. 'It will take me a few hours to prepare the alembic, but I believe you seek to test my skills and more than merely reading and reasoning.'

'Perhaps I do,' Radu said, excited by the possibility that his thrall was indeed fathoming a path through the riddles of the page that had eluded him these long days and nights. 'The path to wisdom entails many obstacles that must be negotiated, and not all of them are obvious.'

'Skin and blood, not so different from bone.'

'An interesting notion. You intend to replicate your experiment from before?'

Casimir nodded, 'Who better to tell you the secrets of the book than the book itself?'

'The writer, perhaps?' Radu said, a trace of irony in his gravelly voice.

'What is to say we can't learn one from the other?'

Radu nodded slowly. 'We might find a home for you here yet, Casimir. Go, prepare your alembic. I will meditate on your progress. Take caution, the test is not yet passed. In every achievement there is failure, in every failure the seeds of achievement.'

CASIMIR RETURNED WITH the rising moon. He cradled the small glass tube of distillate in his hands. He laid it down on the writing table beside the other gewgaws of his invocation.

Without waiting for permission he broke away a tiny piece of the page that contained both skin and blood, and crumbled it into the alembic.

Radu watched, eagerness etched into the deep crags of his vile face as Casimir powdered the root and the glass and began to agitate the tube, taking it through the transitions of colour and clarity until it became pure. The invocation was subtly different this time, the emphasis on the words shifted from syllable to syllable, the tonal quality of his voice more demanding as he called forth the shadow of skin and blood, urging it back to the flesh.

Radu breathed deeply of the Amethyst wind, Shyish, feeling it surge all around him. Casimir's mastery of the wind of magic was undeniable. His voice rose and fell, altering fractionally as he threw his arms wide, urging the wind to gather within him, its dark majesty to recall the man from his parts, bringing back the soul that had flown so that it might sing one last song.

Casimir hurled the tube down between his feet. The distillate splashed across the floor and over the ruined leather of his shoes.

'Return,' he whispered, and more forcefully, 'return!'

It came first as a single wisp curling up from the shattered remains of the alembic.

That one strand thickened, coalescing into a ribbon. A second ribbon curled around it, and a third. The window panes, streaked and bubbled, buckled and shattered to let the sighs of mortal anguish in with the gusting wind. Sorrow was its name. Radu leaned heavily on the support of the fireplace as the sharp-edged splinters of glass cut at them both, swirling and slicing. None bit deep, but they stung.

'Return!' Casimir commanded, bullying the reticent spirit back into shape and form so that it might answer their demands.

Radu tasted its bitterness on the wind, its loathing. He opened his mind to it, drinking in all the grief it cared to share. The sheer unbridled power of it was intoxicating. He revelled in the death wind, losing all sense of self as the vastness of nothing threatened to overwhelm him.

Between them the winds merged with the mist, adding substance to it.

'Return!'

Casimir's bellow brought the first faint features of a hook-nosed face out of the swirling mists. A broad, atavistic brow and cruel teeth followed, sheering the veil as the ghost of the dead man tore and snapped at it, desperate to be free. Its eyes blazed madly, the depths of hatred infinite and vile as the memory of life reared. Radu felt the malfeasance blazing blackly from it.

This was the thing that had given its flesh and tainted blood to create the page; Radu recognised its kind. It was a mortal so degenerate, so far gone that it lived in the filth of the graveyard, so far gone that it fed on the cold blood of the dead, like poison to the children of darkness. The ghoulish entity taking shape before him bared little resemblance to any human that had ever walked the world; it was bestial, a hunched monstrosity driven blood crazy. It was neither the guardian of any great secret nor the creator of the cipher, it was merely a victim. Radu swallowed the bitter bile of disappointment.

Casimir was not so easily deterred, however. He stepped forward, dangerously close to the rending talons of the beast.

He asked a single question, 'Who slew you?'

The answer came back, swallowed in the snarls of rage, 'Korbhen!'

The memory of its murderer was enough to drive all sensibility and coherence from the wretched ghost. It surrendered to paroxysms of murderous rage, teeth tearing at the air inches from Casimir's face. He stepped forward, into it, the ethereal teeth passing straight through his cruel smile. Casimir's goading of the spectre, showing the hollowness of its physical threat, was unexpected. Like the facial tick, Radu thought that he had perhaps learned something worth remembering about his thrall: he was dangerous.

'Why?' Casimir demanded. 'Why did he kill you?'

'Blood… Ritual… Betrayal… of… dead. Let… me… go!' Seven of the eight words were dragged out of the ghost's mouth, so swallowed in grunts that they were barely intelligible as words at all. The eighth was a feral roar.

'We know the maker, then,' Casimir said, turning his back arrogantly on the shade, 'and we know his reason.' He waved his hand, a curiously imperious gesture, and banished the diseased memory of the corpse eater.

'How does that help us?'

'A ritual must be recorded, yes?'

'Not necessarily,' the necrarch said, ruminating on the summoned shade's words. Blood ritual, betrayal of the dead, they did not have to fit together as neat sentences. The creature could barely form a coherent thought, could it be relied upon?

'The cipher unlocks a book, written by Korbhen, or at least pages from the same source, from the backs of mortals gone feral.'

'Where do we find such a thing, if it even exists?'

'The secret has to be hidden within the cipher,' Casimir said. 'Let me see the page again.'

Radu had been over the writing a thousand times and more, and there was nothing in it that resembled directions to some mythical book composed by his sire.

'Here!' Casimir barked triumphantly, stabbing a finger at the centre of the page. Radu hunched over, looking to see what he had found. Casimir snatched up a quill and began inking a series of quick strokes that matched not the blood ink but the spaces it left behind. 'It is not what you see, it is what you don't! Like so much the truth is hidden in plain sight! The master is wise, indeed. Look, the mark of the Man-God,' he rasped, his grin fierce. 'That is what you meant me to find, is it not?'

'An astute find, Casimir. In a world of shadow and death it is not where one looks that danger lurks, but where one is blind to it. Perception is the key. Open your mind to the possibilities. Look where you already looked, but with different eyes. Everything you need to know is in the cipher if you know how to see it.'

'The master is pleased?'

'Very,' Radu said. 'Now solve the riddle, and I shall not cut your tongue out and feed it to Amsel. Fail me, and your usefulness is at an end.'

'Yes, master,' Casimir said, already hunched back over the page, duplicating several of the spaces between the lines to release the truth for Korbhen's elaborate ruse.

RADU WAITED ON the roof of the tower, notions fermenting in his mind.

There was a game being played here, for his sake almost certainly. That Korbhen created the cipher did not surprise him, indeed he had almost expected it of his sire. There were no kindred loyalties between them; Korbhen had walked out on Kastell Metz decades before, in search of a story, nothing more. He had come across an account from the time before the Winter War that claimed a living book had been brought out of the Lands of the Dead. The discovery had become the necrarch's obsession, the intimation of what might lurk within, what power caused it life, too much for Korbhen to resist. So he had turned his back on everything, walking out on all that they had built in this remote corner, hidden away from the

world, and risked discovery and the ruin of everything.

Was the purpose of this page to draw him into
Korbhen's hunt? To manipulate him into dancing
once more to the shackles of his sire?

'I will not,' he said in stubborn denial, but just as
von Carstein's book had wormed its way into every
thought of his sire, this page of secrets and codes to
be deciphered had planted its hooks in him. He
would learn all of its secrets, and he knew that Korbhen understood that similarity in their nature, that
thirst that would keep him digging until he had excavated every last secret from the page.

Casimir joined him just before dawn, triumphant.

'Ashenford!' he said, even before he was halfway
through the door. 'That is the answer to your riddle,
master. The testament of one of the lost prophets lies
under lock and key in the Sigmarite temple in Ashenford.'

'So the cipher is the key to the ravings of a mad
man?'

'Yes, master. It is a brilliant deception cutting to the
very heart of faith and heresy. Hidden within a dream
supposedly received from the Man-God himself, lies
the wisdom of the lords of death.'

'And what is that wisdom?' Radu asked, sensing
that Casimir wanted to say more, to prove his intelligence.

'The cipher is a mix of languages. If I have
interpreted it correctly, this secret will shake the
Empire to its foundations, master.'

Radu raised a hairless eyebrow.

'The hidden incantation is tied to a ritual of blood, as the ravaged beast claimed, an incantation that invigorates the dead.'

'Invigorates? A curious choice of words.'

Casimir nodded and said, 'The text is explicit, the enchantment alters the nature of the risen dead. It stimulates the diseased brain, creating a learning animal, capable of swiftness and more lethally, the most basic of thoughts. Imagine the shambling dead thus changed! Adapting, learning, growing more and more deadly as they understand the mind of their enemy! Imagine the fear that would place in the hearts of the living!'

'You have done well, Casimir. I will not kill you today.'

'Thank you, master. I exist to please. Let me recover this testament. Let me lead a force of bone warriors into the heart of the humans and steal this great truth from beneath their noses.'

Radu looked into his thrall's face and saw the hunger there, the unashamed greed and ambition, and denied him. 'No, you are needed here, with me. I will send Amsel, it is only right as he brought this testament to my attention.'

'You would send the lame one?' Casimir asked, disgusted.

'I would, and I will brook no argument. Do not defy me in this, Casimir. You have done well, do not make me regret my decision to keep you alive. As you said, you serve my will. It is not the other way around.'

'Yes, master. But–'

'Enough. Now leave me to think. There is much to plan if we are to mount a crusade for this lost testament.'

Radu was pleased to see the flare of undisguised hatred in Casimir's eyes as he turned to leave; the servant's naked ambition was a concern that would bear closer scrutiny. After all, he had risen to power through treachery and betrayal and he could expect no less of those he favoured.

CHAPTER FOUR

Drowning in the River Death
Grimminhagen, in the Shadow of the Drakwald Forest,
Middenland
The Autumn of Sacrifice, 2532

REINHARDT METZGER HELD his right arm outstretched for the silver-grey goshawk. The wind was fierce but that didn't slow the bird's swooping descent. It came in fast, wings furled and then opened them at the last moment, arresting its dive. The bird never settled on the leather gauntlet, preferring to sink its talons into the meat of his shoulder rather than be tethered. Their bite was always a sharp jolt but far from agony. When the bird was younger he had worn a leather harness on his shoulder but the goshawk would invariably come down on the other, unprotected shoulder. The skin had long since been toughened by the raking claws. Never once did the old man flinch. He merely waited for the bird to calm down even as the thin rivulets of blood trickled down his chest, and crooned softly to it.

They had been together for eleven years, hunting hares and marmots and smaller denizens of the forest floor, scavengers like squirrels, rats, and field mice.

The sky was thick with thunderheads, heavy as they amassed over the distant outposts, a veil of black threatening to drown the world in their sorrows.

Metzger was in a strange mood, and it seemed as though the sky shared his misgivings. They hadn't had a runner in from the outpost at Brach for two weeks. Orlof, the commander there, was a fastidious soul, and it was quite unlike him to be derelict in any duty. Things happened, of course, the runner might have been taken sick on the way or fallen foul of bandits, or one of a hundred other possibilities. Metzger knew that, but he could not shrug off the nagging feeling that worse was afoot. There was a strict protocol for reporting throughout the protectorates and Metzger had spent years drilling the routines and disciplines into every man that fell beneath his command. As with any fighting force, Metzger's army was only as strong as its weakest man but he had made damned sure that even that man was disciplined and drilled and worthy of holding the lives of his fellow soldiers in his hands.

The goshawk had not been alone in the sky. Darker specks of black smeared the swirls of cloud, banking and sweeping low across the land in their hunt for carrion: ravens. Metzger had a dislike of the birds. They were ill omens. His father had whispered that they were harbingers, psychopomps that carried the souls of the dead to Morr, and had told tales of how in his great-great grandfather's day a bird had been caught with a forked tongue, capable of phrasing the most basic Reikspiel: a talking bird of death. Metzger had shuddered then, and he shuddered now. He had seen those damned birds feed on too many friends to disbelieve anything he heard about them. He was a soldier, facing his fiftieth year. He did not shy away from death, but he was in no hurry to embrace it, either, and carrion eaters were as much a part of his life as was his sword.

He gentled the goshawk. It was a male hunting bird, raised from the nest by his falconer. Metzger had been there in the high woods of the Drakwald when Scharner had found the nest abandoned, and had crouched low over it, whispering, so that his voice and his face were the first things the newborn heard and saw, imprinting on it as would a mother bird. He had cradled its tiny form in his huge hands, soothing its name over and over: Morgenrot after the dawn's red sky.

Metzger often brought the goshawk out when he wanted to unwind the kinks of the day, letting him hunt, but today's black mood would not be shifted, even by the primal role of the hunter.

'Feed, my beauty,' he said, dislodging Morgenrot from his shoulder. The goshawk rose in a flurry of feathers, gaining altitude quickly. He flew in ever-decreasing circles above the fields of the estate until he found his prey. Then he struck, falling from the sky with lethal speed, sweeping low, talons raking the grass, and rising back into the sky with the kill, a dormouse. The rodent was alive, squirming as the hawk released it, a thousand feet above the earth, and then plunged after, snagging it with its barbed talons to open the dormouse, and began feeding even as it tossed the corpse into the air again, enjoying the thrill of the kill.

Metzger never fed Morgenrot from his hand, no cut meat and no pampering. He earned his kills, tasting the meat fresh with blood spilled by his own beak and rending claws, or he did not eat at all. Domesticating the bird would have been wrong in so many ways. They had ridden to war more times than he wanted to remember, and more than once Morgenrot had in some way been responsible for saving his flesh from the damned ravens. That was the bond they shared.

Reinhardt Metzger called the goshawk back with three sharp whistles. He came reluctantly, leaving the small carcass of the dormouse half-stripped.

'We're done for today. See to Morgenrot,' he told Scharner as the falconer appeared, as though summoned by the same three sharp whistles as his bird.

The younger man took the leather gauntlet and hooded the goshawk, making peculiar chirrups and caws as he did, as though speaking to the bird in its own tongue. Scharner had a gift with all birds, just as his father had. He had trained falcons and hawks for the Graf himself before joining Metzger's household.

He sat on the side of the stone fountain that hadn't cascaded water for the better part of a decade. Rainwater stagnated in the bowl. He dragged his fingers in the water, looking back at the house he had done his damnedest never to set foot in, the familial home. Like Metzger, the place had seen better days. Vines clawed up the façade of the fortified manor, choking the brickwork. The facing had chipped away to reveal the dung and hay hardcore centre and the linseed treated timbers were riddled with dry rot and insect infestation that slowly worked away at bringing the once noble manse down.

Alone again, Metzger could no longer hide from the duties of the day.

He had been born into the commission of Knight Protector of Grimminhagen, the duty inherited from his father and his father before him. His family had served as the right-hand of the Graf Sternhauer, making him in effect the second most powerful man in the entire protectorate, for a little while longer at least. In a few weeks he would hang up his shield and unbuckle his sword belt for the last time, and with no son to inherit the role of Knight Protector it would pass to another of Sternhauer's choosing.

He did not know how he felt about that; much of his life had been dictated by honour and servitude and suddenly he would be no one, a retired old man living in his manor on the outskirts of the town. He wanted to believe that he was about to embark on one last adventure but after the better part of fifty years caring for so many people it would be difficult to simply stop. Decades of service were a habit not easily forgotten. Would the new man look upon him as some interfering old fool always prattling on about how he used to do it in the good old days? Would he seek him out for advice at all or ignore him and be his own man?

Metzger knew the answer to that.

Still, for a little while longer he had a duty to Sternhauer.

He swallowed the bitterness he felt rising and retreated to the quiet of his rooms for the best part of an hour, reading the latest missives from the protectorates, before moving on to the quartermaster's monthly rationing reports on supplies stockpiled for the winter, tributes still owed, projected sowing and harvesting returns, building and shipping manifests for imported victuals traded with thieving merchants, even forecasts for the weather, which seemed such a ludicrous waste of time. Better to try and predict the outcome of a cock fight than foretell the foibles of the wild skies, but it was all part and parcel of the business of running the small community of Grimminhagen in the Graf's absence.

The last piece of business was one that always left a sour taste in his mouth: the dispensing of justice.

Kaspar Bohme waited downstairs with the accused, barely a child and with child herself. The charges were serious, the sentence one of public humiliation should he choose to exercise it. It rankled that hunger had become such a crime in his homeland, but having read the quartermaster's predictions, it was easy to see the privation all around without ever having to leave the relative sanctuary of these rooms.

He pushed back his chair and went downstairs to face the accused and mete out his judgement.

Metzger was a good man, which made even such a petty theft difficult to let go unchastised. To turn a blind eye would send out the message that survival within his protectorates had become a matter of cunning and crime, but to shame the woman for needing to eat sent out a message he found even less palatable.

He loitered at the head of the grand stair, beneath so many portraits of long dead Metzgers that there was no space left on the wall. Generation after generation of faces so similar to his own in the artists renditions gazed down on him. He could not help but wonder if there was approval in their oily eyes, or if they deemed him a disappointment for shying away from the harder choices of leadership. Had Felix Metzger harboured the same doubts centuries before, or Ewan, or Kormac or even Montague, the family's one true scholar? Or were they all better men than him?

'Some are born to greatness, some have it thrust upon them, and others live their lives shying away from it,' he said, taking that first step down.

Kaspar Bohme waited at the foot of the stairs. He smiled in greeting. Where Reinhardt was a bull of a man, Kaspar was a wolf, lean, hard of eye and heart, ruthless to the core, and fiercely loyal to the pack. He had been with Metzger twice as long as the goshawk, serving through fifteen campaigns with Reinhardt Metzger's Silberklinge.

The old knight did not match his friend's smile.

'Where is she?' he asked, heavily.

'In your study.'

He side-stepped his friend and then turned and said, 'Have Rosamund bring mulled wine in fifteen minutes,' as though an afterthought, when in truth it was anything but.

'Of course. Do you want me to sit in?'

Metzger shook his head. 'There is no need, Kaspar. My mind is made up.'

'And you will not be swayed?'

'Have you ever known me to be?'

Kaspar Bohme laughed at that, a short bark of a laugh.

'Fifteen minutes,' Metzger repeated and then left him.

The wooden floors were carpeted, the rugs worn thread-bare by the endless passage of bustling feet over the years since he had inherited the old family manse, though he had barely added to the wear so often was he gone.

Briony Neumann might have been comely, once, but no more. She stood in the corner of the study, wringing her hands. To her credit she hadn't tried to flee; there were three large leaded windows in the study, though none of them opened. She looked up from her hands as he closed the door behind him.

He said nothing.

An oak pedestal desk dominated the centre of the room, behind it a leather-backed chair. He sat behind the desk, steepling his fingers as he contemplated the woman before him.

'You have put me in a difficult position, Briony,' he said, eventually. She met his eyes, pleading mercy without saying anything. 'Artur was a good man,' he said tapping his temple, 'and his memory is still strong in here. For his sake I would not see you humiliated, nor harmed, but how would that look?'

'If you are going to take my hands, be quick, I beg you, do not drag it out like some hideous torture. If you loved my man, do that for him at least.' There was a fire in the woman, even now. He admired that and he could see why his Silberklinge had fallen for her. A man of war needed a good woman, perhaps more so than a simple farmer, but goodness was not measured in pretty packages; it was measured in heart and spirit, not the curve of a breast or the swell of a hip.

'It is about perception, Briony. Do you know what I mean?' She shook her head. 'How other people see us, how we see our selves. If I do not deal with your transgressions I appear soft-hearted to other hungry widows and beg to be robbed again and again. Yet if I exact the full penalty as owed to the law I take your hands simply because you were starving. Why did you not come to me, Briony? Why did you not swallow your pride and knock on my door? I would have helped you.'

She had no answer for him.

'Are you not going to plead your case?'

'Your mind is made up,' she said, 'so what is the point?'

'You presume much. Yes, I have deliberated your fate since Kaspar heard the charges against you, and wished they were some ludicrous thing that could easily be denied or even some serious crime that might be refuted by the intervention of witch hunters, witchcraft, consorting with daemons, not something so simple and undeniable as stealing a chicken for meat and bread for your table. Giles would have you publicly flogged, your hands taken and your babe too. That is what he sued for.'

'No!' Her hands went instinctively to her mouth in denial.

'I have no liking of the man, but he is aware of his rights and demands satisfaction, so what am I to do, Briony?'

'Take my hands, but not my child, please. It is all I have left of him.'

That was the truth of it. Artur Neumann had fallen before he even knew he was going to be a father. To rob her of her unborn child would be to rob her of her husband all over again, and no wife deserved that no matter what her crimes. Her husband had been a knight, one of his own, a man of honour. He deserved better even if she did not.

'If I take your hands how will you care for the babe, Briony? You are no common peasant, you are the widow of a knight, but even so you have not the coin to pay for a wet nurse and no indentured servants to see to your needs. So tell me, how will you nurse and change it? How will you cradle it and soothe its tears?'

'Not my baby.' Her heartache was wretched to behold but he had to make her understand.

'No, not your baby, and not your hands. I have another fate in mind for you.'

She met his gaze, challenging him to say what she thought he was going to say. 'You can claim my flesh but it will not be given willingly, and with no love.'

For a moment the woman's resignation hung between them like a challenge. Then he laughed sadly, shaking his head. 'What kind of man do you think I am, Briony? All these years and you think that of me?'

'You are a man,' she said, as though that answered everything, accusing him of every fault imaginable and excusing them all by the root of his sex. 'You have never taken a wife, and if my man was to be believed you never sired any bastards nor anything so ignoble, so perhaps you would claim my boy as your own? Is that what you have in mind?'

'No,' he said, shaking his head again, unable to meet her gaze, as though suddenly their roles had reversed and he was the accused, her his would-be executioner. 'I have never taken a wife, that is true, though I have no idea if I have sired any young. I like to think the Metzger line will not die out with this old fool's passing, but I have no idea. You know me, woman, but you cannot know what happens in the aftermath of battle, as the frenzy of it wears off the flesh. Some men do succumb to the base need to confirm their immortality by sinking into flesh. It is inevitable. Mortality and mindless coupling are inextricably linked in the minds of some, but believe me, I have never forced myself upon a woman, not as the spoils of conquest, not when the blood was pumping and the need to prove my manhood raged hot in my veins, not even when I was angry at the injustice of the world and the death of a friend. There has never been catharsis in those darker passions, never, and I am not about to start.'

'I am sorry,' she said, and broke down into ragged sobs. He moved from behind his desk and went to comfort her, but held back, shy of embracing her even to allow her to weep on his shoulder.

There was a timid knock at the door, Rosamund with the mulled wine. He opened the door for her, 'Just put it on the table and take a seat.' She looked at him askance. He nodded once, and said, 'Please.'

She did as she was asked, settling down into one of the arm chairs beneath the largest of the three leaded windows. 'Take a look at Rosamund,' he told the other woman. 'Take a good look, ask her any question you see fit and she will speak the truth. She has a tongue on her that would cow any man.' The maid shuffled in her seat. Her black skirts trailed around her feet. She looked decidedly uncomfortable with being the centre of attention.

'I have no questions,' Briony said.

'You will, I am sure, but Rosamund can answer them when you are out of the door. Now, I must mete out justice, as law demands. You will hear my verdict?'

She nodded. 'Yes, my lord.'

'Then listen and bide my words well, Briony Neumann, wife of Artur. In the matter of theft against the person of Giles, pig and poultry farmer of this protectorate, you are found guilty by your own admission. Your punishment will be to serve within the house as a scullery maid. It is a long way from the wife of a knight, make no mistake. You will be stripped of all nobility and recognition of rank and treated just as every maid is treated within this house. Rosamund will see that a room is made up for you. It will be nothing fancy, but you will receive three square meals a day in return for your service, to which Rosamund will give instruction. You are to abide by her decisions, for she speaks with my voice in this matter, and the voice of the law you broke.

'Now heed this warning, for I will say it only once, steal from me and you will be cast out, not only from this house but from all the lands the Silberklinge protect. You will be alone, banished but your child will not suffer the same fate, for it is a cruel man who sentences the child for the sins of the mother. Respect my house, respect Rosamund, and there will always be a place for you here, wife of Artur Neumann, disrespect those few simple rules and you are gone. Do I make myself clear?'

'I don't know what to say,' she said, looking not at him but down at her hands.

'I suggest you say thank you,' Rosamund said, rising from her chair to pour two goblets of warm wine. She handed one to Metzger and another to Briony.

'In respect of the woman you were, this is the last glass of wine you will share at my table,' Metzger said. 'When the last sip is supped your new life will have begun. Welcome to our house.' He raised his goblet. 'It is a most peculiar house, but we are rather fond of it.'

'I… thank you. Thank you,' Briony stammered, at a loss. She clenched her left fist as she raised the goblet to her lips. As she swallowed she placed her palm against her swollen belly and Metzger knew that she was thinking about how close she had come to losing both.

KASPAR RAPPED ONCE on the study door and opened it without waiting to be bidden to enter.

Reinhardt Metzger sat alone nursing the last of the now tepid wine. He looked bone tired, carrying every one of his fifty years heavily on his broad shoulders.

'You're a soft-hearted old beggar,' Kaspar said, sinking into one of the armchairs. He put his feet up on the waxed side-table and teased off his gloves one finger at a time. 'But if it means anything, you did the right thing.'

'We'll need to give that moaning swineherd some satisfaction. No doubt he will be hammering on the door
the moment word reaches his cauliflower ears that she
hasn't lost her hands, her child or her life. Have I told
you lately how much I loathe men like Giles?'

'This morning, last night, and at least twice more
since he sued for the Graf's justice.'

'Yes, well, let me just state for the record, men like
him ought to be fed their own bloody tongues to put
an end to their merciless bloody tittle-tattle. They're
worse than old maids.'

'A few coins will buy him off.'

'It's blood money.'

'Aye, it is. But we both know if the shoe was on the
other foot and Artur was dispensing justice to our widows we'd expect some kind of compassion from an old
friend.'

'Damned right we would,' Metzger agreed. 'and he'd
give it.'

'Still no word from Orlof?' Kaspar Bohme said,
changing tack as artfully as any midshipman.

'Nothing.'

'That's not like him.'

'Did I ever tell you you had a talent for stating the
bloody obvious, my friend?'

'Well, there was that one time, at Essen Ford,' Kaspar
said, pushing back up out of the upholstered chair. He
paced the room like a caged animal, prowling back and
forth, back and forth. 'Have you sent scouts?'

'No, I thought I would sit here like a blind man in the
dark rooting for navel fluff. Of course I have, two good
men. One last week, one this.'

'And neither have returned?'

'That's a real talent you have, Kaspar.'

'I say we ride out,' Bohme said, bracing himself on the wainscotting of the wooden window, feeling out the grain with his calloused fingers. Each knot and whorl in the wood depicted more years than either of them had been on the planet. Even at the simplest of times nature was a humbling thing.

'Two old men against the evils of the world?'

'I can think of no one better suited.'

'Go to bed, Kaspar. We'll talk in the morning.'

But they did not; they met in the middle of the night on the landing, drawn by the reflections in the streaked glass and a thicker, unnatural darkness.

'Some foul miasma clouds out the moon,' Kaspar said. 'You know it and I know it, and where there is roiling darkness like this there is some unnatural curse beneath it.'

'We don't have a choice, do we?'

'Would you send someone else out?'

Metzger shook his head.

'I didn't think so. Get dressed, I will meet you in the courtyard.'

'It's the middle of the night.'

'You weren't planning on sleeping were you?'

'No,' Metzger said.

'Neither was I. I believe they call that a coincidence. Now, if you'll excuse me, I've got to go drain the snake. The old bladder isn't what it used to be.'

A quarter of an hour later, still hours before dawn, the two men set off towards the clouds, grim-faced, all joking cast aside. Bohme roused the stable boy and had him saddle up two of the Knight Protector's horses while Metzger woke Briony and had her bag up travel rations for them. They opted for speed over power, leaving behind the chargers they would ride into battle in favour of sleek, fast mares. They knew better than to gallop, moving out at an easy canter at first, resting the animals often as their long strides ate the ground, and still exhaustion claimed the beasts along with the first cry of the dawn chorus.

They were not the young men they had once been, of that the night had made them painfully aware. By midday they were forced to take shelter in the ruins of an old temple. The stripped roof offered little in the way of respite from the elements, but with the statue of Sigmar still standing sentinel in the corner it offered other protections.

They talked little during the morning, wrapped up in their own thoughts as to the origins of the miasma. It appeared every bit as thick in daylight as the darkness had threatened it would be. Bohme struck tinder and saw to the small gathering of dead-fall that he had scavenged to make a fire, while Metzger unwrapped two slabs of meat from the greased paper wrap and skewered them on his long dagger to cook them over the fire. The fat sizzled and spat as it dripped onto the hard stone beneath. The meat, when they ate it, was gamy, and still slick with fatty juices that had them licking their fingers and smearing the stuff on the grass that had slowly begun to reclaim the temple. Done, they grabbed a few hours of sleep before rising again to stalk the miasma through the early evening.

There was more to what Metzger had told Briony than she might have understood, more about his debt to her man. There were different types of leader, as many as there were types of men, but a man like Metzger felt responsibility for those in his service. His scouts had not returned: two good men with five children between them. The loss weighed heavily on his shoulders, and it was a loss. He did not for one minute think that they had suddenly become derelict in their duties. They were either dead or captured, and then as good as dead if they were. He studied the miasmic clouds as they amassed, amazed that the sky could harbour such black hatred for the land beneath it. They had yet to spill their ire on the landscape, but when it came the deluge would be apocalyptic.

It was ever the way of the earth. It cleansed evil and good with equal disdain, scrubbing them from the land as though they had never existed.

'You know what we face as well as I do,' Metzger said after a while.

Kaspar Bohme pushed to his feet and scuffed up dirt to kick out the fire. 'I know nothing, Reinhardt. Neither do you. It's time to move on.'

And so it was for three straight nights, though without the stars they were forced to orientate themselves in the oppressive press of the trees with a loadstone on a string that pointed true north. The pair of them pushed their mounts to the point of exhaustion. Where they could they followed tracks carved into the forest, where it was impossible or impractical they wove their own paths through the trees. Sleep was a luxury for man and beast, though they grabbed an hour's rest here and there, until they woke on the morning of the fourth day to a shivering earth.

Kaspar came awake instantly, sensing that something was fundamentally wrong. He placed both of his hands down, palms flat on the grass, feeling the violent tremors rippling through the soil. He counted out the gaps between the ebb and flow of the shivers, judging the nearness and size of the enemy they faced.

'An entire army is on the march,' he whispered, 'and they are close.'

'The earth never lies,' Metzger said.

The horses whinnied and shied, spooked by their unseen enemy, kicking at the dirt and deadfall and prancing sideways as far as their tethers allowed.

Bohme surveyed the landscape around them. To the left there was little in the way of cover, scrub land leading towards the foothills, to the right, tree-lined slopes, and straight ahead a declivity leading down to the stream-bed cutting through a large u-shaped valley that ran for thirty miles and more. From his vantage point the valley floor was obscured by the overhanging cliff, making it ideal for the safe, unseen, passage of a substantial force.

'I'm going out, give me five minutes and follow,' said Kaspar.

Metzger stayed low, hunkering down beside Kaspar and said, 'Just watch yourself.'

'You worry too much, old man.'

'And you don't worry enough,' Metzger said.

He watched his back as Bohme moved off, skirting the low broken stones of the temple wall. He moved fast, running hard and keeping low. The weight of his body was always on the front foot. Metzger saw the subtle flash of silver in his left hand and knew that Kaspar was not taking any chances. A moment later he disappeared behind a crumbling spar of stone. Metzger wasn't about to sit by idly and wait. He set off in the opposite direction, running for the trees.

They offered little in the way of cover, but anything was better than nothing. He sprinted across the open ground, crashing through the undergrowth. He pushed through low, dragging branches, snapping them back in his haste.

The nature of both men was evident for any observer to see, the bull charging recklessly on, flattening anything in his way, the wolf moving with terrible swiftness, low, sleek and fast. A thoughtful enemy could deduce much from this simple observation, enough, perhaps, to win a war.

Metzger hit the thick trunk of a withered tree. Chest heaving, he glanced back over his shoulder. For all the skeletal shadows and long sighs, the trees appeared empty of any real threat. He crouched and rummaged through the deadfall. There were no obvious signs of passage to announce the enemy's advance, whoever they might be, no broken twigs or brown leaves crushed into the mud. He craned his head, listening, but there were no sounds either, no signs of life; the stillness was eerie and unnatural. In the dusk so many of the forest's natural foragers ought to be stirring, but the place was dead. He cupped his hands to his mouth and, shaping his lips, hooted twice, mimicking the cry of an owl. It was greeted by silence as the forest rose to engulf it. Reinhardt Metzger shivered despite the relative warmth of the early evening.

When he placed his hands flat to the dirt he felt them again, the telltale tremors of marching feet, thousands upon thousands of them causing the ground to revolt at their vile advance.

'Talk to me, mother earth,' he whispered, digging his fingers into the dirt.

There was no miraculous revelation.

He crept forward, deeper into the trees. The first blush of moonlight filtered through the canopy of leaves, scattering its reflection across the forest floor like a wealth of ghostly coins. He moved on, deeper into the trees until quite suddenly the land dropped away steeply beneath him.

What he saw snatched his breath away: a shuffling river of death, rolling back across the countryside for league upon league, rotting skin and bone, dragging feet. He stared in absolute horror, scarcely able to take in the enormity of the force: a crusade of the armies of death, shambling corpses, moving blindly on, staggering and lurching mindlessly.

The column was so wide that he could not see its far edge. Several of the marchers carried torches that threw eerie light across the ranks of the vile army. The dead had no need of light, he reasoned, which meant that the living marched with them. He saw flesh that hung in grey tattered strips and all he could think was to pray to Sigmar that the dead passed by his homestead, knowing the selfishness of that prayer even as he thought it. Their salvation was someone else's damnation and yet he could not bring himself to care about those nameless others. He would willingly carry the burden of their deaths if their sacrifice saved even one of his own people.

The dead marched. Within the faceless ranks of rotting corpses he saw more recent fatalities bearing their wounds nakedly. In his mind he carved out the passage of the dead, using the valley and his memory of the lodestone to orientate his fear. Sickly, he realised that Grimminhagen lay directly in the path of their march.

There was a grotesque order to the force. There was a hierarchy that mimicked the structure of a real army, with the rotting zombies and flesh-stripped skeletons forming the infantry that made up the bulk of the lines, marshalled by more fearsome foes: ghouls, ghosts and wights clinging to the flanks, and black riders on skeletal mounts that snorted smoke and flame that in turn fed the miasma that clung to the dead army. In the centre of the abomination he saw a huge chariot fashioned from bone, and a withered vampire spurring on the corpses that dragged it, flaying strips of skin from their backs with his whip.

Metzger lurched away from the tree, dread, fear, and horror ripping his mind asunder as he scrambled down the hill, tripping and sliding, and digging his heels in to stop himself from pitching forward and falling even as he started to run. His first instinct was to draw his sword and throw himself into the river of shambling dead swinging, but that instinct did not last long. He had to get back to Grimminhagen in time to warn his people.

A hand came down hard on his shoulder and pulled him up short. He wheeled around, blade raised to gut whatever ghoul thought to feed on him, and barely managed to pull the blow when he saw that it was Kaspar Bohme.

'We must away from this place,' Kaspar said, his face bled of all colour. 'Die here and we damn everyone.' It was a simple truth.

Metzger nodded, grimly determined. All thoughts of age and retirement banished, the knight sheathed his blade. There would be time aplenty for swords and violence, but not now and not here.

'How many towns and villages have fallen along the way to feed that vile force? How many families are rotting in this river of filth because no one was strong enough to stop them? How many is too many? One hundred? Fifty? One, that's how many: one.' Bohme had no answer for that.

The moon burned within the dead, augmenting the eerie torchlight of the living that marched side by side with them. The dead were not, as he had first suspected, whole. Decay was rife, pallid skins and sallow complexions turned an ethereal grey. The rot of the grave bared white bones where the flesh had failed. More of the dead men were skeletal, cages of ribs torn open on putrid giblets, limbs stripped of muscle and tendon reduced to lichen-thick bones.

Carrion eaters flew above them, hundreds of black-winged birds that swept low time and again to feed on the soft tissues of the dead as they shambled and lurched and staggered, dancing to the pull of the chains that had dragged them back to this wretched unlife so mercilessly. Ravens clawed at the last remaining strips of muscle, beaks tugging at the wormed fat of gaping cheeks and the soft humours of leaking eyes.

It was a procession of damnation.

He rubbed at his stubbled jaw, the urge to throw himself at them all still strong. He imagined hacking and slashing at the mortal chains that bound them, but no matter how many he freed of their damnation, it could never be enough.

All he could do was prepare his town for the worst.

Had Orlof been somewhere in there marching on with blindly staring eyes? That was what the dead did, after all. They swelled their ranks with the corpses of the men they killed, growing stronger and stronger by the mile.

Metzger turned his back on the dead. Bohme was looking at him strangely. Metzger had seen enough blood shed in hate to know that the things seen in the eyes of others were reflections of the things that burned in your own eyes. They were not secret glimpses of the other man, they were the hidden truths of the self. There had been fear in Bohme's eyes, Metzger's fear.

The cries of the ravens rose, mad caws that spiralled, taking on an almost human quality. It took him a moment to realise what he was hearing within them: the wretched sobs of a baby.

'Did you hear that?' he asked, but Kaspar was already moving, swiftly back up into the next layer of undergrowth where the brambles and thorns tangled around the tree trunks. The cries became more and more obvious and heartbreaking as they retreated back up the hillside, until they found the baby, wrapped in a bundle of swaddling clothes, nestled down beside a hollowed out tree stump, crying and crying and crying for the mother that had abandoned it. Metzger gathered the crying child into his arms and hushed it, offering his thick finger to the babe to suckle on in the hopes of quieting it.

'Who left you here, little man?'

Had the babe's mother fled her doomed village hoping to deliver her child from the procession of the dead? Was she lying somewhere near or had she become a part of the shuffling zombie army? Or was the babe some unwanted bastard brought out to die? It didn't matter. Reinhardt Metzger cradled the helpless child to his chest.

Down the slope he saw the first of the pallid corpses pushing through the trees, drawn by the baby's cries.

CHAPTER FIVE

On Fields of Fire
In the Shadows of the Drakwald Forest, Middenland
The Autumn of Sweet Deceits, 2532

THE ZOMBIE, HE could not think of the wreck of humanity as anything else, came lurching at Kaspar Bohme, the splintered bone of broken-down fingers clawing at his face. He reeled away from the wild, raking blows blocking them easily on his sword. There was no grace or dexterity to its attack, it simply came up the hill swinging, a weird, baleful moan punctuating each missed strike. Though clumsy, it was relentless. He ducked a blow, rocking back on his heels, only for a second to come slashing across where his throat had been a split second before, and even as he compensated for his lost balance, a third and a fourth swing threatened to bowl him over.

'Run!' he yelled at Metzger, throwing himself to his left in an effort to put his body between the dead thing and the child.

The zombie moaned again, lurching forward with its arms outstretched, grasping. There were no words in the sound, only the undertow of grief that it had been shrived of its humanity. It set a chill deep in his bones to hear such an empty sound come from the undead fiend's mouth.

It was alone, calling out to more of its kind. Would silencing it likewise doom them? Bohme wondered, parrying another savage slash. Were the undead like wasps? Would its second death act as a lure for the others as they were drawn to the stink of its ruin?

'Run!' he yelled at Metzger, putting himself between the zombie and the child.

The big man did not need telling twice. He stumbled away up the hill, clutching the bundle of clothes to his chest.

Kaspar Bohme spun on his heel, delivering a scything kick across the thing's midriff. It was like kicking a sack of sawdust. The bones and guts powered inwards, pulverised. The dead man stumbled forward, strings of gore clinging to his torn lips. Bohme hammered a heavy left fist into the thing's face, again and then again, each impact ripping the skin to open a second yellow-toothed leer high up on the side of its face. He stepped in close, avoiding the dead man's ruined fingers, and straight-armed it in the throat. The muscle and bone collapsed beneath the impact of the blow. It would have killed a normal man, after a moment's agony. The thing did not so much as flinch from the crushing blow, with no need of air. It came on again, its elegiac moan calling out to its perverted kin.

Kaspar drove his blade into the zombie's leg, just below the knee with enough force to cleave the cap-bone. The dead man lurched sideways, his leg hideously disjointed, and fell, but even on the ground it was not done. It clutched at Kaspar's ankle, sinking its fingers deep enough to grate against the bone. His fist clenched around the hilt of his sword, and rammed it into the dead man's chest, up between the third and fourth ribs. The blade cut through the dead man's heart. Kaspar jerked it savagely, and jammed the blade down again, working the thing's ribcage open with a crack of bones. A third blow opened it up fully, tearing through the striated muscle, and even as it grasped for his throat, he leaned down to reach in with his bare hands and tear out its heart.

Whatever ungodly force had animated the corpse, rending its heart was enough to drive it out. The thing lay motionless in the mud of the forest floor. Kaspar looked sickly at the thick black blood that had already begun to coagulate around his clenched fist. The tainted blood burned his skin. He tossed the withered organ aside, sick with revulsion, and scrubbed his hands on the mud and leaves of the forest floor on either side of the corpse.

All around him he heard the rising moans of the shuffling dead and knew that he needed to move, to get as far away from this place as possible.

The skirts of the forest were paradoxically alive with the sighs and moans of the dead.

Fear steeled his resolve. Kaspar looked up the hill, where Metzger had run with the child, and then back down, fearfully, at the line of trees that had opened to reveal the zombie moments before. He leant against the bole of the nearest tree. It was a lyme tree, he realised, a maniacal laugh bubbling up in his mind as his fingernails dug into the bark, a corpse tree, said to grow out of the bodies of the fallen where they were buried on the field of battle.

He was alone, for now.

He couldn't stay here any longer than he already had. He knew that. The stench of old death was ripe in the air where he had opened the thing up. He looked up and through the filter of branches he saw, already, the carrion birds circling in and out of sight. In minutes this quiet glade would be swarming with flesh eaters.

The black blood ate into the his sword's blade. He crouched, and cleaned it on the ground before sliding it back into its sheath.

Then he heard the rustle and snap of branches being pushed back and the crack of deadfall being crushed underfoot.

They were coming.

He rose, pushing away from the tree, and ran for his life.

KASPAR RAN BLINDLY, branches snagging at his body and face as he lunged through spaces barely wide enough to squeeze through. Brambles and thorns tore at his legs. Where the undergrowth grew too thick, he cut it away, hacking and slashing at it with his blade.

He welcomed the darkness as it fell, knowing that it offered another layer of obscurity to his wild flight even if it made it more treacherous.

At times he thought he heard Metzger up ahead, crashing through the choking confines of the forest, but apart from the first occasion, when he caught a glimpse of the startled boar his own reckless charge had set running, it might just as easily have been heavy-footed ghosts, always just out of sight as he chased to catch up with them.

That was the curse of the trees.

The consistency of the ground changed, going from firm, hard-packed mud to a mulch, his feet sinking in up to the ankles and deeper as he struggled to maintain the momentum of his flight. The trees showed no signs of thinning out, though many of their lower branches were denuded by the season. Their skeletal limbs conjured up wraiths of shadow as the darkness descended. Again there were no sounds of the forest. It was as though he were reliving an intimately familiar nightmare. He ran with no conscious thought to direction, but only to distance and putting enough of it between him and the swath of mindless dead cutting across the lowlands.

Kaspar stumbled to a halt, trying to get his bearings, but the lack of landmarks even this near to the fringe of the Drakwald left him guessing. Thick spiders' webs clung to some of the high branches, joining the upper canopy of trees together with spindles of white thread. He cupped his hands to his mouth and gave two short hoots, the mating call of one of the owls indigenous to the forest. He and Metzger had been using the same call sign for years. Hearing an owl out in the trees at night was hardly uncommon and during the day Kaspar favoured the howl of a silver-furred wolf.

His call went unanswered.

He risked a second call, and a few minutes later a third, but with no more luck.

He stayed quiet for a moment, listening to the emptiness within the canopy of tall trees. The silence was eerie. Forests were living places, but all around him the obvious signs of life were missing; even the whispering of the breeze and the sly voice of the leaves had fallen quiet. He licked his lips nervously. He turned to look back the way he had come, a small twig breaking off against his cheek. The sharp crack of the wood was loud in the dead stillness. He brushed it aside, turning again. Deadfall crunched beneath his boots. Something wasn't right and he knew enough to trust his instincts. They were all that had kept him alive these long years and they were crying out to him now but he didn't know how to interpret their warning.

The wind stirred, masking a second sound. Kaspar turned through a full circle, not sure what he was looking for, or what the sound he thought he heard meant.

There it was again: a long slow creaking, of wood straining.

Then the forest floor began to rise up beneath his feet. The deadfall stirred, the soil and the broken branches coming together, leaves and mud and grass and worms giving flesh to a fell beast clawing its way into existence. The head came first, broaching the earth in a vile parody of birth, forcing its way out of the ground. There were bones as well as all the mud and rot of the forest, the bones of a dead bird, its tiny skull like a tattoo on the side of the face of the beast. And it was a face, with fully developed features; an uprooted sapling formed its nose, its roots creating the illusion of a muddy leer as more and more of the fell construct clawed its way free of the earth at Kaspar's feet.

Then came the fingers, gnarled tree roots pushing up out of the dirt, the leaves clinging to them as the rest of the hands emerged. Moss and lichen and wood pulp clung to the beast's arms as it heaved itself up. The ribcage of a large animal, a horse or cow, formed part of its spine, along with the pelvis of a smaller animal. The grasses were coated with a layer of slime-like afterbirth, and still it grew, rising taller and taller to dwarf him.

Kaspar stood, trapped by the impossibility of what he was seeing. Even as his mind screamed: run! his legs refused to obey.

He didn't even reach for his sword as the creature of mud and leaves and long dead bones lurched forward, shambling towards him with its claws of rotten wood reaching out for him. It stood almost twice his height, arms dragging the floor, dirt and leaves falling off it as it lumbered forward. Its macabre flesh shifted and writhed, the dirt sloughing from the wood, the brittle bones sliding from shoulder to hip and up through the thing's chest only to work their way back to its broad shoulders again. Not all the things trapped within its ever-shifting shape were dead. Kaspar saw a bird, its wings flapping weakly as it struggled to be free of the cage of roots that snared it. He saw bloated worms and the kicking legs of a vole as the rodent was swallowed by the body of the beast. Vines curled around tree trunks to fashion mighty legs, and more bones added definition to them, shattered vertebrae and fractured femurs. Alive, it roared, its voice gravelly with the detritus of the forest floor. It was a forlorn sound, the voice of a lost soul. Its huge arms raked the canopy of leaves, shedding soil and worms as they dragged through them.

Kaspar staggered back, away from the impossible beast, but even as he did it seemed to notice him properly for the first time. The thing that formed its face had settled around stomach height. It sifted through the mulch until it came level with Kaspar's own face and roared again, an almost human anguish in its strange voice as the trailing roots ululated. As Kaspar reached for the blade at his side the construct's huge hand snatched out and grabbed him, the bones and wood and dirt clenching around Kaspar's waist as he kicked and struggled. The sword fell from his hand and tumbled the fifteen feet down to the ground as the beast scooped him up and shook him as though he were no more than a corn doll.

Part of the ribcage splintered, piercing him like six small daggers along his right side, through the boiled leather of the jerkin beneath his shirt and into the soft skin of his side, drawing blood and screams.

The stench was overpowering, foetid, like stagnant water soaking a foul bog. Rancid sludge dripped from its muddy flesh, down his neck and back, leaking through his clothing. He gagged, trying to turn his face away from it. Kaspar kicked and thrashed in its constricting grasp, but still the verdant hand clenched into a fist, squeezing the life out of him.

He grabbed desperately at the dragging branches, trying to claw himself free of the fist, and then he was falling head over feet, crashing through the low branches as the beast hurled him away. He slammed into the trunk of a lightning-struck tree where it had been split into a V. A long spar of rotten wood pierced his armour, burying itself deep in his shoulder-blade. The pain was excruciating, an all-consuming fire rising up from the blackened wood to spread through his body. Kaspar's screams were wretched as he grasped the spar and drew it out of his flesh. The rotten wood flaked and powdered, leaving splinters beneath his skin.

Through his screams he heard the unmistakable sound of laughter.

He lifted his head to see a sallow-skinned man, rank with the corruption of the charnel house step into the clearing, though to call it a man was a lie. It was dressed like a beggar, and wore the last vestiges of a mortal face like a death mask, the features riddled with decomposition. The cartilage of its nose was gone, leaving a ragged hole in the centre of its face that wheezed as the thing snorted; it did not breathe. Waves of dread radiated from the wreck of humanity. It clutched a twisted doll of twigs fashioned in the malformed shape of the fell beast that had risen up out of the boggy floor of the forest. The vampiric acolyte, for that was what it had to be, manipulated the effigy, causing the construct to mirror the twig-doll's disjointed dance.

'The cost of sight is death,' the creature said, his voice the sigh of lament.

'I saw… nothing,' Kaspar Bohme said, rising to his knees. Blood streaked his shirt. His vision swam in an agony of black.

'You saw us. You looked upon the tide of death creeping silently across the land, and now you join its ranks.' The moon burned through the vampire's dull black eyes. The smell of his blood only served to inflame the fell creature and its pinch-faced master. Kaspar's eyes found his sword, lying in the dirt twenty feet away, the corrosive blood of the dead man still smeared on its blade in places. There was no way he could reach it before the construct snapped him in two.

The laughing fiend stepped closer. There was a sourness to his stink.

The forest around him was reduced to rock and dust and dirt and wood, basic elements.

The creature lumbered towards him, reaching out in the parody of affection, as though to draw him in to its bosom. Only instead of holding him close like a lover it sought to absorb him into its huge swollen gut, digesting him as it had the cow and the birds before him.

Kaspar hobbled three steps to the left, wincing as every footfall jarred, the reverberations moving up through his body in wave after wave of pain. The fractions between agonies became, conversely, ecstasies by dint of the respite they offered from the pain.

'Death,' the vampire repeated, savouring the word.

The leaves and grass that bound the foul beast susurrated with the sibilant breeze, a moan beneath the baleful groan coming from its makeshift mouth. Its breath reeked of the ash of burned corpses more than it did of peaty loam.

'Not today,' Kaspar Bohme said, with a certainty he did not feel.

His glance flickered again towards the sword. He edged a few inches to the left, toying with the notion of hurling himself full-length in a desperate attempt to reach the blade, but even entertaining such ideas was foolish. He would have to make do without the blade, which left the long dagger in his boot as his only weapon, and save for a miracle the pig-sticker was going to be about as useful as a poke in the eye with a sharp stick. The beast roared its melancholy cry once more, convincing Kaspar that there was more to it than merely mud and wood. Somehow the laughing lord of the undead had bound a human soul to the construct, creating a torture within a torture with his black arts. Then it surged forward. Its huge trunk legs uprooted from the earth and came thundering down, the ground shuddering with each violent impact.

It swallowed the space between them in three enormous strides, barely enough time for Kaspar to react. He snatched the dagger from his boot. He felt like a boy with a toy sword facing down a huge dragon of old: worm food.

The beast's wood and bone talons slashed through the air inches from his face. Kaspar rocked back on his heel, spun inside the swing and slashed back, cutting the construct from hip to groin. The wound spilled dirt and stone, but as quickly as it opened up the mud and leaves shifted sealing the cut. Staring at the healing wound cost Kaspar, as the thing spat a cloud of ash in his face. Flinching, he closed his eyes for a split second. It was enough for the construct to land a crunching blow in his midriff that sent him sprawling backwards in the dirt to the manic laughter of the nose-less vampire.

'Yes, today,' his tormentor cackled. 'Finish him, my beauty.'

Kaspar rolled over onto his back as a great leafy fist slammed into the dirt where his head had been a heartbeat before, and then back again onto his stomach as a second gigantic fist ploughed into the dirt where he had just rolled to. He scrambled forward, launching himself face-first. A great clubbing blow slammed into his left leg, below the joint of the knee before he could drag his leg clear.

'Squash the bug, squash the fly, squash the little man, bleed him dry,' the vampire cackled madly, crouching low so he could get a better look at the torment etched into Kaspar's face.

A second pulverising blow crunched into the base of his spine.

'Say good night, sweet prince,' the man mocked.

'Good night, sweet prince,' Kaspar rasped, flinging his dagger underarm. The long blade turned end over end. It wasn't weighted to be thrown, but that didn't matter. It missed the laughing man's face by inches and slammed into his shoulder, cutting off his laughter in a choke of pain.

It wasn't enough.

And he wasn't ready to die.

Kaspar waited for the killing blow but it never came. He struggled to roll over, to face his own death, to look it in the bogged eye. He slumped onto his back, gasping through clenched teeth as another wave of agony surged through him, from the wounded knee up through his chest. The beast echoed his moan of pain. He saw the bite of degradation peeling leaf and bone from the power of its frame, dribbling out like the grains of sand from an hourglass. Through the fog of pain clouding his mind, it took Kaspar a moment more to realise what was happening: the vampire's control of his construct weakened, the fell fiend was coming undone. It was decaying before his eyes, the rot rapid. Soil fell away depositing the stolen bones, until it was nothing more than the muck of the forest sinking back into the ground.

Kaspar's knife landed by his side, the mocking laughter silenced. The vampire discarded his ruined effigy, crushing it beneath his foot. He held his hand to his shoulder, blood leaking through his fingers as he came to stand over Kaspar.

He looked down at Kaspar's ruined leg, harsh laughter bubbling back up through his throat.

'You are dead, little fighter. I shall leave you here to die like a pig in your own filth,' the fiend rasped, spittle flying from his bloodless lips. 'Without food, without water, unable to drag yourself the miles home your death will be so much more agonising than a single crushing blow from my beautiful creation. It will be an ugly death filled with deliriums. You will beg the ghosts to take you, to have mercy. We shall not meet again, warrior. Our fates are not intertwined.

CHAPTER SIX

The Oncoming Storm
In the Shadows of the Drakwald Forest, Middenland
The Autumn of Sweet Deceits, 2532

HE DID NOT die.

Weakness suffused his body but the pain, mercifully, was gone.

His leg was a mess.

He had no idea where he was, or how to get back to Grimminhagen.

He tried to stand, but his leg wouldn't take his weight. Biting back against the flare of pain he sank against the trunk of the nearest tree.

The laughing man had been right, that one blow to his leg had killed him as surely as a knife to the throat.

'No,' he said through clenched teeth, 'I will not die here. I will not.'

As though in answer to his stubbornness he heard the distant call of a hunting wolf, the howl rising sharply at the end. It was a distinctly human sound. It had to be Metzger, Reinhardt had mastered the lupine voice years ago. He was letting Kaspar know he was out there, giving him hope. Kaspar waited, to be sure. It came again a few moments later, and again the howl contained a peculiarly human quality. Kaspar Bohme smiled for the first time in more than twenty-four hours. It was a fleeting smile, gone before he cupped his hands around his mouth and gave an answering call.

He looked around the clearing; there was enough left from the collapsed construct to fashion a splint for his leg and a stick to take his weight. For now all he wanted to do was close his eyes and sleep, but he couldn't allow himself the luxury. Instead he waited five minutes and gave the call again. Metzger answered, noticeably closer. The image of the big man charging through the undergrowth heedless of the risk, to get to his side brought the glimmer of a smile back. There was a reason he had followed Reinhardt Metzger into the jaws of death time and time again. The man was a true hero and the world had so few of them left. He would follow Metzger into the flaming pits of the hellish Underworld to tackle Morr himself if Metzger willed it, so fierce was his loyalty to the man, and it was a loyalty repaid in kind.

Metzger called out again, closer still, his wolf rabid by the sounds of his frantic howl. The babe's cries were shrill, its discomfort obvious even before Metzger found him.

The old knight stormed into the clearing, brandishing his sword in one hand and cradling the grubby white bundle of screaming child in the other. Metzger took it all in in an instant, though what he made of the huge pile of composted mulch in the centre of the clearing, Kaspar hesitated to think.

'What happened to you?'

Kaspar winced. 'My leg's buggered, can't bend it, can't take any weight on it.'

'Don't worry about that, we'll get you home if we have to drag you, won't we, Lammert?' Metzger said to the wailing child.

'You named the baby then? Is that wise?'

'Nothing is ever wise, my friend.'

Metzger slapped him on the shoulder in a familiar gesture. This time it brought a reflexive wince and had Kaspar twisting slightly to protect his injured side. The movement didn't go unnoticed.

'Off with your shirt, let's have a look at that wound shall we?'

He knew better than to argue. He turned his face slightly, so Metzger couldn't see the twist of his face as he raised his arms and pulled the ruined shirt up over his head.

The damage was both less, and worse, than he had suspected; he could see it in his friend's face as he peeled off the bloody leather. The frayed edges of the punctures had pressed into the wounds, and his blood had coagulated around the leather, fusing the ruined armour to his skin. Metzger teased it at first, but it didn't want to come away so he was forced to tear the leather free. Kaspar screamed, tears mingling with the sudden fever of sweat on his face and neck.

'Keep still,' Metzger ordered, placing the flat of his meaty hand beside the first of the line of holes, pressing down around the redness, feeling out the inflammation and the tenderness where infection had already begun to spread. The third puncture still contained some of the filth that had caused it, a shard of old yellowed bone that had dug deep into his side, snapping off as the construct lost its grip on him. 'This isn't good; some of the wounds are already infected. I'm going to have to cut it out, my friend. This is going to hurt.'

'I trust you,' Kaspar said. 'Just give me something to bite down on because I am pig-sick of screaming like a little girl.'

Metzger laughed, offering up one of the branch's that had made up the fell fiend's musculature. Kaspar took it, biting down hard on it as Metzger took the bone between thumb and forefinger and drew it out in a single smooth pull. Kaspar screwed his face up, his jaw clenching so tightly that his teeth virtually sheered through the length of wood in his mouth. He spat it out, panting raggedly as Metzger drew his dagger and placed the silver length of its blade in the embers of the makeshift cooking fire. When it was sufficiently hot he pulled it back out of the flames and cut the pus and dark tissue from each of the puncture wounds, the heat of the blade sealing the blood vessels as it cut through them.

It went beyond pain.

Metzger heated the blade again before widening the worst of the holes in an attempt to cut away all of the poisoned flesh. As the searing hot metal slid into his side Kaspar Bohme lost his grip on consciousness and slumped back against the tree trunk. When he came to

Metzger was done, the dagger cleaned and sheathed, and his ribs and side were bandaged with scraps of the old man's shirt that had been torn into strips and tied tight against the wadding over the cleaned wounds. Metzger sat beside the babe, fashioning a splint out of another length of wood from the decomposed construct. Kaspar didn't have the strength to argue against the irony of using the very thing that had caused the damage to help heal it. Instead, he lay beside the tree and kept his eyes closed while Metzger worked and talked to the child he had taken to calling Lammert.

He worked the wood like scrimshaw, peeling away the coarse bark to fashion a smoother splint with a tiny pocket knife. 'We'll take you to your new home, yes we will,' the old man said softly, making the kind of baby noises Kaspar associated with the feeble-minded. 'It's a grand old house, is the manse on the hill, a real manor. You'll be warm and safe there and nothing will be able to hurt you.' As he said it Kaspar almost believed him, until the memory of the endless ranks of the marching dead walked across the back of his eyelids.

Metzger took up a second spar of wood and began stripping it to match the first.

'We lived in a bigger house once, a castle high in the mountains that overlooked the entire protectorate our family served. There was a lake, and trees like these. It was beautiful, like in a fairy tale. It's gone now, like so much else, but back then, it used to stand sentinel over a mountain pass, guarding one of the old dwarf roads. That was a long, long time ago. I don't know why I am even thinking about it now,' he said wistfully, losing himself somewhere for a moment. Kaspar had never heard his friend talk about the old days and the history of his family. He had heard whispers growing up, about dark secrets buried deep, but had forgotten most of that stuff and nonsense as soon as he had heard it, dismissing it as fishwives with nothing better to do with their time than gossip. Metzger breathed deeply, exhaling slowly, emptying his lungs completely.

'The dead,' he said suddenly, as though that explained everything, 'that's why I am remembering it now. All of those dead men marching through my land, that must have been what it was like back then, like we've stumbled back in time or found a way to glimpse what was once more. Ghosts, that is what they were, little Lammert, ghosts walking the world, cast out from the Kingdom of Morr. There are bad men in this world, little one, bad men who league with things so vile they do not bear thinking about. There are men who own twisted, repulsive souls, yet to look at their face they look just like you or I. We owned a castle once, but it is gone now, lost to five hundred years of elemental torment, the road it guarded long since abandoned.

'This must be how my forefather felt that last morning, waking up to face the day when it would all end with the coming of dusk, the world he knew, the things that were so right he took them for granted. Do you think he was frightened when he walked out wearing his suit of burnished bronze armour? I do. I think he was a real man and walked out to face his death, terrified every single step of the way, and yet he did not run away from it. He felt just like we do now, but we will not run or hide either, and do you know why? Because people like you need us to stand up and be counted. We didn't live our lives turning and running and we won't end them that way, no matter what we face. We fight, and when we do, because we are frightened, we hack and hack and hack and hack and they see us, our enemies and our friends and they think of us as daemons of war, great killing machines, but we are only men, frightened like them.

'That's the great secret of war, Lammert, we are all of us, everyone who raises his sword in defence of something he loves, frightened all the way down to our souls. We hide it as best we can, or we embrace it, and at the end, well, it isn't all happy endings, Lammert, not even close. The monster cut him down and Felix Metzger failed. He lost his fight, all of his men, everything. Courage wasn't enough, just as he must have known it wouldn't be when he took that first step on his own, and yet he took it.

'Do you know why he took it, Lammert? Because he was a hero, that's why. A real hero, like your parents who must have risked everything to hide you away so that you had a chance. That took real courage in the face of despair, and we won't forget that, not even for a day. It isn't for glory or honour or any of that. It is always about protecting the people that you love. That's the life lesson for today, little one. That's what your mother and father did, that's what Felix Metzger did and that is what I will do now.'

He fell silent, the bark stripped clean away from the second spar of wood. He cut them to a length and then pushed himself to his feet and began to cut away some of the thinner tendrils of vine with which to bind them to Kaspar's damaged leg.

'I know you are awake, Kaspar,' he said at last. 'How do you feel?'

'Like I have been beaten and kicked by a herd of snotlings.'

'That good, eh? Well that's something. We need to be moving soon. Do you think you can stand on that leg of yours?'

'Doesn't matter if I can't, does it?'

'Not really,' Metzger admitted, 'we're moving out anyway.'

'The horses?'

'Gone. We're on foot until the nearest settlement. Time is of the essence. We have to get word to Grimminhagen, send for reinforcements, and batten down the hatches. The long dark night of the soulless has begun again.'

'It will come to swords,' Kaspar Bohme agreed.

'And when it does, when the clash of steel is greeted by the death cries of the human storm, when flames and the crack of black powder cannons enshroud the night sky, when Morr wends His cruel path between the press of men on the battlefield, touching shoulders and claiming souls, we will be in the thick of it, my friend, side by side, same as it ever was.' There was no bitterness in his voice, no anger, not even resignation. This was what the bull-necked warrior had been born for, this never-ending fight against the darkness of mankind. Bohme was in no doubt his friend believed he was taking the first step towards finishing what his ancestor had begun: the last great human crusade.

'Same as it ever was,' Kaspar agreed.

Metzger braced his leg, securing the wooden frame tightly with vines, and helped him stand. Kaspar tried, tentatively, to put a little weight on his damaged knee and felt the heat flare within the joint. 'I'll need something to lean on.'

A storm was coming.

Across the land, the dead walked.

Metzger had stripped a third branch while he was unconscious. This one was stout enough for Kaspar to use as a walking stick. Improvising, Kaspar wadded up his ruined shirt, wrapping it around the end of the stick so that he could use it as a makeshift crutch instead. With its support Kaspar walked slowly across the clearing, each step drawing a wince from him. He nodded to Metzger.

The older man gathered up the child, and together they walked slowly back towards civilisation, aware in their silence of the implications of the message they brought with them.

CHAPTER SEVEN

Call To Arms
The Road to Grimminhagen, in the Shadow of the
Drakwald Forest, Middenland
The Autumn of Sweet Deceits, 2532

THE JOURNEY THAT had taken three days going out took eight on its return, fear and urgency driving them mercilessly on through the pain.

Kaspar Bohme could not walk more than a few hundred yards without the fire flaring within his knee; the ligaments had swollen hideously, and the constant weight on it as well as the jarring impacts of step after step never gave the inflammation a chance to subside. The long silences were heavy between them but when they talked it was seldom of what they had seen or what it meant for their small part of the world. Kaspar listened as Metzger named the trees and the birds and countless other things for young Lammert. The child cried, desperately hungry, and they couldn't feed it with meat killed on the move. Unlike them, a child could not hope to live long without food, and there was no way of knowing how long the babe had been abandoned before they had found him. On the eve of the first dawn, when the child's cries were unbearable, Kaspar remembered a small farmstead that ought to have been near: one of the more distant outliers. They made the detour to beg milk for the boy and found a widow nursing her grief only too willing to share a cup of cow's milk and a warm pallet for the men when she saw their wounds.

Although the night beside a warm hearth would have been a blessing it was time they could not afford to waste on comfort. Metzger worried for his friend; he needed the attention of a proper chirurgeon to be sure the infections had been cut out and no ill-humours remained to fester. 'Do you have alcohol?' he asked the woman, Sara, wiping his hands on a rag as he came into the kitchen.

'It's too early to be drinking,' the woman said. She was not unappealing, in a matronly sort of way. She had all the right curves and a softness of body that many men found attractive.

'It's not for drinking, lass. I'm going to check Kaspar's chest wounds and a bit of spirit is good for cleaning out any sickness that lingers.'

'You'd think I'd never dressed a cut in my life,' Sara said, ruffling his hair and disappearing into the cold cellar. She returned with a stoppered earthenware jar. 'Let me.'

Metzger chuckled. 'I could get to like you woman.'

'The novelty would wear off soon enough, I am sure,' she said, bustling out of the small room to tend to Kaspar.

He followed her a while later.

'Is he going to be up to moving on?' Metzger said.

'In a week or so, yes,' Sara said.

'We don't have a week.'

'I know but that doesn't change the answer to your question.'

'Will you stop talking about me as though I am not here,' Kaspar said, twisting his head away as Sara tried to pry his mouth open for another spoonful of broth. 'I'll be fine.'

'Typical stubborn man,' she said, shaking her head in disgust, 'you will not be fine. You'll be lucky if you make it a mile, and what good will that do you marooned out in the middle of nowhere, barely out of a fever, yes that sounds like a great idea to me.'

'Then put me on a damned cart, there isn't time for laying abed. We must leave.'

'Come with us,' Metzger said, without thinking. The words just tumbled out of his mouth but even as he said them he realised he had been thinking about them for most of the day in one way or another. 'Come back to Grimminhagen. We have a house, and men: a community. You wouldn't be alone, and Lammert needs a woman's influence if he isn't to end up like me.'

'No,' she said, dismissing the notion as simply as that.

This time Reinhardt Metzger did not laugh or smile. His mouth tasted of ash and bile. 'It isn't safe here,' he told her, pressing the point.

'It's just as safe as it was before you arrived,' she said.

'Just come with us, please.'

'And be your slattern? No, I don't think so. Now you'd better be on your way if you are in such a hurry to leave. Take my cart and the old dray.'

Metzger reached out, hesitating to lay a hand on her shoulder. 'Please, Sara, it isn't safe.'

'So you say, but you don't say why, so why should I believe you?'

'Tell her, Reinhardt,' Kaspar said.

'Tell me what? Stop talking in circles. If there is something I should know, spit it out.'

So he told her of the bones and the dead, of the shuffling ranks of the soulless, of the fallen stronghold and the war he knew was coming, of the sacrifice of the parents who had given their lives to hide their child, of the first fallen village swallowed by the tide of death marching relentlessly on, of the beast that had risen up out of the dirt, a puppet to a man's dark magic, and he begged her again to come with them. 'Because when they come your walls can't protect you any more than your memories can. I am sorry, I cannot with good conscience leave you behind to die on your own.'

His words shook her, but she didn't for a moment doubt him, this stranger who had turned up at her door with a child in need and a friend battling a low fever. She looked into his eyes, as though they were gateways into his soul that could prove or deny the credence of his claims, and asked, 'Who are you that you can promise a stranger a place to live and safety?'

'I am Knight Protector in the service of the Graf; my family has served the Sternhauers for years. That is who I am, but I am also an old man who watches over the land of his forefathers in a time of ill omen. The dead walk the land.'

'We'd better pack a few things,' she said, giving him the only answer she could.

THE FOUR OF them left long before dawn, the sounds of the earth still muted by the last vestiges of night.

Sara packed few creature comforts, a change of linens, a brooch from her man as a keepsake, the only treasure from a house full of her life, and food: bread and cheese wrapped in waxed cloth, a flask of sour wine, and some thick slices of ham.

She turned on the edge of her land to look back at the home she was giving up. Metzger did not hurry her silent farewell. He had left homes often enough, always wondering whether he would return. Sara left with the certainty that she would not. It was not just the walls and roof she was leaving, it was the life she had made for herself, the life she had shared with her dead husband, the one encumbered by so many ghosts already.

She closed her eyes, touched her fingers to her lips and blew a kiss to the life she would never have, and then turned her back on it.

'I am ready,' she said, and Metzger did not doubt her for a moment. She was a strong woman to be able to make such a sacrifice, to need nothing of her old life to survive and to still manage a smile for the child in her arms that wasn't her own. He could only imagine the emotions conflicting within her, but he was savvy enough to know that Lammert was just another unborn ghost for the woman.

He nodded, and spurred the dray horse on. The cart lurched forward.

'HE IS A good man, Sara,' Bohme said. 'I have followed him to the Gates of the Underworld and back on more than one occasion. If he had need I would step through them to bring him back to this stinking place. I love him as a brother and a father and all the friends I never had because he genuinely cares. That is a rare thing in a fighter. Usually they take their coin and join the cause but not Reinhardt. He follows his own moral compass and answers to his heart. He is a just man, and dare I say a pure man. I would die for him tomorrow if it meant he lived on to make a difference.'

'Do not be so quick to throw it away, soldier, this life is not such a bad place to be,' Sara said, and he knew she was thinking of her own husband but he did not want to ask her what happened. Some truths were best left to come out in their own time.

Metzger talked in his sleep. Like so many others with troubled dreams, he worked out his guilt and anxieties as he slumbered. What she heard then, in those feverish snatches of memory unconsciously shared, opened up a world of nightmares that no normal farmer's wife ought ever to experience. She didn't want to believe the snatches of horror rendered so hideously in his anguished cries, but night after night they grew more and more real to her.

As the days turned Kaspar grew stronger. His knee, though not healed, was able to take more of his weight and his ribs no longer pained him so fiercely.

Their road took them beneath the shadowy over-hangs of rock and between the bosom of rolling hills, along the outskirts of various homesteads and iso-lated farms, each one lying in the path of the dead army. Sara woke Metzger in the middle of the night, shaking him out of the fever-sweats of another night-mare, to plead with him.

'We can't just leave them,' she whispered. 'We can't just leave them in their beds, not when we know what is coming.'

He had been thinking the same thing.

They did what they could, amassing refugees in their desperate flight.

By the time they came in sight of the manse on the outskirts of Grimminhagen they were no longer four travellers. Two hundred more had joined their number, making it a caravan of the dispossessed. The mood was sombre. Metzger talked little, turning introspective. Sara nursed the babe, Lammert, singing lullabies in a voice far sweeter than her slight beauty would have suggested, adding another lie to the myth of looks. None of them carried more than a few of their most personal possessions, the rest left abandoned in their homes. More than double their number had refused to join Metzger on the journey back to Grimminhagen, saying they would stay and face whatever they had to, just as they always had, even when they saw the refugees that Metzger had gathered. They were stubborn people. It might have been different had the old priest, Scheller, joined them, but the Sigmarite was adamant they would fight for their homes not run from the shadows. Others followed his lead, refusing to budge as though a few stones were worth more than their lives.

He did not plead with them; it was enough for his conscience that he had given them the choice and if they refused to accept his protection he could not be held responsible. They would have to make their peace with the implications of their choice when the time came. He told them of the horrors approaching, what more could he reasonably do? Drag them out of their homes and force them to accept his protection? Have the Silberklinge round them up like prisoners? No, everything in this life was a choice, and they had made theirs.

Death would take them, and return them, and they would have a mindless eternity to own their mistake.

They walked and rode. By day it was hot and humid, intensely and unseasonably so, and by night cold and clammy, with thunder in the air and a storm never far off. The bread grew more and more unpalatable, becoming harder until it was unchewable, and the ham grew greasy, the cheese green with mould. What little food they had ran out the day before they arrived back at the manse. No one complained and the subservience disturbed Metzger more than the lack of food. That these people simply accepted empty bellies was wrong. He was already thinking of these few dispossessed as his burden, but he had offered them the choice, just as he had the others. They chose to follow him to Grimminhagen. They chose to throw their lot in with him. He shook his head, unable to lie to himself. They might have made the choice but he had asked them to, and he had promised them hope. That promise of hope made them his responsibility.

The sight of the old manor house didn't lift his spirits, nor did the rooftops of the town a short way beyond it. Even knowing that he was at journey's end and that Kaspar could seek proper care did little for his humour, but then he seldom felt joy with homecoming. A place had to feel like home otherwise returning to it could never hope to be a homecoming.

Crossing the threshold he could not help but wonder if he would have been able to give these walls up as easily as those people he had brought back with him. Despite the intimately familiar aromas of cooking and wood-wax, the fustiness of the threadbare rugs and so much else that was ingrained in his soul, he knew he could, as easily as the first day he had left to fight on a foreign field in another man's war.

He wanted nothing more than to sink into a steaming tub and soak the road out of his skin but there were things that needed to be done, some matters pressing, others less so, but no less demanding of him. The bath could wait.

First he called Fitch, Rosamund's man, into his study, bidding him fetch a physician for Bohme, then he summoned Rosamund herself, bidding her take care of the refugees, find them quarters and work lest they feel like they were living off his charity.

She left him to pen letters, six of them in all, each identical down to the final full stop. The message was concise, outlining the danger they faced. There was no rhetoric or hyperbole in them, no embellishment of the horrors he had seen. His language was deliberately matter-of-fact: a huge force of undead was on the march, already deep into the territory he protected. With the few men at his disposal he could not hope to stand without aid.

He sealed each one with red wax, impressing the Metzger crest into the seal.

He summoned six of his retinue. He gave each a letter. 'Today you are messengers, but make no mistake your errand is every bit as vital as your sword will be in the coming days. Take the six swiftest mounts in my stable, and ride the animals into the ground if you have to, these messages are that important and we have no time. Do you understand?' To a man, they nodded.

'Good. Holzbeck, Delberz, Untergard, Middenstag, Middenheim,' he pointed at each man one at a time, 'and you to Arenberg. I cannot impress upon you enough the importance of your mission, gentlemen. This is no mere ride. Would that it were. I could tell you that the fate of the town rests upon your success and it would be no exaggeration,' Metzger said, sitting on the corner of his writing table. 'Let us consider it on a level we all understand, shall we? Our mothers, our wives, our daughters, that is to say the lives of all of our loved ones, rest upon the swiftness of your ride. The dead are rising. You are to find the Stads Marshall, the Knight Commander, whoever is in charge of each city's defences, and deliver the letter to him personally, not some lackey. Impress upon them what we face, but do not exaggerate or fall into fancy. The truth is frightening enough. They must believe their aid will save the day. If they are left thinking otherwise they will look to fortifying their own strongholds and prepare their own defences, leaving us to the mercy of the dead. They may well choose to send you on to the next link in the chain, if that is so, you are to ride like the wind. Word must spread or we fall. It is that simple. Without their support we cannot hope to stand.'

He looked down the line, from man to man, studying their faces, fixing them in his mind. These were the men their survival hinged upon. Grim determination was etched upon every face that looked back at him. These were good men. He could ask for no more than that. He stood once more. 'Are you with me?'

'Aye,' they said as one.

'The marshals will no doubt ask you questions. Tell them this: word is being sent to every outlying farm, the citizens are being brought in to the shelter of Grimminhagen. Every able-bodied man will be given some instruction from the Silberklinge. We will not lie down. We will meet the dead with steel. Stand or fall, Grimminhagen will give good account of itself. Now go, and may the point of Sigmar's boot spur your horses on.'

FINALLY, HE HAD Briony brought to him. The young woman knocked timidly at the door. She entered the chamber, her hands defensively cradled around the bulge of her belly.

'How far along are you?' Metzger asked, looking up from the report he was penning.

'Sorry? I don't...?'

'How many months until you deliver?'

'The midwife thinks it will be before the next moon, but as a first born it could take as much as another full moon after that.'

'I would ask a favour of you, Briony, but do not think your position here is at risk if you say no. I swear that it is not, and I shall think no less of you if you say no.'

She looked at him then, a little frightened. He smiled, hoping to allay her fears, but a smile, no matter how kindly, was not so much when set against the turmoil that had already shattered her life. He knew there was gossip already, twenty refugees could not pass unnoticed, but the nature of that gossip needed to be watched lest it breed fear, the same fear he saw now in her eyes.

'It is a lot to ask,' he said. 'Kaspar and I found a child hidden by his parents. They are dead and the child is alone to fend for himself despite being no more than a month old. His parents' sacrifice has touched me. I cannot claim otherwise, even though I never met them and am fashioning their bravery in my mind. I would honour them by giving the best I can to the child. He cannot take solid food yet, and rather than simply pay a wet-nurse I would find the child a mother to care for him.'

'You want me to take in the child and raise him as my own?'

'Yes,' he said.

'And what of my own child if there is not enough milk for two? I live on your charity, my lord. I cannot very well say no, but the idea of taking another man's child to my breast does not sit well with me.'

'My household will give you all you need, if you in turn offer the boy, Lammert, all he needs.'

'More charity?'

'No, Briony, it is not charity to care for another. It is human decency, and in a world like this, we need each other more and more.'

'I don't know.'

'Please, at least think about it.'

There was a small brass bell on his writing table and he rang it. A moment later a thick velvet curtain was drawn back to reveal a second door into the study that led to his private chambers. Sara stood in the door, holding the child Lammert in her arms. She smiled as she offered the small bundle to the pregnant woman. 'Meet Lammert,' Metzger said, trusting that when Briony saw the little tyke she would not be able to refuse him.

She took him, holding him close to her chest, her mother's instinct taking over the moment she laid eyes upon the helpless child. Shushing him gently, Briony laid a gentle finger against his cheek. He reached up with his small hands and grasped it, drawing it down towards his mouth to suckle on it.

She looked up at Metzger, her mind made up. 'How could I say no?'

'Thank you, Briony. We are a family here, never think otherwise. Your kindness will be returned to you, of that I have no doubt.'

'Or perhaps I am returning your kindness, Reinhardt?'

'I have no kindness, Briony. I am a crotchety old man looking for a good night's sleep,' he said, winking at her, and both women laughed.

It was good to be surrounded by laughter.

There would be precious little of it soon enough.

'You're a good man,' Sara said when Briony had left them.

'I like to think so,' he said, 'but sometimes it feels like I don't have a choice.'

'You always have a choice, but to a good man those choices are obvious. To take in a child instead of leaving him to die in the woods with no one to know better, to bring home two dozen more mouths to strain your granaries and smoke houses, those are not easy choices but you made them without hesitation. That marks you as a good man, Reinhardt Metzger.'

CHAPTER EIGHT

The Coterie of the Damned
On the March through the Howling Hills of Middenland
The Autumn of Sour Deaths, 2532

THE MIDNIGHT HOUR crawled across the land, casting its dark magic over every hill, every valley, every rooftop and every tower.

The dead walked, like something conjured from the depths of the dreamers' minds. They were a plague upon the land, bringing sickness beneath their feet to wither the long grasses. It was not only the dead, it was the sick and the twisted, the damned. Their taint went deeper than blood. The soil withered, growing parched as all goodness was leached from it by the unholy crusade. A thick black miasma gathered in the sky above them.

Amsel rode in a war chariot of bone in their midst, surrounded on all sides by the rotting flesh of the risen dead. His pride at being chosen by the new master over Casimir had not diminished in the slightest.

He had Radu's trust. He revelled in the little victory, but he could not enjoy it to the full for while he was gone Casimir had their master's ear. To return to the castle without the book, to fail, would undo all that he had achieved. He must follow the clues laid out by Korbhen and once and for all see the back of his rival, cementing his place as the Forsaken's right hand.

He whipped the dead dragging his chariot onward.

The blood taint strangled him, driving all thoughts beyond his urge to please his master from his mind. Time lost its meaning, if it had ever had a true meaning. It slipped and slithered away from him, leaving traces of memory, of what it had been like before, when time had seemed so precious, into what it had become, where time grew irrelevant. It blurred memories of one decade into the next, of one war and one fear into another.

He had had a daughter once, before, when the world had felt so young. The taste of her blood, the final ecstasy of taking her, came back to his tongue. He would never forget that. The rest might go, but the taste of the blood he had given her would remain even as he crumbled away to dust.

He felt no guilt over it, even as he had torn at her flesh for two whole hours, forcing pains beyond description upon his own flesh and blood. There had been no remorse because he had become a beast of instinct, and his instinct was self-preservation. He obeyed the cry of blood when he needed to, but was not reliant upon it. To feast on the living was an indulgence, a whim, not a need. It was a pleasure to sate that whim every once in a while, but every now and again the call of the blood was irresistible.

He felt the pull of generations in his veins, more potent than mere time. He felt the dizzying addictiveness of his sire's blood, the blood he had taken with the kiss that ended and began his life. He tasted the potency of his sire's sire and his sire beyond, like a river of death running back to the well of darkness that birthed them all. They were family, fathers and sons in death, a binding shared between them that was stronger than the coincidence of rutting that joined them to their fathers in life. That was the true power of his curse.

'I will not fail, master,' he vowed. It was a promise that could easily have been given to either elder vampire lord who had a claim on his rotten existence.

The stench of corruption was its own macabre perfume, a heady mix of decay, dissolution and infestation that lingered in the air. It was more sweet than rancid to his nose, a honey to the welter of flies that followed them.

They moved only at night, for they were stronger then, keeping to the dark places, but how could ten thousand corpses hide? They could not, so with every step threatening discovery, Amsel drove them on in search of the disgraced priest's testimony. As they marched so their ranks swelled. As people saw and people died, they were absorbed into the ranks of the dead until twenty thousand marched where ten had set out. He doubted the ease of their mission. For all that he grudgingly admitted that Casimir was ferociously intelligent, and that his deductive reasoning was second only to the master's, to believe that this great secret simply lay under the noses of the cattle in one of their houses of worship just seemed naive.

Layers within layers, that was the way. What was hidden stayed hidden through deception, not ignorance. There would be no treasure at Ashenford, of that he was sure. Ashenford, the ford of ash, ash being burnt wood and pulp, both vital parts of the production of parchment. A coincidence? Or a hint as to what he would find in this place: the remnants of this lost testament?

They would not give up their treasures easily. It was the nature of the cattle to accumulate, to hoard, so he had come prepared to take it from them. They were not so different that way, though his kind grasped and gathered knowledge and power while the cattle clung to useless trinkets and trappings. The expectancy was for war, terrible and swift, blood and death and the wretched screams of stupid sacrifice. He had been out of their society for an age, but he remembered enough of what it meant to be a man. He expected no less from them than he would have managed himself in another time.

'Let them die!' he said to himself more than to the twenty faceless dead that shuffled listlessly around him. They were mindless fodder to do but one job: instil fear in the eye of the beholder. Fear would eat into the courage of the cattle, stripping them of the one thing they needed to hold onto: hope. With that gone he would do what he had to do, and in the process swell the ranks of his host, so much so that the hills would tremble and quake at his return. Let Casimir scheme to oust him then! He would be immune to his petty ploys.

Amsel was no fool; he had brought as many of his loyal coterie with him as he dared. They were scattered throughout the endless entourage of risen dead, unique in their deformities and in the strength their deformities gave them. And what an array of deformities they had. Close to him in the press of bodies he could see Masken, with growths all over his skin; Dugar, with his giant arm, his fist a match in size for his skull; Kofas, who carried her guts outside her body in loops of translucent entrails; Sebastian with hunched back and clubbed foot, and Glick with his distended jaw, split mouth of seventy teeth and his single eye.

These few were his loyal servants. They were not unthinking zombies fresh from the grave, minds rotten with the sweat meats and soft flesh of their corpses, but neither were they fighters. They were cunning, and more: they were survivors. How could they be anything other in a world that would see mothers stone their babes to death at birth should they show even the smallest sign of being different, of being wrong. They all bore the taint of deformity, carrying the scars of disease, and yet they had made it, against all the odds, into adulthood with their twisted bones, their conjoined aspects, their scaled skin and all of the other betrayers of difference writ plain upon their flesh.

Like Amsel, they were survivors.

Beside him, Gehan Volk, the vampiric acolyte, crushed an inquisitive bluebottle that had settled in the cavity where his nose ought to have been. The man bore his mark with arrogant pride. He might

have passed among the living with barely a second
glance had he chosen to wear sackcloth and play the
beggar. It had been common in the years before Amsel
had tasted the blood of his sire for adulterers to be
thus marked, their beauty shorn from their face. Volk
was no adulterer. He had been born with the ragged
hole in the centre of his face.

The soldier's dagger had done damage to his shoulder. The wound was festering, the reek of pus and
soured skin clinging to the acolyte.

Lights on the hillside caught his eye.

They had followed the river to the fording point,
tracing its meanders as it coiled like the Lahmian ser-
pent across the Old World, and the light brought its
own reward. Amsel smiled coldly as he stared up at
the sleeping town of Ashenford.

They would wake, those dreamers, soon enough.

But by then it would be too late.

Death would be among them.

THEY CAME DOWN upon the town like a plague of ravenous locusts, denuding the world of even the
smallest shoots of life. Amsel orchestrated the
onslaught, relying on Volk to deflect the hysteria of
the living as they threw themselves into a pitiful
defence while he sought out their holy place. Their
soldiers came, but one hundred swords were nothing
against the dead. The killing was as brutal as it was
swift. He walked through the battle, smelling blood
and denying the hunger that rose in him. He had no
need to feed; he had purpose, and that purpose lay
wrapped and protected in the musty confines of the

Sigmarite temple. They had wardings against his kind. He felt the repulsive wrench inside his gut, like poison spreading through his blood the closer he drew to the place. It was a poisonous pestilent whore of a place, a brothel of the petty gods, and its nearness stung him like a dose of the pox down below.

Amsel listened to the cries of a woman being dragged out of her home by his damned, begging for the life of her baby. It was a mistake to plead mercy, it only incited Sebastian and Kofus and the rest of their kind to do more mischief. The woman had no time to learn her lesson. By the time Amsel had reached the threshold of the tumbledown temple his servants had pinned her out in the centre of the town square and tore the flesh from her bones in a frenzy of tooth and nails. Amsel was deaf to the screams. They meant nothing to him, these humans. He did not care what happened to them. After all, they were meat, and one did not ask a joint of roasted pig its feelings before the feast.

Amsel paused with his hand on the wooden door, and then pushed it open onto a simple unadorned room. The priest was on his knees before the wooden altar, head bowed in prayer. He looked up, face wrought with fear, and made the sign of Sigmar across his chest. The vampire's lips curled into a smile. He stepped forward and stopped, brought up short by the sudden and brutal stab of revulsion in his gut. His blood burned against the violation. Every fibre of his being refused to cross the threshold and the fear on the priest's face slipped as he understood. He pushed himself slowly to his feet and walked towards the door, mumbling the words of his prayer. He clutched a hammer in his right hand.

Amsel threw himself forward, forcing his first foot over the transom. The fire in his heart was more than he could bear and he staggered back out of the holy anguish of the temple.

'You are not welcome hear, fiend,' the priest said, his voice strained thin. His knuckles where white where they clenched around the shaft of his hammer. Amsel could smell the stench of his fear and the iron tang of his burgeoning resolve. 'Go. In the name of Sigmar, go!'

'I don't think so,' Amsel said, his voice relishing the sibilants. For a moment the world consisted of a single room and two men, one living, the other dead. The rest of the world had gone to damnation.

'Then you will feel the wrath of my holy hammer!'

Amsel laughed at the ludicrousness of the threat. The man was a pompous fool. He would enjoy humbling him. His slow smile turned cunning as he said, 'Is that a euphemism, priest?'

'You do not frighten me, creature.'

'Then you are a pious fool. Your flock is dying. Can't you hear their tortured screams? Their blood sings in the night air. They scream and die, scream and die, over and over while you hide in your temple, a coward against the night's dying.'

'I am no coward!' the priest bellowed, raising his hammer and running at the creature standing in the temple doorway.

'Tear the place down!' Amsel cried, his voice rising above the tumult of the killing. The dead responded to his command unquestioningly, rising from the dirt and blood of the town square, pieces of the fallen townsfolk still in their teeth, dribbling lifeblood down their ruined chins and chests. The front zombie lurched and stumbled, tripping over the body of a faceless knight staring blindly at the starless sky. The creature righted itself. Behind it ten, then twenty then fifty and three hundred of the dead responded to Amsel's call, shambling towards the temple.

The priest's hammer struck the vampire full in the face, the silver burning deep.

Amsel turned the other cheek.

The wound opened the left side of his face up, tearing through cheek and jowl to bare his teeth in a permanent grin. Where the skin tore away it exposed corruption, bloated white maggots eating through the flesh beneath. There was no blood.

The priest brought his hammer up for a second shattering blow that never came. The face of corruption mocked him, daring him to cross the threshold and face him without the protection of his damned chapel. The priest took a step forward, out from under the aegis of Sigmar and into the night. One step was all it took. The vampire fell upon him in savage fury, rending flesh from bone in an arterial spray. Amsel tore the robe from the priest's back, his thick black fingernails slicing through the tendon and muscle above the man's heart, and reached into his chest, forcing his fist through the broken cage of ribs, to lift the still beating organ out. The man died in agony, forced to watch as Amsel's gnarled fist closed around his heart and crushed the life out of it.

The priest's corpse lay across the transom, half in and half out of the temple. It was no hindrance to the dead as they threw themselves at the walls and clambered over each other to get onto the roof. The temple groaned, the stones buckling beneath the press of death, and still more fought their way onto the roof and hurled themselves at the walls, forcing them inwards until the mortar cracked and split and the weight brought the whole thing crashing down, reduced to rubble in the centre of the town square.

Amsel stood removed from the destruction, surveying the fallout of his schemes. Driven by wrath and a furious need for vengeance against the perfectly formed men and women, his coterie were wrath incarnate as they ripped the harmony and solidity of the world apart. There was no protection to be found, no refuge or sanctuary. The walls came down. He felt nothing to see the servant of the Man-God humbled. It did not matter. All that mattered was finding the revelation of the lost prophet and continuing upon the quest that his master had laid out for him.

He would not fail.

He felt the warmth of fire on his back as they burned the rest of the town. Come dawn it would be as though Ashenford had been scrubbed violently from the world.

Amsel explored the wound in his face with his fingers. The flaps of skin ached from where the silver had cauterised the wounds, burned even as it tore through his face. It would never heal, the accursed metal would see to that, but it did not matter. He would wear his maiming as a badge of honour: the disfiguration he suffered to secure the great prize. It would be worth it. He would only need to feel the ruination to remember what it had bought. Amsel breathed deeply, savouring the stench of slaughter. Across the transom, somewhere within the rock, dust and rubble, a world of forbidden knowledge awaited him. He closed his eyes, as though he could seek it out with his mind, calling to it, or as though the lost prophet's words could call to him.

He took a single step, expecting the ground to burn, but it did not. With the temple torn down the earth returned to what it had always been: dirt. It was neither holy nor unholy, hallowed, consecrated, defiled or desecrated. It was dirt. He savoured the shiver of satisfaction that this small part of Ashenford resembled at least the first part of its name, ash.

The hand of the Sigmarite statue lay amid the red clay tiles of the roof, fractured from the rest of the toppled statue.

Amsel stepped over it.

The dead were like rats picking over the building's corpse, rotten fingers grasping up rubble and hurling it aside as they dug through the ruin in search of his glittering prize.

Gehan Volk moved up silently behind Amsel. The vampire did not need to hear him, the acolyte reeked. 'We have matching wounds,' Amsel said without taking his eyes off the excavation.

'The testament is somewhere under the rubble. My children will bring it to me, and I shall in turn deliver it up to you as was our arrangement.'

Amsel clasped his hands together, battling the impatience he felt inside.

The men lay in a pile, stacked as though for a bonfire, their lifeless bodies broken and twisted, heads lolling slackly, arms bent impossibly back on their elbows and wrists. One by one the women were forced to watch the pile grow, their husbands, lovers, fathers and brothers, robbed of dignity in death as they defecated and died begging for mercy where there was none. Only when the men were dead did the deformed turn on the women.

This was death: unforgettable, dirty, endless.

Amsel revelled in it, inhaling it, holding it inside him for an age before letting it leak out of his lungs.

Behind them flames gathered, red tongues laving at the sky.

By the time he turned to face Volk once again a look of utter beatification had settled upon his ruined features. 'This death is a contagion, all of it, inescapable and glorious. The day is ours, the cattle crushed. This is the world as it was meant to be, but,' he mused, thoughtfully, 'death begets more death. That is the way of it. The living will come, they will hunt us and we will run from sunrise to sunrise with them dogging our every step. The sun will burn us and silver brand us, and though we live an eternity the short-lived ones will hound us and stake us, chop our hearts out and burn us. They will always be there, hunting us, and thus the death we wrought today will return to us twofold as the children of these wretched few seek us out.'

'You do not look distressed at the notion,' Gehan Volk observed.

'They will extinguish us, or we them, it matters little which. Today we are victorious. To think that it will be the same tomorrow is nothing more than hubris.'

'Then plan for tomorrow, to ensure the day is won again.'

'You speak as though the whims of my kind are shallow and fleeting. We are here,' Amsel said, stooping to pick up a fragment of temple wall, 'to carry out the plans of a long forgotten tomorrow laid down by my sire. We stand in a ruined temple just as he envisioned it more than two centuries ago. It just happens to be our today.'

'That is... convenient,' the acolyte said, a sneer twisting the last word to escape his lips.

On their hands and knees, the dead tore what remained of the temple apart stone by stone, deep into the night. Amsel watched the perilous passage of the moon, knowing that the herald of dawn could not be far away. 'The first cock that crows,' he muttered more to himself than the man beside him, 'I eat.'

'There is nothing here,' Sebastian said, stumbling on his club foot as he struggled through the rubble to reach them. Dugar came beside him, swinging his huge arm like a club. The hour was late and they had been at it for the best part of the night.

'It has to be here,' Amsel said, no room for doubt in his mind. 'Casimir is right; I have gone over his interpretations again and again. The master intended us to come to this place, to find the revelation.'

'Then someone has taken it. There is nothing here.'

'It cannot be. Look again.'

'But it is.'

'No!' Amsel snarled, 'You are wrong! Look again!'

'You can say that all you like, but it doesn't change things. The prophet's testimony isn't here.'

'It is here. There is nowhere else it could be. How many Sigmarite temples do you think there are in this gods forsaken hole?'

'Perhaps there was another Sigmarite temple. It was common for the people to build a wooden temple first, before they constructed the final stone building.'

'No, it is here, hidden.'

'We have torn the place down to its foundations, master. There is nothing here.'

'Then you are looking in the wrong place.'

'That's what we said. It isn't here.'

'But that is not what I said,' Amsel rasped, turning on his servant with fangs bared. Dugar recoiled, his heel catching on the edge of a piece of rubble, and went sprawling. Sebastian couldn't help but laugh, the sound choking in his throat as Amsel's venomous gaze turned on him. 'The words are hidden, not in some book, turned to the right page on the altar.'

'We have looked everywhere,' Dugar objected, but Amsel was having none of it. He scrambled across the debris and started clawing at it with his bare hands, desperate to prove them wrong.

'You have merely scratched the surface,' he shouted over his shoulder, hurling aside a huge chunk of masonry. The stone hit a slew of smaller stones as it fell, causing a small landslide of rubble and dust. He pushed aside bigger and bigger sections of the wall, digging down to where he knew the altar had to be. It took Amsel more than an hour to dig his way through to the white marble of the prayer block. It was not in any way what he expected to find in the heart of a Sigmarite temple. Indeed, like the heresies of the lost prophet it was completely and utterly wrong. He laid a hand flat on the stone, feeling a curious warmth within it. The sensation brought the smile back to his lips. It was a curious piece of craftsmanship, almost pagan in its design. The carvings, in bas-relief, were all wrong for a place of worship. These were not re-creations of the trails of the Man-God; far from it in fact. As he brushed aside the dust Amsel uncovered depictions of life frozen within the marble that were almost bestial in nature. He traced the lupine features of a wolf walking on two legs like a man and some kind of fertility spirit. There were so many more, each image exquisitely rendered with a skill far beyond the worth of a small backwater temple with only a handful of faithful in its flock. Amsel's smile grew cunning as he uncovered yet more of the altar's vile curiosities.

'It is here,' he said with certainty, his palm flat against the grizzled face of a man and bear either conjoined or consumed, it was impossible to differentiate.

Standing again, he cast about for a stone hefty enough to wield against the main altar block. 'Help me,' he demanded of Dugar and Sebastian, and between them they raised a section of the wall above their heads and jumped away as they brought it crashing down on the altar. Stone hit stone in a cacophony of shingle and shale as the sheer mass of collision cleaved the altar block, a deep cleft opening up. Grinning fiercely Amsel leapt upon the altar and wrenched the two sides of the gash apart. 'It's hollow!' he cried, bringing down a smaller piece of rubble violently again and again to work the crack wider.

He reached into the cavity, feeling around with his fingers until one of his nails snagged on something that moved. He felt a thrill of trepidation at the fleeting contact, and knew what he had found. He reached deeper, his fingers finding the cylinder and closing around it. Amsel withdrew his arm slowly, bringing the bone scroll case into the light for the first time in centuries. Like the altar it was decorated with intricate carvings, and again like the altar none were even remotely Sigmarite in nature.

It amused him that his master had hidden this treasure within the sacred heart of their enemy's faith. Such was his cunning that the haunters of the dead never thought to tear apart their own house to find it. Like the hidden door within Kastell Metz, the scroll-case bore the familial sigil that had belonged to the first inhabitants of his home. He felt the thrill of excitement as he cracked the seal on the tube and eased the curl of vellum sheets out. The pages were brittle to the touch, forcing him to handle them with the utmost care. Reverently, Amsel laid them out on the broken altar, scanning the faded ink.

'How can it be so?' he said, shaking his head in disbelief.

'What is it, master?' Sebastian asked, moving up close enough to see the pages over his shoulder.

'It is incomplete.'

'That is impossible.'

'You are wonderfully simple, Sebastian. There are days when I like that quality in you, and then there are days like today when it makes me want to tear out that pulsing vein in your throat with my teeth and feed. It has to be possible because it is precisely so.'

Sebastian picked up the bone scroll-case and held it for a moment, raised like a weapon, before Dugar snatched it from him with a big fist. The misfit grunted, turning the scroll case in a complete twist of the wrist.

Volk stood by silently, his face impassive.

'What is it?' Amsel asked without looking up from the vellums. The ink had faded so badly that it was barely legible in places. It would take all of his skill and a good deal more patience to restore whatever wisdom the sheets contained, but that was the task his master had allotted to him and he vowed to be equal to it.

'The answer,' Dugar said, looking down at his feet. The big man had worked up a feverish sweat from the exertion. His black hair was plastered flat against his scalp. He wiped his massive ham-hock of a hand across his brow, mopping up the sweat.

Amsel looked back over his shoulder, his lips already curled in a sneer prepared to scoff at the freak's stupidity, when he saw the carving properly for the first time. He saw the details and read beyond the symbolism and the heresy its maker had etched into the bone, but even seeing them was only a part of the whole. Before his temper could flare Dugar looked down pointedly at his feet. Amsel followed the direction of his gaze and saw the patterns mirrored in the stone column the big man was standing on. It was not a perfect replica, though the differences were both minor and surprisingly subtle, but there could be no doubt that it was a part of the same overall design.

'Shall I crack it open?' Dugar asked, reaching down for a boulder.

'Let us not be hasty,' Amsel cautioned. Something about the similarities in the two sets of iconography stayed his hand, or rather the subtle differences. 'He who acts in haste repents at leisure.'

'As you wish.'

'Good, now, hand me that scroll-case.' He took it, and turned it over and over in his hands, marvelling once more at the skill of the craftsman in rendering so many intricate images so immaculately. It struck him as peculiar that, with such obvious skill, the man had made a single glaring mistake, but of course, despite his misgivings, it wasn't a mistake at all, but simply another layer to Korbhen's puzzle. The carving was the key. He ran his fingers lovingly over the lines scored into the bone, but where on the column there was the image of a robed man in supplication, there was an open book on the scroll-case. He tapped the bone against the stone.

'There,' he said, indicating the kneeling man. 'Open it up.'

Dugar nodded and brought the huge chunk of masonry down in a savage blow squarely over the kneeling man's bowed head. The layer of stone in that single spot was paper thin. It crumpled inwards leaving a fine coating of powder over the contents hidden inside. Dugar reached inside with his smaller hand and pulled out a second bone scroll-case, identical in every way to the first.

Amsel took the tube, which again bore the seal of his master's forebears, and cracked it open. The seal gave a soft pop as it broke, air leaking back into the canister for the first time in who knew how long. He hooked a finger into the crisp vellums and fished them out. Amsel lay the second set of pages down beside the first, knowing even as he turned the final sheet that it was not the last, ending, as it did, in the first part of an elaborate alchemical formula. Again the ink was faded to a thin flake of rust. The scribe had used blood of some description, which while potent offered little in terms of longevity for the message it inked out. The quality of these sheets was different from the first few pages. It was thicker, the edges yellowed where the air had bleached them and turned them brittle as marrowless bones. He turned the page over to look at the back, but it was unblemished.

'There is another,' he said, laying the page down again.

'Is this some kind of game?' Sebastian grumbled, looking around the rubble for some sort of clue to the whereabouts of the final pages.

'The master does not play games,' Amsel said, seriously.

'No, no, of course not,' Sebastian said, turning away so that the vampire could no longer see his face.

Amsel studied the scroll-case again, looking for the one thing that would set it apart and lead them on to the next stage of their hunt, but it was identical in every way to the other scroll-case. He drummed his gnarled fingernails on the stone, willing the answer to somehow materialise inside his skull. There were no such miracles. He hurled the bone scroll-case away in a fit of temper, kicking out at the damaged column.

Sebastian turned his back and scrambled away across the treacherous rubble towards the rest of his kind. Amsel let him go. He turned his attention back to the damaged pillar, sensing that the final solution lay not in the bone case but in the case that had sheathed it, a layer within a layer, just like the initial puzzle. It made a poetic kind of sense, and very much matched his master's playful mind, but as he stood there, trying to find whatever final clue Korbhen had left him, all he could see was the wound left by that first inconsistency of the kneeling priest.

With the sun rising and the mournful cries of the dead growing more urgent, Amsel crouched, digging through the rubble to bare the entire column. The frieze was an otherwise perfect copy of the two bone cases.

'The priest in prayer is surely a sign of the first resting place, not the last,' he mused. Then he scrambled to his feet, suddenly sure what he would find if he re-examined the bas-relief images on the side of the altar.

It was there amid all of the fanciful fusions of man and beast: a funeral bier.

Amsel recognised the religious significance of the carvings on the bier. It was a priest's tomb.

'Where would you find a priest's tomb in a temple?' he wondered.

'In the crypt,' Gehan Volk said.

Amsel pointed down at the stone around his feet. 'Clear this mess.'

Volk smiled, and took a gewgaw from the depths of his robes. 'If I may?' he said, and without waiting for permission from the vampire, the acolyte touched the fetish to his lips and whispered a word. He set it down on the broken stones. It was a thing of bone and feather, delicate as it perched over the cracks between two stones. With a second word it sank into the shadows of the small crevice and disappeared. A moment later the stones in front of them appeared to shimmer, like a snake slithering over a hard-baked desert. It was as though a molten thread ran through the hard core of the stones.

'Bring me to the older dead, my charmed one,' Volk whispered, looking back over his shoulder at the pile of broken bodies. 'Not this new meat. Old bones. I want old bones.' Amsel watched as the shimmer coiled, the rock around Volk's feet puddling like mud before it snaked away from him, rippling through the heart of the shattered temple stone for a full twenty paces before disappearing again. 'Over there,' Volk said, directing his dead to begin their digging. Within minutes they had uncovered the trap door down to the crypts.

Amsel stood over the wooden door set in the huge granite slabs of the floor and then threw open the trap. The dead crowded around him, as though drawn by mawkish curiosity.

He descended into darkness.

As a creature of the night his eyes were sensitive to all of the shades of darkness. He had no need of light beyond the sliver of early dawn that followed him down. He stood stock still, allowing his vision to clear. Slowly the details of the chamber began to solidify for him. It was a small room with three cornices, and in each cornice were set three stone sarcophagi.

The air down below was old air, robbed of its vitality by years of entombment.

There were bones not in any coffin, incomplete skeletal remains scattered across the hard-packed dirt of the crypt floor. He kicked aside a desiccated tibia. The bone powdered beneath his foot. Crude markings had been scratched into the ground below the bone. He crouched to examine the three deep scores, like the points of a cloven hoof scuffing up the dirt before a charge. He raised his fingers to his nose, inhaling the redolent earth. He was about to push himself back to his feet when he saw the misshapen skull. Where the other bones had been distinctly human in nature this was without doubt animal in form. He turned it in his hands, studying the powerful jaw-line and the atavistic brow. The skull almost certainly belonged to a bear or some such forest dweller. It made no sense. If the animal had crawled in here to die surely they would have found more of its bones? Perhaps the priest had taken the head as a trophy or an ornament in return for a favour?

He set the bear's skull down at the foot of the first stone sarcophagus.

Again the tomb was decorated with depictions of bestial men cavorting in some vile ritual. It was not the holy tomb of a true Sigmarite, no matter what the temple might have become today, it had once been something far removed from all that this new faith called holy.

'What was this place?' Amsel muttered, his voice echoing in the dank confines of the crypt. He shook his head; it did not matter. All that mattered was finding the final pages of the testament. There was no kneeling priest for him to pry the vellums out of cold dead hands though. He cast about the crypt, nine tombs, three by three by three. He was going to have to disinter all of them, since there was no way of knowing which contained the right priest.

The sun was brighter through the hatch of the trap doorway. It would be full dawn soon, his army would weaken, and he would be forced to take shelter down here. He could not allow that to happen. The ransacking of Ashenford would not be without consequence. To stay here even an hour longer than necessary was a mistake he could not afford. One hundred swords offered little defiance, but in days a thousand or more might be mustered. Snatching defeat from the jaws of victory was a fool's folly, and he was not a fool.

Moving with urgency, Amsel toppled the lid of the first sarcophagus. It hit the ground and cracked into three pieces upon impact. The corpse inside was wrapped in yellowed bandages that had rotted through in several places to expose mildewed bone. He grasped the corpse and heaved it aside. The bottom of the tomb was empty. He toppled the second lid and the third and the fourth, grunting with frustrated anger as the fifth broke at his feet.

The dead man, still recognisably a man with leathery skin stretched tight across his shrunken face lay in peace, as though he had died but yesterday, simply falling asleep never to wake again. His arms were crossed over his chest, his priestly raiment riddled with holes. The priest clutched the final pages of vellum in the calcified bones of his fingers. Amsel pried the fingers back one at a time, the phalanges coming away in his hands as he claimed the pages.

CHAPTER NINE

Walking The Line
Grimminhagen, in the Shadow of the Drakwald Forest,
Middenland
The Autumn of Lost Souls, 2532

REINHARDT METZGER WATCHED his men drill from his vantage point in the study of the manse. So few would make it. He was an old man. He had been listening to lies all of his life. He recognised the sound of a lie even before the words had finished forming in the liar's throat. It was his gift. It had helped make him who he was, and before today it had saved many lives.

Before today.

'A general offering peace while continuing to raise armies is lying through his teeth. Have you ever heard that saying, Sara?'

'I can't say I have,' the woman beside him said. She looked at Metzger with a mixture of admiration and pity, and perhaps something more. It was not uncommon for affections to be transferred during excessively stressful circumstances, and there could be no denying the excessively stressful nature of the events that had thrown them together. Was it love? Misplaced? One-sided? Did it even matter?

'Commit it to memory. A man offering peace should not be preparing for war. It is a contradiction.'

'I will remember,' she promised.

'It isn't all about generals and war, Sara. It is about people. A man promising one thing should never be preparing for another. A man promising to love and cherish you should not be bedding your sister. It is the same.' She nodded. 'Tell me something, do you believe in me, Sara?'

'Believe in what?'

'The stories. I hear the men talk. I am a man alone. I have never taken a wife, never raised children. I gave myself to the service of others. They talk of me as though I am some kind of legendary figure, a hero of old, but you have lived with me now. You know I break wind just like every other man. So, tell me, knowing the real man, do you still believe the stories?'

'Do you want the honest answer?'

'Is any other worth hearing?'

'Then, to be brutally honest with you, sir, no,' she said, a wry smile playing across her lips. 'No man could do what they say you have done. Not all of it.'

'Ah, you are a rationalist. Good, my dear. Very good. You are quite right. I haven't done even a quarter of what the men claim, but I have done many, many things they never speak of. So, tell me, why do I let the stories persist? Why not quash them? They are obviously lies, after all.'

'Because the men need to believe them.'

'Explain.'

'They need to believe you are a giant. To follow you into death they need to believe that you are immortal. Your immortality rubs off on them. By serving you they in turn inherit your immortality.'

'Good, Sara. Very good, indeed. Psychology is a rare trait in a maid. Being able to read a man is a gift. Now answer me this, how many men do you see outside?'

'Eighty, perhaps a few more.'

'And the others?' Metzger persisted.

'Boys.'

'So, tell me, when you look at them, are they immortal?'

'No one is, not truly.'

'Wrong. I am, Sara, and as far as those boys out there are concerned the rest of the Silberklinge are. Do you understand?'

The young woman wiped her mouth with the back of her hand. She stared at Metzger's knights as they drilled the youths, saw wooden swords clashing, the men ducking and weaving, duking it out like pugilists. They were just men, no matter how much she wanted to see them as more. Immortal? Hardly. Even from here she could see the difference between the knights and the others, the butchers and bakers and tallow makers and stable hands. They were less than the scraps of an army. They were not conquering heroes. She saw the ghosts of men soon to be conquered out there on the parade ground, still living, still breathing but ghosts just the same. 'No, sir, I don't.'

Metzger wasn't surprised by the answer. It was hard to look beyond the literal surface and into the figurative implications of those few men striding out to join the boys.

'They made it, Sara. Despite everything, they made it. They offer hope. A slim hope, but hope nonetheless. To the younger men, the ones yet to face another man sword to sword on the field, they represent survival. They faced death and came home.'

'But at what cost?'

'That's not important, Sara. This isn't a game of costs. The fact that they came home is everything. It means hope. Even against the tide of death sweeping our way, their return again and again means hope, and hope, sweet Sara, is the last thing we want to die. Just imagine if these men rode out tomorrow and did not come home. How would those boys feel knowing that better men had failed before them? How would you feel?'

'Hopeless.'

'Exactly. And Sara?'

'Yes?'

'It is all right to be frightened. Remember that. Fear is healthy. In the days to come it might well be all that keeps you alive.'

'Not all,' the young woman said, resting her hand on his broad shoulder.

'Quite right,' Reinhardt Metzger agreed. 'You'll need a slice of luck or two as well.'

Alone, looking at the pitiful sight of his makeshift army being put through its paces it was difficult to heed his own words. Other than his men, hand-trained and loyal, he didn't see heroes down there. He saw children pretending to be men, out of their depth but willing to give everything to protect their home. He couldn't ask more of them even if the darkness gathering on the horizon gave lie to their hopes. There was no safe place.

'I can't save everyone,' he said, more to himself than to the woman at his side. It was the bitter truth, no matter how distasteful it was to swallow. It was impossible to save everyone who looked to him for protection. His protective reach extended far beyond the city skirts, out into the farms and homesteads a fortnight's ride away from Grimminhagen. The riders had gone out to warn the major townships and word would inevitably filter out to the smaller farmsteads. He had to pray that it was enough. He did not have the men to spare to warn all of the people who looked to him for protection, not if he was going to try and see to that protection. He knew that abandoning them to their fate was tacitly signing their death warrants, and that did not sit comfortably with the old soldier but there was nothing he could do. He could not save everyone.

He needed to talk to Kaspar. There were things that needed to be done. He couldn't sit by idly and watch these people, his people, die when it was his job to protect them.

'You can go now.'

'Sir.'

THEY HAD NO time.

The cart had bought them perhaps two days' lead on the dead, but they had lost the best part of it collecting strays. The thought of it burned Kaspar Bohme. He was a warrior, supposed to train farmers' and bakers' boys to defend themselves against the oncoming storm. If he had not witnessed the river of death shuffling through the heart of the land with his own two eyes he might have been able to lie to them and promise hope. But he had seen it, and he could not lie. It wasn't in his nature. No matter that the truth was a demoralising force, it was better for these young men to know that hell was walking towards them and pig-stickers and pitch forks were all they had to fend it off.

No time was nowhere near long enough, but ironically it was perfect. With too much time on their hands to dwell upon their mortality discipline would have broken. As it was, they had hours not days to drill these boys, so naturally they struggled to cope with the drills and the demands he put on their bodies, but it had to be done. It was a fine balance of need and fear, but he would have killed for another month to work with these boys. They were good boys. They deserved the chance to become good men.

Birds circled overhead all the long edgy hours of the day. Their presence promised one thing: that the dead could arrive at any time. Their ceaseless caws cut to the soul of the inhabitants of Grimminhagen. The ghastly sound penetrated the walls of Metzger's fortified manse, from the highest heights of the temple's bell tower to the lowest depths of the cellars hidden beneath. They cut across the houses crowded nearby and Sternhauer's keep off across the rooftops to the east. The black birds circled and watched until Reinhardt Metzger's patience crumbled and he sent

Morgenrot up to reclaim the sky. The goshawk killed with ruthless efficiency, plucking the ravens from the sky one by one, chasing them down until every last bird lay dead in the dirt.

He sent the dogs out to finish the task.

Metzger did what he could to establish the passage of the damned, sending out scouts into the surrounding countryside to give advance warning of their arrival. Even an hour was a luxury worth deploying every trick in his arsenal to secure.

The black miasmic cloud still clung to the sky, thicker now than when they had first spotted it, so thick that it already smothered most of the surrounding land in its choking fug. It could not be used to predict the arrival of the dead, only to demoralise the men further with the promise that they were close.

Bohme had gathered every able-bodied man between the ages of twelve and fifty onto the parade ground and was vainly trying to turn them into soldiers in less than a day. It was an impossible task and everyone concerned knew it, yet it needed to be done. Simple drills gave the defenders a sense of worth, and sold them the lie that their lives would not be given cheaply. By the end of the morning Bohme had them believing that each one of them was worth five of the undead horde. By the mid-afternoon word had begun to spread that the dead numbered thousands. The three hundred and sixty men Bohme had plucked from the tanneries, bakeries, market stalls and farms to swell the ranks of the militia knew fear then, in ways that they had never previously comprehended.

Throughout the afternoon, Briony, Rosamund and the women of Metzger's household brought food and drink out to the men and lingered to watch.

The confidence of the first few hours, the easy camaraderie of sword brothers their shared plight had formed, had died by dusk. The truth spread like a canker in the ranks, its darkness consuming what little hope Kaspar Bohme had begun to instil in them.

'It's hopeless!' Bohme yelled, hurling his spear like a javelin. Frustration ate away at him. Despite everything, all the lies he offered in praise to boost their morale, his rag-tag troop of defenders were, to a man, incapable of mastering even the most rudimentary weapon skills. They waved their wooden swords around like fly swatters. Sigmar help them when they donned armour and tried to fight with real swords. He shuddered at the thought.

There were other thoughts, too, that he wilfully avoided thinking, but one kept returning, every bit as stubborn as his refusal to think it: there were nowhere near enough weapons to equip even these few. Those too old to man a genuine defence slaved all day long and into the night in the forges trying to make up the shortfall of spears, swords, arrowheads and armour, but their skills were laughable. They drilled with wooden staves instead of proper balanced blades, the clash of wood on wood ringing out from first light deep into the dusk, but for all the sweat and effort, toy swords were not the real thing and Bohme knew that come first blood everything they had learned would flee and the boys would be left dying and wondering why the swords in their hands didn't feel like the wooden sticks they had practised with.

He felt like he was banging his head against a stone wall.

The weight of real weapons was so different that even the most basic of moves he struggled to drill into the men was worthless.

It pained Bohme to admit the fact that he wasn't helping these lads but he had promised Metzger that he would do all he could to give them a fighting chance of survival. That fighting chance would almost certainly be what got them killed. He was giving them a false belief in their skills that would see them as dead as if he left them to it. It was a hopeless cause.

He let them believe what they wanted to believe.

What was interesting though was the effect the drills on the makeshift parade grounds had on the wives and would-be lovers. The women came out to watch their men sweat and cheered them on even as they dropped their pretend swords and nearly brained the men beside them with mistimed swings. Their presence gave the men a chance to show off. It was as though the drills had become an extended part of some sort of weird mating ritual.

Undoubtedly, if they survived, nine months down the line there would be a spate of births and a surge of new life within the township. He wasn't about to deny them this last flirtation with happiness. Hell, in their place, he would have wanted to work out some of that nervous tension in as physical a way as possible. As it was he put himself through a series of punishing routines, driving his body as hard as he could despite the hammering it had taken from the sorcerer's construct. He knew he was not even close to half-way fit and that only served to make Bohme push himself all the harder. Most of the boys could out run him and would outlast him in a serious duel, if they had the wherewithal to avoid his cuts and wear him down. So while they were doomed through lack of skill he was damned by a body that would turn traitor at the first opportunity.

Metzger moved up beside him. He had been so wrapped up in his thoughts that he hadn't heard the old man approach. 'Nothing is truly hopeless, my friend,' Metzger said, laying a firm hand on his shoulder. 'Don't make the mistake of underestimating these farmers. They may not be soldiers but they are fighting for their homes, their wives and their children. Today that makes them fighting men because they know if they fail it all ends here. When the time comes they will fight like cornered beasts, and who knows, they might even surprise an old cynic like you.'

'You are talking about desperation, Reinhardt. We both know that won't last. It never does. It might hold off the initial assault but what good is that if they just keep coming? And that's what they do, isn't it? In the face of the dead it won't be enough.'

'One day at a time. That's all we can ask for. Remember the darkness will always be turned back by a single light.'

'You are a hopeless optimist, and I love you for it, but, friend to friend, you sound like a fool,' Bohme said, honestly.

'Perhaps,' Metzger conceded with a smile, 'but ask yourself this: which is more inspiring, the optimistic fool or the weary pessimist telling the world it is doomed?'

Kaspar Bohme looked at the old man as though seeing him properly for the first time. He wasn't just a grizzled old warrior facing one last hurrah; he understood his people. 'Perhaps you aren't a fool after all,' he said with a grin. 'And they do say the gods favour a fool so maybe your longevity is down to the whims of some fickle immortal you have yet to piss off.'

'Go get your spear, we have work to do. The first scout's just reported back. If the dead march relentlessly they will hit us in the dark heart of the night. If they rest they will arrive come first light.'

'When did the dead ever rest?'

'Exactly. I want to divide the men into squads and I want them to get to know each other. They aren't going to learn much fighting in an hour, so now it is down to trust. Their lives depend on it. They have to know that a friend has their back. There is only so much drilling a man can do with wooden swords. And while we are about it, I think we should divide the Silberklinge between the squads, for organisation and because their presence will be good for morale. For each knight we have fifteen trained soldiers. It theoretically weakens our fighting unit, but individually their presence will give each new troop an element of experience that could be vital when it comes to the crunch. We're all lost if these boys lose their heads, remember. This isn't about theoretically turning artisans and farmers into swordsmen, it is about giving ordinary men the tools to survive.'

'Everything you say makes perfect sense, but–'

'You can't get past the reality that it isn't enough?' Metzger said for him, voicing what they both knew to be true.

'Big hearts won't save us.' Bohme agreed.

'Don't you think I know that, my friend? I do, of course I do, but this is my home and these people are my friends. I grew up with them, fell in love with them and will give my life to try and protect them. That is what it means to be Knight Protector.'

'You are a better man than I am, Reinhardt Metzger.'

'I don't believe that for a minute. You're here aren't you? Even when you know it is hopeless.'

'When you put it like that you make me think I must be the fool,' Bohme said bitterly. 'Come on, let's go and talk to our army. One last chance to practise your foolishly optimistic rallying cries.'

THERE WERE NO drills left, and despite the thumping rain and the boggy soil, the wolf-whistles of the women and the lies of the soul that he had propagated, he found himself liking some of the boys.

Bonifaz, the youngest of the Silberklinge, came to find him three hours before dawn. The men and boys sat around nervously in their armour, some of them grasping a sword for the first time. He was a serious young man, bearing twin scars on his cheeks when a tavern brawl had turned ugly. Without them he might have been considered handsome. With them, when his face creased into a smile, he looked almost manic. There was no more ferocious or skilled warrior in the ranks of the Silberklinge, and none more loyal to the old man.

'Fehr continues to show promise,' Bonifaz said, unbuckling his bracer.

'One man from three hundred and sixty,' Bohme said, trying to keep the bitterness from his voice.

'It is better than no men from the same number,' the young warrior said. He scratched at the nape of his neck and then finished unbuckling the leather strap.

'How many others are there?'

'In my unit? None. Cort reckons he has two or three in his group, the butcher's boy, Eugen, and Eva's eldest, Fabian. Fester is less hopeful. He counts for none who might not break ranks and flee at the first sight of the dead coming round the mountain. He urges we cut the farmers free and leave the fighting to the real soldiers. We might be fewer in number but fear is like a plague. If one farmer loses his bowels good soldiers are going to be unnerved, not just the bread-maker and the butcher. Jakob and Ingo are no more impressed, either. I haven't talked to the others, but I reckon it is safe to assume we have maybe twenty boys from the three hundred and sixty that we could, given time, make men out of.'

'Twenty,' Bohme repeated, the significance of the word 'time' not lost on him. Of those twenty, how many would buckle at the first sight of death? It was one thing to swing that wooden sword and look the part, it was quite another to do it in the piss and shit and blood of battle with friends dying all around.

Of those twenty maybe one…

He didn't have time to dwell on it.

The cry went up. The dead had come!

CHAPTER TEN

The Last Testament of the Lost Prophets
On The Outskirts of Grimminhagen, in the Shadow of the
Drakwald Forest, Middenland
The Autumn of the Living Dead, 2532

AMSEL SAT WITH all the pages in front of him, marvelling at the simplicity of the puzzle when all the pieces were in place. The vampire had come to the highest point overlooking the settlement of Grimminhagen, leaving the bulk of his army below, poised to crash down like a merciless tidal wave on the streets of the town. He felt a little surge of satisfaction at having followed the game to the end and brought it all together. It took a special kind of mind to see outside the framework of the conundrum and root out the solution, but then, the master knew him better than any other. He knew his mind and the way he thought and had constructed the clues for him to follow. Korbhen had laboured long and hard to lay out the seeds of his long game, anticipating the covetous nature of his get and the grim determination of his thrall, and planting seeds to please and frustrate in equal measure. Now, on this darkling plain, Amsel knew that just rewards waited over the next horizon.

He took the bones of the dead bird in his hands, gently stroking life into the brittle skeleton. The wing twitched involuntarily. He whispered a sweet word, drawing another barely perceptible tremor out of the dead bird's carcass. He had written the note, cryptic enough to have Radu pacing and cursing his name before he took the time to decipher the message properly, and secured it around the dead bird's leg.

Amsel breathed unlife into the fragile creature, throwing it up into the air. The bird's wings flapped and fluttered as it lurched in the sky, flying erratically. Amsel watched it, willing the creature to rise. When it was high in the sky he whispered the final command, bidding it fly home to Kastell Metz. 'Carry the message to the new master. Bid him come.'

The bird rose higher and higher, angling towards the dark clouds. It would find Radu and in the meantime they would wait.

The prize is not a book but a box long hidden where the bodies are buried in Grimminhagen. It awaits your hand.

The knowledge that it was no mere book they sought excited him. He ran his fingers over the indentations beneath the ink on the page, tracing out the symbol of the great Nagash and recognising the secret strength seeded into the vellum. It was no accident that Korbhen had woven the necromancer's sigil into the warp and weft of the paper. He could read the images as clearly as he could the words, and knew precisely what they meant, but doubts nagged him, still. Could Korbhen really have left such a treasure waiting at the rainbow's end, or was it more lies meant to build up Radu and then crush him when they came to nothing?

'Could it possibly be?' he whispered, daring to hope.

Hope was such a tenacious thing. Once it had its teeth in the mind it did not let go.

He knew what the scrolls promised, and he had told Radu enough to work it out if he dared. A box where the bodies are buried is more commonly known as a coffin or casket, long hidden, or hidden throughout the ages. Could such a treasure truly contain the necromancer's hand? Or was it a metaphor for the power the hand offered? He had some of the answers, but far from all of them. The rest were there to be read by those with eyes to see.

Radu watched the dead bird settle on the battlements among the rest of its kind. Flesh and feather hung from its tiny bones. Its jaundiced eyes roved, finally settling on the necrarch. It hopped forward. He saw the note fastened to its leg and chuckled at the utterly prosaic nature of his thrall's communication. That Amsel would raise a raven from the dirt to carry the message and not imbibe it with the remnants of his own voice but rather scratch out a few hasty words said so much about the thrall.

The cruel wind howled, whipping in from the north. Given time it would bring snow. He grew weary of waiting. Amsel had been long gone with no word, and worse, no reward for his sojourn. Still, here was the bird with its archaic little message. He knew he ought to be grateful that the fool had managed this much, but there was no room for gratitude while every black heart he had surrounded himself with would so willingly feast on his remains.

Below, he saw the filth of life diluted into the desperate act of survival, the few damned and deformed grubbing around in the dirt. He licked his fleshless lips.

'Come to me, little wing,' the necrarch rasped, his voice clotted with disuse. The words frosted in the air like tiny crystals. The bird cocked its tiny head and then hopped forward three steps onto Radu's rotten palm. The wind ruffled what was left of its feathers. He unfastened the tie and unrolled the small strip of parchment. The message was not what he had hoped. He crumpled the paper and tossed it from the parapet. 'Can the fool not be trusted to do anything alone?' he railed, wheeling on his heel to see Casimir skulking in the shadows. The thrall irritated him irrationally, creeping around everywhere.

'My brother has let you down, master?' Casimir wheedled, rubbing his pale hands together in gleeful anticipation.

Radu knew him well enough to know that nothing pleased Casimir more than hearing of Amsel's shortcomings. The bitterness between them would be the death of one of them soon, but even that did not worry the necrarch. Why should it? A second death was weakness. He had no need of the weak to serve him. If one died, how could he ever have been worthy of Radu's wisdom?

'Yes, yes, yes,' Radu the Forsaken muttered, his frustration getting the better of him. Without realising it he had crushed the frail skeleton of the resurrected bird in his gnarled fist. It cawed once, weakly, but didn't die even as its chest cavity caved in and its wings bent and snapped like dry twigs. Radu looked down at the mess in his hand, grunted, and tossed it off the battlements. It fell, but it was not released of the curse that had brought it back. He watched as the fluttering of the wings became impossible to differentiate from the blur of its descent. It would live on until the enchantment failed, a pitiful wreck of a thing.

'What does he say?'

Radu looked up. What should he say? What lie should he spin? What truth should he obfuscate? What, in the end, did it matter what he told the eager Casimir? Let the thrall stew in his own juices and convince himself that Amsel had discovered some rare and exquisite treasure.

'That the promised prize is not what was promised at all but something far, far more powerful. He would have me there for its recovery.'

He watched the covetous gleam flicker across his thrall's slack-jawed face.

'I will watch over your work, master. You need not fear your efforts being undone by time.'

'You are a fine servant, Casimir, faithful.'

The thrall nodded.

Radu could not miss the greed behind his dark eyes. His cravings were every bit as transparent as his brother-in-death's, more so, even. That predictability made him malleable.

'What will you do, master?'

Radu thought about it, drawing the rags of his cloak close about him as though to ward off the wind's chill. The moon danced silver across his lips. 'What I always do, Casimir. I shall take hold of the situation myself. If you want a job doing well, you must, it seems, do it yourself.'

'The master is wise indeed,' the thrall agreed, obsequiously.

'Leave me now,' Radu said turning his back on the lickspittle.

AN UGLY KESTREL banked high in the night sky. Caught in the light of the twin moons its deformities drew the eye. Amsel watched it with a sense of trepidation, knowing the bird for what it was, a harbinger.

A grey empty mist lay on the fields, wisps of fog curling up from the down-trodden grasses. The bones of the skeletons had been allowed to fall to rest, scattered across the fields. The acolytes would rouse them when the need arose. He had better things to do than waste his energies rising piles of bones. This was his moment of glory. The zombies stood still, swaying slightly as they awaited the imperative to attack. For now, the peace was a blessing. The deformed clung to the dubious safety of the trees. Amsel turned his attention from the bird to the mist, listening for the telltale sounds of Radu's approach. For the longest time there was nothing but the loneliness of the mists, but slowly a dark shape began to resolve and the crook-backed necrarch limped out of the swirling fog, strands of ethereal white still clinging to him as he stomped angrily through the remnants of the dead. His grumbles preceded him like the snapping of a black hound. Clutching his lantern, Amsel hastened towards him.

'I do not answer your beck and call like a dog,' the Forsaken rumbled threateningly as he divested himself of his travelling cloak and thrust it at Amsel. Radu's face twisted angrily.

'No, master. I merely thought–'

'You were not sent out to think. You were sent to recover a treasure, and now you tell me you were wrong all along and this treasure is no treasure at all? I should flay every inch of skin from your spine for your temerity and use it to record your failures so that all who come in your stead know not to disappoint me.'

'Master,' Amsel said, bowing his head. The chill of the night wormed its way down his spine one bone at a time, lingering.

'Then... then perhaps I would satisfy the anger that churns away within me, the anger of a man who feels he has been cheated and lied to. Should I cede to that anger, then I would draw the bones out of your wet flesh and broil the marrow out of them for broth to feed that damned coterie you have filled my home with. Is that the fate you want for yourself, Amsel?'

'No, master,' Amsel said, not daring to move, even to shake his head in denial, lest the necrarch's temper flare and he make good on his threats. Radu was nothing if not a volatile man, and capable of great pettiness should the whim strike. It did no good to snivel or plead. The necrarch had no respect for weakness, despite the underlying irony of that loathing. Begging would only worsen the punishment. Amsel merely waited for reason to reassert itself in the necrarch's mind. Such was the new master's capricious personality that in an hour or two the man would be lost in thoughts of the great gift his thrall had uncovered, but for now his imagination was no doubt ablaze with tortures galore, each one burning to be unleashed on Amsel's body.

He needed to divert Radu's attention to the discovery. It was more than any mere book, more than a trinket or a gewgaw. It was a relic fundamental to their heritage. It was, in truth, their birthright.

More than that, it would change the world.

That would appease the Forsaken.

Radu turned up his nose as though catching a scent on the wind, turned his head and walked beyond Amsel. 'Show me what you have found, and pray that it is enough to defer my disappointment.'

Amsel scurried after him, hurrying to catch up.

It was a narrow track forged by animals who had made the side of the hill beyond Grimminhagen their home. It wound up the shallow slope in a series of slow curves, taking the line of least resistance up to the summit. Moonlight and lantern combined to turn the ground to his left gold and silver while darkness claimed the thick grasses to the right. Beneath, behind and between Radu's curses, Amsel heard the night sounds of the forest: the low croak of tree frogs, the susurrant whisper of the leaves in the trees, the rustle of snakes, badgers, and rats in the long grass, and all the small creatures that made the shelter of the hillside trees their home. They followed the trail up towards the rocky plateau that overlooked the town. Mountain goats chewed at the side of the track, bolting at the first whiff of decay.

Radu moved with an awkward, clumsy, gait, struggling up the incline.

The higher they went, the lower the tree branches dragged down.

The wind tore at Amsel's rags as he struggled to match the necrarch's determined stride.

Finally they stood together at the summit, on the rocky outcrop that overhung the tallest of the trees. They were not alone. Volk stood to the side, clutching the three bone tubes that they had rescued from the ruins. The lights of Grimminhagen lit up the valley below them. The candles and oil lamps looked like a thousand fireflies hugging the lowlands. Slightly removed from the town, but still within the walls, lay a manor house, and outside the wall, the silhouette of garrisons and the shadow of Sternhauer's keep. Even in the low light of the night it was apparent that parts of the town had been built and rebuilt, the dark stained silhouettes of the buildings that had not been reconstructed marking out darker lines in the grass that had overgrown them.

'This is what you brought me to see? A sacked town? It is not as though any of this devastation is newly wrought, so what am I supposed to be looking for?'

'The answer is in the marks in the grass, master. I did not see them at first, for the light is not good, but if you wait, the moon will again catch the angles you need.'

'Explain.'

'Come, come, here, look,' Amsel said, waving Gehan Volk over. Without a word the acolyte uncapped the scroll cases and unfurled the three vellums, laying them out to correspond with the town down below. He saw Radu studying the man, and in turn saw Volk's ruined face with its ragged wound instead of a nose curl in contempt. 'Do you see?' he asked, causing both men to look at him instead of each other. It had been an accident but once Amsel had glimpsed the similarities between what appeared to be random brushstrokes and the black shadows in the dirt of fallen ruins, he had understood. The vellums were literal and figurative maps to the treasure.

He brought his lantern closer.

Looking at the map and the darker patches of grass he could rebuild the town of Grimminhagen as it had been before invasion had levelled it, before Korbhen had stashed the casket away. Layer upon layer of plans became apparent.

'What am I looking for?' Radu asked impatiently.

'The town today is not the town that it was. It's clever, beyond clever. Look at the penmanship.'

'Sloppy at best,' Radu said, dismissively.

'Not at all, every stroke is immaculately rendered. Together they form the final jigsaw piece. Look again and then look down at the patch of ground on the far side of the town, slightly removed from the streets and new houses, but still within the wall. The dark patches in the grass?'

'I see them.'

'Now compare them with those sloppy brushstrokes.'

'Amazing,' Radu crooned, seeing it at once. Amsel could not help but smile. 'A temple?'

'I believe so, master.'

'Hidden away all this time, but how could the man who penned this document have known that the outline of the temple would still show through the earth today? Was that not a great risk to take with such a treasure?'

Volk cleared his throat. 'If I may make so bold, there are many possibilities. None of them demand that the scribe knew the fate of the temple, after all the image might simply be a key and does not have to be a literal outline for outline match. What we have here is the building schematic of a Sigmarite temple. It could be any temple. It is the written clues that direct us to this corner of the Empire. If the temple still stood it would be equally obvious to the beholder where the treasure might be found. That said, perhaps the document was inked after the temple's destruction, or then again perhaps the writer witnessed its fall or brought it about. This place has a history of war and pain. He may even have been the one who hid the treasure within, or merely heard a rumour and this is all some wild goose chase. Whatever, this is undoubtedly the place.'

'Absolutely,' Radu said, his face lit up with greed. There was an ugliness in Radu that went beyond the flesh. All the words he said were lies and half truths, all he touched, as tainted as defiled dirt. He was weak, sickeningly so, with the madness of greed, a canker that grew where his mortal soul had once been.

He was nothing now but a maker of illusions, the great deceiver.

A cheat, a coward, a liar, a fraud, he was all of these things.

Amsel looked at the avaricious glee in the vampire's eyes as he rubbed his hands together contemplating the great treasure his cunning was about to earn, and revelled in the repugnance of it all. Layers within layers, he told himself patiently. Korbhen had recognised all of these failings in his thrall, Radu knew. The true master had seen through all of the deceptions. Hence the game of power now, riddles within riddles, leading towards a single goal. He felt instinctively that he knew what it was, what it had to be and his dead heart raced imagining Korbhen's return. How could it be anything else? The true master was returning to vanquish the vainglorious upstart that had usurped his power with sour deceits.

All of Radu's supposed great magics were founded upon the genius of those around him, stolen through guile and cunning.

That greed would be his undoing.

Eager to hasten the end, Amsel bustled the vampire towards the edge. 'It is down there, waiting for you.'

'But what is it?' The necrarch asked, his voice grating.

Amsel moved in close beside him, so close that his decayed lips grazed the air beside the necrarch's ear. 'I believe,' he said, his tongue wrapping itself salaciously around the words, 'a casket lies within the bone yard of the old temple, and within the casket a relic of the Great Necromancer.'

'Nagash,' Radu crooned, stepping forward instinctively, closer still to the edge. The rock crumbled beneath his feet, sending a thin shale falling out into the nothing above the treetops. Down below, the wind whipped up, tearing the last of the low mists to shreds. The night shone bright on the town of Grimminhagen, the moon's radiance lingering on the sacred ground where once a temple had stood.

A step behind him, Amsel nodded.

'Then it is best we recover this treasure before sunrise, before the living awake to find their world awash with walking bones.'

'Master,' Amsel agreed.

CHAPTER ELEVEN

Dawn's Dead
On The Outskirts of Grimminhagen, in the Shadow of the
Drakwald Forest, Middenland
The Autumn of the Living Dead, 2532

THE DEAD CAME down to Grimminhagen looking for
more than souls to steal.

They crept and slithered and shuffled and stumbled
and swayed, bones creaking arthritically as they went.
The living met them head-on with steel, rank after
rank of breastplates and brandished swords in the
moonlight. The dark of the battle was eerie in its
quiet. The living did not scream or cheer. They fought
grimly and died frightened. All around them, the dead
clambered over the walls, bringing a reign of torture
and cruelty the like of which the living could not hope
to withstand. The moon reflected off the bone transforming the field into a corpse riddled with rot, the
bone the pus within the wounds. There could be no
blissful ignorance. Even as the living swarmed towards
the tide of slaughter, their lines holding formation as

183

ten by ten they threw themselves into the fray, still more of the skeletons tore at the dirt of the old temple, eager to unearth its foundations, but they could not get far with their excavations. The fighting held little interest for the necrarch. After all, any creature could fight and he cared little if they lined up in neat formations or scattered wildly in a frantic melee. The dead would triumph, that was all that concerned him. The treasure would be his.

Radu walked towards the wound in the earth.

He was thrown from his feet to the crack of magical energy. It was sharp and brutal, charged with elemental power. The air around them reeked with the aftertaste of lightning. Radu levered himself to his feet and dusted his brown suit off. All around him the skeletons moved to the machinations of the acolytes and his thralls, matching the swords and knives of the defenders with bone that shattered and not once did they scream or cry out because it didn't matter. Every broken bone was ignored or turned into a weapon to hurt the living.

Radu looked down at his suit. More of the material had singed through to the bare bone. He studied the exposed stone with distaste, angry with himself for being taken so easily off-guard. The faintest traces of a rune were etched into the rock. It had worn away to almost nothing, yet the power within it was undeniable. He reached out again tentatively, only to trigger a second shock that hurled him off his feet no less vehemently than the first had.

'Bring me innocent blood,' he rasped, reasoning that he needed someone pure, and how he detested that word, to cross the threshold. 'I will not be denied by petty hedge magic.'

'Master,' the damned thrall said, scraping his heel in the dirt.

'Go, now.'

He watched Amsel limp off through the fighting in the direction of the nearest house and then turned his scrutiny to the black marks in the earth. How many more runes were there? One? ten? Were they all wards or worse? He did not need to ask who had placed them. Korbhen had led him here and no doubt thought him slow enough of wit to be undone by a few scratches in the dirt. How wrong his arrogant sire was. He crouched, studying the marking, and recognising within it the one flaw he had already suspected would be present. It was poised to be triggered by the taint of unlife and any living breathing thing could wander happily across its barrier.

'How simple a trap,' he said to the acolyte, Volk, who stood at his shoulder. 'There is no artifice to it at all.'

'Did I not see you sprawling in the dirt a moment ago?'

Radu wheeled on him, raising a long finger threateningly. 'Do not overstep your mark lest you want your tongue turned to rot and your flesh to dissolve from within. I am in no mood to be mocked by anyone.'

'I was wrong,' Volk said artfully. 'It must have been your thrall making a fool of himself. One rotten face looks much like another in the half-light. My apologies.'

Great horns blared a fanfare, sending a warning out to the barracks, the manor house and the keep itself. The fighting turned savage.

Radu did not care. He would have the treasure delivered into his hands by some witless child and would delight in outwitting his sire with such a simple ploy. That was all that mattered.

His minions orchestrated another wave of violence. Watching the attack was tantamount to spying on an elaborate ballet of death. The bones jerked and twisted mimicking the savage movements of Amsel and Volk and the other acolytes, anticipating the cut and thrust of the mortal's weapons. The flames of brands slashed at the air, snapping and sizzling as they charred rot-riddled flesh. Volk, he saw, revelled in the slaughter. That was his madness and that was how the pair differed. Killing was not true strength. Any fool could kill. It was the mastery over death that brought power with it, the banishment of time and its treacherous tinkering. In that way Radu was different.

Radu placed a gnarled hand over his unbeating heart. Life in the silence where the frailest organ of mortality had once drummed out its rhythm of existence, that was strength, power, might and all of the other synonyms for potency he could conjure.

It was a strange sort of homecoming, not that Grimminhagen had ever seen Radu's home, not this Grimminhagen, at least. He had lived ten lifetimes since he had last set foot on this defiled dirt. There had been a temple then, and houses of adobe and wattle and wood, and cattle grazing in the field. The memory came back to him with the vivid clarity of grief, of fields of fire. He turned in a circle, and around again, the sounds of fighting and fire bringing to life the recollection. They had brought his woman, Esther, out and pinned her down with iron nails, driving them into the earth and even as her lifeblood leaked out into the black dirt, they had lit the grain crop effectively murdering every last man, woman and child of the township. He remembered Korbhen's gaunt face, his leer as he licked his damned lips and laved his tongue across Esther's throat and the grin he shared with the man he had yet to break.

Had he planted this 'treasure' back then, even as his parasites had burned his home?

Was his sire capable of such premeditation?

Listening to the screams of his ghosts he knew that the answer to both questions was yes.

The regret Radu felt was fleeting. Indeed it could barely be called regret. It was a half-remembered spectre, nothing more. His link to the man he had been had withered away to naught centuries before. Even now, turning back to face the tear in the earth where his minions had cut into the heart of the old temple, he saw it all in a curiously detached manner. It was as though he remembered the thoughts of a stranger, those thoughts a translucent veil draped over the here and now. It was this place, he knew. Once it had been the world now it was nothing more than its elements: wood, stone, and dirt. It meant nothing.

With that realisation the screams of the ghosts melted away leaving him with the screams of the living.

The peasants could not hope to stand against the naked ferocity of the dead. Their neat lines were ragged, their metal frail protection from his minions. Radu watched for a moment, enjoying the desperation of the enemy. It was only a matter of time before the hopelessness of the fight sank in and the sensible broke rank and fled while some few valiantly stood their ground. The dead drove them back, turning their homes into traps, pressing them up against the walls so that they could not fight back. Crushed up against their homes, they died like the cattle they were, slaughtered, gutted and heartbroken. Some few found it in themselves to fight back. Their heroics could only delay the inevitable. Even as the horns of the rallied militia and the destriers of the roused knights joined the fray it was never going to be enough for them.

He saw an old man in the centre of the violence, anger driving his blade as he cut and parried, his face bathed in sweat and grim determination. For all his age he was more than a simple old man. He radiated strength and power, his skill with the blade unmatched by any that faced him. The living flocked around him, answering his cries as he dictated the defence, ordering the militia to flank around on the right, and the knights to close the pincer on the left. For all that strength Radu could smell the old man's lifeblood straining through his veins, forcing his heart close to rupturing. Yet there was an awesome vitality to the town's defender that belied his years. So much purity sang in his blood it was sickening.

'You will die, old man,' Radu whispered.

In the thick of the fighting the grizzled warrior looked up, as though hearing the vampire's promise. Their eyes met and for a moment the world was reduced to the two of them and then the fighting closed around the old man, the sheer weight of the dead bearing him down. The knights came to the old man's aid, hacking a path through the bone-puppets to get to his side. There was an air of inevitability to the scene.

Radu turned his back on the slaughter, taking no great pleasure in the killings. He wanted one thing out of this night and one thing only: the treasure his sire had hidden, be it a gift or a curse. Amsel had been right in one thing, it was his birthright and he knew instinctively where they would find it buried. There was only one place it could be: the same patch of graveyard dirt where Korbhen had taken Esther. There was a poetic symmetry to it that his sire would not have been able to ignore. The prize was personal. It always had been.

He turned his head, seeing Amsel drag a young girl out of the fighting by the hair. She wept hysterically and struggled against the thrall's grip, but Amsel was merciless. Her knees buckled as he dragged her over the churned dirt and broken stones. Blood dripped down her scalp where her struggles tore her hair free. Amsel slapped her and hauled her back to her feet.

'She retains her innocence,' the thrall declared, as he pushed the child at Radu.

'Good.' Korbhen's treasure would soon be his.

The girl's face was streaked with tears. Sobs hitched in her throat.

'I do not intend to kill you, child,' the necrarch said, his mellifluous voice anything but reassuring. He knelt, ignoring the slaughter, and grasped the girl by the shoulders, his long fingers hooking into her flesh. She cried out as his withered nails drew yet more blood from her but did not dare struggle against his hold. 'You are going to do me a service, and then I shall send you back to your mother,' he lied smoothly. He had no intention of passing up her innocence. He would take the treasure from her hands and then he would draw out the second more intimate treasure from her meat. There was nothing like the taste and texture of innocent blood. She stared back at him blankly, uncomprehending.

'Go down into the dirt. There is a casket hidden within that is mine by right. Bring it back to me and you shall live a while longer. You want to live, don't you?' He lost himself in a ghost, remembering a time when he had stood on the same dead earth. 'There was not always a temple here,' he said more to himself than the girl. He pointed towards a patch of grass much like any other patch of grass. 'You will find it there. No doubt there will be markings in the stone around it, much like the one you will see as you cross the threshold to begin your descent. Let the markings guide you to the box. Bring it back to me and you will be rewarded with your life. Do you understand?'

The girl nodded, tears and spittle staining her otherwise pretty face.

She understood more than just the words. She understood the subtle knife beneath them, the glorious reward he promised.

She knew she was dead even before she took her first step into the belly of the earth.

What she didn't know, what none of them could know, was that her first step was the culmination of hundreds of years of cunning that would ultimately bring about more than just her downfall.

CHAPTER TWELVE

Phantoms
Grimminhagen, in the shadow of the Drakwald Forest,
Middenland
The Autumn of the Living Dead, 2532

BONIFAZ, CORT, AND Bohme fought like daemons possessed to reach his side.

Reinhardt Metzger felt his heart breaking. It was not some metaphorical agony. It was a very real, very physical pain that lanced through his left arm and into his chest. Metzger winced, forcing his shield arm out to take a hammer-blow from a rotten corpse. The impact resonated through his blood and bone, fresh agony firing his heart. He turned on his heel, delivering a crushing blow that cut through the lower jaw of his enemy, sheering the bone in two and leaving his mouth flapping open stupidly. Spots of fire blazed across his eyes as the horizon swam. Metzger felt the fist clench around his heart, crushing it in its merciless grip. He took another hammer blow on his shield, from what looked like a razor-toothed bone blade.

The impact cleaved into his shield, opening a deep tear in it. The sounds of death and dying took on a surreal distant quality in his ears. He twisted, thrusting the point of his blade deep into the rotten corpse of the creature that had risen up before him. The sudden and shocking flare of pain rippled out across every inch of his skin like sunburn. His knees buckled.

The sounds of battle muted down to the drum of blood in his ears and he knew he had failed everyone. It was that, more than the understanding that his courage was bigger than his old heart could hold, that undid him.

He let out a roar of anguish and swung the sword in a vicious low sweep, but he didn't finish the move. The blade slipped through his fingers and fell to the dirt by his side.

Through the pain of his heart's betrayal he saw the hideous face of the vampire mocking his failure. Metzger held the beast's gaze until a second savage twist of pain attacked his heart and the world went black. He pitched forward onto his face and the dead fell upon him.

Cort reached his side first, the Silberklinge's twin short blades cutting a swathe of destruction through the ranks of the dead. He moved with the grace of a natural born killer, his swords weaving a pattern of murder between them that was almost beautiful to behold. He turned the blades into a reaping hook, disembowelling and beheading all that fell across his path. Bonifaz and Bohme came in his wake, adding their steel to the danse macabre. It did not matter that the fight was impossible, that Reinhardt Metzger's heart was one foe they could not vanquish with skill, steel or sheer bloody will. Neither one of them was about to abandon their friend to the teeth and claws of the vampiric horde, even if it meant laying down their lives to save the dying man for a few minutes longer.

There was an eerie silence to their foes who surged forward in wave after endless wave without a single groan or sigh even as they were cut down. The only sounds of battle were the clash of steel and the cries of Grimminhagen's fallen. It sent a cold shiver deep into the core of each of them, but it was the very unnaturalness of the battle that spurred them on to reach their fallen comrade. They did not care about winning the fight or saving the town, that was beyond them. They had a single purpose, to protect Metzger.

He was unconscious when they reached him, but alive, barely.

The three swordsmen formed a circle around their leader, talking incessantly as they blocked, parried and thrust desperately. It took every ounce of their skill and more still of their indomitable will to drive back the silent ranks of the dead.

The fog of battle broke, leaving him with room for respite. Through the blood and spittle, Bohme saw the miller's girl emerge from the ground clutching a wooden casket to her breast. He began to run towards her, seeing the creatures all around her. A withered vampire took the box from her with grasping hands, and then laid it aside and caught her by the shoulders. In the space between footsteps the creature sank its feral teeth into her skin. She offered no resistance, simply going limp in those vile arms. Before Bohme could get close, he saw the boy, Fehr, fighting to reach her with a stubborn determination that outmatched his little skill, but it was that fierce will that would see him live even though there was no hope for the girl.

A corpse lurched for Bohme's face. He cleaved it open, taking its jaw from its ruined face and leaving its rot-addled tongue hanging. He finished the wretched creature, dragging his sword out of its bowels. As the corpse fell Bohme saw Fehr run, screaming, at a man with no face. Bohme knew him: the vampiric acolyte that had summoned the bones from the earth to fight him. Hatred boiled up within the warrior. He pushed aside another shambling corpse and ran flat out to reach Fehr's side. Before he could reach him Fehr thundered his blade clean through the gash where the acolyte's nose ought to have been. Again and again Wolfgang Fehr drove his blade into the ragged wound, until the body ceased its twitching.

As he died, all across the field hundreds of bone creatures fell, the will binding them together undone.

Bohme cracked his fist into the face of a blood-smeared woman, blood exploding from her nose. He cast her aside, thrusting the long blade in his right hand into the gut of the man at her side. These two, he realised, bled, and worse, screamed.

Bohme dispatched another stricken foe, buying himself a yard of breathing space. He brandished his blade, keeping the deformed at bay. At his side Bonifaz was bleeding badly from several cuts; most were superficial but the worst ensured that he would never be thought of as handsome again.

He saw Metzger fall, and reversed the direction of his charge.

A dozen yards away Fehr looked around stupidly, realising that he had abandoned the safety of the line. He cut down three rag-clothed creatures. A fourth threw itself at the young man only to pull up short, Fehr's blade emerging bloody silver from its back. As the damned creature fell from his sword Fehr saw the three Silberklinge and ran towards them.

'Make me a path. I'm going to get him away from here,' Bohme barked. Bonifaz moved with renewed ferocity, his blades tearing a hole through the press of the dead. There was an economy to his swordplay, his blades never cutting an inch more than necessary to deliver the hurt. The man was a daemon possessed.

Without a word, Kaspar Bohme knelt to cradle his friend's body and lifted him.

With Fehr and Cort protecting him on either side, and Bonifaz cutting a path back to the safety of the buildings, Bohme carried Metzger out of the worst of the fighting.

'Don't die on me, old man,' he whispered like a prayer.

CHAPTER THIRTEEN

The Hour of the Man
Grimminhagen, in the shadow of the Drakwald Forest,
Middenland
The Autumn of the Living Dead, 2532

RADU THE FORSAKEN's long fingers trembled as they caressed the wooden case.

He crouched beside the wound in the earth that led down to the hidden temple, the dead girl cast off to the side. Amsel lurked at his shoulder. The pair were removed from the slaughter, but not by much.

The box was a simple thing, devoid of ostentatious decoration. Bronze hinges clasped the casket and where the keyhole ought to have been a small face had been rendered in the wood. He let his fingers linger over the elaborately carved features, feeling out the hatred in its expression. The craftsman's mastery was evident in every embellishment. He felt the coils of gorgonian locks that cascaded from the face, probing for the trigger that would release the mechanism and spring open the lock.

'We must away from this place,' Amsel said, staring down covetously at the wooden casket.

'Yes, yes, yes,' the necrarch agreed without looking away from the engraved face.

'We have what we came for,' Amsel pressed.

'Yes,' Radu crooned, though not in answer to his thrall's urging. The thrill of sheer raw power was palpable. Whatever the casket contained hungered to be free. He felt its siren call sing through the tainted blood in his veins.

He traced the line of the nose, and then, understanding, placed his thumbs on either side and put out the carving's eyes.

The spring-loaded mechanism responded with a soft click as the clasp released and the lid opened.

Radu opened the box.

'Oh, yes, yes, yes.'

Within, set in a bed of red velvet, sat the withered stump of a hand. The flesh had shrivelled tightly around the bone but rot had not touched the hand. He reached into the casket to hold it and felt its coolness. The fingers twitched in response to his touch. The hand was still alive. All thoughts of treachery slipped from his mind as he clasped the hand, hungry for all that the relic might give him.

The necrarch whispered reverently, daring to speak the name of the dread lord. Could it truly be a treasure of the Great Necromancer? He laughed maniacally as he thrilled to the desiccated touch of the hand. Such a treasure could not literally be the flesh of the necromancer, but it was almost certainly an artefact imbued with his might.

'We must go,' the voice said, like a bee buzzing irritably around within his head, refusing to leave him alone.

THE DEAD FLED the field, leaving the living to cope with their losses.

Of the three hundred and sixty butchers, bakers and farmhands over three hundred had fallen. Beside them lay more than half of the militia, another three score nursing life-threatening wounds, fifty more carrying light wounds. Metzger had lost twenty of the Silberklinge and another thirty were sorely wounded. The town had faired little better. All the streets around the outskirts, from Metzger's fortified manse in to the well at Grimminhagen's centre, resembled rock dust and rubble. The bracing walls had come down spilling terracotta roofing slates all over the ground like the blood of the buildings.

Bonifaz and Cort joined the militia men in gathering corpses while Wolfgang Fehr joined the rest scavenging for the huge funeral pyre. The necessity sickened Bohme; the dead deserved the rest of the funeral gardens or Morr but given the nature of their enemy burning was the only sure way to prevent the fallen villagers from rising. Fehr had fought well. Indeed, of all of them he had without doubt claimed the prize kill. It had not gone unnoticed among the men that the corpses fell as the link between them and their vile master was severed, nor that it was Fehr's blade that severed that link. That they rose again as some fresh master claimed their servitude did not matter; it demonstrated that the links between the creatures and their puppets could be broken. That was enough.

Every able-bodied man moved with purpose, aiding in the disposal of the dead, dragging corpses to the huge flames and casting them into the fire. There was no time for grief. The aged priest of Morr stood beside the pyre offering nameless blessings as the dead flesh spat and hissed in the flames.

The eight sisters from the Shallyan temple moved with purpose, summoned by the men as they found more and more terribly wounded survivors out on the killing grounds. There was a reassuring grace about the women as they tended the wounded and the dying. How many lives they saved in that first hour it was impossible to say, but their presence was enough to cast a calm across the field, their touch taking away more pains than any small town ought to bear.

Removed slightly from the suffering, in what had until hours before been the town square, Bohme sat with Metzger. Now the tavern and the smithy were reduced to smouldering timbers and gutted wattle. He sat with his back against the well, and did not leave the old knight's side. On the surface Metzger's wounds looked fearsome, but none were more than superficial. There was plenty of blood, but when it was washed away the cuts did not go deep. Metzger had suffered much worse in his day without so much as a complaint. On another day he would have sat against a tree and stitched the worst of the cuts himself.

He looked grey, his skin waxen.

Bohme touched his fingers to the thick vein in his friend's neck, feeling out the weak, erratic pulse.

'Your heart always was too big, old man,' he muttered, shaking his head. Seeing the truth like this frightened Kaspar Bohme more than all of the assembled dead had. Age was the one foe that neither skill nor stubbornness could match, and whether they admitted it or not, they were all succumbing to its silent assault.

He did what he could to make Metzger comfortable.

He sat beside his friend deep into the night. The funeral fire blazed high, the huge light marking the human cost of the raid. The survivors were subdued, dealing with their losses alone. No one was left untouched. The worst of it was that most of the corpses on the pyres belonged to the very young, the women, or the elderly: people who on any other day would never have been called upon to fight. They had died protecting their homes. Their sacrifice would not be forgotten, not by those left behind. In time the tragedy would serve to unite them, but this close to it they had no wish to share their grief while it was still so personal.

None of them wanted to hunt down the enemy.

The fight had passed beyond their walls. It was someone else's now. The selfishness of it counted for nothing.

The woman, Sara, walked amid the survivors, moving in the light of the pyre. She held the babe Lammert close to her chest as she sang an elegiac farewell to the fallen. Her voice was beautiful and heartbreaking. Her lament touched the souls of those left behind, lifting them up. Tears streaked her cheeks, reflecting silver in the firelight. Though she hardly knew these people, her grief was pure. It was the grief for her own, the friends and lovers that had joined Morr today and on every other day that the dead had marched across the land.

Bohme closed his eyes, losing himself to her voice.

When he opened them again he saw another woman he knew well, Rosamund, Metzger's house-keeper. Like Sara her face was streaked with tears, though they were of a more intimate grief than the girl's. She knelt close to the huge pyre, Fitch's unmoving body in her arms. Her man had been one of the first to fall, running recklessly in to the thick of it with a rusted sword that had never been swung in all its years of corrosion. It broke his heart to see a good woman like Rosamund suffering so, but they were all suffering. To highlight the grief of one was to diminish the grief of many.

Beside him, Metzger groaned. He was awake but weak as a lamb as he struggled stubbornly to sit. His face twisted in pain and Bohme had to catch him before he fell once more. Metzger tried weakly to shrug off his helping hand. 'Rest a while longer, Rein-hardt. There is nothing to be gained by killing yourself now.'

'No,' Metzger said, his voice was weaker than he had ever heard it. 'I need to know. I need… to see.'

'You can see later, my friend, and what is to know? We are alive, that has to be enough,' Bohme said, not unkindly.

'Just help me up, Kaspar. I need to be seen.' His words broke away as another jag of pain speared into his chest.

'You always were a stubborn old fool,' Bohme muttered, shaking his head.

'These are my people. They look to me.'

'And what good will it do them to see you like this? By rights you ought to be dead. You need your bed.'

'Then I still need to rise,' Metzger grunted, levering himself up onto his elbow in the dirt. 'So you might as well help me up now rather than later.'

Together they walked slowly through the ruin of their town, Metzger leaning on Bohme for support. It was a difficult journey, and not merely because of the physical pain. The enormous pyre burned against the bruise-purple sky. Loved ones knelt before the fire, heads bowed in farewell as the sweet stench of burning flesh filled the air. He imagined he could see their ghosts in the flame, watching over those left behind and sharing their grief at the sudden parting.

Metzger made a point of standing beside each mourner, sharing a prayer and sad words with each and every one of the surviving townsfolk. Bohme could see the grief reflected in their eyes but knew in the days to come that they would draw some small comfort from the fact that he had come to them. He laid a reassuring hand on the cooper Dierdrich's shoulder, making a whispered promise to the old man to avenge his three fallen sons, and hugged the woman he recognised as the tanner's wife, promising that he would not rest until her husband's and daughter's killer gave restitution. It was the same with others whose names he did not know but whose faces he recognised: the same moment of intimacy accompanied by the same solemn pledge. They loved him for it. They always had. He was not some distant fighter or stoic protector. He was a man, like them, not some colossus, not some mythic hero. He was one of them, he lived among them, he called them friends and never hid from the demands of their lives. That was the kind of man he was, a man who grieved alongside them for all that the town had lost.

But Bohme knew he was in no state to make good on those promises.

Worse, he would probably kill himself trying.

The woman, Sara, saw them standing beside the fire as Fitch's corpse was fed to the flames, and came to join them. She was no longer singing. Her shawl wrapped tight around her throat she looked as though she had lived a thousand lives in one night. She laid a hand on Rosamund's shoulder. The older woman looked up, red-eyed. She had no smile of greeting. There was no need for words between any of them. The women stood awhile in silence, sharing the company of grief. Reluctant to intrude, Bohme lost himself in the dance of the flames. The orange tongues of fire took on an almost hypnotic quality as they cavorted to the chill wind. In the hush that accompanied the aftermath of battle, voices carried; they said the same things with different words. That, too, was the nature of grief, it owned a vocabulary of its own. The wind was a welcome reminder of mortality. It cut through the steel rings of his armour more effectively than any sword, driving its ice into his aching muscles even as the death fires warmed his face. That duality of fire and ice was in itself the paradox of survival, that the body was capable of both, simultaneously, and both to the point of extremis.

There was something else that kept the distance around Kaspar Bohme: the difference between him and Reinhardt Metzger. Where Metzger was adored by his people Bohme and the other Silberklinge were respected. There was no intimacy in respect. They did not share his grief, or more accurately he did not share theirs. He was in the town but he had never been of it. In that he was alone.

'What did they want here?' Rosamund finally asked the question that Bohme had asked himself a hundred times in the last hour, and even though he had seen the miller's girl delivering the wooden box from the bowels of the earth, he had no understanding of the answer.

Metzger shook his head. 'Truthfully, I do not know.'

'I do,' the boy, Fehr, said. Bohme had not heard him approach. He looked at Fehr, seeing the man he could become if this war did not kill him first. There was a strength to the boy that would serve him well in the days to come. He showed no outward signs of grief despite the fact that the pyres burned every last member of his family. Of all the survivors he had almost certainly suffered most.

'Tell us, lad,' Metzger said.

'The box,' Wolfgang Fehr said, as though it made all the sense in the world.

'And what box might that be?'

'Jessika brought it up out of the ground. The creature killed her for it.'

The lad was right; it had all been about the contents of that box. The realisation set a chill in Bohme's heart. 'Name it for what it was, Fehr. There is power in a name, but there is also power in knowing it. Name the creature. Calling it anything else gives it a hold over you,' Kaspar Bohme said. 'Claim the creature.'

Fehr looked at him, stared. The young man's dark eyes seemed to shift from hues of brown to silver-grey and back under the Silberklinge's scrutiny. It was a subtle shift, a trick of the firelight.

'The vampire killed her for it,' Fehr said, naming the necrarch for the bloodsucking daemon it was. Bohme nodded. 'I couldn't reach her in time,' the young man said, his voice breaking as he relived the memory of it. Bohme had seen it all, but hadn't seen it true. Sometimes his misunderstanding of human nature frightened him. She might have been the miller's girl but she was also Fehr's sweetheart, that much was obvious now.

'If it wasn't for you, lad, none of us would be here now,' Bohme said, knowing that the truth was no consolation.

'Show me where it happened,' Metzger said, holding out a hand for Wolfgang Fehr to lead the way to the tear in the belly of the earth.

They walked through the rutted ground, picking a path through discarded swords and fallen shields, kicking aside rotted bones as they splashed unseeing through puddles of blood. They crossed the killing ground in silence, humbled by the proximity of the fallen, towards the blacker rent in the earth.

The dead had left the ground blackened, the grasses withered beneath their feet. Bohme knew the place for what it must once have been. The scorched outline of the ancient temple's foundations stood out starkly against the ruined grass. The blight affected stalk and stem of grass right up to the ruin's perimeter and beyond that mark the protection of the hallowed ground could not have been more obvious: the grass remained lush, green and unsullied by the dead. It was as though nature had rebuilt the ancient foundation. None of them doubted for a moment the miracle of what they saw.

Fehr crouched down a little way to the side of the hole, resting his palm flat to the ground. Bohme recognised the spot as where the girl had fallen. The young man lifted his fingers to his nose and sniffed them as though trying to breathe her last moments of life into him. When he looked up, tears streaked his dirt and bloodstained cheeks. He did not need to say what had happened. They understood.

'No!' BOHME ARGUED vehemently. 'Enough of this foolishness, old man. You are not well enough.'

'You expect me to lie abed like some cripple?' Reinhardt Metzger roared back, anger giving him strength, but even as it fired his blood it betrayed him, sending a sunburst of pain across the back of his eyes. He winced, knowing his temper had proved his friend's point. He was far from fit enough to lead a crusade against the monsters that had ravaged his home, despite all of the midnight promises he had made to the bereaved.

The po-faced Sister of Shallya left the room. The men had been arguing as though the healer were not even there. She had tended Metzger in his private chamber for three days, feeding him with tisanes and changing the poultices on his wounds.

The curtains stirred as the draught found its way through the cracks in the window frame.

'That is exactly what I expect you to do. Use your head. We cannot do this alone. We are not invincible anymore, my friend. Age has slowed our blades and weakened our hearts.'

'Then what do you suggest?' Metzger asked reaching across his chest to massage his side with his right hand. It was an unconscious tell that betrayed the continued pain his heart gave him.

'We send out runners and call in every favour we believe we are owed and beg more from those we call friends and neighbours. We petition for the state troops to join us, we continue to train the lads we have hear, bolster the militia, hell, we finance the recruitment of knights and mercenary soldiers from our own pockets where necessary, but we gather ourselves an army. Talk to Sternhauer, have the Graf dip into his bottomless well of gold and bring us the money we need if we are to protect his people. This is a fight for younger blood, my friend, and older heads. It is time we admitted too that neither one of us is the hot-headed youth we once were.'

'I hear you,' Metzger said, the fight leaving him. Bohme was right, just as he always was.

CHAPTER FOURTEEN

The Last of the Great Liars
Grimminhagen, in the shadow of the Drakwald Forest,
Middenland
The Autumn of the Living Dead, 2532

DAYS ABED TURNED into weeks, as Metzger gathered his strength.

The po-faced sister returned with her vile tasting tisanes and took away the soured poultices. There was nothing sweet in her demeanour but she most certainly had a healing touch.

There were mornings when Metzger awoke sure that he had died in the night and woken in the underworld, a prisoner of Morr, but then the pain bit and he knew that he was still alive. It was funny how the same thing that threatened to kill him became the thing that told him he was alive. It was an exquisite irony.

The men mustered. He sat in a wicker chair, watching from the window as Bonifaz and Cort put them through their drills, driving them hard. No one complained, the deaths of their friends and neighbours still fresh in their minds. The sound of swords rang out from dusk til dawn for a month and the rhythm of the drills changed, hinting at the growing proficiency of the men down on the parade grounds. Bonifaz visited night after night, the sweat still clinging to him as he sank into the chair opposite to report the day's news. 'We'll make fighters of them yet,' was the most common conversation starter between them, followed almost always by, 'Six men arrived from Merz,' or 'Five more came in from Genz,' or some such.

They were building a small army one soldier at a time.

It wasn't enough, the old knight knew. He had seen the things the enemy could do, raising swords from the grave and turning the casualties back on their friends before their blood had stopped gouting from their wounds. It was a perversion but it was only one of many that the enemy was capable of. Bohme was right: the enemy could not hide. The earth revolted at their vile presence, all of its vitality touched by the blight of unlife as the dead walked. In their wake they left a path of disease and decay.

More than anything, he felt helpless. It galled him to have to beg for aid, his own sword arm not strong enough to do what was necessary. He missed watching the goshawk fly. He missed the sweat of honest toil training side by side with his men. He missed being able to trust his own flesh.

'Enough with the self pity, old man,' Metzger berated himself. He knew he had reached a fork in the road. Stay in the chair and slip into dotage as a feeble old man, or push himself to his feet, get dressed and get back to whatever little life his heart permitted. Better to die defending what he loved than live like a dotard swaddled in blankets and drinking pulped vegetables with a wooden spoon listening to some well-meaning Shallyan nursemaid cluck and croon about what a good boy he was. That wasn't the death he had imagined for himself, certainly not the one he had fought for time and again. He had earned the right to something better.

With that fixed firmly in his mind, Metzger pushed himself out of the chair.

'There is only so much coddling a grown man can take,' he told Sara as he saw her on the stairs. The woman smiled and hugged him. The warmth in her eyes shamed him. He had done nothing to deserve it. He almost told her as much but stopped himself, realising it was self-pity and anger that fuelled the thought, not the truth. He walked slowly, favouring his left side still, out onto the parade ground. For a minute or more the drill continued, the men forcing themselves through the motions. Again he was struck by the notion that watching them was like watching an elaborate dance. There was most certainly grace to the movements and rhythm to the footwork. He smiled as Cort rapped one of the young men on the knuckles with the flat of his blade; it stung his fingers open and sent the sword tumbling. Cort shook his head as though despairing. It was all an act, Metzger knew. The man was incredibly proud of the leaps and bounds his recruits had made. In a few months they had gone from farm boys and stable hands to soldiers, and watching them now, Metzger knew that was exactly what they were.

They have just enough skill to get themselves killed following an old man to his doom, he thought bitterly.

Then they saw him and one by one the swords ceased swinging. Fehr started it, sheathing his blade and clapping slowly, and it was taken up by the others until every man on the field was applauding him. Someone else cheered, and suddenly more cheering rang out.

'Come to join us?' Bonifaz said.

'Not today, my friend. I'm just stretching my legs,' he said. Then with a wink he added, 'We've got a long ride ahead of us if we are going to hunt down the whoresons responsible for all this senseless death.' He swept his arm out around him, encompassing the silence that had until recently been a bustling town. That was in its own way the worst of it, the lingering emptiness where a town once stood. There was no laughter or cheering now, as the reminder sank in.

'We're ready,' one of the men, Sirus, pledged. Until two months ago he had been apprenticed to the tallow maker, now he was ready to die with a sword in his hand to fulfil the demands of honour.

Metzger nodded. 'I know you are lad, I have been watching you from my window. You do not think I would leave the comfort of that damned chair if I didn't know that all of you were ready? Of course I know lad, that's why I came down, to show you that I was ready to join you. There will be blood, my friends, and there will be a reckoning.'

'Aye,' Sirus said, nodding thoughtfully. 'I count on sending ten to the flaming pit for each one they robbed me of.'

'They robbed me of an entire town,' Metzger said, meaning it. 'I'll match you on that ten, lad, and throw in a few more for the hell of it.'

As THE NIGHT wore on the conversation turned to the practicalities of what amounted to a crusade. Metzger summoned Bettan Moyle, wanting his wisdom. He joined them in Metzger's ill-lit study. While Cort and Bonifaz and to an extent Bohme were all veterans there were aspects of fighting that remained almost magical to them. Not so for Moyle. The man had served as Metzger's quartermaster for the best part of a decade and knew the logistics of combat inside out.

'It is more than merely an understanding of maps,' Moyle said, marking out an area of ground with the sweep of his finger. 'On any given day this area here could be relied upon for foraging, but given what we know of our enemy we cannot rely on the land to support us. Instead we need to look after our own.'

There was a frightening truth to that simple statement. Metzger recalled the blackened soil and withered grasses. With the enemy's passage blighting the land the ramifications would bleed over into so many other areas they took for granted. There would be no feed for the mountain goats or sheep and no grain crop. They could not simply forage for survival as they moved deeper and deeper into enemy territory. They needed to read the world and make appropriate countermeasures to ensure survival, otherwise they were as good as beaten before they even saddled up.

Moyle had a way of looking at lines on paper and reading into them things that no one else seemed able to see. They had several maps laid out between them, and Bonifaz had marked off the routes between the watchtowers that had failed to report, plotting in reverse the advance of the dead. It was nothing more than supposition, Metzger knew, but they had to come from somewhere. They did not simply crawl out of the ground in the middle of nowhere; there had to be a zero point, an origin. He feared he knew all to well where that point was.

'It's folly,' Moyle said, not for the first time that night. 'Is this what you intend for your legacy, Reinhardt? You want people to remember your army that starved to death?'

'I made a promise to them,' Metzger said, his voice barely carrying across the maps. 'I intend to keep it or die trying.'

What was he supposed to say? That it was a campaign of punishment? Revenge against the vampire for destroying the lives of the people under his protection? That he felt the unbearable weight of failure on his shoulders and needed to make amends? Or should he say that he feared the beast would return? They would believe the second, but there was no truth in it. He wanted to make the beast pay. He wanted to recover his faith in his own body. He wanted to drive the beast back to its lair, and something more, something he dreaded giving substance to by forming it as a thought: an ancient shame carried close to his heart.

Moyle shook his head. 'Be reasonable, man. The numbers don't add up. An army marches three leagues a day at best. It isn't like you or me going for a stroll. An army is only as fast as its slowest wagon unless you want to break the supply lines. You've marshalled almost seven hundred fresh fighters, knights, halberdiers, infantry spearmen, and rank and file militia, but you know what? It doesn't matter how skilled they are, they all eat the same amount of bread and meat at the end of the day. So that's more than a thousand hungry men, three hundred of them on horseback. Forgetting the animals, that's a thousand mouths to feed, every day for as long as it takes to march to their doom and back. You know, if you are intending to come back?'

'Don't be facetious, Bettan, it doesn't suit you.'

'Fine,' the quartermaster said, 'even marching for a week means providing forty-two thousand meals: three meals a day out, the same back. You can discount probably sixty per cent of the victuals needed for the return journey, putting them down to casualties. Like it or not, people die in war. So even if we are only looking at thirty thousand individual meals we are talking enough coin to drain your treasury dry, never mind the logistics of trying to transport that much food.'

'You paint a grim picture, my friend.'

'That's because it will be bloody grim, and make no mistake about it. We aren't talking sweet meats and delicacies either, we are just talking the staples, grain for bread and the like. If you don't keep their bellies full come the time to fight you'll have ranks of hungry, dizzy, tired men barely able to swing their swords.'

'So what do we do?'

'Stay at home,' the quartermaster said earnestly. 'You don't have the resources for this war, not if you expect to provision an army.'

'Yet without an army we cannot hope to prevail,' Metzger said. 'You saw them, Bettan.'

The quartermaster nodded. 'I'm not denying it, but is vengeance worth a winter of privation for those left behind? If we emptied the grain silos and culled the cattle to dry the meat we'd barely have enough to see the town through to the turn of the season. Forget the fact that we would be without milk and eggs and other stuff. Take that to mount your crusade and you are killing those left behind as mercilessly as the bastards who set this whole sorry mess in motion.'

'But if it could be done?' Metzger pressed, 'How would you do it?'

'There are so many practicalities to think about. Food aside for a moment, think about the horses: three hundred mounts. It's a safe assumption that each one will throw at least one shoe before journey's end, and a lame horse is no good to anyone, so you need three hundred shoes hammered out for starters. Then there is cooking pots and pans. Seven hundred mouths take a lot of feeding. How many blacksmith's are there in town?'

'You know very well there is only one forge, my friend.'

'And you know how long it takes Mac to hammer out a single shoe. Even with the fires burning day and night it will be a week before he has made even half the shoes, and that is not allowing him to sleep. With the cook pots it will be a month before he's done, and then you need someone to fit the horse shoes and patch the pots, sharpen the swords and hammer out the shields, so you have to find a way to take him and his fires with you. You know all of this, Metzger. It isn't as if you've never been to war. You know that even the best laid plans will go awry because of boggy ground or some other unforeseen nonsense.'

'Yet still I need to find a way to make this happen. There will be a reckoning for the dead of Grimminhagen, mark my words.'

WITH THE QUARTERMASTER gone, Kaspar Bohme took his friend aside.

He had watched Metzger for weeks. At first he had thought the old man was coming to terms with what had happened, but now he was not so sure. A different thought had wormed its way into the back of his mind and refused to be shifted.

'Look me in the eye and tell me you intend coming back,' he said, grabbing Metzger by the shoulders and forcing him to meet his gaze.

Without pausing, the old fighter said, 'I have every intention of coming home.'

'Now I know you are lying,' Bohme said.

CHAPTER FIFTEEN

Swords Against the Damned
On the March, Deep in the Heart of the Howling Hills,
Middenland
The Winter of the Faithless, 2532

THEY MARCHED INTO the teeth of the storm.

Aside from his loyal Silberklinge Metzger had recruited thirty knights from the Order of the Twin-Tailed Comet, who rode at the rear of his force while Metzger and his Silberklinge rode alongside the foot soldiers who marched eight and ten abreast where the road allowed.

The winds howled through the hills, their mournful cries making it painfully obvious to every one of the men how the rocky peaks had got their name. It was a harsh landscape made harsher by the brutality of the weather. Storm clouds gathered overhead. The infantry carried the banner of the Sternhauer family, the pennon matted with the dirt of the road. It had been a long time since they had sampled the creature comforts of home. These simple men were not fighting for money or honour, but were miles from home for the most basic of reasons: love. They were not knights who had sworn oaths to protect the weak, they were men who had lost something more precious than honour. They had lost one of the most basic human rights, that of the sanctity of hearth and home, the safety of their loved ones. So they had given a vow to Metzger; they would follow him to the end of this road he was on and they would fight, and they would slay the vampire and its horde and restore the illusion that all was well with the world and that their four walls were protection enough.

Metzger had not made it easy for them to make their pledge. He had assembled them on the parade grounds and spelled out the hardships they were volunteering for, making a point of facing each man eye to eye and holding them to the same need for reckoning that drove him. Months on, hungry, cold and with the threat of snow heavy in the sky not one of the men doubted their promise. They remembered the parade grounds and Reinhardt Metzger's words. It wasn't that he had inspired them, or even roused them to a righteous fury. He had simply reminded them. It had been enough then and it was enough now.

The difference between Metzger and Ableron, the Preceptor of the Twin-Tailed Comet, could not have been starker. Ableron was cold and disdainful of the infantry, preferring the company of his own men. He rode his charger, his armour immaculate, even his hair groomed and chin shaven while Metzger let his beard grow out and did not care that mud stained his cloak. Metzger understood the more basic needs of the raw untested troops under his command. They might have been fighting for a cause, they might have believed that Sigmar walked with them towards righteousness, but that didn't mean they did not need a connection with their leader, that they needed to know he was one of them, willing to get mud as well as blood on his hands, and that they were more than merely cannon-fodder in the game of knights.

They had ridden the paths of the dead, following them back through the ruins of ghost towns and the broken stones of homesteads and farms, every day encountering another reminder of the human cost of this war. Their path was laid out plainly for them: the dead had left their blight all across the land, withering crops down to rotten kernels of corn and husks of wheat, brown grasses and withered trees.

There could be no mistaking the sickness they wrought upon the land, nor the cost of their passage. The rolling hills transformed into wind-blasted places bereft of shelter, the valleys clogged with fog and the echoes of lost souls. Riding down into the fog was never less than chilling, the trailing wisps conjuring spectres, each one wearing the face of one of the fallen. There was not a man among them who did not shed a tear for the lost somewhere along the road, reminded by the world of what they had once had. The ruined towns were worse than the ancient burial mounds because their ghosts were newer and more intimately connected to the soldiers' crusade. Each abandoned house served as a reminder of Grimminhagen.

It wasn't just that they found empty buildings, for they found so much more in the way of cruelty, but not once did they find a corpse.

The dead took the dead with them.

Metzger was stronger, his recovery plain in his face. He had taken to flexing his left hand, clenching his fist again and again, and curling the arm to build up the muscle through sheer repetition. He did not talk to the other men much, leaving the bonhomie to Bohme. The irony of that turnabout amused Kaspar. He had never considered himself a man that others would die for, that had always been Metzger's department. It was Metzger who commanded the loyalties and admiration of the men and it was Metzger who inspired them and made them want to die for him. They did not like Bohme, no matter how much he might have wanted it to be otherwise. They respected him for his skills and they admired him for the honesty of his tongue and for the truth that he would lay his life down for any one of them unquestioningly, but there was not a man among them who actually liked Bohme.

He did not need them to like him. He only needed them to listen and act on his command.

So this was new to him, riding side by side with knights and infantry, getting to know their names, drilling with them on the long road. He walked amid the rank and file, and though he could not know them all, he took the time to let those he recognised know that he did so, and that they were every bit as important to the animal that was their army as any knight. It happened slowly, without him realising, but it happened, nonetheless. The men began to look to him, to seek out his experience, and perhaps even to like him a little.

The thought of it frightened Bohme. He had never needed friends, nor sought them, especially not from among the ranks of the doomed.

'How do you do it?' he asked Metzger. The pair rode at the front, between the outriders who scouted a mile further down the road and the main body of their tired army that lagged a mile behind. They needed this alone time.

The old man looked at him slyly. 'What?'

'Don't pretend you don't know what I'm talking about, you old fox. How do you do it? How do you cope with knowing that they all think of you as a friend?'

'I am their friend, Kaspar. They need to believe that if I am going to ask them to die for me, don't you think?'

'Bollocks to that. You're twisting my words around. You know very well what I mean.'

'Probably,' Metzger said. Kaspar noticed that he still favoured his left side slightly. He had seen men before who had lost all movement and mobility down one side of their body after some particularly vile humour attacked their brain. His friend clenched his fist around the reins. That simple gesture was in itself an ever-present reminder of their mortality.

'So how do you do it? How do you cope with knowing that you are leading half of these men who think of you as their friend to their deaths?'

'I made my peace with death a long time ago, my friend. When you understand that it comes no matter what we do, then it loses much of its power to frighten. It doesn't matter if we run all our lives or if we stand and fight, you can only run so far before you fall down, your heart worn out.' He rubbed subconsciously at the side where he had first felt the pain of his heart so close to bursting. 'A sword in the back to hurry it along or a withered corpse tucked up in bed, which would you rather?'

'Neither,' Bohme said with a wry smile.

'Exactly, but it isn't as though we have much of a choice, so knowing we are on borrowed time it is best to truly live. So, I make damned sure that every man that serves with me knows I am prepared to put my life on the line for him, and that I would ask nothing of them that I am not prepared to do myself.'

'But how can that be enough?'

'Who said it is? You asked how I coped.'

'You're a complicated man, my friend, truly bloody complicated,' said Bohme. Metzger smiled at that. 'It's not a compliment.'

'No, I am leader. What would you say if I told you I know where we are going? That this is not some blind crusade against an unknown enemy but rather a quest to lay to rest a lost hero?'

Bohme looked askance.

'Do you remember the story I told you? My ancestor's last stand?'

Bohme nodded.

'There is more to it than death,' Metzger said. 'Death would have been mercy from what I understand of it. We all have things in our life we are not proud of, but sometimes we are presented with the opportunity to right what once went wrong.'

'You aren't making sense, my friend.'

'There was a survivor from that day, a single soldier who fled the field of battle in fear. He carried a story back to the family. The vampire did not kill Felix Metzger, it turned him into one of them. That is the secret shame of my family, the protector turned predator. Every story needs an end. That is why we march to war, because unless we do it will never be over.'

Bohme had stopped listening as he saw the three bodies lying in the middle of the rough track. All he could think was that they weren't coming home ever again. There was no sign of what had killed them, but the way they lay left him in no doubt that they were dead. Even without seeing their faces Bohme knew who they were. They had sent three scouts ahead to read the road. Three men lay dead one hundred yards ahead of him, and even though the horses were nowhere to be seen it did not take any great wisdom to put two and two together.

The road cut between twin peaks, both covered with rough scrub and gorse thick enough to hide any number of archers. At that moment nature was reduced to useless beauty and hidden threats. Bohme scanned the ridge looking for telltale reflections, for any glint to give away the hiding places where their ambushers lurked. He saw none.

Metzger raised his fist above his head and drew it down sharply, the signal to the men behind that something was wrong and that they must proceed with care.

'See anything?' Bohme asked, shielding his eyes against the morning glare.

'Nothing,' Metzger said, 'but that doesn't mean I don't know exactly where the whoresons are. To the right, up high, see the line of bushes.'

'I see it.'

'Watch for movement. Something will give them away, even if it is something as basic as the need to fart. They're up there,' he said, resisting the urge to make any sort of gesture in their direction. They were up there, Metzger was sure of it. He knew death well enough. 'You, you and you,' he called, picking out three of the men from the ranks, 'go and bring the bodies home. Keep your wits about you, lads, this place reeks of ambush.'

They nodded and moved cautiously towards the three corpses that lay in the road.

'Form up,' Metzger called, urging the front ranks of the infantry to move into defensive formation. Word moved quickly down the line with the men shifting ranks. Because there was no enemy in sight the Silberklinge broke away from the mass of the men, forming a circle at the head of the line while the infantry merged into an apparently solid block, shields up and swords and pikes out to form a wall of steel. The narrow confines of the path made it impossible for the block to properly form, and where the pass choked the road the Two-Tailed Comet were isolated from the main body of the army. Metzger could not see them, but had faith that Ableron would react as the formation shift moved down the ranks.

Bohme took in the lie of the land. It didn't take any great strategic genius to know that they were in a bad place. The path took them right between the twin peaks, both towering several hundred feet above them with plenty of outcroppings and overhangs to offer shadow and shelter. There was no obvious way around the peaks, making it the perfect spot for an ambush. Had they not been talking they would have seen it easily, but it was a long road, they were tired and hungry and the thirst for vengeance would only sate the mind so far. Beyond that, mistakes became inevitable. What it meant was that for more than a quarter of a mile they were easy pickings for any half-decent bowman.

But it was not bowmen they needed to fear.

In the long silence the fear of the men facing their first real test as a fighting force was palpable.

Bohme looked to the sky but there was no help to be had there.

They needed to draw them out; the horses were useless against an elevated foe. His mind raced, rejecting implausible thought after implausible thought as he hatched and dismissed a dozen stupid plans for getting the dead out in open ground so that the Silberklinge could tear into them.

Then the first bone spear arced through the air, slamming into the ground beneath his horse's hooves. Bohme wheeled the mighty roan around, spurring it into a gallop as the animal surged towards the ranks of armoured knights. The second shaft sailed harmlessly overhead. There wasn't a third.

It was only then, facing the wrong way on the track, that Bohme saw the true nature of the trap: the iron

jaws of the damned and deformed springing tightly
shut behind them cutting the fighting men off from
their supply wagons and leaving the knights of the
Twin-Tailed Comet stranded from the body of the
main force. It was a simple manoeuvre, and one they
would not have fallen into had they known the terrain
better, or been more alert, but such thinking was best
left for the regrets of the dead.

He spurred his horse on, feeling the immense power
of the animal beneath him as a dozen bone spears
streaked across the sky and hammered into the grain
barrels. They made hellish sounds as they flew, the
bone whittled in such a way as to turn the long shafts
into instruments as well as weapons. Their's was the
music of slaughter. A dozen more shafts of bone hit
other victuals, and a single well-placed spear split the
wooden brandy keg. The reek of alcohol was fierce as
it seeped into the wood of the cart and into the sacks
of grain.

The sudden stench of burning flesh was overpowering. Bohme saw the burning man stagger out of the
undergrowth moving jerkily but with obvious purpose. He lurched forward, flame eating into his flesh,
with his arms held out in front of him, grasping for
the cart.

'Stop that thing!' Metzger bellowed beside him.

Two of the knights reacted instantly, bringing their
mounts around and charging at the burning man.
Their swords cleaved into the wretched creature, hacking off one of its arms and half of its head but still the
zombie lurched on, collapsing against the side of the
cart. As it reached into the flatbed, the flames burned

down its hand and ignited the alcohol. The cacophony of the explosion was deafening, the splintered shrapnel lethal as it roared out of the flames as they engulfed the supply wagons on either side.

The detonation acted as a signal for the dead to come streaming out of the undergrowth, screaming and howling as they swarmed down both sides of the valley. They lurched at the ranks of the horses grasping and clawing at the frightened animals. There was no cohesion or strategy to their assault, the mass of rotten flesh surging out of hiding, pieces of undergrowth still clinging to them where they had lain in the foliage.

More corpses came shambling out of the mouth of the pass ahead of them, effectively cutting off any hope of escape. The valley was thick with the dead.

This attack was far from mindless. Bohme saw a hunchbacked figure on a nightmarish black steed snorting steam and wisps of smoke as it thundered forward. The wretched rider gesticulated wildly. The dead danced to his frantic waving. Bohme remembered vividly the effect the vampire's death had had on its minions at Grimminhagen: as Fehr cut the creature down all of its constructs had collapsed, but the fiend rode within the mass of zombies, unreachable.

From the first shriek to the first clash of steel three hundred more swarmed over the supply wagons, gutting the cooks and the servants and all the vital machinery of war, and those that fell upon the knights went for the horses, not the warriors as they cut and cut and cut. The horses cried out, fell or shied, the men struggling to keep them under control with the stench of blood fresh in their nostrils. In such close-packed quarters it was almost impossible for the mounted warriors to do anything.

With nowhere to run, it turned into a bloodbath in moments.

Bohme drew his sword and threw himself into the thick of the fighting.

There was no place for skill or swordsmanship. Bohme swung his blade brutally, in vicious wide stabbing arcs. There was no finesse to it. Each swing was aimed at delivering maximum pain for minimum thought. He hacked away at the first man that stumbled into his path, thrust a vicious blow into the throat of the second, opening a second ferocious grin beneath the first, and disembowelled the third in a matter of moments. It carried on like that, his sword moving of its own accord in a danse macabre. It was a world of blood, Bohme, Cort and Bonifaz at the centre of it, each beloved of Morr as they sent more and more souls into the Underworld with ruthless efficiency.

'To me, Silberklinge!' Metzger bellowed, drawing the knights towards the front. A dozen still on horseback rode to his side, the rest cutting a path to join him. They read his intent immediately. They had to open up a path for the infantry to retreat.

Metzger dug his heels into his mount and spurred the animal forward at a charge. The mounted knights formed an arrowhead, sitting low in the saddle, swords held out like lances as they drove into the ranks of the dead.

The knights hit the line of skeletal warriors, splintering the bones upon their swords and shields as they crashed down upon them mercilessly. The unhorsed knights charged in their wake, their blades cutting and cleaving into the decimated ranks of the undead.

Metzger was a beacon in the centre of the carnage, his sword plunging and rising and plunging again to fountains of blood as it cleaved deep into vile flesh and opened blackened veins, fighting relentlessly towards the mounted cadaver that played general to the undead horde. The knights fought their way to his side, punching a hole straight through the unbeating heart of the dead's disorderly line.

The foot soldiers swarmed in behind them, turning the tide of the battle by sheer weight of numbers and the momentum of fear.

Bohme found himself turned and turned about, hacking and slashing away at the macabre faces pressing in all around him. He took a blow to the side of the head that rattled his brains inside his skull. Dazed, he stepped back. Through the blood mist Bohme saw young Fehr fighting desperately against a dozen foes, barely keeping them at bay. It was a battle the lad was destined to lose. Loosing a savage roar, Kaspar Bohme threw himself forward, using all of his anger to force a path through to the young man. The din of battle subsided momentarily, the world in his ears reduced to the snap and cackle of flame and the groans of the dying. He saw Fehr turn, presenting his back to a huge warrior clad in black leather with twin ebon blades, and run. Rather than cut him down, the giant mocked him. His laughter rang out, chasing the coward off the field of battle. The words stretched out in a deep, almost lupine howl, 'Ruuuuun man child! Ruuuuun!'

'Face me,' Bohme challenged, his blade thick with the ichor of corpses. His voice carried to the leather-clad giant. The man-thing turned, cocking his head quizzically, and then laughed, raising twin blades above his head as though mocking the sky. He lumbered forward, gathering momentum like some huge colossus as he charged through the ranks of the knights. The undead giant wore a leather mask over the right side of his face. The left remained uncovered, featureless, the skin like melted wax where the hideous burns had caused it to slip over the mildewed bone. His milky white eye fixed on Bohme, half of his mouth splitting into a grin as he brought his swords up to cross them over his chest.

Bohme had no time for such niceties of ritual.

He flicked out a deliberately weak feint. The move was telegraphed, ostensibly little more than a test to gauge the skill of his opponent, and meant to feed off the man's arrogance. Even as more laughter rumbled in the beast's maw, Bohme rolled his shoulder and swivelled on his heel, changing the angle of the strike to slice high, towards the few inches of bare flesh left unprotected at the giant's neck. The laughter died in the big man's throat. The blow cut deep enough to open up the thick muscles all the way back to the jagged bones of the neck. There was no blood. Surprise filled the beast's milky eye. For a long moment he tried to fight on, delivering a wild clubbing swing with both blades scissoring in at the same time, looking to remove Bohme's head from his shoulders. His head lolled sickly on his neck as maggots bubbled out of the undead warrior's throat.

Bohme gagged at the sight of the corruption. The huge warrior delivered a crushing blow that took Bohme high on the left shoulder, twisting him around. Bohme rolled with the momentum of the blow, turning with it. He reversed his blade and thrust hard into the boiled leather of the warrior's breastplate, driving the monstrosity back a step. Its head hung slackly on its neck, the black-clad warrior lacking the muscle to control his gaze, stared with his one eye at the dirt beside Bohme. Bohme stepped in, cleaving the masked head from the giant's shuddering shoulders, and planted the sole of his foot against the dead man's chest to topple him.

He turned away from the corpse a fraction of a second before a rusted blade could deliver him a matching fate. The sword registered instinctively in his mind, his body reacting without thought, and still he barely brought his blade up in time. He took the full vehemence of the blow across his knuckles. His gauntlet saved his hand. It was a stupid lapse of concentration but he had no time to berate himself. He rounded on his would-be killer and dispatched him to whatever fate awaited such soulless abominations.

He was alone, deep in the ranks of the dead, surrounded on all sides by leering eyes and slack jaws, cut off from the rest of the men. Out of the mist of blood he saw Metzger and Bonifaz fighting through the zombies to reach the hunchback on his nightmarish mount.

A blade thrust in towards his exposed back. He blocked it on the flat of his blade, barely turning, and hammered his elbow into the face of the enemy fighter, rupturing his nose and spraying blood into his eyes. He drove his blade into the man's belly and left him to die.

Metzger and Bonifaz fought side by side, barking out orders to the others. The word passed down the line. Discipline replaced shock and within a minute the Silberklinge were fighting with controlled fury, pushing back the swords and spears of the enemy. Those that succumbed to their fear fell victim to the savagery of the corpse warriors. Such was the ebb and flow of any fight.

Bohme cut through the enemy to reach their side.

With the heat of the fires on their faces, they bought a few yards of breathing space. Bohme delivered a vicious riposte, rolling his wrist around a blow aimed at his heart, and stepped in to open his surprised enemy's belly from stem to sternum. The zombie fell, clutching at its guts as its black heart slithered out of its corpse, rendering the beast dead again.

He could not see the knights of the Twin-Tailed Comet beyond the ragged lines of the foot soldiers. No doubt their rearguard action mirrored the break-out manoeuvre trying to punch a way through the press of the dead to open the pass behind them. There was no way of knowing how they fared, and no sense in worrying about it.

A horn sounded four sharp blasts behind them: Ableron's herald announcing that the pass was clear.

The sound meant more than that, though. It signi-fied the turning of the battle. Bohme smiled coldly. After the initial shock of the ambush Metzger's men had stood their ground, the fire of battle tempering them as a fighting unit.

A dozen keening corpses lurched and staggered between him and Metzger. Another dozen stood between him and the ranks of the infantry.

THE OLD KNIGHT fixed his gaze on the mounted hunchback. It was obvious that the fiend orchestrated the ambush, his razor-sharp fangs bared as his wild gesticulations puppeted the zombies across the field, throwing them against the raw recruits of Metzger's crusading army. The creature was unlike anything the old man had faced in his years of combat, dressed like some shamanic priest of the old ways. Fetishes and gewgaws hung from his belts, including shrunken skulls, the withered tongues of fallen foes, and so much else besides. It turned its baleful eye on the old warrior fighting his way towards it, and recognised the threat immediately, casting some grim enchantment from its cadaverous finger.

The ground around Metzger's feet buckled and cracked. Dead roots dripping bugs and worms clawed up towards his feet trying to snare him. Metzger kicked through the grabbing fingers of the roots, his sword ruthlessly cleaving a path through the keening zombies towards their master.

The vampire levelled a finger at Metzger's chest and uttered a single arcane curse.

Pain erupted within the warrior's chest as an unseen force invaded his body. Ethereal fingers clawed through his veins, the death in his blood answering to the creature's black arts. He felt the blood choking inside him, his heart seizing, but gritted his teeth and forced himself forward through the sheer black agony.

The wizened cadaver cackled, hissing more words of power to bring Metzger down to his knees. The old man's legs buckled but he did not fall. Determination kept him on his feet as a fresh wave of pain tore through his body. He lurched one step forward, and then another and another, pushing on through the pain. The sight of fear writ on the acolyte's twisted face was enough to drive him on. Metzger blocked out all sounds of the battle and all thought of anything beyond reaching the beast's side. Waves of dread and fear hit him over and over, bearing down upon him as they assailed his mind. He could not shake them. His muscles stiffened, threatening to betray him. His heart hammered wildly in his chest. He felt his sword arm tremble, gripped by fear. Metzger loosed a blood-curdling scream-come-challenge and lurched forward another step, forcing himself to move through the dread just as much as he forced himself to move through the grasping roots, and felt the lethargy and pain lessen. The beast had ceased its chanting, he saw with grim satisfaction. Metzger raised his sword and began to run.

The dead could not stop him.

He hit the vampiric steed hard, ramming his blade through its neck even as the great beast reared up. Metzger wrenched the sword clear, severing the horse's lower jaw as the steel cut through the meat. Any natural beast would have fallen but the great black stallion reared again, kicking out for the warrior's skull. Metzger ducked beneath the hooves, thrusting the point of his sword in through its cage of ribs and into his heart. He clung on to the hilt as the beast thrashed, its immense weight impaling the creature on Metzger's sword. The steed tossed back its mane, a gurgling cry escaping its ruined mouth as it fell sideways, dead again. Metzger dragged his sword free and turned on its rider.

Before he could cut the vampire down the air around him shivered and thickened with smoke. A moment later the beast was gone and in its place a bat flew erratically up into the sky.

'Bring it down!' Metzger bellowed. Spears launched, falling short as the bat fled the battle.

BEFORE KASPAR BOHME could reach his friend's side he saw the vampire transmogrify, shifting shape to flee. He felt a surge of anger that there would be no single death to win the day, knowing that it condemned more good men to dying. He turned his back on the fight and rallied the Silberklinge. Three of them were on foot now, their mounts cut down beneath them during the slaughter in the valley.

The horn of Ableron's knights sounded again, cutting across the low moans of the zombies and the clash of steel.

The remaining riders of the Silberklinge responded to the call, bringing their mounts about and galloping back to bolster the defence of the foot soldiers. Bohme and the rest continued to fight like daemons, opening the path through the dead wider and wider, allowing the knights and the infantry to adopt a proper defensive formation that held firm as the enemy were cut down, their fall met by ragged cheers from the foot soldiers as they too understood that the day was won.

It took the living less than an hour to drive off the dead, but at such a cost it did not bear dwelling on.

Their vampiric master did not return.

In the lull that followed the slaughter, they were left with too much time to reflect upon the ramifications of it. Behind them, the supply wagons smouldered, their food gone. Their most immediate concern though, was water: the barrels had burned leaving them with nothing to drink.

The men sat in clusters, tending to the wounded, stitching and bandaging shallow wounds. More than a dozen though were not fit to be moved. This presented a dilemma for Metzger: did they leave them behind in the heart of hostile territory or sit with them while they recovered, sitting ducks? Bohme knew it wasn't ever as simple as either or, but the new boys didn't. They saw the badly wounded and would judge Metzger on how he treated them. Bohme remembered seeing the old man weep as he was forced to cut the throats of three of his own men rather than leave them behind, and didn't dare to think what such an act of honest soldiering would do to the morale of the raw recruits.

For every enemy they had cut down, one of their own had fallen.

All but a baker's dozen of the knights had lost their mounts, including Ableron's men.

More than two hundred of the militia had fallen.

Worse, another hundred of the boys from Grimminhagen had fled in fear from the field.

The survivors were subdued as they went about the business of assessing the damage. They were a long way from home, in a wilderness that did not welcome them, without water, and to a man, wounded. The experienced warriors would ride on, without question, they were soldiers. They followed orders even if those orders took them to their deaths. That was the soldier's lot. They died for what they believed in. It was the others, the butcher's boys and the stable lads and all those who had marched with such fire in their bellies, those were the ones Bohme worried about. Now that the fires were burned out and the game of soldiering had come to a brutal and bloody end, what would happen? He had been through enough fights to know that some of those who had fled would return, shamed by their cowardice, but the others were gone, good lads turned into deserters by fear. He hated the truth of that knowledge as he thought about the young lad. The boy was gone. He would come back or he wouldn't.

That did not change the fact that desertion was a crime punishable by death.

That was the harsh reality of it.

Every soldier relied upon his sword-brother. It was more than just a lesson in brotherhood, those swords were all that any of them had as an ally against death. They needed to be able to count upon the men at their sides unequivocally. There could be no lingering doubts.

Those doubts were precisely what this skirmish had put into the mind of each and every one of the men left behind. Who could they trust with their lives when it came right down to it? The answer was no one.

An army could not withstand such a canker eating its way through the ranks, Bohme knew. What he did not know was how to cut it out.

He sought out Metzger and found him walking among the corpses of the enemy, revulsion on his face. 'Will this threat ever cease?' the old warrior asked. Bohme had no answer, at least none that he wanted to voice. 'We need to burn them,' he said instead, offering the simple expediency instead of a true answer. Metzger nodded and summoned the nearest foot soldiers to see to it.

They found Cade, Cort's youngest brother, lying in the dirt. His leg had been severed above the knee where the dead had cut him down from the back of his horse. He had lost a lot of blood and there was little that could be done for him save cauterising the wound with flame or slitting his throat.

Bohme looked around for Cort and saw him stitching a wound in his shoulder with a thick steel needle. He called his friend over. Seeing his face, the knight understood, or at least thought he did. Then he was faced with the sight of his little brother lying helpless, delirious with the pain as his courage threatened to give out. 'Do not scream, little wing,' Cort said, kneeling down beside his kin.

'Cort? Is that you?'

'It is.'

'I cannot see you, brother. Am I dying?'

'Yes.' Their could be no lies between them now, at the last.

'Can nothing be done?' the wounded knight asked between clenched teeth.

'Precious little,' Cort said, truthfully.

'I would be whole when my spirit crosses,' Cade said, his words barely a whisper as the pain swept them away.

Cort looked up at Bohme, his eyes red-rimmed with uncried tears. Bohme nodded, and collected a brand from the smouldering ruins of the supply wagons. He fed it to the flames, stoking the life back into its charred stump. By the time he returned Cort had torn away the garments around his brother's severed leg. The others held the young knight down. Cort held out his hand for the flaming brand and warned Cade, 'this is going to hurt like hell,' as he rolled the fire across the bloody flesh until it blistered and blackened into a hard crust. The air stank of the bitter sweet tang of burned meat. Not once did Cade cry out.

Bohme saw why. Death had taken him even before the first lick of fire had touched his flesh. There was mercy in that.

He laid a comforting hand on his friend's shoulder. 'He is gone,' he said simply, and left Cort alone to mourn his brother in peace.

It was the same all across the field. People he had laughed and joked with only the night before lay lifeless in the dirt. The lucky ones tended deep cuts and shallow gashes, each one insisting they were fit and that the wound looked worse than it in truth was. Bohme knew better. They were fighting men and that made them liars when it came to their injuries. None wanted to be left behind.

Bonifaz walked up beside him. His face was bruised and swollen from the battering he had taken but the young fighter was in as good spirits as his nature ever allowed. He itched at the twin scars on his cheeks, digging the caked blood-rust out of the whitened wounds and then knelt beside one of the corpses of the damned. As he opened his mouth to say something more it sprouted a mildewed bone shaft where his tongue ought to have been. The bone spear emerged from the back of his neck, splitting the vertebrae. The shock registered in his eyes even as the blood bubbled up out of his throat and he fell.

Bohme threw himself forward as a second bone spear whistled an inch away from his ear. He hit the dirt and rolled.

Skeletons reared up in the dirt, their silhouettes picked out by the sun as they hurled the rest of their bone spears down into the valley below.

The dying was not done for the day.

CHAPTER SIXTEEN

Bloodstained Hero
The Secret Places within the Howling Hills, Middenland
The Endless Winter Night, 2532

WOLFGANG FEHR RAN through a world of shadows and half-truths where images glimpsed out of the corner of his eye became the beasts of his imagination, hungry to hunt him down and consume him.

His dreams were haunted by deformed faces.

The skin slipped away from chins and jaws like wax and milky eyes stared into him while bestial growls mocked.

They were the manifestations of his guilt, he knew, but knowing did nothing to banish them.

He stumbled on, knowing that he could never turn around and go back. The sure and certain knowledge that he was alone in the wilderness of the damned ate away at him like a canker. He had left the crusade, abandoning his sword-brothers to the rusted blades of the beasts they sought. He had failed them. It was as simple, and yet as profound as that. There could be no excuses, no forgiveness. He had failed his friends.

Twice he had stopped running and turned to look over his shoulder, not in fear but in longing, wanting nothing more than to return to the fold, to go back to the easy camaraderie of the men beneath Metzger's command, but he could not. The penalty for his desertion was death; there could be no forgiveness for his cowardice. Over the days and nights that followed one truth became clear to the young soldier: he hated himself for what he had done.

Tears of rage stung his cheeks as the bitter wind curled around him, its caress harsh.

And so he ran until he could run no more.

He took shelter against the leeward side of a huge boulder, using its bulk to shelter from the teeth of the wind. The night was black and bitter cold, so far from even the nearest farmsteads that the stars, a thousand points of light for the dispossessed soul, offered the only light. He heard movement in the undergrowth, ignoring it as the more restless daemons of his psyche, and set about finding food. It was unforgiving countryside. He could not subsist on dead leaves and mud. He found blue berries clustered on the vines of a bush. He could not bring himself to care as he stuffed them into his mouth and bit down on the bitter juices, swallowing the mouthful whole. His stomach cramped in revulsion, but he stripped another branch of the small berries and forced them down his throat. A few minutes later he threw them back up again as his stomach purged itself.

Primitive instincts took hold. He crawled on hands and knees gathering the twigs and kindling he needed for a fire.

When it was lit, he crouched over the small pit and offered a prayer to Morr for the souls of the men he had abandoned, begging their forgiveness. There was no divine revelation, no sudden warmth in his heart that told him the dead forgave him. He rubbed his hands briskly over the fire.

He heard it again, a rustle in the bushes. The sound was too substantial to be the wind through the leaves. He felt his heart trip a beat against his chest. 'I can see you,' he called out, his voice crackling like the flames. Fehr pushed himself up to his feet, grabbing a brand out of the fire. 'Come on then,' he called, his voice full of false bravado. Still the sounds of movement ghosted around him, their maker always just out of sight. He struggled to see beyond the red glow of the fire, but the relative brightness of the flame left Fehr night-blind. He slashed out with the branch, stepping forward, almost into the fire. The flame trailed through the black without revealing any of the night's secrets.

Fehr spun left and right, brandishing the flame like a weapon.

It all happened so fast. In the cackle of the fire he heard a low-throated growl filled with menace and hunger. He lunged towards the sound, and as the fire in his hand spat and popped eating away at the branch, the yellow eyes of a feral wolf blazed out of the darkness, frothing jowls peeled back on vicious fangs. The wolf pounced, teeth tearing at his throat as the shock of its huge weight took him off his feet. Fehr lost his grip on the firebrand as he fell, sprawling backwards. It guttered and died in the mud. He thrust his arm up desperately, screaming as the wolf's jagged teeth sank into the soft flesh of his forearm.

For a moment they were locked together, beast and man, and Fehr saw his eyes reflected yellow in the beast's ravenous gaze every bit as feral and wild as the wolf's.

Fehr tore his arm free of the wolf's mouth, shredding the muscle agonisingly, and reached around, grasping either side of its head in his hands as it snapped and snarled. Ignoring the agony firing his flesh, he sank his fingers into its eyes, forcing them deeper and deeper until he felt them rupture and the wolf's growls became yelps and finally whimpers as he robbed it of its sight.

The animal reared away from his clutches before he could snap its neck, and loped off blindly into the dark.

Fehr rolled over onto his back, panting and shivering as the adrenaline slowly left his body. In its place came pain. He didn't dare move. He lay in the dirt, pressed close up beside the huge rock, staring up at the stars and yet blind to them through the haze of pain. He heard nothing beyond the mocking of the fire, but as far as he was concerned any night predators were welcome to feast on his bones, such was the depth of his self-loathing. It was another lie he told himself though, his desperation to cling to life betrayed that much. He did not want to die, not on the battlefield, not here like some piece of carrion. He felt out the extent of the damage the wolf had done to his arm. His good hand came away sticky with blood. Muscle and tendon were ruined and hung in ragged tears. The pain as his fingers came into contact with the shredded flesh was indescribable. He had nothing with which to stitch the wound or staunch the bleeding. Biting down on the agony, Fehr pulled his shirt over his head, tore off the sleeve and used it to bind up the wound. In less than a minute it was clotted black with thick, sticky blood.

As the night wore on the blind wolf's baleful cries haunted him but the wounded animal did not return. It would find its feed elsewhere or it would die. In that way they faced the same fate, man and beast.

Deep in the dark heart of the night Fehr lapsed into unconsciousness; it could not be called sleep.

FEHR WOKE TO the first fat drops of rain falling on his face. The weather worsened, the blustery winds gathering momentum. The cold and wet seeped through to his skin. For a moment he was utterly lost, and then it all came back to him: the ambush, his panic and flight, the wolf. He cast about in the darkness, looking for his sword. It was over by the fire pit. The fire, as pitiful as it had been, had burned out while he slept. Pain flared through him as he reached down too quickly, stretching the new wounds. He almost blacked out with it, sunbursts in negative erupting across his vision, black holes of agony that threatened to overwhelm him. Fehr slumped to his knees, clutching at his stomach as he heaved his guts out into the charcoal of the pit.

He wiped the spittle from his lips with his good hand and crawled away from the pit.

He sat with his back against the stone, the sword across his lap, while the rain streamed down his face.

He had never felt so completely alone.

A jag of silver lightning split the sky. Three heartbeats later the distant rumble of thunder rolled across the hills. The elemental rush made the darkness and isolation easier to bear. Fehr pushed himself to his feet, cradling his damaged arm as he strapped on his sword-belt. The makeshift bandage was stiff with dried blood. He needed to find water; the wound needed cleaning and redressing, otherwise the germs the wolf carried in its saliva would fester and the wound would become gangrenous. A second spear of lightning forked across the bruise-purple sky. Wolfgang Fehr imagined the shapes of so many unnamed daemons out of the shadows thrown down by the wrath of nature.

He started to stagger, trying to keep low, his body bent over to protect his arm. His head swam sickeningly.

The thunder chased him.

He didn't know whether to seek high ground or low, whether to seek shelter in the trees or stay in the open. This time the lighting was so much closer that it seemed to leap from the ground into the sky rather than the other way around. There was no lag between the flash and the bang as the thunder cracked. He felt it like a physical blow, like hands on his chest bowling him off his feet. Fehr stumbled and fell to his knees. He looked up in time to see a three-pronged fork of lightning lance deep into a promontory of rock, splitting it asunder with the sound of the mountain itself dying. Stone split and crumbled, a landslide of scree tumbling down from on high. Fehr lurched to his feet as another bolt of lightning tore up the sky and in its afterglow he saw, beyond the ruined spike, the silhouette of an old abandoned fortress. Without the intervention of nature he never would have seen it. He ran towards it, thinking that the dilapidated towers offered salvation.

FEHR STUMBLED FORWARD, struggling against the ferocity of the storm. The ghosts of the brutal battle burned bright in his mind, resurrected with each fresh lightning strike. The wind and rain battered him, biting at his face, drawing the heat out of his blood and through his stinging skin as it cut him. He shivered, drawing his damaged arm in closer to his stomach protectively.

The lightning revealed the high towers of the ruin, and it was very much a ruin. Each one crumbled as though the stones were being reclaimed by the island it rested on. It looked like no place he had ever seen outside of nightmare, with leering gargoyles and daemonic faces carved into the broken stones. Withered trees shrived of life bordered one side of the path down to the ruined castle, and before it lay a huge lake in which it seemed to stand. There was no drawbridge or any other means of reaching it that he could see. As he neared the afterglow of the lightning made it appear as though the stone creatures writhed and twisted, the stark shadows adding to the nightmarish quality of the vision. It took Fehr a moment longer to realise that there were subtle movements within the stones, and a moment more to understand that the worms of motion he thought he saw were actually a madness of ravens swarming in and out of the cracks between the stones.

Fehr felt eyes watching him as he neared and tried to convince himself that the only spies looking down on him were avian. He didn't believe his own lies for a minute.

He stood at the water's edge. The great ruin loomed over him, full of menace in the storm. He could not hope to cross the water with the rain lashing down in torrents. Fehr stared across the churning lake to the castle gates. But for another jag of lightning he would have missed it: a path led back from the gates, running close to the wall and then around the lake. It was well hidden, and almost invisible from this side of the water, making it a deceptive defence. He followed the line of the path with his eyes as it skirted the lake on the furthest edge and then followed the line of trees. Fehr stumbled towards the trees, and halfway there saw that the illusion of the water was even more cunning: the lake was a naturally formed horseshoe of water. Despite how it appeared from the pass, the ruined castle was not actually on an island within the lake but set behind its bowed waters.

He stumbled on, dragging himself around the lake. Twice he needed to rest, first using the trees and then the curtain wall for support, before he reached the gate.

The arch of stone over the huge ironwood doors of the castle offered some slight protection from the elements. Another fork of lightning and crescendo of thunder lit the doors in stark relief. They were banded by black iron and deeply pitted with woodworm. Like the rest of the ruin the doors retained little of the integrity they had had when they were new. The ironwood crumbled like sand against his fingertips. Beneath the corruption a hard wood core remained. He pushed at the door but it did not open. Thinking it was just the resistance of disuse, Fehr put his shoulder to the wood and pushed. Still, it did not open. Grunting, he dug his heels in but the door didn't budge so much as an inch.

Above, the ravens mocked him, their caws like laughter as they rolled beneath, behind and between the thunder.

He looked up, and for a moment fancied he saw an ugly face leering back down at him through one of the murder-holes set into the stone arch.

Fehr hammered on the heavy wood with the flat of his hand.

The last thing he expected was for it to open, even if only a crack.

Through the crack he saw a curious bloodshot eye peering out at him.

'What do you want?' the mouth beneath the eye rasped, chipped and broken teeth turning the question into a single elongated sibilant hiss: Wathdyouthwanth?

Fehr lifted his damaged arm, showing the gatekeeper that he was helpless. 'I need water and bandages first, though I would not refuse shelter from the storm.'

'There is no place for you here.'

'Please,' Fehr said, stepping closer to the door. 'One night, then I will move on. If I cannot treat the wound it will fester. I am starving, cold and in agony. Have mercy.'

'That is not our concern, stranger. There is no mercy in this place. Go.'

'Please,' Fehr repeated. There was nothing else he could say. He held out his arm as though he hoped it might inspire pity in the man behind the door.

'Come closer,' the gatekeeper said, pressing his face up into the crack, tongue lolling between his yellow teeth as he sniffed the air like some rabid dog. 'Who are you boy? And what brings you to our door?'

'Fehr,' he said.

'Fear?' The gatekeeper repeated, missing the inflection. 'You are fear or fear brought you to our door?'

'Both,' he answered, honestly.

'Wait,' the man said, but instead of pushing the door open he slammed it closed in Fehr's face. He heard the drag of wood on wood as the beam was dropped in place to lock him out. With little other choice, he did as the peculiar gatekeeper had bid him.

As the minutes stretched into a full hour Fehr sat slumped against the foot of the curtain wall, staring blindly up at the stars. The rain streamed down his face. He found himself picking at the scabrous crust that had hardened over the damage caused by the wolf's bite. He broke the crust, causing the wound to bleed again.

Behind the door, Fehr heard the wooden brace being lifted. He scrambled to his feet in time to see the huge door open wide enough for him to walk through. He didn't. A young girl of perhaps ten or twelve stood in the doorway, her face wrinkled with concentration. She was a pretty young thing. She smiled at him, the warmth in her eyes causing him to smile in return. She was dressed in a simple white shift, the hem blowing around her legs. The rain matted her long blonde hair, causing it to curl into ringlets. He had no idea who she was, or what she was doing awake at such an ungodly hour, or why the gatekeeper would summon her to greet him. None of it made a lick of sense to him. Her feet, he saw, were bare. The right was small and dainty like the rest of the girl, but the left was withered and twisted with the relics of polio or some other heartless disease.

'Give me your hands,' she said, holding out her own, palms up.

She was trembling with the cold.

Fehr crouched down before the girl and offered up both hands, wincing as the skin beneath the scabs stretched painfully. Her fine-boned fingers closed around his and she drew them up towards her face. She placed them on either side of her face. Her cheeks felt like ice to the touch, the cold going deeper than the bone. She smiled reassuringly at him as, with questing fingers, she picked away at the makeshift bandage covering his wounded arm. Before he could stop her the girl dipped her head and licked at the crust of blood. Her face came away slick with crimson.

She looked up at him with a misplaced longing in her eyes and nodded as she let go of his hands. 'You are welcome here, Fear. Your running can stop now. Let Kastell Metz be your new home.'

He caught himself about to correct her pronunciation of his name and then he realised what she had called this ruin. Kastell Metz? It couldn't be. Metz was back in Grimminhagen. He had grown up playing in the fields beneath the fortified manse. This place, this ruined fortress, wasn't Metzger's ancestral home.

She opened the door wide and stepped back so that he might see the place she had bid him call home.

He did not move.

Fifty rag-clothed wretches gathered on either side of the door, waiting to welcome him. They wore the shadows as protection against ridicule. He saw one-legged women shuffling uncomfortably, pox-addled pickpockets itching, he saw a twisted hunchbacked dwarf of a man, and a woman whose face seemed to have melted beneath an angry flame. They were the wretched, the sick and the twisted. They were monsters to a man, woman and child.

They moved back to let him through.

She looked at him strangely, tilting her head. 'Do not be afraid, Fear,' she said, misreading his hesitation. 'They are like you, refugees here. We do not judge, we do not condemn. We find a little peace in this isolation, and the master is kind to us. You will not be a pariah here. You are one of us. This is where you belong.'

Here, he thought, as she beckoned him, here among the freaks and killers that took Jessika and destroyed my home. This is where I belong? He wanted to scream at the stupidity of the thought. He belonged nowhere. The dead and the damned had seen to that when they murdered his friends and tore down the walls of his town. He looked at the little girl, lost, it seemed in this macabre flock. His eyes drifted down to her shrivelled foot. She was one of them. Touched by some cruel deformity she had taken refuge behind the crumbling walls of the castle and made herself a new life amid the damned, and that was truly what they were, each and every one of them. Abandoned by mothers and fathers through fear, left out to drown or bundled in sacks and beaten to within an inch of their lives, these wretched souls were, like him, survivors. The similarity, when he thought of it in those terms, rocked him.

Fehr reached out his ruined arm and the young girl took his hand, leading him into the wilderness of lost souls.

There was so much pain all around him, and beneath it, an underlying hatred that was shocking in its intensity.

'Let Messalina see to your wounds and then we will find you a place to sleep.'

He nodded, mutely.

Messalina, it turned out, was a haggard-faced weather-witch who had taken up residence amid the clutter of rags and barrels and other refuse at the far side of the bailey, making her home out of a garish swathe of tent cloth tied to wooden poles. She shuffled forward on her knees as they neared, her grey hair hanging over her eyes in greasy wet ringlets. Her clothing was every bit as garish as her makeshift home, though thick with mud and grime and soaked through from the downpour. She looked up at Fehr, nostrils flared as she sniffed the air like some mindless mutt. 'You bleed,' the woman said. 'Agnes, you bring a bleeder into our home? Lucky the master is away, lucky indeed. Such temptation, such foolishness.'

'Fear needs our help, Messalina.'

'Does he now? Does he indeed? Can Fear not speak for himself?' She rounded on him, her eyes thick with cataracts that made them as grey as her hair.

'A wolf bite,' he said, holding out his arm again.

'I can see what it is, Fear. You are a lucky man. Be grateful the Forsaken one is gone chasing treasures. You would not want to meet him with your life exposed so. He does not feed on our kind often, but the temptation of the blood is too much for his sort. He would wring it out of you greedily, make no mistake. Now, sit, sit, let me put water on the fire and find some rags. We will clean and bind the wound before it draws them out of the tower.'

He did as he was told. All this talk of blood and the Forsaken one feeding swam around sickly in his head. That they were so obsessed with the ramifications of blood told him all he needed to know about the nature of the Forsaken. There were few such predators that feasted on blood, and only one he could imagine making its home in such a noble ruin. Wolfgang Fehr had unwittingly staggered into the lair of the vampire that had damned Grimminhagen. On all sides he was surrounded by the dead and the damned. He did not belong here.

* * *

HE SCRATCHED AT the clean bandages.

For all the filth they lived in, Messalina and her kind were fastidious when it came to cleaning away blood. He pieced it together in his head: they talked in fearful whispers of one they called the Forsaken, a withered ancient as old as the hills where he made his home, cursed to life eternal even though his flesh passed the way of all things, into rot. The Forsaken made his home in the highest tower of the castle, with those few he trusted, and seldom walked among the brethren gathered below. The rest, those wretched souls marked with deformity and sickness were given shelter but this was not their home. They did not enter the keep unless bidden, living instead beneath canvas and other scavenged shelter. They feared the vampire's wrath for its capriciousness, just as they feared his thirst; neither were predictable.

The creature spent day and night closeted away in the darkest places of the castle, slaving over mad experiments. Now and then he would wander out into the courtyard and snatch one of them, dragging them back into the damned castle to feed his lust for power and understanding. That constant fear was a small price though for a place of relative safety away from the judgements of mankind.

The name Fear stuck to him. The little girl, Agnes, was much loved by the damned of Kastell Metz. She drifted amongst them all, claiming hugs as she passed from wretch to wretch, nuzzling up against the ugliest of them. At night she would seek him out to tell him stories of her day. That night, for the first

time since his arrival, she spoke of the creatures
from the tower, confirming what he had always
known: they only came out at night, beneath the
shelter of the moon, and save for Amsel, who in his
own way cared for them, they kept themselves to
themselves. Amsel had gone months before, taking
with him the vile Volk, and Radu, the Forsaken, had
not been seen for two cycles of the moon. Casimir,
remained behind. The night before he had snatched
Elis, Agnes's brother from his cot and dragged him
screaming into the tunnels beneath the castle.

'He is dead now,' the girl said, as though offering
an indisputable matter of fact.

'You don't know that,' Fehr reasoned, worming a
grubby fingernail beneath the wrap of cloth to stab
at the wolf bite. The wound was still sore, but it was
healing, the flesh pink and healthy.

'I do,' Agnes said, resting her small hand over his
as though he were the one in need of comfort. 'I
cannot feel him. When I search inside my head Elis
isn't there. He was always there and now he isn't.'

He did not know what to say to that so he merely
stoked the fire with a twig, causing sparks to dance.

'Tell me about him,' he said in the end, not taking
his eyes away from the flames.

And she did, for hours, her voice an enthusiastic
babble as she took him through her childhood. Fehr
closed his eyes as he listened and found that she
painted such a vivid image with her words that he
could almost see the stories playing out across his
mind. Her tone changed though, as her words
brought them back to Kastell Metz, and eventually

the beast that had killed her brother. 'Casimir is a monster,' she whispered, looking around fearfully as she did so, as though she thought the vampire's thrall might be there now, wreathed in the shadows, listening and waiting to punish her for her loose tongue.

It occurred to him then that the little girl might well be the answer to his prayers.

Perhaps, with her help, there was a way for him to go home.

OVER THE NEXT span of nights Casimir proved himself a petty and vindictive beast.

He came out of his tower with the full moon.

It was the first time Fehr had seen him. The thrall stalked though the shanty town of rags, kicking through the detritus of their wretched lives, hunting for something, or someone. They recoiled from him, pressing their flesh up against the stone curtain wall as though trying to disappear into it, all except Fehr, who sat before his fire picking at his wounded fore-arm.

The vampire came up to stand beside him. The fire's shadows cavorted eerily across the beast's gaunt face, conjuring life and movement where there were none. 'I do not know you, human,' Casimir said, his voice thick with malice.

'And I do not know you,' Fehr said, surprising himself as he looked into the eyes of the monster. 'They call me Fear.'

'Because you cower from the shadows, no doubt, like the rest of your wretched brethren.'

'Because I do not know the meaning of the word.'

'Then you are a particularly stupid mortal,' Casimir said dismissively.

'Perhaps,' Fehr agreed, 'but then I am not the one who shies away from the yellow sun.'

'Where is the girl child?' The vampire asked, ignoring his barb.

'How should I know?'

'I smell her on you. Do not try my patience. I am in no mood for lies.'

'What do you want with her?'

'Her brother hungers for her company,' Casimir said, eventually.

Fehr looked up. 'Her brother is dead.'

'Yet still he misses the girl child. Tell me where she is so I might offer them a tearful reunion.'

'No,' Fehr said.

'Do you dare defy me?'

'I think I do, yes.'

Out of the darkness, Fehr saw others beginning to stand. At first it was just one or two of the freaks but as he refused to hand over Agnes to the vampire more gathered the courage to rise up until, as he said 'yes' fifty or more of the rag-clothed damned closed in around his small fire. There was something about the way they looked at the vampire; it was not only fear that burned in the firelight reflection in their eyes, Fehr realised, there was hunger there as well, and need. They looked at the beast and saw something in its dead flesh that they craved. They might have appeared human as they pressed in around the fire, but mentally and spiritually they were bereft. These wretched souls craved the unlife.

'You,' Casimir said, grabbing the one-legged whore by the scruff of the throat, 'where is the girl child? Tell me and I shall spare you your suffering.'

The woman shook her head.

The vampire cast her aside violently, his face splitting in a vicious snarl as he rounded on the witch, Messalina. 'Where is she, woman?'

'Where you cannot harm her, Casimir.'

'I will feast on your wrinkled carcass, hag. Where is she?'

Messalina stiffened and straightened her back as his filthy claws hooked into the loose-hanging skin at her throat, digging deep.

'Where is the girl?'

'I am old, Casimir. I have lived my life and more beside. You do not frighten me. Take me. Let me taste your blood. Make me your servant. Only then will I surrender the girl to you, master.'

'You lie,' the vampire rasped as his nails opened her throat. He licked his lips, savouring the tang of her ancient blood in the fusty air.

The old woman's eyes widened in fear as the intimacy of death reached her heart and mind, but shook her head in mute defiance.

'There will be no blood kiss for you. You are not worthy.' Casimir leaned in and with shocking ferocity tore out her throat. Her blood sprayed out in a huge arc, soaking the faces of a dozen more around the fire. The vampire looked up, the weather witch's throat still in his mouth. He spat the flaps of skin out and wiped the thick crimson juices from his lips as he stared at each and every one of them in turn. 'You will all suffer the same fate if you do not surrender the child.'

'Why do you want her?' another asked. Messalina's blood ran down the side of his face. He did not move to wipe it away.

'She is mine, as you all are,' the vampire hissed. 'You reside here under sufferance, you feed our thirst for knowledge. That reason, and that reason alone, is why you live.' His hand snaked out to punch clean through the man's ribcage and tear out his still-beating heart. It took a moment for the shock to register on his face but by then he was already dead. The vampire sank his teeth into the bloody organ, taking a deep bite from the soft, succulent flesh before he cast it aside. 'You do understand how the reek of blood drives my kind to madness? I can smell your fear. It is a violent delight just waiting to dribble down my throat. Your suffering is my ecstasy. Deny me the girl and I will take particular pleasure in devouring each and every one of you. Now, where is she?'

'Here,' Agnes said, pushing between the legs of the adults. 'I am not afraid.'

'You should be,' the vampire said, holding out his hand for her to join him.

'Why? Elis came to me. He promised me he would be there to meet me. Why should I be afraid of you if it means seeing him?'

The vampire's grin was cruel, 'Because, sometimes, child, there are worse fates than death.'

'Harm her and I will kill you,' Fehr said, crouching to wrap his arms protectively around Agnes. She was tiny in his arms, shivering with the cold.

'Oh, such tender bravado, but I don't think so, Fear. I think you are aptly named for the coward you are. Now let go of the child before I run out of patience and kill you both here.'

'No,' Fehr said. The beast was right, he was a coward. His heart beat wildly against his chest. His mind raced with imagined pain. She wasn't shaking, he realised, feeling the tremors worsen. He was. Like the rest of her foul kind she craved the unlife that the beast's kiss offered. Yet still, he did not give her up.

'Then you are a fool, Fear, and you have damned all of your cohorts with your stubbornness. I trust you are happy with your new-found courage?'

'Mock me, beast, it matters not. Call me a coward, you would be right, call me a fool and you would be equally right, but for all my failings, for all my fears and weaknesses, I am not the sort of man capable of surrendering a child to murder.'

He remembered Jessika's face as the beast had compelled her into the earth to retrieve the box, and worse, by far, he remembered her fear.

'Pretty words. Did you practise them? A dying man should say something important with his final words, don't you think? Now give me the girl and let this miserable charade be over. I am bored with it.'

Fehr said nothing.

Agnes wriggled out of his arms and went to the beast.

Fehr could not bear to watch as the creature led the little girl towards the darkness of his tower.

THEY BURNED THE weather witch and the other hapless fool who had got his heart torn out. There was no ceremony to it, no dignity. Two men dragged the corpses through the dirt by the heels, tossing them into the fire pit. For a while, as they all stood around and watched, it did not seem as though the flames were fierce enough to sear away the flesh and bake the bone, but as the juices dripped out of their bodies the flames roared and the heat forced the mourners back step after step.

Then they brought the pieces of their lives, the weather-witch's gaudy tent and the geegaws of her magic, and threw them into the flames beside the bodies. The clutter of life was quickly reduced to smoke and ashes. The flesh took considerably longer but it too went up in the sickly smelling clouds, and like that they were gone.

He had lived amongst the deformed death seekers for the best part of a month and still he had no idea who the man had been, only that he had lost his heart for the little girl they all adored in their own way.

Fehr felt sick.

He wanted to tear the place apart stone by stone. He wanted to bring it down until it was nothing more than a pile of dust. The strength of his anger surprised him. It seemed disproportionate to the death of a child he barely knew, but then it wasn't about Agnes and it wasn't about the old woman Messalina or the fool who had lost his heart. It was about Jessika and his parents, his home, the four walls he had been raised in, the grass outside the kitchen window where he had played as a child. It was about Metzger and Bonifaz and the soldiers he had betrayed in fear, and most of all it was about him.

More than anything, he wanted to beat down the tower door and confront the vampire face to face even if it meant dying.

That thought meant he was just like the rest of them: a seeker of death. The only difference, slight though it was, was that he did not seek immortality in the endless night of the soul. He sought oblivion.

He did not throw himself at the door. Instead, Fehr watched the flames as though it was his own life they so greedily consumed. The pattern they wove was hypnotic. There was a tragedy here above and beyond the existence of these wretched folk, above even the beast that haunted their nights. It was the tragedy of the human condition and it's ability to survive where truthfully it had no right to. It was the confession that mankind was nothing more than another parasite feasting on the bloated corpse of the world. It was the blight of this unnatural selection that had the dead walking hand in hand with a youngster too willingly naive to know that her brother couldn't be waiting for her.

He might crave death but he did not belong here. He never had, no matter what Agnes had said.

He didn't belong anywhere.

It had never been so obvious. He was not one of these pitiful creatures. He refused to be. And yet what was he? Fear? Were they right in naming him? He could feel the pull of the place. It grew more insistent day by day. Their wretched ghetto was claiming him for its own. He could feel it seeping into his blood like a rot had set into his will.

He looked down at his clothing, the shirt with the torn sleeve and the trousers caked thick with mud that had dried into a crust. The toe of his boot had worn through. His belt was little more than a frayed rope that kept his trousers on his bony hips. He looked every bit as pitiful as the next man in the castle. He turned away from the fire, hating what it showed him about himself. Instead he clung to the anonymity of the shadows along the curtain wall. His breathing was harsh, ragged. His skin itched, not just the pink flesh of the healing wound, but all of it, every inch of skin. Fehr looked up at the moon and wanted so desperately to howl out his frustration. He had to cling fiercely to the knowledge that there was one subtle difference between them: he did not yearn to be some bloodsucking monster.

Fehr huddled up against the chill brace of the stone wall and wept for the girl, Agnes, and for himself, for all of them. He had to get out before the ghetto claimed his soul as fully as it had claimed his body.

When he thought of what he knew about Kastell Metz and its wretched denizens he couldn't believe it would be enough to buy his life back from Reinhardt Metzger. No, he needed to know more. He needed to know all of its most intimate secret places. He needed to strip it of its mysteries. Within those hidden things lay its weaknesses. With those, perhaps he could buy his life back.

CHAPTER SEVENTEEN

Nine Lives
Kastell Metz, Deep in the Heart of the Howling Hills,
Middenland
The Winter of Buried Grief, 2532

CASIMIR DRAGGED THE girl behind him.

She did not kick or struggle; it might have been better if she had. No, she was lifeless in his hand. The irony of it did not escape the necrarch's thrall. Shadow shapes twisted as the baleful wind coiled around the tombstones. Curls of mist roiled around the withered stems of twisted thorns. There were no flowers in the boneyard. Huge stone sarcophagi and mausoleums leaned drunkenly, their foundations slipped over the centuries of disuse and disrepair. Each slumped silhouette cast another gnarled show across the cemetery lawn. Shadows of gargoyles leered, their faces stretched by the moon. He dragged the girl between standing stones and behind echoing mausoleums towards the subterranean tunnels that led down to his hidden workshop.

Together they descended into the earth and along the dank tunnels to the pit beneath the graveyard where he laboured. The chill of emptiness stole into the chamber as he pushed open the heavy wooden door. It was the same chill that crept into Agnes's hand, born from a similar emptiness. The child had given up the vitality of life even before he had fed her to the machine. He was almost disappointed, almost. He would have been but for the fact that she was precisely what his little experiment needed.

He pushed open a second oak door and propelled her through in front of him, down a narrow flight of stairs carved into the clay of the earth, and deeper until he emerged into a second, lower chamber hidden away beneath Radu's workshop. Alchemical globes lit the vast space. It was not as grand as the necrarch's but it was secret, and it was his. The globes did not gutter in the draught that blew through the open door. The machine stood in the centre of the pit, itself sunk in the centre of the room. It was an elaborately welded bronze and tin framework of beams and cross braces, and in the centre of the machine were the leather cuffs waiting to harness the little girl beside what remained of her brother.

She did not recognise the wretched creature as her kin, but how could she?

The boy had at least looked like a boy when she had last seen him.

Not so now.

Now he bore little resemblance to anything remotely human. His musculature had been torn apart, his heart kept beating by arcane manipulations even as his skin was peeled back and the muscle and tendon drawn away from the bone to wrap around another skeletal frame, this one fashioned of brass and tin. The notion of replacing the skeleton, so brittle and pointless with something unbreakable fascinated the vampire. Could the essence of the boy, Elis, survive or would the new creation be new in every way? There was so much he did not know, but the processes would reveal the truth; that was the beauty of scientific reasoning, the truth could not hide from it.

He stood behind the girl, imagining his creation through her eyes: part man, part monster, which was which though was more difficult to differentiate. The metal frame was eight-limbed, like a giant spider, for balance. Because of that it needed more than one body to flesh it out. It needed several, eight, in fact. All eight hearts still beat on in the centre of the construct, one set in the cavity before each of the limbs, still linked by veins and arteries to the flesh of the dispossessed. Likewise the grey matter of their brains had been placed within a web of pulsing blood vessels, still controlling the most basic automotive functions.

The girl was to be the final element, the soul of the monster. Once fastened into the framework he would open her skull and fuse the eight to her one mind so that she might will life into his great creation. She would be its mind, its eyes, its very core. She would turn eight into one and become a creature of immense power in the process.

He saw a thing of great beauty, a thing that could not have existed without his vision. For all his age and wisdom, Radu could not have done it, but then he was capable of so little, bastardising the genius of those around him. The thought of Amsel having the power to fuse flesh and recreate life so immaculately was laughable. No, he was unique in his vision as well as his gift. The others were ciphers, pale shadows of their kind. How could such noble ancestry be diluted into this weak blood? How could their sires allow it to happen? But he knew, of course, the insidious whisper of the truth niggled away at his mind as it had done for years. They allowed it to happen because they wanted it to. Paranoia prevented them from allowing their gets to truly inherit the gifts of their kind. Instead they subjugated them, undermining them, leading them into failure whilst gleaning what little they could of their genius.

Not so Casimir. He had out-thought his brethren. Soon his scheming would come to glorious fulfilment and he could throw off the shackles of the servitude he endured. The vampire gritted his teeth, a physical manifestation of his will to overcome.

He pushed the girl towards his creation, close enough for the rancid stink to overwhelm her senses and sting tears from her eyes.

'Such a noble beast,' he said with conviction. She did not disagree. She said nothing. She did, however, shiver. He relished that single tremor.

Casimir shoved the girl towards the metal and flesh monstrosity. 'In,' he demanded.

She did as he bade her, clambering into the belly of the construct. He fastened the harness, buckling the leather straps at ankles, wrists and throat before adjusting the tin pins to hold her head forever in place. When she was secured, he tightened the pins, drawing beads of blood where they burrowed in to the bone. He walked around the frame, tutted and furrowing his brow. He took a saw-toothed blade and cut through her screams, first slicing down to the bone and tearing away the girl's scalp, then deeper, through the bone, careful not to bite into her brain lest he damage it. Carefully, he opened her up so that he might affix the dreadful tissue of the eight freaks from Amsel's coterie that had preceded her into his great creation and fuse them all together.

She screamed again, the pins holding her in place even as the blood streamed down her face and her cheeks and ears, but he did not hear so much as a stifled sob, an artfully crafted glyph on the floor absorbing all of her torment so that he did not need to hear it.

On another day he would have savoured the suffering of a mortal but today he needed to concentrate. There were a dozen glyphs set in a circle around the frame, each serving its own specific purpose: one to hold back the inevitable moment of death that ought to have greeted his invasion, another to hinder the putrefaction of the meat and yet another to dampen the maddening lure of the blood. There was a sigil for every eventuality and complication he could anticipate. That, too, was a gift of the scientific method. The theoretical drove the practical, and step by step it offered solutions for all that could possibly stand between his creation and its rebirth as a glorious monster.

The vampire offered no platitudes to the child; there was no need. In that single sawing cut through the sanctity of her skull she had learned the truth. There were things worse than death, many, many things. He began the slow ritualistic chant, drawing the bloody flesh together. Ropes of the stuff ran slick with blood between his fingers. He did, however, offer a chilling smile as the light of recognition flared behind her frightened eyes, her brother's thoughts melding smoothly with hers.

Before she could begin to come to terms with the presence of a second mind within hers, the ritual opened her up to the third and fourth, the screaming minds of the freaks drowning out any trace of sanity the child might have retained.

He walked the circumference of the circle around the infernal machine. The line was drawn with fine gold filament laid deep into the stone, forming an unbreakable cage for his rituals. Too many times Casimir had read of great sorcerers and daemonologists undone by careless preparation. The use of gold, smelted and poured into the runnels carved into the floor was one of many safety measures that he had taken to ensure he did not end up a cautionary tale for scientists. At each of the seven points within the circle, where the gold triangle and square set inside connected with the outer ring, he stopped to utter another line of the incantation. Within the geometry of gold, the construct sculpted around the girl mutated, embracing young Agnes into its heart. As he left the third point, there was little of her left side that was not somehow melded with the muscle of the frame. By the fifth she was unrecognisable as the young girl she had been. By the seventh she was unrecognisable as human, so complete was her sacrifice.

Even so, Casimir did not know if she would survive to breathe life into the marvellous creation. One by one he needed to remove the glyphs, knowing that in doing so he was breaking the sorcery that supported the child's life with no guarantees that her flesh was strong enough to survive the transition.

His creation could still prove to be stillborn despite the months of secret labour that he had devoted to bringing it to life.

He could not allow doubts to creep into the ritual. Even the slightest flaw in the intonation of a single syllable could have untold ramifications. Casimir held up a hand, like a puppeteer manipulating phantasmagorial strings, and reverently commanded the creature of nine souls to, 'Dance.'

And it did, slowly, with no rhythm or coordination to its spasmodic movement.

A cruel smile curled across the vampire's bloodless lips. He made a second pass around the circle, scrubbing out the magical symbols that he had so carefully inscribed. With each one Casimir held the breath he no longer needed to breathe, willing his creation to live on independent of the sorcery that had thus far bound it together.

With the collapse of each warding spell and protection, it survived, until with all of the glyphs removed his creation of nine minds fused into one glorious whole, lived on.

Casimir threw back his head and laughed, his cry of, 'It's alive! It's ALIVE!' filling the subterranean laboratories. Mammut, the beast of Nine Souls, was a perversion of magic and madness but it lived!

WOLFGANG FEHR CROUCHED, the side of his face pressed up against the wall.

There was a crack in the mortar and brick of the wall that allowed him to peer through and spy upon the vampire's vile experiment. He shivered impotently. He knew, even as he watched, that his failure to intervene had cost him a part of his soul. The chill sweat of fear ran down the ladder of his spine, making a mockery of his new resolve. He had followed the beast back into its lair, his mind fired up with thoughts of confrontation, of saving the girl and going back out to the others as a hero.

Moving through the workshop with its mad scrawls on the walls and piles of bones was akin to walking through the gates to the Underworld. He could not breathe for the cold hand of dread around his throat as he slipped through the second door and began to descend still further, sure that he would never again feel the luxury of the sun on his face or the wind against his cheek. The sickly subterranean light cast its pallor across the clay stairs exposing their thick cracks and many more deep fissures in the walls as though the passages and chambers cut out of the earth were buckling from the constant pressure bearing down on them from above.

Instead, he was on his knees, his face squashed up against one of the widest cracks, shivering violently as he watched Agnes absorbed into the hellish monstrosity of the necrarch's making.

He retched, helpless to prevent his body's betrayal.

The sound of his revulsion echoed loudly in the hollow earth.

Fehr sank forward, the contents of his guts spilling across the cold stone of the floor.

On the other side of the fissure the beast turned, drawn by the noise. Its face shifted in the shadows cast by alchemical light. Shock at the intrusion was quickly masked as the vampire's pale brow furrowed. Its cheekbones narrowed, casting deeper shadows as its jaw distended. In the silent echo between heartbeats the vile creature shifted shape from the withered old man into something primal, animalistic. The vampire tossed back its head, nostrils flaring as it scented his vomit on the stale air.

'How dare you?' the creature rasped, moving with shocking speed across the floor.

Fehr lurched to his feet and tried to run for the stairs but his guts cramped and he vomited again. Behind him the oak door slammed open as the vampire burst out of the workshop to snatch him up off his knees and hurl him into the wall. Fehr hit the stone hard and slumped down into a pool of his own vomit.

'You invade my sanctuary,' Casimir said, driving his boot into Fehr's gut, lifting him bodily to the snap of ribs. 'That is a violation, Fear. I suffer your existence for my master, but at a distance. You are a fly on a dung heap to me, a necessary evil. I should have killed you when I had the chance.' Then he broke off, distracted by a sudden notion. His lip curled back on feral teeth. 'No, no, this is better. This serves a purpose. It is ordained. You were brought down here to feed my child. Of course. Yes. You desperately crave freedom from your hellish existence. I understand you now, Fear, you are just like those other wretched mortals. You seek oblivion. Should I share my blood with you, Fear? Or should I share yours with Mammut of the Nine Souls?'

When Fehr did not answer the vampire's smile spread, the beast taking his silence as tacit agreement. 'It is good yes, very good. She needs to feed. You understand her needs. You always did, that was why you gave her to me. I see it now. I understand. It was not the child you surrendered, it was yourself. How many times have you spied on me down here? How many times have you crawled on your hands and knees so close to my beautiful creation longing to be a part of it? I ought to punish you, but I will give you what you want. I will feed you to the Nine, though I do not think she will absorb you, merely digest you, a coincidence of needs. How opportune. You, Fear, will be meat for the beast.'

Fehr lifted his head as another cruel kick drove into his chin, snapping it back.

The beast grabbed him by the wrists and dragged him into the workshop, and across the floor, throwing him bodily inside the gold circle, then hunkered down beside him. Casimir stroked Fehr's cheek almost tenderly. 'I can smell your fear, little man. It oozes out of every pore, soaked into your sweat. It is such a delicious stench, fear.'

'Please,' Fehr begged, drawing his legs up to protect his damaged ribs.

'Do not beg, Fear. It is a revolting trait, so mortal in its pointlessness. Think instead that what you are doing is a great thing, a noble thing. You will not be forgotten. You will live on within Mammut. Surely that is better than the unremarkable life you have fled from?' Casimir took Fehr's bandaged arm in both hands, drawing back the cloth to expose the soft pink under-skin that had healed over the bites. He lowered his head to the wound, his nostrils flaring as he savoured the thrill of the blood so close to the surface. Their eyes met and their gazes held. It was the perfect parody of a lover's moment, broken only when Casimir's teeth pierced the raw flesh, opening the vein. The beast suckled at the wound, savouring each pulse as he swallowed. When he drew his head back up his chin was covered in a thick crimson smear.

The circle did not dampen his screams.

'Are you ready to become a part of history?' the vampire crooned. He wiped the blood from his lips and moved in close to the cluster of meat and muscle that had been the girl Agnes, and held out his hand until a ragged maw opened and a grotesque tongue laved across his fingers, Mammut of the Nine Souls tasting blood for the first time. Casimir smiled his satisfaction.

'Run,' he said, without turning, and chuckled as he heard the frantic slap of Fehr's hands trying to protect his face from Mammut's reaching talons as the monstrosity sought to bury them inside Fehr. He screamed and thrashed out, but the beast was relentless and remorseless in its hunger.

Fehr's screams were pitiful.

The more he resisted, the worse the pain became as the bones of his chest tore apart to breaking point, his struggles opening him to fresh agonies. He refused to die here, like this, grubbing in the dirt at the feet of the vampire's pet. He needed to live. He needed to carry what he had learned to people with the strength to put down the rabid animal. He owed them that much having failed them so many times before. Wolfgang Fehr lifted his head defiantly, feeling the bite of bone breaking. He pulled his good hand away from the suckling flesh of the bloodstained mass of flesh that was Mammut. The abomination's juices had dissolved patches of skin, stripping it down to the muscle beneath.

He scrambled away from the monster, cradling his ruined arm against his broken ribs.

The vampire stood over him, eyeing the hurts appreciatively. 'Death becomes you, Fear. See how willingly your flesh succumbs? You are truly one of the damned.'

'No,' Fehr said, stubbornly. His voice barely carried the inches between them.

'What was that? Resistance? You seek to deny me still? You are a curious creature. Such spirit for a coward. I did not expect that. I had you down as a runner, Fear, a man always taking to his heels come the pain. Tell me, Fear, did you think I could simply allow you to walk out of this place with your head full of our secrets?' He swept his arms around to encompass all of the walls. Like the workshop above they were covered with meaningless scrawls of formulae and invocation.

Fehr shook his head. It was a frantic desperate denial. 'I don't know anything,' he promised, but he knew that he knew too much. How could he not? He had seen the kind of diabolical experiments these mad creatures were capable of, and in them glimpsed the true nature of their dead hearts.

'So much for those gallant final words, Fear. To die with self-confessed ignorance on one's lips is less noble by far, but it is good that you have rid yourself of those heroic notions of saving the world.'

The vampire turned, as though hearing some inaudible voice over his shoulder.

He nodded, and inclined his head.

Still with his back to Fehr the vampire said, 'Perhaps I won't kill you, what then?'

Fehr did not dare hope the question was anything more than another part of the beast's cruel madness.

He said nothing.

'You cannot leave like this, oh no. No that would not be right, but then, you cannot stay. I have no need of you if you are not to feed my child. No, but perhaps you can be used,' he said, turning around to look at the wreck of a man curled up on the floor. 'Can you be used, Fear?'

'Anything,' Fehr said, and knowing even as he said the word, he meant it.

'Good, good. Perhaps we have a second coincidence of needs, you and I?' Casimir knelt taking Fehr's face in his hands and pressing lightly with the index fingers of each one, pushing the grubby nails through the layer of skin as though thinking to probe the man's mind with heavy hands. Blood trickled down Fehr's temples. 'You want retribution. It burns in your blood like every one of your wretched dreams. You would strike down the monster that ruined your life.'

It was a trick of petty fortunetelling. It took no great skill to guess that revenge motivated the majority of the tortured souls in the old world. He bore the stigma of loss, made plain by both his reluctance to hand over the child, and his failure to protect her. It marked him out as clearly as any leper's mark. That, at the last, he had still tried to save her was as pitiful as it was heroic and smacked of a need to salve his own daemons.

'If I could offer you vengeance, would you take it? If I could give you the vampire that destroyed your life, would you slay him?'

'At what price?' Fehr asked.

'Your immortal soul,' the vampire said, and then threw his head back and laughed, not the menacing laugh of maniacal evil, but honest laughter. It took him a moment to realise that the beast was making a joke. 'I jest,' Casimir said, grinning. In that moment Fehr had a glimpse at the man the beast might once have been. It was a shocking revelation in that they were not so different, the two of them. 'I want what you want.'

'It can be arranged,' Fehr mumbled, still unable to move from the beating he had taken. 'Give me a piece of wood and I'll drive it through your heart right now.'

'Believe me, Fear, I am not the one you want to kill. Like you I am a mere servant. I do the bidding of another. We are both soldiers in a fight that is not ours, no? You serve your master, I serve mine and neither of us is our own person. That is how it is the world over, a power play of master and servant, no? We are not free. No one is. Your life is controlled by the whims of another, just as mine is. You seek approval and fear that you disappoint in everything that you do. So you strive to do more, no? Even now you are thinking how you might bring about my undoing and thus save yourself from the cowardice that brought you to my door. That is how it is. Life reeks of subjugation. I would be free of the shackles that bind me as a thrall. Yet the master returns.'

The promise chilled Fehr. He lay at the feet of the vampire, broken, being taunted by the fact that a greater evil neared. He felt as weak and helpless as a newborn fly trapped in an infinite web. 'What would you have me do?'

'Only what you would do anyway: betray us to your masters.'

And so the vampire proposed an alliance that neither man could trust. 'Radu nears. I can sense his presence in my blood. The press of his will on mine has been long absent, leaving me my own master. I would have it no other way. I will deliver the master unto you and yours, in return for the peace I crave.'

'And in that peace you will continue with this?' Fehr asked, nodding towards the monstrosity that was Mammut, his face unable to mask his revulsion.

'I will be no threat to you,' Casimir said, not answering the question. Fehr did not believe him for a moment. 'Ask yourself all the questions you need to, Fear, but do not allow superstitions to cloud your judgement. You can avenge your people or you can die here like a wretched piece of offal smeared beneath my feet. Vengeance or failure, which is it to be?'

'You will deliver your master to us? You are willing to betray him, and yet you ask me to trust you? I was not born yesterday, vampire. Your kind are masters of deceit. You promise one betrayal, why should I not expect a second? Why should I think beyond these words of yours being the sprinkle of sugar to bait a bigger trap? I would be a fool to trust you.'

'And you will be a dead fool if you do not. There is a way out of here through the old tunnels. It takes you beyond the lake's edge. Return to your people, Fear. Bring them back to our door. Or don't. Stay and become one with the damned. I could taste their taint in your blood. Day by day you weaken, becoming more and more like them, don't you? You sense it within yourself. You have twin destinies, Fear. Which do you choose?'

CASIMIR STOOD ON the high tower, savouring the elemental fury of the storm. The wind howled around him, bullying him but he was not about to back down from it. It was a risk, but then all of death was a risk. Fear was out there now, somewhere in the wilderness, running for his life. He closed his eyes, listening to the symphony of nature's instruments as they played for him. It was a beautiful and haunting melody, so simple, so pure, and yet so cunning in its construction.

He moved close to the edge, clambering up onto the parapet. The movement frightened the ravens into flight. Black wings swirled and flapped around him, and for a moment, even set against the moon, the vampire was invisible. It was a subtle deception, as simple as a sleight of hand trick, and as effective as the most powerful of magics. One moment he was there, the next he was gone.

The birds broke with the wind, riding the thermal currents to settle all along the battlements.

Their scattering did not return Casimir. The illusion was complete. The vampire took to the air, merging with the madness of ravens, and became one of them.

The master had chosen to side with his precious Amsel. He would regret slighting Casimir.

The seeds of his downfall were even now scattering to the four winds.

Along the battlements a raven cawed, sighting the master and his entourage returning. The cry was taken up by all of them save one. Likewise, all save one bird took flight, filling the sky. That one bird remained on the battlements, watching, waiting, and imagining what it might be like to be truly unfettered.

CHAPTER EIGHTEEN

Lost Rites and Resurrections
Kastell Metz, Deep in the Heart of the Howling Hills,
Middenland
The Winter of Rancid Flesh, 2532

THE SIGHT OF the castle lifted Radu's withered heart.

His birds took to the air in greeting, filling the sky with tenacious feathers as he walked around the long path skirting the lake. A grey empty mist lay thick on the ground.

'Soon,' he whispered, caressing the simple wooden box he clutched tight to his chest. 'Soon.'

He had not let the object out of his sight since the girl had brought it up from the earth, but neither had he dared to open it again, not out here where so many eyes might see.

No, the contents of the casket were a secret worth savouring. It was enough that he could feel its presence through the wood. It stirred with his touch as though whatever lay hidden was somehow alive, though rather than sentience he suspected it was the proximity of his flesh that triggered the excitement. He had tested the hypothesis with one of the Amsel's loyal creatures, bidding the miserable wretch place his palm flat on the lid of the casket and describe what, if anything, he felt. The man's answer had been an utterly unremarkable, 'Wood.' Then Radu had placed his own hand down alongside his. There had been no need to ask again; the man recoiled in shock as the casket pulsed with hateful life. That single touch had been enough for Radu.

Amsel fussed around him. He saw the covetous way his thrall looked at the casket, and the hurt in his eyes when Radu snapped and snarled and drove him away so that he might have some peace. Worse though was the way he acted. The prissy little fool carried on as though he had somehow gifted Radu with such an amazing thing. Did he not understand that Radu's hand had been slowly steering him towards the relic's resting place? It was pitiful, really.

Amsel spent most of the march with his wretched coterie, pretending to be their master. It was a miserable charade. Watching the birds, he made a silent vow to remind the thrall of his place within the scheme of things.

But first things first, he was eager to return to his laboratories and fully examine the treasure they had found.

He scuttled spider-like towards the great gates. Behind him the waters of the lake rippled, the mist spreading to mask it completely from view. The trees might have been emaciated sentinels watching his return, their gaunt spectres casting black shadows through the thickening banks of fog that rose up in his wake. The coterie of damned hauled the black iron-bound gates open at his approach, and then scuttled away back to their hovels in the outer bailey and courtyard. Behind him Amsel's few loyal servants grunted and cheered, their chants spiralling as they marched in step to the rhythm of the noise. There was no army now, and no need for one. He had allowed the bones to fall, leaving the skeletons to rot where they fell, and cut the tethers on the zombies, allowing them to shuffle mindlessly, his last order imprinted on their minds: fight! When the imperative failed, they too would fall, their resurrection temporary.

Casimir was not at the door to meet him.

Radu had no interest in the ugly faces that stared at him as he entered the courtyard. The casket pulsed in his hands as though it sensed that the moment of revelation was near. Twisted thorns were carved into the brickwork of the walls, a relic from the castle's past life. Set into the abutments and wall braces death masks and chiselled faces fell under the shadows of the twin moons, their visages hideously twisted by the elongated shadows. The wretched death seekers huddled beneath their canvases, their faces every bit as twisted as the shadow-tortured carvings. Ignoring them, he walked through the courtyard, the lord returned to his demesne. He craned his neck, scanning along the wall walks to the high tower, the disused chapel, and then across the outbuildings and back in a slow circuit.

He hissed back one of the damned who dared approach, and swept through the courtyard, his cloak flapping around his legs, eyes fixed on the door ahead that would lead him down to his arcanum and work-shop.

'Soon,' he crooned again feeling the heat radiating from the box. Radu hunched over it protectively. There was no sense of homecoming as he bustled over the threshold. Nothing had noticeably changed in his absence. 'Casimir!' he barked, throwing open the tower door. The thrall did not come running. 'Wings clipped, that's what it needs, yes, yes. Put them in their place. Put them down.'

He scurried down the narrow hall towards the stairs that led down towards the underground laboratories.

'Casimir!' he called again at the foot of the stairs.

There was no sign of the thrall.

He was more at home in these dank tunnels than anywhere else in the world. He was a nesting creature, a hermit crab squatting in the shell of Korbhen's great triumph. He knew all that but it did not matter one whit. These tunnels were his just as much as if he had carved them out with his two bare hands.

It was impossible to tell if it was the casket or his hands, so violent was the trembling as he pushed open the door to the arcanum. 'Casimir?' he called out again, but his shouts fell upon deaf ears. It did not matter.

It felt good to be back in the familiar room, sur-rounded by the scrawled sigils of his formulae, and the objects of his craft: the pipets and tubes, the ampules and clay tablets cultivating festering moulds and growths that defied naming as well as more arcane paraphernalia that cluttered the acid-burned benches.

He closed the door behind him, and then set the box down reverently on a marble slab, marvelling again at the lurid simplicity of the faces for a moment before depressing them to trigger the mechanism. Each pressure point was met by a soft snick and increasingly frenetic vibrations. As the third lock was released the wood grain of the lid shifted rather like the opening of a puzzle box, the metal plates falling into place. Radu closed his eyes, savouring the moment.

'Patience, patience,' the necrarch crooned, his hands lingering over the unfastened mechanisms. It was easy to preach calm but inside his thoughts were a tempest, seething with anger that seemed to emanate from the box and plant itself within his mind, such was the wrath contained within the casket. He felt out each and every grain of wood in the surface. There was so much hatred carved into the simple lines of the wood, so much that he could feel it, like fire burning the tips of his fingers, like ice biting into the turgid blood in his veins. The anger called to Radu, its insidious voice whispering talk of destiny. Right then, right there, the necrarch knew that the casket had been waiting for his hand to break the seals and return the relic to the world of the flesh.

Breathing deeply of the dead air, Radu opened the box for the second time. Even though he knew its contents, he gasped slightly at the sight of the grey mottled hand that lay on plush red velvet just the same. The fingers were withered and hooked around on themselves like a raven's claws. There looked to be no physical decay; there were no obvious signs of mould festering or other such malignant contagion eating away at the hard crust of leathery skin. It was in a remarkably well preserved condition given the propensity of flesh to rot. Buried away for centuries it almost certainly should have been grave dust. Instead the ragged wounds in the flesh were still readily apparent from where it had been hacked off at the wrist. The flesh beneath was clearly dessicated, all the juices of humanity that kept the hand ripe, soft and supple, leeched away by time, but it could be restored. He had that skill.

Radu held the hand in his, and felt the overwhelming rush of anger and hate wash over him as the fingers of the severed limb clenched into a fist beneath his grip. Images of places he had never visited, deaths he had never wrought, pleading, begging and pitiful screams filled his mind, and with them came the fierce joy of power. It flooded his system, energising his coagulated blood. The final image, of a man on his knees, pleading as a bone knife severed his hand at the wrist left him in no doubt, from the strength of the flesh's memory that this was the same hand he saw in his vision. It did not matter that it was not the Great Necromancer's own flesh. That he had possessed it, perhaps even crafted it, was enough. The hand was imbued with such lingering magic that even now it was as strong as any relic he had ever touched. The necrarch's hands trembled as he lifted the hand out of the casket.

Behind him, someone coughed.

He had not heard the door open.

Radu wheeled around to see Amsel standing in the doorway, contrite, head bowed. When he looked up from his shuffling feet an unholy hunger filled his eyes and he asked, 'Is it all you dreamed, master?'

'Everything and more,' Radu admitted. The power seethed within him, barely constrained by the bounds of his flesh.

'What is it?'

'My birthright,' Radu said.

'A fetish? A totem? Some kind of arcane component? An incantation?'

'Far more than any of those, I think,' Radu said, wallowing in the memories of agony that filled his mind's eye. He had connected with the force that lingered within the hand, but not with the man. Despite the snatches of memory that tormented him, he had no clue whose the hand might be. 'There is much I have yet to learn of this treasure and much study to be done. Watch,' he said, holding out his hands. Within them the severed fist unclenched reflexively.

'It's alive?'

'I do not think so, no more than you or I are,' he said, the irony causing Radu to smile.

'Do you control it?'

'Yes,' the necrarch lied smoothly. With the lie came an overpowering vision, so real that it pulled him out of the subterranean chamber. In it he learned the secret of the hand and how it might be used.

He saw a thick muscled man bound to a sacrificial stone, vents and raging tongues of flame hissing and steaming. He was part of the vision, living in its centre. He stood over the frightened man, looking down at the elaborate pattern of blue woad tattoos inked across the well defined musculature. In the patterns he saw the ghosts of gods long forgotten by man and the faces of devils and daemons lost even to the most superstitious of fools. They were in some infernal pit, the twin midnight moons casting their silver and green across the landscape although the venting flame gouts turned the centre of the pit day bright. The clash of steel rang out and the necrarch reached down with his withered hand, forcing the hero's muscle and bone apart to expose the great weakness of the living: the heart. Slowly, with tenderness, the necrarch's vision-self closed his fingers around the still-beating organ and wrenched it out of the man's chest. Despite the primal screams of pain the man did not die for a full agonising minute in which his blood-starved brain refused to look away from the horror of the vampire clutching his heart.

The vision swirled around within him vertiginously, the necrarch losing the fixed point of reference within the scene as though coming unanchored from himself, his sight spinning furiously. He tried to take in the hellish magnificence of the pit, catching flashes of metal and bone constructions lining the walls, and the grim-faced dead who manned them working with laborious precision. Each movement possessed a weirdly choreographed fluidity. There were hundreds of them toiling in the heat of the fires, bathed in the grime of the pit. In the centre he fastened the heart of a nameless hero within the grasp of a severed hand and laid it within its velvet-lined box.

With words writ in blood across his ruined body the warrior rose to stand beside him, born again.

Then the vision crumbled, slipping away like grains of sand through his clutching fingers. Amsel looked at him with a mixture of concern and confusion on his ugly face. He had not been ready for the vision to fail. There had been so much hidden within the layers and textures of it for him to learn, savour and understand, but as suddenly as it had come, it was gone. It did not matter; he knew what he must do.

'Bring me a man.'

Amsel looked perplexed by the command.

'I said bring me a man,' Radu rasped. 'Do I need to beat the order into your head.'

'A man?' the thrall repeated stupidly.

'A warrior. Bring me a warrior of great strength and heart. Bring someone to inspire terror and awe with his martial skill. Bring me the corpse of a hero, I would raise a champion!'

'I do not understand, sire.'

'I will take the greatest they have and remake in him my image, Amsel.'

'You wish to sire another?'

'Hardly, I have no need for a third lickspittle. No, I will raise a warrior whose might will make the ground beneath his feet tremble with fear, a killer immortal. I will raise a legend! I will raise a bringer of death like no other and the world will understand what it means to live in fear! Now go! Bring me my hero!'

'So it shall be, master,' Amsel said, bowing and scraping as he turned to leave. Then, almost as though an afterthought, he turned and asked, 'Should this hero be alive or dead, master?'

Radu's smile was imperious. 'It does not matter, such is my command over the veil. Bring me the corpse of the greatest warrior who ever lived and I shall make him rise as my butcher, or bring me the living breathing embodiment of mankind's obsession with heroes, and I shall break him into my bringer of death.'

'Very good, yes, yes,' the thrall muttered, turning and fleeing the great laboratory in search of a hero of the human cause to appease Radu.

NOT ONE OF the mortals within the castle was fit for the new master's scheme. With the winds howling around him, Amsel scoured the gravestones of the castle cemetery, reading the names. It was impossible to judge the heroism of the dead, and though he was tempted by the largest of the mausoleums, assuming it marked the greatest of the warriors, that could not be taken for granted. The storm broke. Fat heavy rain began to fall. In a matter of minutes it was pouring from the heavens. The ground quickly turned to a sucking mire of mud.

He had to find a suitable corpse, a fallen hero: a colossus.

He thought of the black knight with the ruined face. The man had been a brute in life, and had died like a coward pleading for his worthless hide, but in death he had been a giant. He had died truly, cut down by a better warrior, a true bringer of death.

Amsel knew what he needed to do, and precisely where he would find his heroic corpse.

He ducked his head and shuffled through the sludge towards the heavy ironwood door that led out through the wall. The rain lashed down as he skirted the lake, transforming the skin of the water into a drum. The fog was thick now, thick enough so that he could barely see beyond his outstretched hand. He pressed close to the fortified walls, using them to guide him around the hidden waters of the lake. The footing was treacherous but he moved slowly, placing each foot with great care. Still he lost his footing on the narrow path more than once, barely avoiding falling in.

The deadfall of leaves and branches provided the timpani to offset the rising water. He drew his ragged travelling cloak tightly around his shoulders, only his bald pate and grey knuckles exposed to the downpour. He walked with purpose, keeping to the dark places along the fringe of the trees and the treacherous slopes, through the broken peak, and then across the marshland working his way back towards the battlefield he had barely escaped with his death.

The memory was still fresh in his mind: the old man cleaving through the ranks of the dead towards him. Amsel recognised him then, and now, for what he was: a hero, the kind of man that stood as a fulcrum around which the events of history pivoted.

He would bring the old man to the castle.

Amsel drew the image of the bat into his mind, giving his form over to it so that he might catch the wind and rise with it. He felt the aches of the flesh subside and the freedom of the air covet him, and then he was flying, flitting across the night landscape in search of the battlefield. He flew along the tree line, weaving in and out of the branches, and then across the long open expanse of marsh, skimming low across the rank bog, the stench strong. He no longer saw the world, he heard it, rebuilding it in his mind through the sounds it fed to him. Amsel flew, drawn by the stench of death that still clung stubbornly to the land, for the land was not unlike the mind, it cradled memories of pain and locked them in stone. It did not forget.

Dead or alive, the new master had said, and there were heroes galore freshly buried down in the valley where the living and dead had clashed.

It was deep in the night that he found the familiar landmarks of the narrow passes. He settled into the form of a man and crouched, pressed up against the rock behind a thin line of scrub bushes. The rain brought out the scent of the bushes: lavender. He scanned the fields below, reconstructing the fight in his head. Had the old white-haired warrior fallen after Amsel had fled the field? Or was he alive still? Amsel sniffed the air but he could not tell one reek from another, so powerful still was the taint of blood on it.

The living had abandoned the field, though he doubted very much that they would ever find the castle they sought. A number of simple obfuscation charms combined with the natural protection of the geography made the place almost impossible to stumble upon if you did not know precisely where it was. The master took few chances with their privacy. An army could march for months within a few square miles and never realise they had passed the ruin a dozen times, the great gate close enough to breath upon.

Expedience would have them burn rather than bury the dead, but they would not burn a hero. That was a peculiarity of mortals, somehow they viewed the flames as less than a corpse left to rot and feed the worms in the Garden of Morr. It was folly, as was much of their thinking, based on a falsehood of logic. There was beauty and glory in the flames of a funeral pyre. Any truly worthy corpse would not have been burned.

Scorched earth marked the remains of the ruined supply wagons. Along with the deep scores in the dirt that marked the graves it was the only remnant of the battle with the Imperial force. The few actual graves were honoured with marker stones, though one was honoured with a sword thrust into the earth.

The storm had turned the ground treacherous. Amsel prowled the graves. It was obvious which belonged to the mightiest warrior. He grasped the hilt of a mighty blade driven deep and drew it out of the soft earth.

The sky was framed a soft silver by the distant stars. It ought to have been an image of beauty but there was no place for beauty in such a harsh landscape. Only a hero would wield a blade of its like, Amsel reasoned. Only a hero would have been spared the burning. This was his white-haired warrior. This, buried here beneath the blood-soaked dirt of the field, was the master's heroic corpse. Amsel stabbed the sword back into the dirt and began to dig. It was a shallow grave. After a few minutes he tossed the weapon aside and finished the job with his hands, pulling handfuls of soil out of the hole until he saw the twin scars on either side of the dead swordsman's face and his hands clasped across the hilt of a second blade that matched the grave marker. Rust had eaten into the second blade. Amsel cast it aside as useless and dragged the corpse from the grave. It was not the white-haired hero but another. Rot had ruined his skin, decay and worms eating into the muscle.

He gathered the corpse into his arms. He could not carry the blade, but there were other swords. The master needed bones not steel. Amsel carried the dead man the many leagues back to the subterranean warren and his expectant master.

All the way, the storm raged, all the forces of nature unleashed in mourning for the loss of the hero given over to the earth's protection.

'You HAVE BROUGHT me a worthy corpse?'

They were in the necrarch's subterranean arcanum, the workshop where he quested for knowledge.

'I have, master, yes, yes, most worthy, a true hero of the living.'

'Let me see,' he said, rubbing his hands together expectantly as he bustled through the tools that he had prepared for the ritual of resurrection. The visions had intensified, the consciousness contained within the hand sharing more and more of its secrets, and with them, its power. Radu hungered to feel, touch, taste, experience all of it.

The necrarch studied the corpse. There was no obvious cause of death until he drew back the hair and saw the exit wound punched out through the back of the dead man's neck. The arrow had entered his mouth, tearing out the back of his throat, breaking the bones in the process. He could repair it. He had mastery over blood and bone. Otherwise the corpse was only now beginning to be consumed by the lividity of death. The dead man's back was deep purple where the blood had settled post mortem.

'Lay him on the slab, and then leave me,' Radu said, fetching the necromancer's hand from the casket. He would not allow unwanted eyes. None would share his secret. This magic was his and his alone. He cradled it close to his chest, stroking it lovingly as he shuffled back towards the slab and the exquisite corpse.

He heard the door close quietly behind him as his thrall left.

Radu had marked out the same arcane sigils that he remembered from his vision, as well as emulating the great flame gouts with strategic alchemical globes and candles of black wax. Lighting each in turn he intoned a single ritualistic line of offering in a long dead tongue, and with each new illumination the ambient temperature of the room dropped another degree until the air was like ice.

Still, the corpse did not rise the first time he intoned the invocation. The flesh twitched and trembled but in the end lay lifeless. Radu cursed. He charged around the room grabbing things and hurling them to the floor in his frustration. Then he turned to beating his fists down to pulp and bone against the walls while he struggled to find his focus.

He returned to the slab and demanded the dead man rise.

For a moment it looked as though he might; the corpse's head came up, as did its shoulders.

'Yes, yes!' he hissed, only for the dead man to collapse again, inert.

Then he placed the withered hand in contact with the dead flesh. With the contact the invocation came naturally to mind, but only while both he and the corpse were in direct contact with the dismembered limb.

'As death demands the heart of a noble warrior to give heart to the fiercest fighter, so we take heart,' Radu whispered reverently, caressing the mottled skin with a crooked finger. His blackened nail raked across the pale nipple, digging into the thick muscle protecting the silenced heart. He looked at the warrior's beatific face. 'Come to me, my champion,' Radu commanded, forcing his hand into the dead man's chest, hooked nails puncturing the skin and tearing through the layers of muscle until they reached the bone cage over the heart. Grunting, he forced his hand deeper, cracking the bones until his hand closed over the lifeless organ. He dragged his hand clear, turgid black blood clinging to his wrist where the jags of bone had torn into his flesh, such was the force of the violation.

He placed the dead heart into the clawed grasp of the necromancer's withered hand and set it back into the casket. As he closed the lid he saw the heart beat, once, the blood within it pumping out of the torn veins with the convulsion. Radu closed the lid and returned to the body on the slab.

An hour later the necrarch's hand ceased trembling as he sewed the last suture, closing the dead man's ruined chest. He wiped the blood off his hands and whispered the final word of power to complete the resurrection.

A gust of wind rose up from nowhere. The candles guttered and blew out. In the soft alchemical light, the necrarch saw his scar-faced warrior reborn.

The corpse that had been Bonifaz the Silberklinge opened its eyes.

THE RISEN KNIGHT was unlike the zombies he had caused to return. That much was apparent immediately. The scar-faced warrior was not some mindless automaton to do the bidding of its master like a marionette. Far from it. In the silence after the corpse of Bonifaz opened its eyes, the necrarch could see the Silberklinge's final, and greatest fight being played out behind his dilated pupils. The dead man's glazed eyes roved wildly back and forth, widening with sudden clarity as the essence of the necromantic displaced the consciousness of the hero.

In that instant, as the last remnants of Bonifaz died, a scream was ripped from the dead man's lips.

It was a primal sound, rooted deep in the soul of the human. As it died on the dead man's lips, so too did the last fragment of his humanity. The creature that stared back at the necrarch was utterly alien.

The warrior rose from the slab to stand at Radu's side.

From its ruined mouth came the simple truth, barely intelligible as words, 'I am reborn.'

'You are my death-bringer, warrior.'

'Death-bringer,' the dead man said, the word hanging like a promise in the stale air. There was a hollow echo to his voice filled only by the sucking rasp of air. Its eyes blazed with cruel intelligence. Almost hesitantly, the scar-faced warrior touched the rough stitches that drew the mottled skin tight across its chest, and then moved down to the empty sword belt still on his hip. 'Sword?'

Amsel scurried forward carrying two exquisitely-wrought blades like an offering, resting on his palms.

The dead warrior took them, cutting the air again and again and again, slowly and awkwardly at first, but with gradually more precision before sheathing them. It was a slow, macabre, dance, the steel describing arcs in the air, cutting high towards his throat and low, snaking out to emasculate the necrarch.

Radu did not flinch.

'Incredible,' he breathed.

It was no mere zombie. It was learning how to move again, clumsy and awkward like any shuffling dead at first, but, as though rediscovering its own corpse, the death-bringer was beginning to fill the skin and bones. Risen corpses were puppets to the will of the summoner. They did not practise weapon katas or demand their blades. This death-bringer was more, a zombie yes, but one capable of improvement. Could it eventually become a true warrior of the dead? The thought excited the necrarch.

'Come,' Radu said to the scar-faced warrior, 'I have such delights to show you.'

The dead knight inclined his head and followed as the vampire scuttled out of the laboratory and deeper down the labyrinthine twists and turns of the tunnels hollowed out beneath Kastell Metz towards the vast chamber of bones beneath the graveyard where Casimir was toiling over the bones of the dragon.

The thrall looked up guiltily, his hands black with oily residue. He wrung them out like some miser over a pile of coins and shuffled towards Radu.

'Progress?' The necrarch demanded.

The thrall shook his head. He was lying; Radu could always tell when his underlings were trying to keep things from him. They thought themselves so clever with their schemes but he knew better than to trust either of them. No, Casimir was hiding something. There had been progress.

Radu looked over the clutter of the laboratory but could see nothing out of place. In fact everything was exactly as he had left it, weeks ago, meaning that Casimir had been toiling over his own experiments while he was alone, not proceeding with the task Radu had charged him with. It was a petty betrayal but indicative of the thrall's burning ambition. He thought himself above menial labour. How long before he turned on his master? It was all dependent upon how hungry Casimir was for his freedom. Radu knew the burning need well enough; he had felt it for centuries, chafing beneath the constant battering of Korbhen's iron fist. He saw it now, smouldering in the thrall's dead eyes when he looked at him. The question was when, not if.

'The dragon will be reborn today. I feel it in my blood.'

'Master?'

'The song of the dragon, can you not feel it, Casimir? The ancient spirit of the beast is with us today. It is time. The beast will rise.'

He could see that the thrall had no idea what he meant when he talked about spirits and songs of the blood. Good, let the arrogant fool think there is some secret he has not yet learned. It will serve him well to be humbled a while, Radu thought.

'What is this?' Casimir asked, looking beyond the necrarch. The scar-faced warrior met the question with a curious tilt of the head, as though it had not yet considered who it had been, or who it had become.

'I am two. Bonifaz... called bringer of death,' the dead rasped. It was, Radu thought, almost as though the dead warrior had reasoned it out, not merely repeated the words he had heard.

'Another misfit for your menagerie, master?' the thrall said, though rather than looking at the scar-faced Bonifaz he stared squarely at Amsel beside him.

'Quite,' Radu said, twisting the implication subtly. 'Now, we must apply intellect to our quandary, not brute force. We are not thugs of magic; we are engineers of the arcane. There is dignity to what we do, majesty in what we fashion. So, my greedy brethren, let us bring this damned beast back, shall we?'

Radu walked across to the wall with its maddening scrawl of arcana and reached out, touching the scratches of a dozen aspects of the formulae. 'Yes, yes, yes,' he muttered fiercely, familiarising himself with the challenges of the chant he had begun to unravel so long ago. There was genius in the workings, the daemons buried deep in the details. Quickly he bustled across to the far side of the chamber, pulling open a draw and rooting through the collected miscellany until he found what he was looking for. The necrarch pulled out a candle quite unlike the others already laid out around the room. The black wax was merely a stub compared to the rest but that did not matter. He lit it quickly from one of the others and then moved into the centre of the room, shielding the flame so that it did not blow out. He planted the candle within the jaws of the great skull, allowing the molten wax to dribble on to the bone. Even as the candle burned down it did not burn out. Radu stepped out of the summoning circle, clapping his hands thrice, sharply. On the first clap the candles around the room guttered. On the second they failed, leaving only the soft glow of the alchemical lights. On the third the room was plunged into darkness.

For a moment there was only the sound of that tiny flickering flame of the black candle stub that he had placed within the dragon's skull, and then Radu spoke, framing the words of the invocation. Behind him both Amsel and Casimir took up the intonations of the chant. Slowly, inch by inch, the skull rose, the shadow beneath it receding as the lone candle burned on. The pitch of Radu's voice rose, the intensity of his words heightening as the invocation tripped off his tongue. The sound of bones gnashing against one another filled the darkness, as all across the floor, the skeletal remains of the dragon rose.

This time the fell beast's remains did not crumble and collapse. The words of binding held it.

CHAPTER NINETEEN

A Mad Man's Dreams
In the Shadow of the Howling Hills, Middenland
The Spring of Bloated Parasites, 2533

WOLFGANG FEHR RAN for days that bled into weeks. He had been travelling in circles, it seemed. Landmarks that he thought were familiar kept being rediscovered as he crested new hills. Lakes and trees all looked the same to him, but could they have actually been the same? He scavenged the barren landscape for berries and roots. They left an ache in his belly that went beyond hunger. He stumbled and staggered, ran on and collapsed, into the marshy ground, on the rocky abutments to the hills, in the shadow of the grim... It all blurred into one single hellish geography of torment.

He lay on his back looking up at the sun or the stars.

They were as unreachable as any other form of freedom.

He was a fugitive, a deserter, a traitor.

His life was forfeit.

He had thought about hunting Metzger's men. He harboured some vague notion of returning to the ranks of the army he had fled, a hero, buying back his life with the secrets he had learned from Casimir, and delivering the beast and his vile kin up to the swords of the Silberklinge.

Those thoughts were naïve. He was not a child. He knew that it didn't matter what secrets he brought back to Metzger, there could be no forgiveness for his crime. That was the hopeless truth of war: cowardice was a pandemic. If one ran, others would. He had undermined the cohesion of the crusade, worse he had betrayed his friends.

Only one fate awaited him if he ever returned.

So he banished all thoughts of going home.

His flesh was rank. It had not rained in weeks and the foetid swamp water had bled itself into the weave of his clothes. With the sun up he stank like one of the dead. He found a shallow stream, stripped and jumped in. The shock of icy water was like a fist buried deep in his gut; it doubled him over as he sought to minimise the cold. Even so, he submerged his head beneath the brackish water and came up spluttering for air. He swam for the bank, and then pushed off and swam for the opposite side, forcing his arms and legs to pump hard to get the blood circulating. Then he crawled up to get his clothes and soaked them. With no lye or soap he wasn't really cleaning them, but anything was better than the rancid reminders of the swamp wafting up from his breeches.

He crossed the river, and laid his sodden clothes out on the grass. Fehr lay on his back on the riverbank, utter exhaustion bullying him into sleep while the sun dried his skin and his clothes beside him.

His skin crawled as it contracted beneath the sun"s warmth. His dreams were haunted by faceless creatures stalking him. He awoke sweating, the remnants of the nightmare lingering. He struggled to unravel them before they whispered away to nothing and were forgotten like all the other dreams that had filled his flight from Kastell Metz. There was nothing substantive to hold onto, only subconscious symbolism. It wasn't difficult to work out what it all meant. He was a lamb in a world of wolves.

He rolled over onto his stomach and forced himself up. The clothes were still damp, but it didn't matter. He dressed quickly and set off again, moving towards the lowering sun. He saw curls of smoke in the distance, from a hearth fire. Without thinking about it, his path had carried him back towards people. He berated himself for his carelessness, but the gnawing in his belly kept him walking towards the distant farmhouse.

He started to run, in his head making up lies to tell the farmers in return for a hot meal and a bed for the night before he moved on. The first thing he noticed as he neared was the disrepair of the fences around the higher fields. The corn husks had been left to rot, unharvested from the year before. In the lower fields emaciated cattle had butted into the planks again and again, splintering them. Nails had torn loose leaving timbers dragging in the dirt. Despite the smoke coming from the chimney breast this was not a working farm. It had been once, but not for the best part of a season, which meant one thing: the farmer had died leaving his widow alone and unable to cope. All the lies he had been brewing fell apart as his mind raced.

A widow alone?

His first thought, and he hated himself for it, was that he could simply take the farmstead. How could a woman hope to stop him? He could snap her with his bare hands and bury her in the dirt of the yard and no one would be any the wiser. The thought was not his own, or at least he needed to believe that it wasn't. Growing up, Fehr had always believed he would be the hero of his own life. When the time came he would fight and do right by those he loved and who relied upon him. When Jessika had fallen he had fought. He had run in without thinking and buried his sword in the necromancer's bloated belly, but there had been no heroism in the charge, only grief. Now, instead of doing the right thing he entertained thoughts of butchering a helpless old woman and digging a hole in the yard to hide her remains from the wolves. Those were not the thoughts of a hero.

'What has happened to me?' he asked aloud. The wind had no answer for him. The sky above still clung to the last shreds of blue before fading into black, the clouds full and soft and white. It was an ordinary sky, unremarkable in any way, just as it was an ordinary wind. Yet it was not an unremarkable day. Far from it, it was the day when that naïve dream of heroism died once and for all.

He walked on through the fields of rotten corn husks and the chewed-out meadow of grazing cows, along the side of a narrow brook, all the while heading towards the curls of smoke.

The house was small, the white-wash daub of the walls cracked and broken to expose the wattle beneath. A rat scurried across his path, disappearing into the cattle shed. The old shed itself was dilapidated, the doors hanging drunkenly on their hinges. The stench of mulch and rotten hay filled his nostrils. The farmhouse was little better; the windows were covered with grime making it impossible to see in or out, and the timbers around them were riddled with woodworm. He walked around the outside of the house. There were no neighbours within sight or sound of the place, no dogs yapping. The tools he saw lying out had been abandoned for so long that they had begun to rust; the blade of the hand plough was red with the stuff.

Fehr knocked on the door and waited.

He heard the woman bustling about behind the door before she opened it. She peered out through the crack as though with myopic eyes, straining to see him in the failing light of the day. Fehr stepped back, making sure that she could see him properly, and smiled what he hoped was a warm, reassuring smile.

'What do you want? I ain't got no money, ain't got no work, neither, so if it's either of them two, you'd best be on your way,' the woman said. Fehr saw more of her as she opened the door wider. She was not the doddering old maid he had expected, far from it. She was no more than a handful of years older than him, plain but handsome, good breeding stock as his old man would have said.

He found his voice and said, 'I'll work for food and a bed for the night, nothing more. Put me to use around the farm, mending the fences, tending to the tools. I'll feed and water the livestock, clean out the cattle shed, whatever you need in return for a meal and a place to lie down out of the elements.'

'Ain't got nothin' that needs doing,' the woman said, crossing her arms defensively over her ample breasts as though that small gesture made her argument irrefutable.

He stepped forward, and she bristled. He knew then exactly how it must seem to a woman alone, a stranger who despite his recent dip in the river, looked like he had been dragged through a hedge backwards kicking and screaming, and was still pungent. He looked like what he was: trouble. He held up his hands. 'I'm not looking for trouble, honestly. I don't even need to set foot in the house. Let me sleep in the barn. I'll work my hands bloody for a decent bite, and then I'll move on. Please.'

'It ain't fittin' for a man to beg none,' she said, shaking her head.

'I am just so tired. Give me a blanket and I'll sleep in the straw. You won't be bothered by sight nor sound of me, I promise. I just need a place to sleep.'

'You'll work the fields?'

'Whatever you want.'

'Straighten up Klaus's tools?'

He nodded, assuming Klaus was her dead husband.

'For a meal and a blanket?'

He nodded again.

'Yer bad news, ain't you, boy? You gonna break in here in the middle of the night and cut my throat? That yer plan?'

Fehr shook his head. 'Just a bed,' he said again, but he couldn't shake the image of a hole dug right beneath his feet.

'I oughta drive you off my land, you know that, don't you?'

'But you won't,' he said, and it was not a question.

FEHR SLEPT IN the barn that first night, deeply and well for the first few hours, his dreams untroubled. He woke deep in the heart of it, sensing the woman's presence even though he could see nothing in the darkness but shadows and shapes.

He lay there silently, his face pressed into the mulch of the rotten straw, breathing deeply and listening to the sound of it swelling to fill his mind.

He did not move, but then, neither did she.

The woman stood framed in the doorway, content, it seemed, to watch him sleep.

He watched the deeper shadow where she stood with one eye open while he concentrated on keeping his breathing shallow and even, feigning restless sleep. Fehr shifted slightly. Instinctively, she matched his movement. The more intently he stared, the greater definition she took on as his eyes adjusted to the lack of light until he could see her clearly. A glint of silver in the moonlight caught his eye as she turned a meat carver over in her hand. After a dozen minutes of silent watching, she left him and returned to the farmhouse. He did not close his eyes until he heard the soft snick of the door closing.

He did not sleep for the rest of the night.

AFTER A BREAKFAST of hard bread and mouldy cheese, the woman worked him like a dog. He began by clearing out the barn and burning the rotten straw, scrubbing down the surfaces with water and lye, and patching the broken slate that let the rain leak through. He spent the afternoon with the whetstone grinding off the rust from the blade of the plough and the other hand tools, and oiling them once he had honed an edge. The widow came out to watch him work three times, standing a little way off with her arms folded across her chest, without saying anything. He did not even know her name. He supposed it was unimportant; after his meal he would be moving on. There was no need for them to be best friends forever. Come sundown she fed him a bowl of stew with chunks of meat in it. It was the best thing he'd eaten in months.

They talked a little.

'My name is Wolfgang,' he said, between spooning mouthfuls of the steaming soup down his gullet. He wiped his lips with the back of his hand.

'Irena,' she said.

'I will be moving on tonight, as I promised.'

She nodded. 'There is still a lot to be done,' she said after a moment. Fehr spooned a chunk of stringy meat into his mouth. 'Another day would not hurt. After all, it is getting late for being out on the road.

Stay the night if the barn suits your needs. I will not chase you out.'

'My thanks,' Fehr said.

So IT WENT for several days.

Fehr worked his fingers bloody, dead-heading the husks and burning the chafe, and then turning the soil and replanting, and night after night they shared a quiet meal. For a while it was as though he had stumbled into a normal life. He slept out in the barn, his muscles burning with the ache of honest toil, and it felt good. He didn't sleep deeply, and his dreams were often troubled.

For the first two nights Irena came out to watch him. She stood quietly in the doorway, the steel carver in her hand. She did not enter the barn, but simply stood in the doorway, watching.

At the start of his third day working the farm she invited him into the house. He came willingly. Irena talked more openly about her life and her man and how he had died a year before, and about the loneliness he had left her with. In turn, Fehr told her about Grimminhagen and Jessika and, in the darkest part of the night, about the dead.

'I see him each time I look in your eyes,' she said.

He rolled over onto his elbow and looked at her. She was not pretty, not in the girlish way of girls he had known, but nor was she ugly. She had a strength about her that lent its attraction. 'I am not going anywhere,' he promised, but even as he said it he knew it was one of those lover's promises, rash and unkeepable, like, 'I will always love you'.

'Your eyes!'

He reached up and touched his face. He could feel nothing wrong.

Then she started laughing at herself. 'I could have sworn they were yellow,' she said shaking her head, trying to dislodge the tricks of the candlelight.

'Are they yellow now?' Fehr asked.

She shook her head.

Fehr found himself in those long nights. It was during the day that he lost himself. He threw himself into the chores of the farm, seeding and furrowing, herding the cattle, milking the cows, clearing away the burned chaff and so much more. He relished the burning in his blood and for a while he forgot about Metzger and Bohme and the armies of the damned.

At night he dreamed, and in those dreams he was not hunted. In those dreams he was a father.

LIKE EVERY LIE he had ever told, it could not last.

It was not a normal life. In the daylight she could not bear his touch and would not look into his eyes, no matter what colour she thought them.

Fehr was on his knees in the top field when he saw the outriders coming down the hill. He hid, curled up beside the brambles, and watched them. He recognised one of the two men as Cort, the Silberklinge who had worked them so rigorously on the drill fields with Bonifaz and Bohme. His heart hammered against his breastbone. His hands sank into the rich black loam. He kept his head down. He did not dare move as the pair rode passed. He watched them all the way down to the farmhouse, praying fervently to whichever god or daemon watched over deserters that they would ride on by.

They did not.

The two warriors dismounted and approached the farmhouse.

Fehr was torn. He did not know whether to run towards them or as far away from them as he could. In the end he stood rooted to the spot, watching as Irene opened the door to them. After a moment both men turned to look up towards him. They were like ants down there but he fancied he could see the most minute of details: Cort raising a hand to shield his eyes from the morning sun, his companion licking his lips. He could smell them on the wind. They had ridden hard, their sweat dried into the wool of their under-tunics. He breathed it in. They were weary, tired of being afraid in this hostile hell of a place, so far from home with no means of return. Fehr licked his lips, not sure how he could know any of this. His blood pumped through his veins, his heart racing. He strained to hear, despite the mile or more distance between them. Cort and his companion saddled up and kicked their mounts into a gallop, riding straight for his hiding place.

She had turned him in. For a moment he could not believe it. He had thought… what? That she loved him? That they would be a normal happy family? He laughed bitterly at the ridiculousness of the notion. She could not even bear to look at him when the darkness did not hide his face.

Fehr ran.

They came fast, spurring there mounts on. The horses were grateful to be given their head. Like the men, they were frightened in this place, though their fears were more primal. They smelled death on the wind, death and predators. Fehr stumbled, grasped a wooden style and threw himself over it. The mud of his freshly furrowed field sucked at his feet slowing him down. The horses' hooves drummed loudly in his ears. He looked about frantically for a place to hide, but the landscape offered little shelter: a line of trees up ahead, the bank of the shallow stream off to the left, or wide open fields of burned chafe to the right. He ran for the water.

HE DID NOT reach it.

They rode him down long before he made it to the riverbank, driving him down onto his knees with blow after blow from the flats of their blades. Tears streamed down his cheeks as he collapsed, but he did not beg.

Cort dismounted and came up to stand on his shoulder. He grabbed a fistful of Fehr's hair and yanked his head back.

'I know their secrets,' he pleaded, clawing at the fist that held him.

'What rubbish is this?' the warrior's companion said contemptuously. He drove a booted foot into Fehr's gut. Cort's grip on his hair prevented him from doubling up in pain as a second savage kick hammered home.

'Hear me out,' Fehr gasped, refusing to plead even as he felt something inside him break as a third kick crunched into his ribs.

'Speak plain, and speak fast, boy,' Cort said. 'No lies.'

'I have seen inside the vampire's lair. I have lived

among his wretched kin. I know where they hide away. I can take you there.'

'Impossible!' Cort's companion rasped, driving in another brutal body blow. 'There is no lair! We have walked these hills for almost a month, being turned there and there about by the mists and the crooked paths. There is no castle here. There is only death. Kill the traitor!'

'No. That is not for us to decide,' the Silberklinge said, and then he brought the hilt of his sword down hard against Fehr's temple. The last thing he heard as he blacked out was the warrior saying, 'Bind him.'

CHAPTER TWENTY

The Hollow Man
In the Shadow of the Howling Hills, Middenland
The Spring of the Beast, 2533

KASPAR BOHME SAT with his head in his hands.

He felt hollow.

They had walked and walked, hunting high and low, but there was no sign of the enemy nor its lair. Before it had been easy, tracking the damned; their passage was burned into the earth, but after the confrontation at the pass the blight had faded. They followed signs that led them in circles. The mists that clung to the lower land hid the truth of the landscape, but even that couldn't explain the fact that they could walk towards mountain peaks for a week without appearing to get any closer, and then turn around and see the same peaks behind them, their path all turned around. It sapped the will and left the men thinking that they would never get the justice they craved, which in turn left the craving weakened, their resolve undone.

The crusade had taken its toll on all of them.

That was the truth.

They sat in the valley basin, either one hundred leagues from where they had battled with the dead, or just over the next line of hills. They were lost in more ways than one.

There was something inherently sickening about bringing judgement on one of his own men. He felt as though he had failed young Fehr, rather than the other way around. He was the experienced warrior. He was the one who had walked into hell and back time and again. He was the one who had watched his family and friends lowered into the ground. He was the one who had lived and died a thousand times. How could a mere boy be expected to pay such a huge price for a moment's panic? He wanted to tell the boy he was forgiven, that there was still a place for him among the men. Then he remembered the look of shock on Bonifaz's face as the arrow took him and he knew he could not. The men needed to see strength from him, not compassion. There was nothing to say that had Fehr held his nerve Bonifaz or any of the others would still be alive, but that was irrelevant. Fehr had run, as had others, and their sword-brothers had paid the price. Now it was up to the youngster to count the cost of that decision.

'I am sorry,' he said, and he was.

'I don't want to die,' the prisoner said without looking at him.

'That's the one truth of life, lad. We all do it.'

'There's no one left to mourn me,' Wolfgang Fehr told him. There was something terribly sad about a young man being so alone in the world, but that was the way of life. There were fathers who outlived their sons, no matter if they fathered one or one dozen. Life was not a list of checks and balances, it was cruel and capricious and ultimately unpredictable.

'There's no one left to shed a tear for me, either,' Bohme confided. 'That's a soldier's life. Why'd you do it? I saw you at Grimminhagen. You are no coward, lad. You saved us all that day, and don't think we've forgotten it. Soldiers have got long memories. We might not say much, but we don't forget. Had you been anyone else Cort would have brought your head back. You know that, right? That's all an officer needs to instil discipline, the head of a traitor. He brought you back because of the blood debt he felt he owed you, and now you're my problem.'

'I'm sorry,' Fehr said. It was too little, too late, of course, but it was the truth.

'I don't doubt it for a minute, lad. I just wish you had come back rather than kept on running. That's the part of this whole sorry mess that's going to cost you your life.'

There were only five hundred of the men left. The crusade had seen two hundred fall, and a hundred horses besides. The atmosphere in the camp was subdued. The realisation had settled in long since that they were not going home. This was Reinhardt Metzger's last crusade. It wasn't some noble adventure. The old man had come to this place to die, and he had brought them with them. Each and every one of the men was content with his fate. They were soldiers. This was what soldiers did: soldiers died.

The initial anger over the slaughter at Grimminhagen had faded, dulled into an ache and then more until all that remained was a deep festering need for justice. 'Every one of the men lost someone that day,' Bohme said, 'not just you lad. I know you feel like your life was ripped apart. I'm not going to waste platitudes on you, but tell me, why all the lies about being a prisoner in the vampire's lair when you were happily rutting away with the merry widow?'

'They aren't lies,' Fehr said, stubbornly.

'Really? You expect me to believe that you lived in a shanty town with the freaks and they didn't gut you like a fish? Why would they spare you, Wolfgang? That's what I don't understand. Why would they welcome you as one of your own? Your story doesn't ring true. In fact, it sounds to me like a story you've concocted in the hope of buying your life back. That's what I think.'

'I can show you,' Fehr said. This time there was an edge of desperation in his voice.

'Lead us into a trap, you mean?'

'No, you have to believe me. They want the vampire dead as much as we do.'

'My enemy's enemy is my friend,' Kaspar Bohme said.

'Yes! Exactly!'

'Do you take me for a fool, Wolfgang? Is that it? Do you look at me and see an idiot?'

'No.'

'Then why do you expect me to believe that they would send you back to us with a promise to betray their evil master? That all we have to do is follow you to the door of their hidden lair and they will throw the doors open in welcome? Can't you hear how preposterous it all sounds?'

'But it is true, I swear on my mother's–' he had been about to say life, 'grave.'

'Then Metzger will want to hear your story,' Bohme said, not unkindly. 'So you will die another day.'

'Two old men waging a war against the beast and his dead army,' Metzger said. The old man paced back and forth. They had struck camp three days before and it had begun to take on an air of permanence. The landscape was familiar in that he was sure he had seen the same line of trees and the same cleft of rocks three times since they had entered the hills. The castle was here. It had to be. The location fit everything he had ever heard about his original ancestral home. It had to be magic masking the landscape, turning them around and hiding the place in plain sight. There would be a way to break the charm and he would find it. He couldn't ignore the possibility that maybe the lad, Fehr, was the key. 'How pitiful does that sound in your ears, my friend? I have to admit that in mine it sounds like the grandest folly.'

'No more foolish than two young men going into battle alone against arrayed mercenaries of a petty baron because the bastard raped the daughter of a friend,' he said, chuckling bleakly at the memory.

'Ah, but those lads were fired up with the passion of youth and driven to see justice done. The world had yet to beat the idealism out of them.'

'Whereas the old men have seen all the shit the world has to throw in their faces and still want to see justice done. I don't know who I would be more afraid of,' Bohme said, wryly.

'Do you think he's telling the truth?'

'He is too frightened to spin such a compelling lie.'

'Perhaps not, perhaps he is just frightened enough.'

Bohme shook his head. 'You don't believe that.'

'You're right. I don't, but there's something ugly about his confession.'

'I know what you mean. Why would the damned simply let him walk away? It makes no sense unless it is a trap.'

Metzger shook his head and said, 'No, not that, though what you say is a reasonable assumption. No, why would they welcome him in the first place? That's the bigger question, I think.'

The old man rubbed at his thick growth of salt-and-pepper beard. His eyes were still as sharp as ever. The wind had its dander up and was blowing in fiercely from the west. The ground was still moist with rain from the morning. Looking at the sky another shower was moving in. That was spring in the lee of the hills: fierce winds, intermittent showers and glorious sunshine as the meadows bloomed all at once, life returning to the world.

'But not one we need to worry about,' Kaspar Bohme said as a tree frog crossed his path. 'Either we walk knowingly into the trap they've laid, or we don't. Strip away the bullshit and it is as simple as that.'

'Hardly simple, then, is it?' Metzger said.

Bohme grunted out a miserable laugh. 'I think I know you well enough to know just how simple it really is.'

'The lad'll lead us to their door. They'll be expecting us but this time we'll be expecting them as well. That makes all the difference in the world. We won't be walking blind into some ambush on the hill. There're five hundred of us and a whole hell of a lot of them, so we'll end up fighting like bastards when they come at us. If there're ten more of them to every one of us we'll have to kill ten of them each. It'll be bloody but we'll kill every last one of the bastards or die trying.'

'Sounds like a plan,' Bohme said. 'One last grand huzzah!'

'One last grand huzzah,' Metzger agreed.

'ARE WE GOING to die?'

'Eventually, but not today. I don't know about you, but today I intend to live,' Kaspar Bohme told the young man at his side. It was true. They would not die today, but that did not mean they wouldn't die tomorrow.

They had struck camp and started marching that morning, and had walked deep into the day, following Fehr's directions. He did not trust the lad.

'Then why have we left the wagons?'

It was a question that only had one answer: because the wagons would slow them down, and because after tomorrow it was unlikely that any of them would need to feed again. They would meet the enemy on the field of battle and they would do what soldiers did best. They would die. It wasn't the kind of answer that needed to be said aloud, but they had been through enough together to be spared lies, 'Because tomorrow is another day.'

The young man nodded and said, 'Does it ever frighten you, sir?'

Kaspar Bohme looked at the young man. In truth he couldn't have been much more than a boy, but the last few months had taken their toll on his youth. He carried the grief of the world on his young shoulders. 'I've had a good life, lad. I went to war before you were born, and I've yet to go home. When I was twenty my best friends Maren and Nate died as they stood on either side of me. When I was twenty-three it was Horst and Mort. When I was twenty-four it was Lucan. When I was twenty-six it was Felix and Kurt and Darius. I've lost more friends than most men have in a life-time. If I die tomorrow they'll be there waiting to tell me how much better swordsmen they were, or better with the women or funnier, or more attractive, or simply how much more they could drink than me. I'll be back among the easy camaraderie of friends. That doesn't seem so bad to me.'

'Do you really believe that? That the dead will be waiting for us when we fall?'

'No,' Bohme admitted, 'but it makes a pleasant thought, doesn't it?'

The young man nodded but there was disappointment in his eyes.

'What's your name, soldier?'

'Kane.'

'Well, Kane, when the fighting begins, stick by my side, eh? A soldier needs a man he can trust watching his back and I can't think of anyone else here I'd rather have looking out for me.'

'Sir,' the young man said, 'but what if?'

'There are no what ifs, soldier. We deal in absolutes, your sword and my sword. That's what the world comes down to in the end.' He patted the young soldier on the shoulder and rode to the back of the line, where Metzger was riding with Cort.

'You were right,' he told the old man, without telling him what about.

THEY DRAGGED FEHR along in chains like a dog.

When the others ate, he was given a cup of water. When the others drank he was left to go thirsty. He neither begged for more nor complained.

They no longer followed any roads, trudging across the country. The remnants of Ableron's Twin-Tailed Comets struggled with their mounts. None of the horses of the Silberklinge survived. The animals had been put down for their meat when they started to founder in the impossible terrain, tearing fetlocks and splintering hooves, nature humbling the mighty animals. Their deaths brought the men more time in their quest. The ground beneath their feet turned to marsh, bogging them down. Fehr constantly looked around, trying to get his bearings. He knew they were close to the castle of the damned and deformed, that the marsh would eventually cede to the tidal lake, but memory was a tricky thing at the best of times and one strand of trees and outcropping of rock looked much like another with someone whipping your back.

'Where now?' Cort rasped, kicking him forward.

Fehr shook his head, trying to clear it. The chain chafed at his neck, burning into his skin where it rubbed. He stumbled forward on his hands and knees. Then he caught the scent of the freaks, so close, over the next rise, and wondered why the others couldn't smell it. It reeked.

'This way,' he said, pointing towards the lightning-shattered peak two miles distant across the boggy plain. 'Over the ridge there is a body of water, and beyond that, the castle.'

'So we are close?'

Fehr nodded. 'A league, no more.'

'So we are close enough for the fighting to begin at any minute?'

Fehr had no answer for that.

The warrior drew his sword and took a moment to very deliberately study the blade for nicks. Satisfied, he said, 'Then we're close enough for me not to want a whoreson like you within a mile of me.'

Cort hammered the pommel of his blade into the back of Fehr's skull, leaving him sprawling in the boggy ground like a drunkard. 'Get this bastard in the brig,' he ordered two younger men, survivors of the Grimminhagen militia. They ran to do his bidding, dragging the groggy Fehr between them to the cramped wooden box that had been cobbled together by two of the men the night before. A deep-throated feral growl rasped between Fehr's clenched teeth as he lashed out, trying to bite and claw at his captors. A moment later, wild-eyed with terror he was on the floor at their feet whimpering and begging, 'Help me… I don't know what is happening to me. It burns. My blood burns.' They hit him again, savagely this time, knocking him insensate. They kicked him when he was down, and then manacled his wrists and ankles, shackling him before they lifted the lid and forced Fehr inside. Before he could so much as scream, they slammed the lid back down on him, and while one leaned all of his weight on the box, the other nailed him up inside.

Even in the relative chill of the spring, in an hour the claustrophobic box would be unbearably hot, the air breathed so many times that all of the goodness would have been sucked out of it by fear. In three hours the dead air would be suffocating, and but for the small hand-sized hole cut away from one of the timbers, in five it would be a coffin.

That small hole was no mercy though, it merely prolonged the inevitable, another layer to the torture of the box.

The hole was set low enough for the deserter to reach out with his fingers for any small scraps the men he had betrayed might offer. It was a barbaric punishment, but it was not death. Though given a day or two in the box Fehr might wish it was.

But then in a day or two they would almost certainly all be dead so what did it matter if the traitor died chained in a box or free with a sword in his hand?

The two men hoisted the box on the carrying poles up onto their shoulders and marched, bringing up the rear of the line. The ground sucked and pulled at their feet, as though trying to drag them down. They marched out without complaint, even as the weight of the carrying poles dug deeper and deeper into their shoulders. It was not pity for the prisoner that stayed their tongues, it was fear of what waited beyond the shattered peak.

Grey wraiths of mist clung to the field, coiling up towards the steely sky.

The boggy ground made it difficult to keep rank and file as they marched, the lines losing all order and cohesion the deeper they got into the wet ground. For the first five hundred or so feet the earth retained the semblance of solidity but that quickly gave way to a shifting landscape of tussocks of tall reeds and thick grasses and instead of the brackish water sloshing around their ankles it was up to their waists making any kind of haste impossible.

'We're sitting ducks out here,' Bohme commented to Metzger. The old man didn't disagree. He checked the prevalent wind direction, licking his finger and holding it up to the breeze, and then gestured for the front line to wait for the rear to fall into line. Bohme turned to watch the rabble splashing and stumbling behind them. The sight did little to instil confidence in him. He watched one of the militia boys go over, screaming like a girl as he fell much to the amusement of the men behind him. That amusement died in their mouths, stillborn, as the marsh water around him turned red with his blood. His body buoyed back up to the surface. His throat had been torn out. It was as sudden and shocking as that.

The closest to the soldier's corpse splashed back away from it, reaching instinctively for their weapons.

Two more went down a moment later, kicking and splashing wildly as they went under the black water. They were dead before they were fully submerged.

'What the hell's happening?' Cort shouted.

'Everyone stop! Stand still!' Bohme yelled, eyes frantically scanning the surface of the black marsh water. Discipline was a soldier's closest friend. The order got through the panic to them. To a man they stopped mid-step. The bog became eerily silent, the only sound the low susurrus of bodies swimming stealthily beneath the dark water.

Bohme looked down and saw a dead face looking up at him, the reflection of the lowering sun shimmering on the skin of the water. He stabbed down fiercely with the point of his sword, driving it into the corpse's rotting skull. The blow severed the dead man's spinal column and left the decapitated head to drift away with the undertow. Flaxen hair fanned out like the fingers of a grasping miser, tangling around his legs.

'They're under the water!' one of the men shouted, pointing at the eddies caused by the sinuous corpses as they curled about the men.

A moment later a fourth soldier cried out, dragged from his feet by mottled hands.

Metzger boomed out a stream of orders, and the men struggled to respond to them but it was impossible to obey. They stumbled and splashed trying to form up, and fell back as the ground shifted, leaving them wide open again. By stopping them he had turned them into ripe plucking. 'Form up! Form up!' he bellowed. 'Defensive lines! Protect your right!'

Another man hacked at the water, seeing one of the dead drift up against his thigh and reach up for him. Then all was pandemonium as the dead rose up out of the water, pallid skin and mottled bone grasping at the armour of the living. A dozen warriors were dragged under, a dozen more thrown off balance and left floundering as the corpses swarmed over them. Swords hit the water and sank beneath the surface. Men screamed, slashing out desperately, not caring what they hit.

Kaspar Bohme swung his sword at the head of a putrid corpse. The creature threw up an arm in desperate defence, the blade slicing off the bone and burying itself in the dead man's throat. Bohme wrenched it clear. Another blow scythed in at him from the left. Bohme took it on his shield and reversed a cut, hacking into this new foe's thigh deeply enough to sever the tendon that kept the corpse standing. All around him the battle was joined. It was a mêlée. The living fought back to back, driving back the dead only to have more corpses swim up around their legs and drag them down, screaming, into the black water.

For a moment he was clear of the slaughter. Bohme saw that Metzger had hacked his way into the very thick of the furore, his blade dripping with the gore of the dead. The old man was surrounded on three sides by clutching dead with rusty blades. They swung ponderously, Metzger battering the blows aside as he stepped in close and hammered his shield into the face of the nearest, driving the dead man off his feet.

Bohme pushed through the deep water to meet him. He caught a surge of movement out of the corner of his eye and barely brought his shield around in time to block the blow from a rotten axe. The wooden shaft shattered in the corpse's wretched grip, leaving the axe-head buried in Bohme's shield. Unbalanced, Bohme lost his footing and fell sideways, sending up a spume of stinking swamp water as he slashed out desperately with his sword. The blade lodged in the ribcage of a corpse. Before he could wrench it free another empty-eyed skull lurched up in front of him swinging a huge hand-and-a-half bastard sword.

Bohme threw himself forward, relinquishing his hold on his sword in a desperate attempt to dodge the corpse's almighty swing aimed at parting his head from his shoulders. He barely made it beneath the blade, but hit the water hard, and fell to his knees, up to his chest in the turgid water. The corpse thundered another scything blade at Bohme. The sword slashed across his face.

Then the young militia boy, Kane, hurled himself bodily at the corpse, taking its wild blow on the flat of his blade and even as the impact staggered him, reversing his swing to slash straight up through the dead man's chest. Kane's sword opened the corpse from stem to sternum with clinical precision. He deflected a weak blow from his dead foe, and then drove the point of his sword through the reanimated creature's heart. He wrenched it free and delivered the coup de grace, beheading the corpse and kicking it aside contemptuously.

Bohme crawled forward on his hands and knees, the water getting in his mouth as he wrested his sword free of the corpse.

He nodded to the lad and held out his hand to be helped up.

The two fought side by side as the dead came at them again and again from below the water, rising up, dripping the ichor of the swamp as they lurched forward with decrepit weapons. 'Hold the line!' Metzger shouted, crashing his blade into a skull and splitting it. Still the dead came up, snaking up around the legs of the living and dragging them down into the murky depths of the bog even as they cut and thrust and parried, fighting for their lives.

The sounds of the battle haunted the landscape.

Metzger's men were in disarray, his shouts for discipline falling on deaf ears as the invisible threat from the black water dragged more and more of them down.

The box bearers dropped the prison. The box fell on its side, the air hole in the water. From within Bohme could hear the desperate hammering of Wolfgang Fehr as the black water swelled up around him. For a moment he thought about letting the lad drown. Then he fought his way through to the box and heaved it up so that the hole was out of the water.

More than one hundred of them drowned in under an hour.

Wolfgang Fehr did not.

Bohme could read a battle. He had been in enough of them to sense the moment when the balance shifted. The elements of surprise and horror had faded and the dead were no longer coming at them in relentless waves. Down the line, Cort issued a piercing cry and threw himself forward, hacking into the dead so ferociously that he drove the creatures back and back. The Silberklinge grinned wildly as his blade opened a path through the dead. 'Drive them back to the pits of the underworld!' The warrior yelled, to the cheers of the men at arms. The living rushed forward, pushing the dead further into retreat, until Bohme and the others were standing in the 'V' left by the shattered peak, looking down at the dead as they fled towards the lakes.

METZGER'S FACE PALED as he looked up at the walls of the castle and the towers.

Dark clouds festered in the sky above it.

A storm was brewing.

The castle seemed to stand betwixt and between glittering expanses of water, its crumbling gothic walls and towers filling the glowering sky. It was like a vision taken from his childhood memories and warped through the filter of a nightmare. What should have been familiar and comfortable was utterly alien and wrong, and yet it seemed somehow fitting. Good men died in the rain not in the glorious spring sunshine, fighting before the portals of nightmarish bastions, not family homes, he thought bitterly as he stared at the machicolations. His men, the men he had dragged from their homes and families on his damned crusade, charged down the hill towards the lakes, brandishing their weapons and hammering them against their shields in a cacophony meant to scare their undead enemy. It had little or no effect other than to break the silence. That in itself was a blessing.

This was his birthright. It seemed impossible looking at it now but he knew it was true. This was the true Kastell Metz. This was the place where Felix Metzger had fallen to the necrarch fighting the hopeless fight for what he believed in. This was the secret shame of his clan, the ancestral home they had lost to the mad dead. He did not know what he had expected to feel, confronted with the past, but it wasn't this. He stared at the walls, and the huge lakes traversed by a wide causeway and felt nothing, no pull of homecoming, no vengeful return. Instead there was an immense hollowness within him.

He stood there, aside from his men, alone on the hill. He was the last man to go over the top.

As he walked down the scree, he was reminded of so many truths about his life. He was a hollow man on a fool's quest for an unattainable justice. It was little wonder he felt empty as he stared at the home he had never known.

THE LIVING DROVE the dead down the hill and into the cleft between the lakes where the causeway ran. Roaring defiance, the men of Grimminhagen charged after them. It was chaos, but there was an element of order within it. The living came together in a driving wedge, Cort at the front, his sword slicing again and again at the stumbling dead. It was butchery. Stripped of their hiding places beneath the black water the dead were a slow, lumbering foe. But something niggled at the back of Bohme's mind. The living ran and screamed anger and hate at the fiends that had snatched away their friends, and the dead were pushed back towards the castle gates.

He had fought the dead before.

This was the first time he had seen the enemy routed.

'Back!' he yelled, realising it was a trap. 'Pull back!'

No one could hear him above the clamour of combat. The chill ghost of fear gripped the nape of his neck as he stared down at Cort rushing the dead. The Silberklinge's charge drove the shambling enemy back onto the first slick cobbles of the causeway.

Slick.

The failing light clung to the lichen encrusting the stone like oil.

It took him a moment for it all to fall into place: the dead driven back, slick cobbles.

It was there, in the front of his mind but he couldn't grasp it. Something about the landscape was wrong. He stared and stared, frantically trying to see what it was, but he couldn't see anything that he hadn't been warned about by young Fehr. It was a blighted place, of that there could be no doubt but it was more than that.

Dark clouds gathered overhead, a storm front rolling in. There was a palpable shift in the air pressure.

Cort drove the dead towards the middle of the causeway fifty men with him. Bohme stared at the cobbled causeway and the skeletal limbs of the trees beyond the far shore of the lake. The dead splashed and floundered, stumbling back towards the huge gates of the castle as Cort cleaved into their panicked ranks. Above them ravens circled, cawing hungrily as they rode the winds.

The box carriers pushed by him, grunting and straining under the weight of the mobile prison. He could hear Fehr weeping inside. Fehr. What was it the lad had said when he was sketching out the lie of the land?

Something about the lake.

The castle is bordered by a huge lake.

Not: the castle is bordered by two huge lakes.

There was no mention of a causeway dividing the lake.

It hit him as he looked up at the walls of the castle and saw the misshapen silhouette of a man gazing down over the fighting. It all came together inside his head. The dead hadn't been driven back. They were mindless puppets; they had baited the trap and drawn the living forward onto the causeway and into the middle of the lake.

'Cort! Cort! Get them back from the causeway! Look at the water!'

He started to run down the scree covered slope, skidding and sliding as his arms pin-wheeled desperately. He did not fall. Bohme yelled at the top of his voice but with the discordant symphony of the mêlée, his voice couldn't carry to those out in the middle of the no-man's land that until recently had been submerged beneath the water. He yelled again, crying himself hoarse, and still his warnings couldn't rise above the din.

It was subtle at first, the lake water lapping against the edge of the causeway's cobbles as whatever force had driven a tidal line down the centre of it ceded its hold over the water. Then the water was up around their ankles, and deeper, around their knees in a matter of moments. The men out there realised then, turning to flee the trap before its watery jaws could snap shut and drown them.

It was too late.

The water banked up into steep waves that came crashing down, the sheer elemental force of nature surging around the living, driving them off their feet and under the frothing white-caps. It carried them off the relative safety of the causeway and out into the deeps of the lake where more submerged dead swam, grasping and clutching and keeping the desperate soldiers from getting their heads above the waterline.

Then they were down and they were drowning, their forgotten blades dragged away from limp fingers to the bottom of the lake.

He stood watching in horror as one by one the corpses of his friends bobbed back to the surface of the suddenly placid lake, only for the weight of their armour to drag them back down as the air leaked out of their dead lungs.

Within minutes they were gone, and it was as if they had never been.

Bohme stood on the edge of the lake, balanced as though hovering over the edge of forever beyond which the endless night waited, staring at the still waters, and then at the cackling figure on the wall walk.

The emaciated hunchback threw up his arms as though trying to pull down the sky and the storm broke. A single jag of lightning and a deep rumble of thunder heralded the downpour. He saw a ghost within the white light: Bonifaz. There was a cruelty to his face in death that had never been there in life, marking him more indelibly than his twin scars ever had.

There were no more screams.

CHAPTER TWENTY-ONE

Blood Crazy
Outside the Walls of Kastell Metz, Deep in the Heart of the
Howling Hills, Middenland
The Winter of Scars and Grief, 2533

'IT BURNS, IT burns in my veins,' Wolfgang Fehr whimpered, scratching at the wooden walls of his prison. 'Help me.'

But no one heard him.

The darkness within the box ate him, gnawing into his mind. His hands were warm and sticky where his nails had been pulled back and broken off with his desperate clawing. It was only when he reached down for the tiny hole that he saw the blood and the damage his claustrophobic fear had wrought.

The sounds of fighting had been dampened by the wood, the anguished screams of the dying muted. Now there was only darkness and silence. Even the motion of the box had ceased leaving him lacking any sensory perception beyond the pain of his ruined fingers and the fire in his blood.

It was worsening by the hour.

At first he had believed it to be a sickness, swamp fever or even the blood plague ravaging his veins, but as it progressed he knew it wasn't. Primal images filled his mind, visions driven by the most basic, animalistic urges. The hallucinations took on integrity and shape and soon became more real to him than the walls of the box and the darkness.

Inhaling the musty air of the wooden prison he breathed in the cadaverous reek of the slaughter. Closing his eyes he found he could differentiate the disparate tangs and textures of the blood, old dead blood against the fresh vital blood spilled by the living. That chilled him.

'What is happening to me?' he begged the darkness.

It harboured no answers, only more secrets.

There was another sort of blood, too, neither living nor dead, but tainted like his. He felt its pull in his blood, not in his nose. It was thicker, bonded to the world in a way the spilled blood wasn't.

Fehr clawed at the wood, needing to be out of the choking confines of the box. He pressed his face up against the tiny hole, sucking desperately at the air.

Time did not merely lose its meaning it ceased to be.

The world was reduced to fragments: one when the box shook as someone kicked it; another as someone left a canteen of water within scrabbling distance of his fingertips, though he could not drink it because the hole was too small; and another as the voices came, whispering up against the hole, goading him to die. Finally he lost control of his bodily functions, the pain in his gut and bowels so intense that he could do nothing to prevent them from emptying. The stench of faeces and the acrid tang of urine transformed his prison into a new kind of hell.

As the hallucinations worsened he imagined he was a wolf, and saw his own yellow eyes burning back at him. He prowled, hunting, stalking the beasts whose rank blood seared his nostrils. He saw himself rending flesh with tooth and claw, lapping greedily at open wounds and somewhere within those dreams his mind broke.

The images shifted in intensity and focus as the beast rose from within. His body responded in kind, the arc of his spine lengthening, the grasp of his hands becoming claw-like.

The darkness existed for a single reason: to taunt him with the smell of blood.

Desperately, he pushed at the walls of his prison.

'Let me out! Help me! Please! Please! Let me out!' He roared and raged, hammering against the walls of his stinking prison, his mind conflicted as the human struggled to stave off the all-consuming rage of the beast. It was a fight against nature that he could not hope to win. Somewhere in that timelessness the man that had been Wolfgang Fehr ceased to be. All that remained was the mind of the wolf.

Then the walls of his prison came tumbling down.

REST WAS IMPOSSIBLE, but without it they were doomed.

In the grim shadow of the beast's castle, Metzger ordered the men to strike camp. After the initial ambush the dead had not sallied forth, content to barricade themselves up behind the high walls where they could not be reached. With the sun fully risen they would not strike out. The men needed to rest whenever they could. With the lake between them Metzger wrestled with guilt. His men were down beneath the water somewhere. They deserved a Sigmarite burial, or at least they deserved not to bloat and rot and float to the surface in a month's time, ruined husks with no trace of their humanity left to them.

But what could he do? Dive after them and drag them back? Hardly.

Let them rot?

He could see little alternative, and it sickened him.

This was his death, not theirs, his last hurrah. A silent tear rolled down his cheek, over the bone. 'How did it come to this?' he asked the man beside him.

Kaspar Bohme shook his head and said, 'The same way it always does, my friend. The same way it always does.'

Four hundred and fifty of the seven hundred men who had left Grimminhagen still looked to him for leadership. None of the Twin-Tailed Comet had survived the lake. He felt the sharp twinge of pain in his left side but refused to acknowledge it.

'We can't very well go under the walls,' he said, looking at the lake. Using sappers was out of the question; the water from the lake would have seeped down to permeate deep into the rock undermining any chance they had of digging tunnels beneath the walls. The weight of the earth pressing down on them would cave in any excavation they tried and almost certainly result in dozens of men being buried alive. He could not imagine a worse fate. 'And a protracted siege is out of the question. We don't have the supplies or the men to starve them out or batter down the gates.'

'Not to mention how you starve the dead out of anywhere,' Bohme said. It was a poor joke.

Reinhardt Metzger ignored him.

He only had eyes for the man standing on the battlements who was in turn watching them.

'Is that...?' He didn't have the stomach to name the dead man looking down at them. His stomach twisted, dread taking root. He couldn't be sure who he was seeing. He didn't want to be sure. It was impossible. It was horrible. He stared up at the man on the wall.

Bohme nodded. 'Bonifaz.'

'He looks different.'

'He's dead,' Bohme said, 'of course he looks different.'

'No, it's more than that. He looks... inhuman.'

'He is waiting for us,' Bohme said. The notion, now voiced, sent a cold shiver down the ridges of Metzger's spine. 'He always believed he was the best of us.'

'His chance to test that belief will come,' Metzger said bleakly. No threat, no bluster.

'Do you think they will come at us tonight?'

'Why would they? We're like flies buzzing around their stinking carcass. Soon enough they'll reach out to swat us away, but right now we are barely even a nuisance.'

'So what say we make a nuisance of ourselves?' Bohme said, with a fierce grin.

'What do you have in mind?'

Before he could answer, the sound of wood rending tore through the thick silence. It took Metzger a moment to place the sound, so out of place was it in this blighted place. He turned as the side of the brig-box splintered and Fehr's hand came reaching out through the tear. Only it couldn't have been the lad's hand, Metzger thought, seeing the thick clumps of reddish hair that clung to the back of it. The fingers were inhumanly long, the joints twisted and spindly, hooking the misshapen hand into a vicious claw. The wood frame buckled against the pressure from within, the metal nails tearing free. The rest of the arm, as weirdly malformed as the hand emerged, the musculature distorted and overly thick around the joints. Then the box shattered completely and the wild-eyed Fehr lunged out of the debris, his face bestial with rage as he ripped away at the wood with his bare hands.

The manacles shackling the deserter stretched tight as he threw his arms up above his head, forcing them apart beyond the limits of the metal's tensile strength. The chain snapped with a shocking finality. Fehr launched himself at the nearest man, lashing out with the dangling chains transforming his imprisonment into a weapon. He slashed the man across the face again and again, moving with dizzying speed. The chains bit deep, cutting mercilessly through the soft flesh of the soldier's cheek and eyes. Again and again Fehr lashed out, driving the man to his knees and then onto his back, screaming as the chains cut him up.

Fehr crouched, chains dangling, and looked left and right, his face contorted with animalistic rage.

Moving with unerring agility he threw himself forward, rolling away from a wild sword slash, and came up on his bare feet, kicking up dirt and dust from the lake shore as he scrabbled backwards. He threw back his head and barked at the rising moon.

Two of Metzger's militia moved to intercept the prisoner before he could flee, only Fehr never intended to flee, that much was obvious by the way he rounded on his would-be captors and snapped them like brittle twigs. His hands reached out, grabbing the closest of the men by the wrist and forcing it back to the point beyond which it could bend, until it snapped. Then he jumped to his feet, wrenched the soldier's arm out of its socket and dragged him in close. Fehr's mouth opened in a feral snarl, and then with shocking swiftness, Fehr ducked his head and tore his teeth into the screaming man's throat, ripping the flesh out in one bloody mouthful.

Metzger ran towards Fehr as the deserter spat a clotted lump of flesh out onto the dirt at his feet.

The second man died through carelessness. He came too close to the bloodstained chains. Fehr lashed out, but not to hit or hurt. The metal links wrapped around the man's legs and with one quick tug Fehr pulled his feet out from under him. He fell upon the man, biting through the cartilage of his nose and tearing it off in a fountain of blood. The man's screams were as sickening as they were short-lived. Swallowing down the meat and gristle, Fehr sank his claws into the soft stuff of his eyes, hooking deep into his skull as he jerked his head back and bit deep into the pulsing vein at his throat, driven crazy by the siren song of the rich blood.

He pushed himself forward, into a crouch, ready to spring at anyone who came too close.

Fehr looked at the old warrior; and such pain and grief there was in the jaundiced eyes that looked back at him. In that moment, gazes locked, the beast that Fehr had become was painfully obvious to Metzger. Stripped of his humanity, abused by his captors, caged and bound, beaten and humiliated, he had lost whatever held his mind together only to find some deep buried primal instinct: the animal within. He howled again, all traces of humanity shorn from his ragged cry.

Metzger moved in cautiously.

Fehr lowered his head, a low growl purring deep in his throat.

Then he spoke, only two words, 'Help me.'

Metzger nodded, reaching around to draw his sword.

'In death there is mercy,' Metzger said, and he almost believed it.

CHAPTER TWENTY-TWO

Wolf's Hour
Outside the Walls of Kastell Metz, Deep in the Heart of the
Howling Hills, Middenland
The Winter of Scars and Grief, 2533

BEHIND THE OLD man and the beast, their dead friends rose up out of their watery grave.

Skulls broke the placid skin of the lake, followed by lank hair tangled with strands of water-weed and scum, and worm-eaten eyes and mottled skin. One by one the drowned resurfaced. Many of them bore no weapons but then they needed none. They came out of the water, moving slowly with the sickening grace of swans gliding over the smooth surface of black water.

The filth of the lake clung to their armour and flesh.

The shell of the warrior, Cort Angiers, opened its mouth to scream. Lake water bubbled and frothed out of it, followed by a low keening moan that slowly shaped itself into a word, a challenge: 'Metzzzzgeeeer-rrr!'

* * *

REINHARDT METZGER HEARD his name but did not turn to face his challenger. His knuckles whitened as his fingers closed around the leather wrap of his sword's hilt and slid the blade out of its sheath. The blade sang as he dragged it free.

It felt utterly natural in his hand, like an old friend.

He felt a stab of pain, sharp like needles piercing his chest, and numbness flow down his left arm. It was as though the blood were somehow leaving that side of him empty. He clenched his fist and hammered it off his breastplate in defiance of the pain and in challenge to the beast that he faced.

Fehr sprang.

AT THE SOUND of Metzger's name, coming out of the water like the voice of Manann himself, Kaspar Bohme turned. His hand went instinctively for his blade, but he fumbled it. The cold steel fell through his fingers as the sight of his fallen comrades emerging from the lake ripped into that part of his mind where fear lay nascent.

'Look to the water!' He yelled, bending to retrieve his blade.

The men were ill-prepared, stripped out of their armour, swords laid aside as they readied themselves for the respite of night before the dawn of war. There would be no sleep this night. Beyond the dead, Bohme saw the hunchbacked figure up on the high tower, a madness of ravens circling around him like a feathered cyclone, and beside him the unmistakable bulk of the dead Bonifaz. The hunchback cavorted like some demented dancer, throwing himself around like some dervish. With the moon at their back the pair looked like a faceless manifestation of death.

Bohme straightened. His sword hand itched.

'To me!' he shouted, and ran headlong at the line of corpses shuffling up the lake's shore.

The men reacted, grabbing shields and swords. Some ran bare foot, others with breastplates partially strapped in place, buckles hanging loose. They charged down to join Bohme as he ducked beneath gasping hands and drove his blade hilt deep into a familiar face. Dragging it clear, he spun to block a blow raking in from the left, taking it on his arm. The pain shivered through him, almost wrenching the blade from his hand. He hacked into a third drowned knight, his blade clattering off the dead man's rusted breastplate and sliding up into the bloated white flesh of his neck. The blow barely slowed the drowned man. Bohme stepped in and drove his fist into the dead man's face, snapping his head back, and then brought his sword arm up savagely, the blade sliding up through the gap between the plate and skin, disembowelling the corpse. His insides spilled down over the blade, soaking Bohme's hand with blood and gore. Bohme slid the sword clear.

Then he was no longer alone in the shallow water, cutting and splashing and struggling desperately to stay on his feet as the lake-bed shifted treacherously beneath them.

The world around him was reduced to sword and bone.

Bohme broke away from a clinch, forced to draw a short stabbing dagger from his opponent's sodden belt and ram it into the dead man's gut to buy himself a few feet of calm. He found himself once again side by side with the young warrior, Kane. There were no grins between them this time. Tears stained the youngster's cheeks as he fought, all discipline gone from his movement. Seeing the facial similarities between Kane and the vile corpse he hacked away wildly at, Bohme knew all too well why.

He stepped in close enough to reach around and drive the point of the dagger deep into the eye of the warrior's brother. He dragged it clear and stepped away from the corpse as it fell, the motors of its brain ruined.

Still Kane slashed wildly at the air where his brother had stood, his face torn with grief as his blade slashed again and again at nothing. He fell to his knees in the shallow water and threw his head back in a pitiful scream as his brother's corpse brushed up against his side. He reached down, sobbing, to cradle the dead man in his arms, oblivious to the battle raging around him. He was locked in his own personal hell.

Bohme could not comfort him, but he could keep him safe as the dead came on again and again.

FEHR HIT METZGER so hard that the old man staggered back and fell, sprawling in the mud. He lost his grip on his sword, and then lost sight of it as Fehr came down on top of him.

Nothing of the man remained in the deserter's face. Even the bone structure beneath it had shifted, elongating and becoming almost lupine beneath the blazing yellow eyes. Unshaven facial hair grew in across his cheeks and up to those jaundiced eyes, while his hairline had crept down low across his brow, and even as the lost boy looked down at the old man, his wild hair became more of a mane than a ragged mop. His mouth opened on sharp canines while his jaw distended like a snout. The transformation was as horrific as it was incredible.

There were tears in his yellow eyes as he reached out with thickly muscled arms and wrapped the rusted chains that dangled from his wrists around Metzger's throat.

'Help me,' he pleaded, slowly choking the life out of the old man. Then he shook his head brutally, and whatever last vestiges of Wolfgang Fehr clung to the beast's sense of self were gone. 'I can smell death within you, old man. It's in your blood. Killing you will be a mercy.'

'You talk… too… much,' Metzger said, the chain biting deep into his throat as it choked off his breath. He reached up, clawing weakly at the length of chain with his left hand in a desperate subterfuge. He reached down with his right hand, fumbling blindly for the hilt of the dagger sheathed in his boot. His fingers snagged it, drawing it an inch out of the leather, and then another inch until they could wrap around the leather binding.

The chains bit so deep into his windpipe that he couldn't swallow down even a mouthful of air.

He flapped weakly at his throat with his left hand and closed his eyes, counting silently to five in his mind. Then he brought his right hand up with terrible swiftness, ramming the short blade into the side of the beast's neck. It went in up to the hilt, the metal cutting easily through the soft flesh of Fehr's throat, opening the thick vein and parting the windpipe in a single cut. Metzger wrenched the dagger's hilt sideways, opening the wound wide. The wet sound of the beast sucking air through the ragged hole was accompanied by a weak, gurgling rasp as Fehr's eyes rolled up inside his skull and he slumped forward.

Metzger rolled out from beneath him, untangling the chains from around his throat. Gasping hard, trying to swallow down gulp after gulp of air, he rolled Fehr over. The taint of Chaos that had so brutally transformed the boy into a monster remained. He had died a beast, not a man, but there was some small mercy in his dead eyes. The yellow stain had left them. There was hope at least that his soul had gone on to Morr released and that in death he had somehow found his humanity again. Metzger could not dwell upon it. Down by the water the fighting had reached a tumult. He pushed himself to his feet, and as he did, another fierce stab of pain lanced clean across his chest, tearing away at the muscles. He staggered forward a step, his knees buckling as the world swam around him, threatening to go black. He closed his eyes and shook his head, 'Not now. Not yet. Just give me an hour, that's all I ask.' Metzger grunted, willing his vision to come back into focus.

For a moment the world retained some of its clarity, though the sharp edges remained blurry. He looked around for his sword and found it lying beside the corpse of a broken soldier. He bent down carefully to retrieve it.

With one final look at the empty battlements, Reinhardt Metzger walked resolutely down to the water's edge to join his men for one last time.

The shadow of death had come down from the dark tower to join them outside the gates of the castle. Ravens circled, the braver birds settling on the fresh corpses already, picking over the best of the meat.

Slowly, the huge iron doors groaned open.

CHAPTER TWENTY-THREE

The Traitor's Game
Behind the Walls of Kastell Metz, Deep in the Heart of the
Howling Hills, Middenland
The Winter of Black Hearts and Tainted Blood, 2533

As THE ENEMY approached the gates, Amsel stared at their flag, a glimmer of recognition stirring in the back of his mind as he watched the ragged cloth pennon snap in the wind. He knew the crest. There were still doors within the old castle that bore the matching mark. They were not the frightening force they had been. From his vantage they appeared battered and broken, yet still they came on. It was the strength of their humanity that made them most dangerous now.

There was one that the master had forbidden him from opening until the end, though how could he know it was the end? The world went in circles not lines. Events lapped and overlapped; they did not run side by side. Yet this, here and now, was the end, he knew.

He saw Radu and the scar-faced dead man striding along the walls towards him.

He could not stay. There was much to do. 'A door to open,' he mumbled, turning his back on the new master and scurrying away.

'Wait!' the necrarch barked as Amsel reached the narrow flight of cracked and broken steps. He did not. He descended quickly and fled across the courtyard, chased by the sounds of fighting and dying. Radu and his new plaything did not follow.

'Soon,' he crooned, a spring of anticipation creeping into his step as he approached the main building. He slipped through the open doorway and in no time was stalking through the tunnels far below.

His footsteps echoed hollowly in the musty passage. Dank rivulets of water seeped down through the ceiling from the lake above, tracing wet lines down the walls. The vampire paused at the corner, smelling the corruption that lingered in the dank air.

'Soon,' he breathed again, a promise to the dark corners beyond the alchemical lights.

He dragged a hand across the slick stones, feeling the earth shiver with revulsion. A deep tremble ran all the way through it as somewhere up above Radu the Forsaken unchained the bones of the dragon.

There were things that had to be done despite the press of time. Things that the master, the true master, had entrusted to him.

'So little time,' he grumbled, scurrying like a rat through the warren of twists and turns. He knew each one intimately having walked the rough stones of the tunnels smooth with his shuffling feet. Then he reached the hidden door, though it looked nothing like a door. It was marked with a single stone, the crest of the old family chiselled into it. He had seen the crest somewhere else, somewhere outside of this place. The vampire rested his hand upon the stone and pushed until he heard the faint click of a rusty mechanism falling into place and the tumblers being released. It was as though the sound crystallised the half-forgotten memory for him. He knew then where he had seen the sigil: on one of the gravestones in Grimminhagen, close to the hole where the girl had descended into the earth to retrieve the master's treasure.

He pushed the false wall open to reveal a small cavity, more akin to a tomb than a room. The vampire's palms itched as he reached up to adjust the alchemical globe so that he might better see into the recess.

What he saw confused him.

There was an empty funeral bier, or rather a bier without a body. Instead, a wonderfully wrought sword had been interred there, deep in the hidden places of the castle. He eyed the blade covetously, not sure precisely what he had expected to find in this hole in the wall, but this relic of the keep's old masters was certainly not it.

Had Korbhen hidden it or Radu himself?

It mattered little.

Amsel crouched and reached into the cavity, his cadaverous hand closing around the hilt of the blade and thrilling to its touch.

'How long since someone held you?' Amsel crooned. He might well have been talking to a widow, so intense was the longing in his voice as he stroked the flat of the blade. It was a wondrous piece, the metal folded and folded and folded time and again in the tempering process. The flame-scalloped edge was serrated like the teeth of some great beast, and still maintained a deep onyx lustre. The hilt added to the illusion, the grip covered in black leather, the pommel, guard and centre an antique brass with what looked like bone accents set into the cross-brace.

Why open the door now, only at the last with the wolf at the door?

Why, unless there was more to the sword than folded metal?

He ran his crooked fingers along the blade again, feeling for any residual taint of the arcane within the metal but there was nothing magical about the blade. There were no daemons bound to it, no runes etched into its metal, no Chaos hunger that would leech the soul of the living into it, no entrapped wizardry. It was merely a sword, a beautiful sword, no doubt with a story to tell, but a sword just the same.

Then he understood the master's plan. It was so simple in its genius.

This was the last secret of Radu the Forsaken, a sword from another life with a story to tell to the right listener. It was not some trinket or superstitious gewgaw; it was the truest of relics binding the necrarch to his past life. There were no coincidences. Korbhen had laid out a pattern of cause and effect that spanned miles and years to culminate in this place, at this time. The subtleties of it were intricate and far-reaching but undeniable. It was no accident that the casket had lain hidden so long in Grimminhagen, the matching crests of the family Metzger proved that. No, this was akin to the blossoming of a perfect rose, each petal a layer of intricacy to the schemes of the necrarch lord, another aspect to the subtlety of the lies that Korbhen had laid out across the land to inflict one final torture upon the warrior he had sired so many long years ago. It was vicious and vindictive and an utterly exquisite vengeance.

He would see the new master humbled and shed the yoke that ground him down. There was only one mind in this place worthy of apprenticeship to the true master.

Amsel hefted the blade. Despite the fact that he possessed no skill of arms he could feel how well it was weighted and appreciate the perfect balance between hilt and blade turning the wielder's wrist into a fulcrum around which death pivoted.

It was a hero's blade.

A hero should wield it. He grinned fiercely as the thought crossed his mind. 'Yes, yes, yes,' he crooned delightedly. It was so obvious. All the signs pointed to this final deception.

With no way to conceal it, Amsel clutched the great sword as he hurried back towards the surface in search of the hero to wield it against the necrarch.

CASIMIR CLIMBED THE stairs to their summit.

The tainted warrior, Fear, had brought the enemy to their door just as he had planned. All that remained was to open it and let the living in.

He stepped out onto the roof of the great tower, treachery in his dead heart.

Out on the killing fields below the fighting raged, but it looked so artificial, comical even. He watched with curious detachment as the dead rose up out of the lake and shambled towards the shore, only to be met with the old man's steel. His mane of white hair streamed wildly in the wind, untamed. He was an oddity, this ancient in the midst of such vibrant and desperate youth, leading them on this hopeless crusade.

And it was hopeless, or it would be without a few traitorous manipulations. Forget the coterie of the damned and deformed, men and women blighted by disease and the touch of plagues and other evils. Forget the scar-faced warrior with his heart in a box down in the subterranean laboratories, risen dead but no longer some sluggish, mindless zombie, but a deadly foe. Forget even the necrarch's parasitic touch. Down and down, deeper than the bones of the old gravestones lay the skeletal remains of the huge dragon, chafing at the chains that bound it. Cut the beast loose and none of them would survive, such was its threat.

He watched the living playing at their game of soldiers.

The world, he thought, as sword clashed with bloated flesh, could be divided into two: predators and prey. For all their fight, the old man and his little men with their swords were prey.

He could not unbind the dragon, neither could he slay the scar-faced one, but he was not alone. He could call on Mammut of the Nine Souls, and what such a beast was capable of even its creator did not know. His smile was slow and cunning.

'Soon,' he told the wind, savouring the taste of betrayal on the wind.

Radu could not have discovered Mammut. Since his return the necrarch had been caught up with the dragon and the dead knight, too cocksure in his power. Hubris would be his undoing, the same as it ever was.

'Who would be master then?' Casimir asked the moon, for there was only one in the sky. Morrslieb eclipsed Mannslieb. It was an omen. The death god was coming to claim his dues this night. Casimir welcomed the deity, and though he had no soul for the lord of the underworld to harvest, he still thought of death as his only friend.

The tower's ravens gathered around him, a hundred or more birds fighting one another to get close to the vampire. Those that were closest pecked at his ankles and feet, their beaks digging into his emaciated flesh and chipping away at the brittle bones beneath. He lashed out, kicking at the birds, first with his left foot, then with his right, and then with his left again. He threw his arms up, cawing loudly in imitation of the carrion eaters, and then jumped and twisted, flapping his arms in a mad caper to scare the ravens into flight.

They took wing in an explosion of oily black feathers and vicious caws.

Down on the battlements beneath the tower he saw Radu looking up at him. Casimir sneered, knowing there was no way the necrarch could read his expression from so far away. It was a petty rebellion, but gratifying just the same. Radu could surround himself with all the powers of the natural world, but they would not save him. Casimir's time had come.

He left the tower. First he would slip the bar on the great gates to let the living in behind the walls. Then he would free the beast that was with nine souls.

There would be blood tonight.

RADU WATCHED THE slaughter from the high wall. Anger seethed within his tortured body as the battle ebbed and flowed. It was an organic thing, killing. The living cut into his dead, even as he raised them again and again, and the dead cut into the living, giving him more corpses with which to defend his bastion. The way Amsel had fled the wall did nothing to appease the paranoia fermenting within his turbulent thoughts. The wretch made no secret of his split loyalties, mumbling about his old master all the time. Could he not see how much greater Radu was than Korbhen had ever been? He would show him, yes he would. Well, Radu would drive a stake of bone through the ghost of his sire once and for all. Amsel could plot and scheme and play with his demented followers to his calcified heart's content. It mattered little now. His petty ambitions were about to be crushed. Radu had always known that the thrall must die.

He looked up at the tower. Bathed in the sickly moonlight Casimir watched the violence unfold.

Radu turned his attention back to the slaughter.

'You dare come at me?' he whispered, barely forming the words. The necrarch shook his head, his skeletal fingers digging deep into the crumbling masonry of the low battlements. The stone wept dust, so fierce was his grip.

The warrior cleaved into the bloated corpse that shambled into his way, cutting clean through the wet flesh of its neck and bringing his blade around to gut a second. It was not graceful but it was brutal and effective. The white-haired warrior led the line. Others fought beside him, forming an arrow-head of steel that cut towards the barricaded gates of the castle.

'Then come, dead man,' Radu said. It mattered little that the warrior could not hear him. 'Come and let us be done with this dance.'

The old man floundered in the shallow water with his sword raised above his head.

Radu laughed cruelly but the sight brought with it flickers of distant memories that stole any mirth from the situation. He saw the ghost of himself out there, looking up at the walls, his heart swollen with fear. He had been another man, his intellect harnessed by the wretched sword in his hand. Steel proved nothing. It was not power. The result of true power stood at his side, scars marring his beautiful face. True power allowed him to reach beyond the veil and drag a hero back to the mortal plane to do his bidding. True power granted him immunity from weaknesses of the flesh. True power conferred its immortality upon his shrunken bones. True power was unlocked by the rigours of the mind, not the strength of the sword arm.

The white-haired warrior was a dead man walking. Radu could smell the corruption eating through his blood from where he stood. It was rank.

He recognised the banner they marched under. It had not changed in all the time since he had carried it.

He almost pitied the fool for his bravery, only it wasn't bravery at all; it was suicide. It was a motivation he was well familiar with. After all, it was the same one that had brought him back to these very doors.

'Death will come to you soon enough,' he promised the old man, enjoying the exquisite irony of it all. Circles within circles; it was a complex pattern of life and failures. The man was like a flea picking away at his corpse, but there came a time when all the flea-carrier could do was scratch.

Perhaps he would sire the warrior, just as he had been sired at the gate? Close the circle once and for all?

With Amsel disposed of he would have need of willing hands to do his bidding while he immersed himself in his work.

There was a curious appeal to the thought.

Radu looked up at the eclipsed moon.

It was time for the living to learn how truly pitiful they were. Let them tremble and fall upon their swords. Let them beg for mercy that he did not possess. Let them die.

He relinquished his hold over the drowned men, breaking the incantation, and threw up his arms, shouting, 'Arise! Arise!' The world shivered beneath the force of his will, the very ground quaking at his might. At first it was no more than that, a ripple through the dirt, a convulsion that ran from the walls of the castle through the courtyard and the outer bailey and back, across from the disused chapel to the graveyard. By the time the tremors reached the graveyard the earth around the tombstones began to sift down through the cracks and the stones yawed like broken teeth in a cemetery smile.

As the drowned men fell, a fork of lightning rent the black sky, spearing down into the heart of the earth.

With a pitiful shriek, the ground was torn asunder.

The gravestones fell away into the huge cavity that opened up beneath them, the bones of the long-dead sliding down to back-fill the wounded earth. For a moment the cacophony of falling soil and stone and corpses buried the sounds of the battlefield.

Then a swarm of bats erupted out of the belly of the earth.

'Arise!' Radu roared, throwing his hands wide.

Thousands and thousands of bats wheeled in the air, banking, rising and falling erratically. Their screeching had the men on the ground dropping their swords and covering their ears as the madness of sound clawed into their skulls.

'Drums?' Bonifaz said, staring down at the fight below. He breathed in deeply. 'No, hearts,' he corrected himself, the wild hammering growing louder and louder in his ears. 'Hearts and fear.'

Beneath it came a deeper sound, a rumbling far down in the heart of the labyrinthine tunnels beneath the castle, down where the bones of the dragon stirred.

'Arise!' Radu bellowed. A flesh-eating worm burrowed its way out of his death-mask of a face, exposing the bone beneath the rotten pulp of flesh. 'Arise!'

Lightning pierced the sky once more. The wind whipped up into a savage bluster that bullied the bats across the lightning-bright sky.

Beside him the scar-faced death-bringer fingered the hilts of his twin swords as he watched the old man and his blades struggling against the tide of the dead rising up from the lake bed. Each scream sent a thrill through the cavity where his heart had been. Quietly, he whispered, 'Suffering,' and Radu had no way of knowing if it was a promise to him, or to the men down there.

AMSEL FELT THE earth fall away beneath his feet, and even as he stumbled and fell, he saw the dirt of the roof come crumbling down like filthy rain.

He forced himself back onto his feet and pushed on, deeper into the warren of tunnels.

He knew the dark ways intimately, having spent so much of his unlife exiled in them. There was a comfort to the dark, and with it a sense of self that the vampire did not feel when he was up above with the moon on his face, and yet he must rise, he knew that. He could not hide out here forever hoping that the end of all things would pass him by. It had begun.

The ground shifted beneath him again, like some volcanic shiver tearing through the crust of the earth. Amsel pressed up against the beams that supported the excavated wall. The wood had buckled and splintered beneath the enormous weight of the collapse. It was only a matter of time before the stresses being brought to bear on the beam's wooden core found the weaknesses within the grain and the supporting strut tore apart. One of the alchemical globes along the tunnel fell, shattering on the floor, its eternal flame extinguished as crudely as that. Amsel shuffled towards the dark spot. His footsteps dragged loudly in the echo-trap of the subterranean walkway. He clutched the sword to his chest.

He heard other noises down in the deep: a susurrant rush of dirt and rock out of the cracks in the wall, the grating of bone on stone as the graves from up above poured down to fill in the cavities beneath them, the groans of the straining support beams buckling grain by grain, and so much more that could not be explained: sounds of the earth.

The air around him grew hotter the deeper he went, uncomfortably so.

A sharp crack behind him preceded the collapse by a moment.

Amsel started to run, his robes tangling around his legs and the fetishes that hung from his rope belt getting in the way of his long strides. He ran hard, gripped by panic. He had died once before. Death held no fear. Living did. His mind filled with frightened thoughts of being buried deeper than the bones of the castle, trapped in the torment of the unlife for an eternity. He could imagine no worse torture than the dirt and the broken stones pressing into his face and down his throat, pinning his arms by his side, the claustrophobic weight on his chest pressing down mercilessly. He could imagine nothing worse than being unable to move, unable to feed, but equally unable to let go of consciousness and thought, unable to let go, and so driven mad by an eternity of nothing.

He ran, if not for his life, then for his death.

Before, there had always been a loneliness to the dark places, but the chorus of collapse stripped them of that. Now there was only noise and fear.

The ground cracked again. He clutched the sword's blade so tightly that its flame-scalloped edge bit into his hands. He barely registered the pain. The grating of the rock above his head swelled to fill his mind, and he understood. The world was not collapsing, but that did not help him. The tunnels were still caving in beneath their added burden. The ceiling of the subterranean laboratories had been opened up, causing the seismic shifts as the world contracted to fill the empty spaces beneath it.

'Time, time, time,' Amsel said, the words like ghosts taunting him. He looked up at the stones above, willing them to hold until he had found his way back to the world above.

But if Radu had released the dragon he had no hope.

A single imperative galvanised him: I will not fail the master.

Amsel stumbled on towards the wooden staircase and the hidden trap that opened up within one of the false graves of the bone garden.

CASIMIR GRABBED THE woman by the throat, his dirty nails digging deep into the vein that pulsed at her throat. She was one of the coterie, a faceless piece of flesh that he had never given a second thought to. Now she was imperative to his plan's fruition. The wind and the shrieks of the enemy howled all around the courtyard, bringing it close, making it all so real.

'Listen, woman, and listen well,' he rasped, pushing his face up to hers, so close that they might have shared the most tender of kisses. 'The message is simple: he has been betrayed. Tell him that. Tell him that Amsel has betrayed him. Tell him the wretch has made a pact with the living and led them to our door. Do you understand me, woman?'

She nodded.

'Then tell me what you are to tell the master?'

She licked her dry lips. 'We know of the betrayal because we are supposed to be his secret army, to rise up and help the living when they enter the keep. There are men within our number who will turn on the necrarch at the last, delivering him to the old man with the white hair. I know this because it is the vampire Amsel's doing. He is loyal still to the one they call Korbhen. I do not know who, so none are to be trusted.'

'Yes, yes. It is important you name the threat. Feed his paranoia. Good. Now go.'

He pushed the woman away. She stumbled, catching her filthy skirts, and fled towards the stairs that would take her up to the battlements and the great necrarch himself.

Content that the seeds would be sown, Casimir moved through the cluster of tents and wooden crates and all the filth of humanity that festered within them, towards the gate.

No one moved to stop him, but why would they? He was untouchable, the master's most loyal servant. He was Radu's left hand, full of sinister purpose. Who would dare suspect him of treachery? Who apart from that wretch, Amsel?

A self-satisfied grin touched his lips at the thought of that lickspittle being undone by a few words.

'Arm yourselves!' he demanded. 'The wolf is at the door, and the beast won't be content until we are all purged from this place by fire and sword. Let us give them the fight of their lives!'

There were no cheers to greet his rousing words. Some of the men moved away, grabbing makeshift weapons, spears and staves and whatever else lay to hand, while others rooted around in the rags of their lives and pulled out rusted old blades that had seen better days.

He left them to get on with it, turning once, halfway to the gatehouse. 'Protect the master at all costs,' he called back. 'It is imperative!' The lie was an easy one but then they all were. With one well-placed lie Radu would believe some within the coterie meant him harm, with another the damned and deformed would do all they could to remain at the necrarch's side believing it their duty to protect him. It was delicious the way they all tangled up within themselves but he could not allow himself the luxury of enjoying it, not yet.

It was never about the might of swords or the mastery of magic. Fools believed in those tools of power. Men of power understood its nature better. It was about greed and lust, those base instincts had primacy. The weak craved more, the strong craved more. There was no difference between them outside their ability to take it. That understanding made all the difference in the world. A simple word in the right ear at the right time could undo the strength of any sword arm. It was the nature of magic to gnaw away at the practitioner. When the world became a mutable thing it became much more difficult to believe in the truth of the eye. A word at the right time, whispered to feed the right doubts, could undo every strut and support that held together the paranoid's world. Those were the powers that ruled the world, whispered words, not the thud and blunder of swords or the flash and bang of mages. Casimir understood this. He always had.

He barely noticed the rain as it came down, bustling up to the abandoned gatehouse.

As the air filled with the shrieking of bats, Casimir lifted the wooden brace that held the huge door closed, and grasped the great mechanism beside it, turning the spigots that in turn dragged on the ropes that pulled the hidden cogs. Slowly the gate began to drag open.

It amused him to think that it could all be undone by such a simple thing.

AMSEL FOUND THE staircase and climbed up out of the grave.

He had never thought to enjoy the feel of the air on his face again, but as he emerged into the night a sigh of contentment slipped out of his lips. He had come up behind the line of fighting, between the lake and the old graveyard, though there were no gravestones now, only a vast pit from which thousands upon thousands of bats streamed up into the night, the press of their hides so thick that they blocked out the moon.

Amsel moved fast, keeping low as he ran. The bone and feather fetishes on his belt bounced against the atrophied muscle of his thigh. He twisted left and right, constantly looking up towards the walls, sure that the new master could see him from his perch.

The killing had shifted its emphasis away from the lake, the living clinging to the narrow trail that led around it, skirting the line of trees, to the castle gates. He could not tell if it were a trick of the dark, or if the huge black iron-bound doors truly were grinding open on themselves.

He ran towards the fighting, thinking only to reach the white-haired warrior that led the line. He had seen him at Grimminhagen, and now here, fighting with controlled fury. That the living flocked to his side to fight with him told the vampire all he needed to know. He had to get the blade to the old man.

Before he could take another step a soldier loomed up out of the darkness, full of righteous fury at the sight of the vampire's rotten features, and rammed his sword hilt deep through Amsel's chest. The shock of it was like fire lancing through his corpse. The blade tore from his chest, its teeth tearing so much of his insides out that Amsel felt his body coming undone. His hands refused to obey him. He tried to offer the sword up, to speak to the warrior, but the man's blade drove in again, opening his throat as fully as it had opened his gut. Gagging on the sudden swell of rank black blood in his throat, Amsel dropped the sword and fell to his knees. He reached up weakly towards the steel still embedded in his throat, thinking only to wrench the wretched metal free.

The sword, he tried to say, but the words would not come out.

He looked down at the blade lying in the mud, pleading silently with his killer to understand.

But there was no understanding for the vampire in the man's eyes, only the cold hatred of the living for the dead.

The man wrenched his sword clear of the vampire's throat, tearing out the tubes of speech and sawing deep into the vertebrae.

Amsel lowered his head, reaching out, groping blindly in the mud for the flame-scalloped blade. As his hands found its hilt, a surge of triumph flared through his veins, and for a moment, for a mote in the eye of time, it felt right. He surrendered to the rage and allowed his bestial aspect to rise from deep within his skin. His lips shrank away as his jaw distended and his teeth sharpened to venomous fangs. He looked up, meeting the warrior's frightened gaze, and roared. The animalistic venting sprayed blood and spittle as he drove the sword upwards, but Amsel was no swordsman.

The warrior moved at the last moment, bringing his sword round to deflect what should have been a killing thrust. Instead of driving deep into his gut the blade glanced off the curve of his breastplate, slipping between the crack and sliced viciously into his side. It bit deep enough to hurt, but not enough to kill. It wasn't a clean blow, the serrated edge opening more of the man than a normal weapon would as Amsel dragged it clear.

Then, in the silence between life and death the nameless warrior gripped the hilt of his sword resolutely, and with every last ounce of strength left to him, he scythed through the vampire's neck, severing meat and bone.

The sword broke, but it did all that was required of it.

The steel took the vampire's head before its weakness snapped it clean in two.

AT THE GATES, Casimir's skull pounded with the drumming of countless heartbeats beating wildly and erratically. The reek of blood in the air turned his mind feral. It had been so long since he had tasted fresh blood.

He clutched at his temples, digging his fingernails into his scalp. The pain served to drive the thoughts of blood way. It was an intoxicant, not a need. He did not need blood, not now. He willed himself to hold to the task as he cranked the spigot around again and again until the great gates stood open, the way into the belly of the castle wide open.

The rain came down so hard that it drummed six inches back off the dirt. He looked up at the sky filled with bats. The reek of blood was overpowering. He felt the beast slipping out from beneath his skin, drawn by the vital fluid. He knew he could not stay out there for long. With each passing minute the stench of blood rose, thicker and more viscous, and with it rose the beast within him, that primal aspect of the vampire. He could barely keep it in.

Behind him the coterie of the damned and deformed formed up, their makeshift weapons clutched tightly in trembling hands. They cut pitiful figures in the downpour, utterly tragic with their rags soaked through and the filth streaked across their faces. They stood in a dozen lines that stretched the width of the courtyard, those with real weapons at the front. They were ready to die for him. He savoured the thought, backing away from the gate.

'They come!' he said, throwing back his head. He tasted the rain in his throat and it tasted of blood.

The damned raised their weapons and stamped their feet ever faster in some mad tribal dance, whooping and hollering as they slammed their clenched fists off their chests. Behind each one lurked a ghost that would be released before the night was over. They were truly damned.

'Do not go gently. Fight. Make them hurt for every hurt you have ever suffered at their hands. They are the parents that rejected you, the villagers that shunned you. They are the bastards that tried to drown you in their sacks or dragged you out into the forest and left you to die. They are all of these people. Dig deep. Find the taint within your blood, savour it, draw it to the surface, let it consume you, and then, when it has and they are so close you can smell their rancid breath, use it to take from them everything they took from you!'

They cheered him, even as the doors behind him were torn asunder and the living poured in, led by the white-haired warrior.

Casimir stepped forward, the rain blurring around him as it appeared to hiss and sizzle off his body, forming a thick white mist that hung between them. When the rain finally tore through it, the vampire was gone.

CHAPTER TWENTY-FOUR

The Knight of the Last Hour
Kastell Metz, Deep in the Heart of the Howling Hills,
Middenland
The Final Spring Night of an Old Man's War, 2533

THE YOUNGSTER, KANE, looked down at what remained of his sword: the leather-wrapped hilt in his hand and a broken stub of steel. His knuckles blanched white where he gripped the hilt. A weakness in the blade had seen it sheer in two as it cleaved into the vile creature's neck.

He stood over the dead vampire, breathing hard, hurting from the deep cut in his side. Of all things it was the broken sword that betrayed him, accentuating his trembling. It wasn't that he was afraid; it had gone well beyond that. In the last few hours he had seen his brother, Blaine, drown and had barely had time to grieve for him before his corpse came shambling back out of the lake that had claimed his life. He had killed him again, but in the process something inside Kane had broken. Like the sword, he thought.

He had tried. He had stood next to Bohme ready to follow the man into hell, but when the gates had groaned slowly open to give them a glimpse of the freaks lined up behind them, he hadn't been able to do it. He had no thoughts of revenge or retribution. Instead he imagined his mother and his father in their shared grief and wondered how he could possibly tell them it was his sword that had finally put his brother in the dirt when he had promised them that he would protect Blaine? And he fled.

Kane lifted the broken blade, seeing his grief-torn reflection in the steel. He could not bear to look at himself, and though it hurt to discard the blade, that one swing had rendered it useless. He tossed it aside. The sword had been a coming-of-age gift from Blaine. That it had broken in his hands, just one swing after delivering the blow that turned him into a kinslayer seemed so fitting.

It was a sign.

He had tried to flee and the battle had come to him. His blade had possessed one last blow before its weakened core had splintered, but that one blow had been enough to save his life. Did he run again, leaving the others to die? Or did he turn around and go back to the dying? He harboured no illusions: that was precisely what they were doing here, dying. The choice was simple, run now to die another day, or return to fall beside the men who had over the last few months become his surrogate family. It was no choice at all. He knew what Blaine would have done in his place, so how could he do anything other?

He took a single step. Pain flared through his side as the movement tore the wound wider. He told himself there was no way he could run. The ground buckled beneath his feet, every fixed point his balance depended upon betraying the sudden fluidity of the earth. He stumbled, gritting his teeth against the fresh wave of black agony as it threatened to overwhelm him. For a moment the sound of the rain drumming down on the lake, the shrill screeches of the bats clogging up the black sky and the seismic groans of the earth failed to silence the screams of good men dying beyond the castle wall, and then they came together to drown out everything with the agonies of the world.

Kane steeled himself, his breath still coming quick and shallow. His hands were trembling and the blood ran freely down his side from the cut delivered by the vampire's sword, but he marshalled the will to turn back towards the lake and face the castle beyond it.

The bats smothered the moonlight but the vague shadows of the corpses were unmistakable.

One amongst them was his brother.

He knew what he had to do. It wasn't about resolve or revenge. It was about dying. He wanted to die. But it wasn't as crude as suicide. If it had been he could have simply fallen on his broken sword and let the damned steel claim both brothers. It was about standing beside the others. He was a soldier. Soldiers died. Kane turned back to the vampire's decapitated corpse. His vision rolled unsteadily. This time it was not the earth that betrayed his balance, it was the loss of blood. Tentatively, he explored the wound, pressing his fingers into his flesh. It was deep and wide, and without being treated would almost certainly see him unconscious in a ditch. His hand came back thick with blood. The sight of it made his pain all the more real.

'Tonight's as good a time to die as any other,' he muttered, casting about for a weapon because dying was all well and good but he wasn't about to do it without a sword in his hand. His broken sword was neither use nor ornament. There were blades aplenty, the lakeside was littered with them. The swords of hundreds of men lay in the mud beside the fallen, but there was nothing close at hand. He had run too far from the battle in his panic.

That wasn't true. There was one weapon, but Kane had no intention of wielding the vampire's flame-scalloped blade.

The lightning transformed the world around him, lighting the skeletal limbs of the trees and the bloated bodies of the bats as they swarmed above him. For a moment he might have been standing on the bottom of the lake, looking up at the surface thick with the flotsam and jetsam of death floating above him. Then the residual glow faded and the world returned to the night side.

He had enough ghosts; he did not need to go looking for more.

Pushed beyond desperation, he took up the beast's blade and, clutching his bloody side, ran towards the fighting within the castle proper.

The world lurched beneath his feet again, venting a terrible scream of dirt and stone.

The bleached white skull of a great dragon breached the line of the wall walk, bursting into the sky, huge rotten wings helping it climb.

He saw the necrarch on the wall, obviously commanding the creature with the strands of its vile sorcery.

Suddenly the sword in his hand felt tiny and inconsequential: a pig-sticker that would barely graze the monster's bones, either of them.

More and more of the creature rose up behind the castle walls, its bones brittle ivory in the diseased moonlight, until it took its place amongst the bats. The thing was immense, its wings fashioned from hundreds and hundreds of bones fused together by some vile magic. The skeletal beast merged with the bats, the leathery wings of the smaller mammals fleshing out the dragon. It hung there in the sky above him, blacking out the moon, a huge spectre of death hanging over the castle. The bone dragon loosed a hideous cry, and swooped low, its immense jaws closing around the kicking and screaming body of a soldier. The beast climbed high into the sky, flapping its wings languidly as it rose higher and higher, until the screams became one with the rain. At the height of the scream, it opened its mouth and let the man fall out of the sky.

He was dead long before he hit the ground.

Reinhardt Metzger gritted his teeth as another savage cramp tore into his chest.

He barely brought his shield up high enough to catch the wild swing aimed at taking his head off his shoulders. The impact jarred through him, shaking him all the way down to his boots. The warrior stepped in, leaning heavily on his right foot and drove his sword up into the belly of the wretched freak that stood in his way.

For a moment he was out of the rain, sheltered by the arch of the huge castle gates. Two hundred of the men he had brought with him hadn't made it that far. Rainwater overflowed from the wall walk above the arch's keystone and drilled into the straw roof of the stables, soaking through to the sandy soil beneath. Metzger looked to all points of the castle, left to right from the stables, across the lower bailey to the well, the shadowy keep and the great conical tower to the wall curtaining off the main bailey, and behind the wall, the main buildings and what once must have been the chapel, getting his bearings. He counted six staircases cut into the curtain wall, leading up to the wall walks and the battlements.

Metzger stepped back out into the storm.

There were no rousing speeches, no calls to arms. Every man beside him knew why he was fighting. Any words would cheapen their sacrifice. Metzger barrelled into the front line of the damned, seeing the faces of everyone who had ever done him wrong, everyone who had hurt those he cared for. He brought his blade around, hacking into the face of a woman, not waiting for the rusted short sword to slip from her fingers before he pushed her corpse out of his way and thundered a crippling punch into the face of the man beside her. Metzger fought like a daemon possessed, his matted white mane a beacon for the living and the damned.

Bohme fought at his side.

Each was so familiar with the other's movements they could anticipate and move into the spaces left behind by the other. The lower bailey quickly became a scene of carnage. Men and women fell, slopping and sliding in the mud as they struggled to fight. The discipline of the lines collapsed, the freaks swarming over Metzger's men. From above cocktails of fire oil were launched, chased by flaming arrows.

A bottle sailed through the air. Metzger barely managed to get his head out of the away and avoid any back-splash as it shattered against the head of the man three steps behind him. It was followed a moment later by a scream and a soft crump as a burning arrow slammed into the man's shoulder. Metzger followed the burning arc of the arrow's flight, helplessly captivated by it as the flame's heat singed his cheek. He saw the arrow bury itself deep in the warrior's shoulder, saw the look of shock, horror and sudden understanding as he frantically grabbed at it.

Before the warrior could wrench it free the flame caught the oil in his hair and transformed him into a living fireball. There was a bleak moment of doom when the man knew he was dead even before his flesh was consumed. He did not try to cling on to his sword, he simply cast it aside and stumbled forward, almost colliding with Metzger as he reached out with groping hands. Make your death count was every warrior's motto. This man did. It did not matter that his screams were horrific as he ran blindly, ablaze, into the centre of the ranks of the freaks. What mattered was that he brought death into the heart of their ranks, clutching at anyone trapped in his way and smothering them in his fiery embrace.

Metzger threw himself into the man's burning wake, cutting to the heart of the enemy's ranks. He did not look to see if Bohme followed. A fury burned within him as bright and fierce as the fire that consumed the man stumbling before him.

The burning man fell.

Metzger did not.

He blocked an overhead cut and answered it with a stunning riposte, slashing across the face of the ugly man before him. Ugly became uglier as pain twisted his features. Metzger stepped in and plunged his sword into the man's chest, ending his pain. He wrenched his blade free as a burning figure stumbled towards him. He gave the wretch a merciful death, opening his throat.

The second death bought him a few feet of breathing space. He scanned the wall walks and the bat-filled sky. The shrieking of the shrivelled creatures had become indistinguishable from one another in the battle. He felt a curious contentment with his sword in his hand, Bohme at his back. That contentment burned out in the shadow of another burning man, when he looked up at the sky and saw the stark silhouette of the great winged wyrm climbing for the eclipsed moons. It was a vision ripped from a hellish oblivion and made real. Then he saw the man falling, flailing and screaming soundlessly before he disappeared behind the wall. Bohme felt his resolve buckling, his limbs slack with fear. Despite all that he had seen nothing had prepared him for the sight of this new twisted parody of death.

The great bone drake bellowed at them, a sound like nothing else in the world, and streaked down towards the swell of bodies. Metzger could only watch in horror as the great grinding jaws snapped up three fighters. The creature's slaughter was indiscriminate. It took two of his men and one of the castle's wretched denizens and dashed their brains out against the red tiles of the conical roof of the dark tower before it swooped down again, huge jaws wide, straight for the white-haired warrior.

Sheets of flame roared out of the skeletal dragon's maw, roasting across the heads of the combatants, raging out of control, and Metzger stood in the path of the flame.

It seared towards him, great gouts of fire, but he could not feel its heat. His armour ought to have melted against his skin, his hair shrivelled away, his skin burned and blistered, but as the dragon's fire consumed him it did no such thing.

Reinhardt Metzger stood in the heart of the fire, untouched.

The dragon chased the ghost fire. Unlike the flames, the mildewed bones were still every bit as powerful as they had been in life.

Metzger threw himself to the side. The old man lost his grip on his sword as he sprawled in the mud at the feet of a dozen rag-clothed misfits. Each of them clutched either fistfuls of stone or snapped poles with ragged ends, still tied with strips of cloth. Metzger barely avoided the dragon's eight-inch long incisors.

He tried to push himself back to his feet but the sodden ground sucked at his hands and knees as he struggled to rise. Then the first stone hit the centre of his back. Another cracked off the back of his skull. Then they used the poles to beat him back down into the mud. Metzger tried to protect his head from the beating.

He looked up to see the deformed faces staring down at him, hungry to cause the old man hurt.

and hideously twisted limbs, but the path he had cleaved had closed up behind him, leaving the old man trapped.

Kane ducked away from a thrown stone, only to be hit square on the chest by a second. An astringent reek blossomed beneath his nose, stinging his eyes. It took him a moment to realise it hadn't been a stone but rather a clay vial that had shattered upon impact, splashing a viscous fluid across his chest and up across part of his cheek. He reached up with his free hand, touching the liquid. It stank but it did not sting, but as he stepped back out into the rain he realised that the water did not wash it away. That struck a chord of fear in his heart. He clenched his fist around the hilt of his borrowed blade and launched himself at the wall of men.

A corpse with rank boils all down the side of its rotten flesh reared up before him. Kane swung. The sword hissed as it sliced though the air. It sliced bloodily into the man's groin. As the man buckled, Kane swung again, cleaving the dead man's neck and severing his spine. It was only then that he realised the man had no weapon. He couldn't allow himself the luxury of pity. It was not killing, he told himself; he was simply banishing them from the life that was not theirs. He was bringing them final peace. He forced himself into the mêlée. He banished the second corpse as ruthlessly as the first, with two cuts, one high on the thigh, the other across the thick vein of the man's neck. There was no arterial spray.

The third, with his rusty sword, took longer, but not much. He lunged forward on the front foot, going for a swift kill through the heart. The move cost him. The wound in his side opened up, the pain from it blinding him for a moment. The deformed man parried the thrust with surprising skill and delivered a return cut that grazed Kane's cheek, opening up a thin trickle of blood. It could have been so much worse but his vision cleared in time to fend off a second cut. They traded blows, cutting and slashing, Kane driving the man backwards step by step, until his back was pressed up against the men behind him. The wretched zombie blocked, moving back still further. A path seemed to open up for him and Kane realised that he was being led into the mass of the enemy. He went in willingly. He felt himself beginning to tire, the loss of blood taking its toll. He feinted a second desperate lunge at the last moment shifting his balance and cutting the creature's legs out from beneath it. Two more went down in the space of a single moment as Kane slashed out in a huge sweeping arc, the flame-scalloped blade cutting through their bellies and unravelling the rope of their guts.

Then he saw the old man lying on his back in the sucking mud. The rain streamed down across his eyes, cold on his face. Metzger was in trouble. A dozen of the deformed freaks swarmed all over him. He had his arms up trying to protect his face but he had no sword.

Three more men stood between them. He did not know if they were living or dead. He did not care.

The first came at him hard, and he staggered as the man's improvised staff thundered off the side of his skull, barely blocking the follow-up as the jagged teeth of the broken end of the pole lanced towards his ribs. The exertion tore open his side-wound even further. The fire inside was agonising, but Kane dug deep, finding strength he did not know he possessed, and surged forward. He opened the man's throat, stepping over him as he slumped forward, choking on his own blood. The second died with a blow to the face that opened a gaping hole in the centre of his head. He would have made it all the way to Metzger's side but for the sudden stabbing pain in his back.

At first he thought he had been punched in the base of the spine, but he felt his knees begin to give out even as he tried to force another step out of his legs. He blinked, rain in his eyes causing his vision to fade in and out. The pain of the punch didn't fade. His blade met that of the last man, who blocked three successive blows, each one coming at greater and greater effort to Kane until he was moving purely on instinct, no conscious thought behind his attack. The man came back at him, a huge rusted broadsword sweeping into his gut. The blade rattled off the plate of his mail. The shock of it was brutal. Kane fell towards the man, crashing his left fist into his face and exploding the gristle of his nose. He followed the punch with a vicious thrust, disembowelling the last man that stood between him and Metzger.

The old man was only five paces away when Kane's legs buckled and he slumped to his knees.

Blind with the pain, he reached around, his fingers finding the wooden shaft of an arrow embedded deep in his back. It had punched through the metal of his backplate. He tried to rise but couldn't.

A second arrow came down out of the sky, trailing out of its arc with a tail of flame. It struck the young warrior in the shoulder. A moment later his chest went up in flames. The agony of the naphtha eating into his skin was brutal as it tore into his face, melting away the skin through to the bone.

He reached out with the sword, still trying to reach the fallen warrior, and then through the flame he thought he saw his brother striding towards him. He lost his grip on the sword, falling forward onto his face, and as the light finally dimmed, the castle and the carnage lost to the endless night of death, Kane reached up to take his brother's hand.

METZGER WATCHED THE lad burn in horror, unable to understand the beatific expression that settled on his face even as the flames melted it away.

The dead man's sword had come down inches from his fingers, closer by far than his own. It taunted him with a chance of life, if he could just close his fingers around it. Metzger stretched out his arm, desperately trying to snag it.

The sharp ends of broken poles pounded on his chest. He felt his heart skipping arrhythmically, each missed beat sending a spasm of pain through his muscles. His fingers grazed the sword and then he had it in his palm. He brought it around blindly, sheering into the legs of the men standing over him.

The sky above filled with the angry red of the bone dragon's ghost fire and it was as though the gates to the Underworld had been dragged open. The dragon came down to settle on the great wall. They stood side by side surveying the slaughter. The necrarch climbed the ladder of the giant wyrm's vertebrae and rode it into the rain-filled sky.

KASPAR BOHME LOST sight of Metzger when the dragon scorched the earth.

The rain came down in a black veil, drowning the sky and everything beneath it. The bats disappeared over the tops of the bare trees, banking and swirling swiftly as they rose. They were not what interested the Silberklinge. He only had eyes for the dead man walking with an arrogant strut down the worn-smooth stairs leading down from the battlements.

Bonifaz's scarred face split into a broad grin as he reached behind him and drew his twin blades with practiced efficiency. They whispered clear of the scabbards strapped to his back. He turned them over and over in his hands, the steel circle lazy at first but by the time he reached the bottom step it was a lightning-fast blur.

'We buried you,' Bohme said.

'Dug up,' Bonifaz rasped, launching himself forward with a blistering series of cuts, each blade met by Bohme's, barely. 'Better now.' The words rasped wetly though his mouth and the ragged wound in the back of his throat. It would have sounded comical if not for the nightmarish quality it took on in the storm, surrounded by the squall and the thunder. Instead it was a sound that would haunt Kaspar Bohme until the end of days.

Twin swords slashed in again. He blocked the first but the second opened a bloody gash in his left cheek, and before he could fend it away a third blow opened a matching line down his right cheek.

'Brothers,' the dead man said.

The cuts were shallow, more humiliating than painful.

'What has he done to you?' Bohme asked as he circled Bonifaz slowly, keeping a distance that was not quite safe between their blades. 'Are you his puppet? Do you dance to his tune? Is it even you in there or am I talking to the bastard beast himself?' Bohme lashed out. Bonifaz blocked the blow easily, turning it aside with a negligent roll of the wrist.

'Me.'

But Bohme refused to believe that was true.

Bohme was good, but Bonifaz had always been the better swordsman. His only hope was to make this brief. The longer the circling and the testing blows went on, the more tired he would become and in turn the slower he would be. He was already aching bone deep. Bonifaz's blades licked out, six cuts in rapid succession, each one softly nicking the armour protecting his biceps, just enough to scratch the mail but not dent it. The dead man was mocking him. It occurred to him what he needed to do to stand a chance of making it out of this uneven duel alive. He loosened his grip on the hilt of his sword ever so slightly, a hint that he was tiring, and then dragged his trailing foot in the mud a fraction longer than he needed to, compounding the hint. He saw the predatory gleam enter the dead man's eyes as he sensed his opponent weakening. Bohme traded a dozen more blows, each a fraction less forceful than the one before. He breathed deeply, the air leaking out of him like a sigh. He let his guard drop an inch.

It was the signal for Bonifaz to come in for the kill.

He did just that, launching a lethal combination of fast left-right-left cuts aimed at opening Bohme from groin to throat, disembowelling him, but the older man was ready for it, feinting left and launching himself backwards. The momentum of the dead man's lunge carried him forward off balance. Bohme brought his blade up and the dead man staggered on to it, the sword sinking hilt deep into the centre of Bonifaz's chest. He looked down at the weapon protruding from his chest, and then up at Bohme. He shook his head slowly and drew himself off the blade. There was not so much as a single drop of blood spilled. 'Not the end.'

Kaspar Bohme said nothing.

He did not need to. His fear was written plainly in every line on his face.

Before the dead man could bring his blades to bear, Bohme threw himself forward, swinging wildly. The blow cut deep into the dead man's neck, biting through the bone cleanly, but it was not enough to sever his head. It hung on a strip of tendon, and rolled back so that the dead man stared up at the sky.

He finished the job with a second savage cut, and still it did not stop Bonifaz.

CASIMIR STOOD STRICKEN, staring at the weight of rubble that had come down to crush his dreams of vengeance and freedom. Somewhere beneath it Mammut lay buried, alive or dead he had no way of knowing.

He threw himself at the wall of broken stones, grabbing chunk after chunk and hurling them aside in his desperation to get through to his glorious creation. For each rock he removed a dozen slid down from above. Choking dust clung to the air.

There was nothing he could do.

The ceiling above him groaned perilously, the weight on it threatening to bring even more of the corridor down.

At that moment he loathed Radu more than anything else that had ever lived.

He wanted to hurt him but without Mammut of the Nine Souls he was impotent against the necrarch and his legion of death-bringers.

He had to leave, now. He had to run. He could not bear to be trapped down in the depths of this place.

But, he thought covetously, there were such treasures close to hand, and one in particular, the casket the necrarch had scoured the world looking for. The master had crushed something of his. In turn he would crush something of the master's.

Covered in the dust of the collapse, he ran through the tunnels, tracking back on until he came to the stairs that led back up to the same level as the vast laboratories. Even though the huge complex was abandoned, he hesitated before entering.

The destruction was near-absolute. The ceiling was gone, ripped open to the sky. The walls had crumbled, all of those secrets so close to resolution lost as the clay cracked and fell away from the stone, only to shatter on the floor. The pit where the fettered dragon had been chained after its resurrection lay empty.

There was nothing of value left to be salvaged.

The objects of their experiments lay in ruin, the equipment mangled.

He looked around frantically, but he could not see it. He fell to his knees, clawing through the detritus, hurling aside rock and rubble as carelessly as he did fragments of twisted arcanery. He could feel the heat burning up through the stone. It was down there, buried beneath the ruined walls. He would not be denied twice. He refused to be. He tore away his nails and the flesh from his fingers in his urgency to get through to the source of the heat.

Then he felt the thrill of power surge through him as he touched the plain wooden casket. Casimir dragged the box clear, the rhythmic dub-dub, dub-dub of the scar-faced warrior's heart bounding ceaselessly inside his skull.

He released the lock mechanisms and opened the box.

For a moment he stared down at the heart beating impossibly within the clutch of the withered hand, and then he tore it free.

His head filled with silence as the heart was stilled.

Not content, Casimir raised the dead man's heart to his lips and tore into it with his teeth, chewing and swallowing it one mouthful at a time.

Only when he had finished did he flee the tunnels, clutching his stolen treasure to his chest.

RADU WATCHED THE arrow trail away harmlessly as the great bone dragon swept low across the upturned heads of the fighters, cackling delightedly as the beast snatched up another hapless fighter and scrambled up through the sky to dash his brains out from a thousand feet.

A second arrow lodged into the dragons huge rib. For a moment it appeared to be burn out, but then the last dregs of the flame licked the pickling oil that they had used to preserve the bones. The oil ignited, the flames spreading quickly across the beast's skeletal frame, charring deep into the calcified bone and eating away at all of the moisture that prevented the old bones from crumbling to dust and blowing away on the wind like motes of dust.

Soon every bone was aflame, the great wyrm streaking across the sky like a comet, blazing a trail.

Radu hurled himself off the back of the burning beast, and for a moment, fell, tumbling out of the sky, the wind tearing at his clothes. Then he found the form of a great black bat, his body twisting and mutating as it plummeted.

Empty rags blew away on the wind while a lone bat flitted across the sky. It did not follow the same way as others that had gone before. Instead it settled on the roof of the old tower.

THE BLAZING BONES of the dragon fell from the sky, streaking through the darkness like the fiery tales of comets as they burned and burned, brighter and brighter still as they fell. The air filled with the maddening shrieks of the magic undone. The ragged flaps of scale and wing shrivelled, their ash falling like black snow on the up-turned faces of the fighters.

Then the bones of the beast crashed into the lower bailey.

The fires consumed its bones utterly, until there was nothing left to burn.

BONIFAZ FELL.

Bohme didn't understand why and he didn't care.

He bled from a dozen shallow wounds inflicted by the headless warrior.

He stared down at the corpse, half expecting it to rise up again.

It didn't.

Behind him the lower bailey burned, but the heavy rain had already begun to extinguish the small pockets of fire. Before him, he saw Metzger charging through the carnage towards the doors of the tower.

The old man turned and waved for him to follow. Even as he did, he clutched at his chest. He disappeared inside the tower.

'He who scorns his own life owns yours,' the warrior said, setting off after his friend without a second thought.

HIS HEART WAS on fire as he climbed the spiral staircase. He forced himself to run on, even as a fresh wave of pain engulfed him and the confines of the stairwell turned black before his eyes.

Metzger had watched the fall of the flaming bones, a peculiar flutter of motion catching his eye. Its erratic flight betrayed the bat. While others, he was sure, watched the creature's empty clothes drift down on the wind, Metzger followed the bat with his eyes, tracking it back to where it settled on the roof of the great tower.

He burst out through the door to see the vile creature standing over the parapet, grinning ferociously at the devastation the burning bones had caused. The necrarch turned to face him, the corruption that claimed his face absolute.

Metzger stepped onto the roof, finally face to face with the creature that had savaged his protectorate. It seemed hardly credible that this withered husk of a thing could be behind such pain and suffering. The vampire looked down at the blade in his hand and whatever words of mockery lay on its lips died. 'My sword? Where did you get my sword?'

Metzger said nothing, moving forward resolutely.

Another ferocious spur of pain tore into the white-haired warrior. His entire left side suddenly numb, Metzger clenched his fist around the blade's hilt.

He stared at the beast who neither moved to flight nor to defend itself.

Despite the ruin, and as wilfully as he wanted to deny the truth of his own eyes, he saw his features mirrored in the beast's.

Another paralysing wrench tore at his heart.

His face twisted, betraying him to the beast.

'You slaughtered my people. You must pay for that.'

'I don't think so,' the necrarch said smugly, oblivious to the ruin all around him.

Metzger lurched on another step, closing the gap between them to just a few paces. He brought the sword up.

'You butchered women and children in your lust for power. You must pay for that.'

'I don't think so,' the necrarch repeated. 'Who is left to extract a price? You? Do not make me laugh, you can barely lift your blade. The fire of your life has burned out, old man, but I could offer you salvation.'

Metzger managed another step before the pain erupted again, bringing him to his knees. The sword slipped through his fingers.

'I need nothing from you,' he managed through clenched teeth.

'Oh, come now,' the necrarch said, almost affectionately. 'It pains me to see my own kin suffer so. Look around you, all this could be yours again. This is your heritage, your birthright. Embrace it before that treacherous heart of yours gives in. I can smell death on you.'

'No,' Metzger said, his head swimming.

The necrarch walked around him slowly, circling like a vulture. He trailed a filthy finger across his matted hair, and then leaned in close to his ear and whispered, 'Very well, I won't make you beg. Think of this as a gift, from me to you.' Then he sank his teeth into Reinhardt Metzger's throat.

'Now,' Metzger pleaded, 'Finish it...' He never finished the sentence.

BOHME REACHED THE top of the stairs to see the naked, decrepit form of the vampire hunched over his friend, suckling at his neck.

He chose stealth over speed, moving silently across the rooftop to stand over the crook-backed creature as it sucked the last of the life out of his friend. He would not allow the parasite to claim the old man. Bohme drove his sword deep into the beast's back, and as its head reared back, tearing out lumps of Metzger's throat, he rammed the blade in deeper, yanking it upward viciously so that it opened a wound more than a foot long along the line of the vampire's spine. The beast's cries were terrible. Bohme did not flinch from the task. He wrenched the blade clear, and then grabbed the vampire's head, digging his fingers mercilessly into the wretched monster's eyes. He pulled the vampire's head back, baring its throat so that he could saw through it.

Then he tossed the head over the side of the tower.

He stood silent vigil over his friend, not sure whether the beast's bite alone was enough to contaminate him. He said a prayer to Sigmar, begging forgiveness for what he was about to do, cutting through his friend's neck, hacking away until the bone and tendon had come apart and he was holding the head of the man he loved in his hands.

Bohme slumped to the floor, tears of grief streaming down his face.

This was victory, but at what cost?

They had lost everything.

There was no glory, no satisfaction. They had given everything to slay the beast.

Now he was alone.

He felt utterly hollow.

In time he would go back down to join the survivors, few as they were. In time he would find the strength to bury his friend. He would bury the two of

ABOUT THE AUTHOR

British author Steven Savile is an expert
in cult fiction, having written a wide
variety of sf, (including Star Wars, Dr
Who and Jurassic Park) fantasy and
horror stories, as well as a slew of
editorial work on anthologies in the UK
and USA. He won the L. Ron Hubbard
Writers of the Future award in 2002, and
has been nominated three times for the
Bram Stoker award. He currently lives in
Stockholm, Sweden.

WARHAMMER

RUNEFANG

Find the sword, save the Empire

C L WERNER

ISBN 978-1-84416-548-3